# LATENT STATE

Ben Winter

Cover art:

Illustration © Tom Edwards
TomEdwardsDesign.com

Please visit me online and follow me on Twitter for updates.

www.benwinter.co.uk
@TheBenWinter

JRH

# STATE 00

I ran past abandoned buildings – a drizzle-soaked nightmare of corrugated metal roofs. They reflected the garish discotheque of Neo-London across the river.

I was in the heart of the old city – broken and knackered, a remnant of the mobile revolution that had swept before it. The Thames embankment a dividing line where the wealth had fractured.

A homeless man hunkered beneath a holo-display. *Biggest explosion since 2052; links to terrorists suspected,* the floating neon text read.

He muttered something under his breath. It was mostly incoherent. Surprised irritation mixed with a reflexive request for a handout – wild, bloodshot eyes peeking out beneath a filthy scarf.

I ignored him; it was easy to ignore the mad. There were too many of them – castaways who didn't fit the new infrastructure or were driven to despair because of it.

The night sky was black. Dank pollution blocking out the stars and bouncing neon haze to Camden. We ran past the ancient, dried-up lock. A muddy bed filled with acidic rain and ramshackle tents. A place for tramps to take refuge.

Onwards. We could con drugs from the homeless, or steal from their unconscious bodies, but tonight we had more lucrative errands.

"You still with me, Daryl?" Sebastian called back to me, his feet splashing on rain-soaked paving.

I wheezed an affirmative. He knew I was there, but he was checking if I was out of breath. I wasn't as fit as Seb, and keeping up was a chore, sometimes to the point of puking. We didn't have time for that; we were on a schedule and running behind.

Would his tip pan out? He had a habit of exaggerating, but to hear him talk, it was rock solid.

Between alchovials at the sim-shop, Limbo, Seb's dim-witted mate, had let it slip. His sister worked as a dispatcher for a security firm supplying night guards. One abandoned building in Camden had been given strict instructions: never deviate from prescribed routes.

That left much of the place unmonitored. Limbo thought that was weird. Weird enough to mention it to Seb, who'd picked up a reputation for poking into things. It was our speciality.

Seb had played it down, telling Limbo the buildings in Camden were old and dilapidated and the guards kept to safe routes for insurance reasons. There might have been truth in that, but he'd held back – he knew something else. Camden, before removing state welfare, contained treatment centres for homeless addicts. Places where half-dead, brainless freakers could try to get off their habits. That, along with social funding, was a thing of the past, but Seb's hunch was some drugs may have been left behind. He'd mentioned something called *morphine* and thought it was worth getting our hands on. Nothing like the intense delirium of SP1N, our beloved Synthetic Psycholoid #1N, but it would have niche appeal, and that meant we could sell it.

Why would anyone leave valuable drugs lying around? I'd challenged, and Seb agreed; it was a long shot. But why keep guards so carefully on their routes unless there was something worth hiding, let alone guarding? I had no answer to that, but we both knew it wasn't for their safety. Limbo was a dumbass.

Rounding a corner, we skidded to a halt in front of an alleyway stained with graffiti. "This is the place," Seb whispered. His face was soaked, hair plastered to a stubble-coated cheek. Eyes open and sharp.

"You sure?" I laboured between breaths, eyeing where the alley led. It didn't look much. A random collection of squat, grey buildings, huddled together in disrepair. A wry smile from Seb and a glance upwards. I followed his gaze. At the top of the alley, embossed on a rusty sign, hung a three-dimensional cube symbol. Beneath it, faded but readable: *Hive Ltd*. It was the name of the company Limbo's sister supplied security to. Yeah, this was it.

I looked around cautiously. I wasn't sure about this place; it looked like a rathole, but Seb seemed confident. He had instincts for spotting things, intuitions that saw us right more often than wrong. When things were at their worst, he'd turn up with two tabs of SP1N and an hour's credit at the sim-shop. If a dealer was breathing down our necks for money, he'd scrounge it together in the nick of time. And when I'd told him I needed steady income, he'd pulled some strings and got me a job at the Vault.

I considered the thick steel door and large double locks – the building was sealed up tight.

"How do we get inside this tin can, Seb? And what makes you sure security won't turn up?"

"Don't worry about that, Daryl-lad." He grinned, unconcerned. "Limbo says the security firm isn't exactly shipshape. The day guard always knocks off an hour early and the night shift starts at midnight. And hey, look at this ..." He tapped the watch tattoo on his left index finger. It was 10.54 pm.

We hunkered down behind one of the bins lining the alley, out of sight of the security door. My rain-soaked jeans clung to me, clawing at the hairs on my legs.

Seb leaned back, stroking his jawline, a considered look replacing the grin. "How's the Vault going, Daryl?"

Really? He wanted to discuss that now? I suppose I wasn't surprised. Seb never wasted an opportunity to chitchat. I shrugged and pulled a *not bothered* face. "Okay ... I guess."

He inspected the back of his fingernails, then continued raking them across his stubble, dissatisfied with the answer. "Only okay? I used a charm offensive on Pete to get you in there. How about a bit more detail for your brother?"

I forced back the creeping annoyance. Seb could small talk any time, even right before a job; it was part of his nature. I was different. My heart was in my throat and I could feel pinpricks of cold, anxious sweat breaking out over my head and armpits. I took a breath. He'd keep asking, so I'd better say something. I forced a smile. "Sorry, Seb, just preoccupied, you know ... But yeah, job's okay. Steady work. Good for keeping alchovials in the fridge and a tab of SP1N ready to go."

Seb nodded, but a frown appeared. "And good for keeping real food in you too, I hope?"

My face went hot. "Oh, yeah, course." I lied. I'd barely eaten more than rehydrated pasta for two weeks.

"Remember ..." Seb continued, parental. I wanted to groan; he'd activated *lecture mode*. "... You're eighteen now. You can't survive on just that rehydrated junk. Gotta keep proper stuff in you or you'll get sloppy." He stopped stroking his stubble. "That's how the folks screwed up. They didn't take care of the basics. That's why they got taken. But we won't let that happen to us. We take care of the basics. Right, Daryl?"

It was a rhetorical question, but I answered anyway, unsure if he'd seen through me or guessed. "Yeah, okay, Seb. I got it."

He grinned, and the mood was reset. "Good lad. Anyway, it's been five minutes. Time to get going."

At last. I didn't know which was worse. The mini-lecture or the anxiety waiting to do the job.

A few moments later, on time (or rather, an hour early, as predicted), a security guard appeared from behind the door. Sebastian put a finger to his lips, pointing to the floor; indicating I wait behind the bin. He slipped something from his pocket, sneaking out and sticking to the shadows.

"Seb!" I whispered after him. What was he up to?

The guard turned as he tried to secure the door, fumbling with the locks. He was oblivious to the shape creeping down the alley. A moment later, Sebastian was on him, and seconds after, the guard collapsed, motionless.

I jumped up and ran over, slipping on the rain-soaked floor as I came to a stop. "What the hell did you do to him, Seb?"

He winked, showing me the skin-gun, its porous, high-pressure nozzle still hissing. "SP1N – Full tab. He'll have an awesome time but won't be vertical for at least an hour."

My jaw dropped. The attack or losing the SP1N – I couldn't tell which was more shocking. "Crap, Seb, a full tab? We could have used that!"

Running his thumb over the top of the device, he removed the leftover residue. "Don't worry, we've got a score coming. Besides, it was my tab." He licked his thumb, savouring the chemical flavour. Then looking around, he scooped up a broken bottle-end lying on the ground. Fit for purpose; he jammed it in the door's hinge, preventing it closing.

I couldn't believe he'd jumped that guy. Too big a risk. It might draw the attention of Neo-Guards. And a whole tab? What a waste!

Unless … he'd scored extra without telling me? The thought crept in from nowhere, unjustified. I shook my head; it was post-SP1N paranoia. It had been a few days, and seeing the dose vaporised into the guard had brought on my withdrawal. Seb wouldn't do that. He'd banked big, expecting a decent haul. I hoped his enthusiasm was justified; it had been a while since we'd had a break. Was tonight the night? It really needed to be.

Anxiety in check, I stepped over the guard. He lay curled on the wet paving, face twisted in ecstasy. A pang of longing washed over me. It was unusual to use that much in one go; it rendered you immobile – the guard would experience a huge, hot rush.

Eyeing his thin, short-sleeved shirt rewarded me with a follow up dose of guilt – it was a cold night. SP1N made you feel hot because blood got pushed to the outside, sucking warmth away from the core. It wasn't uncommon to die of hypothermia if you took it in the wrong place. Somewhere like here.

I groaned. Seb was already gone, eyes on the prize, but I'd feel bad if this guy died, and it would definitely create a Neo-Guard investigation, which wasn't good either. I'd have to move him on my own.

I grabbed his wrist, warm to the touch as the SP1N worked its chemical magic. Straining, I yanked him behind a bin, fishing out some dry cardboard to cover him up. If Sebastian asked, I'd say I was keeping him out of sight. Seb considered all forms of security 'conformists' – even private guards. His annoyance would be clear if he thought I'd expressed any concern.

I hurried inside. The building was dark and smelled of mould. Medical beds were strewn about, mattresses long since removed, leaving rusty, metal husks. Defunct monitors and drips hung from walls, wet where the ceiling had leaked.

"Seb," I called, my voice echoing.

Somewhere in the distance, out of sight, I heard a reply. "Look around, dipshit. We've only got an hour before the next guard comes on duty."

I gritted my teeth. If he hadn't left the guard, I would have been looking already!

I switched my ARO to illumination mode, thankful as always for the multi-functional device attached to my left shoulder. Sebastian had shown me the old style of com used decades ago – phones. Flat black rectangles, made mostly of glass. Silly handheld things, stowed loosely in bags or pockets where they rattled around and picked up scratches. They looked so fragile, and the battery only lasted a day.

In contrast, the *Anterior Retracting Omnicom* locked to the shoulder. Robust and with a vast array of functions, its screen folded discreetly against the body to keep it protected. And the housing was mostly battery – it would run for weeks.

An analogy to a quiver of arrows had been made, and the acronym-come-abbreviation ARO was soon ubiquitous.

We were better for it. I couldn't imagine retrieving a delicate glass square from my pocket every time I wanted to access information or call someone. What a hassle.

The light illuminated the corridor. Reflecting off the cracked, mirrored cabinets and scattered shards.

I poked through anything that wasn't completely in bits, trying not to slice my hands on jagged edges.

The anxiety that had abated was back in force. But it was worse now, mixed with a sense of dread. This place didn't feel right. I'd been in plenty of dilapidated buildings, but something was off. It was colder than it should be – the darkness more resistant to light. Hunching my shoulders, I kept moving, trying not to imagine movements in the shadows I knew couldn't be there.

My head twitched, the atmosphere prompting my withdrawal again. I'd get the shakes soon and that would make everything twice as hard. I had to keep it together.

Reaching a T-junction, I listened out in both directions. I could hear Seb rummaging through lockers somewhere on my right, grunting and muttering to himself. I took the left, heading deeper into the darkness.

I swore under my breath as I stumbled on debris. The ceiling had crumbled, leaving lumps of plasterboard all over the floor.

I must be on the right path. If the guards had come this way, they would have cleared the obstacles. I was in unexplored territory.

I wandered down the corridor, flanked with rooms. I checked them as I went, but I soon gave up. Aside from the odd bedpan or useless piece of medical paraphernalia, they were barren.

I felt sure I could hear rats nibbling – gnawing at imagined corpses left behind, unseen in the darkness. I swallowed with a dry mouth and kept moving. Stick to the corridor. Wherever it was leading was likely what the guards were warned away from.

After what felt like an eternity of stumbling, but was probably less than a minute, my ARO reflected something back at me. It hovered out in space, yellow and white, criss-crossing my path. It was reflective tape, cordoning off the area ahead. A metal sign hung from it: *HAZARD – keep out.*

I shouted out to Sebastian, but the corridor had narrowed and the sound didn't carry. I flipped out the screen on my ARO and punched up his speed dial.

A second later his voice crackled over the connection. "Yea, bro ...-wha ... need?"

I frowned, my anxiety intensifying. Why was the signal weak? Something must be interfering. "I've found a restricted area." I hoped the crackle hid the wobble in my voice.

"Can't hear ... restric? ... Cool ... foun ... freezer ... checkin ..."

Freezer? That made sense. Drugs often needed refrigeration. It was a good place to look. "Okay, come this way when you're done. I'll turn my geolocation on."

"... kay." Seb crackled and vanished.

I was relieved to hear it go off. The sound of a weak signal was worse than the imagined sound of rats any day. I switched my ARO's geolocator to DISCOVERABLE and tried to push thoughts of disconnection aside. If we lost coverage, we were a few hundred metres from the outside where it would re-establish. And it wasn't like it was gone altogether, just weak. It'll be okay, I told myself; a silent dribble of sweat ran down my face, confirming my doubt.

A shiver passed over me as I pushed through the tape. The psychological effect of a hazard warning more powerful than the security doors. The tape came away easily, the glue holding it long since rotted.

The conjoining corridor was no different to the preceding one, but it *felt* different, like the temperature had lowered again. Surely my imagination? I turned my collar up and pushed on. There had to be something down here worth seeing.

There were no more side rooms to investigate, only featureless grey corridor. Then, abruptly, it ended, and I was confronted with a large symbol nailed to a closed door. It took a moment to interpret what the fan shape meant. I recalled holovids of decaying nuclear plants, the sort that still powered much of England.

I put my hands in front of my groin, as if the sign itself would cause my balls to shrivel up. *Radiation*. It was showing there was a source of radiation nearby.

But why? An old X-ray machine? Used for treating injuries on-site rather than sending patients to hospital? Possible, but did X-ray machines hold value? They were old tech but still in use, so yeah, they probably did.

Every part of me wanted to get away from the door. The sign held a promise of sickness and death, but if I left now, I'd never hear the end of it. I could practically hear Seb's voice: "Don't be daft, Daryl! It's a warning to stay back when the X-ray machine's on. There's no power to the building, let alone the machine!"

Sighing, I steeled myself against the panic and pulled my hands away from my groin. The handle rattled loosely. Locked and defiant.

I kicked myself for leaving my lazeblade at home. It would have sliced through the flimsy lock in no time. And annoyingly, the door opened outwards, so any attempt to kick it in would be futile. Not that I was capable of such a feat of strength anyway.

My breathing had become heavy. A raspy sound, echoing in the narrow space, mingling with the occasional drip of moisture. I had to stay calm. There must be something that would get the door open.

Scanning the corridor, I spied an abandoned metal bed leaning against the wall. One of the crossbars was rusty. It might be encouraged out with a bit of force.

I readied my steel toe capped boot and took aim, directing a hard kick squarely at the most rusted section. It connected cleanly, the crossbar clanging free in a burst of rust and dirt. It coated the air with mist smelling vaguely of blood.

Nice one. I picked up the bar and inspected it. It was jagged at both ends where it had shattered, but the centre looked strong. I pulled it against my knee. It didn't give in any direction – a satisfactory tool for the job. I thrust one of the broken ends between the handle and the frame where the lock should be and heaved. The wood groaned, splintered, and finally popped – the handle and lock wrenching from the frame. They landed on the floor with a satisfying thunk.

I stepped back to survey my handiwork, allowing a small amount of smugness. Moreover, I was relieved. There'd be progress to show when my brother arrived.

I peered inside. The light from my shoulder cam illuminating the dark interior.

It was empty. A featureless box. No different to the ones lining the corridor but without even the rusty furniture. If anything, it had been cleaned – no debris or dust at all. I could even make out the original white walls rather than moisture-stained grey that had been so pervasive up until now.

All that for nothing! I hated this place, but I couldn't mask the disappointment of finding nothing. I hoped Seb had found something in his freezer or this whole trip would be a waste. And worse, we'd have burned that tab for nothing!

I turned to report the anticlimax, stopped, and looked back, a nagging thought pulling at me. Why a locked room with nothing in? What was the point? If there'd been a source of radiation, an X-ray machine or something else, it was no longer there, so why bother taping off the area? Had I missed something?

The air wheezed out of me. I was sick of this misadventure. I wanted to be outside again, where the signal was strong, but Seb would grill me on the details, catch me out. One last check, then I'd head back.

I stepped inside and cried out in pain – assaulted by blinding light. It was coming from everywhere, filling my head with hot, white brilliance – a furnace behind my eyes! I dropped to my knees, feeling them crack on the concrete. What was this? Images cascaded through my mind, each one a painful blur.

I saw myself speaking to Sebastian by the collapsed guard. A third party to the scene that had unfolded earlier. Not part of it, but watching. The image switched. He was rummaging through the freezer, still muttering to himself – something I'd imagined but not seen. The picture changed again. I was eight years old, prodding a dead frog. Sebastian, thirteen, laughing along beside me – a decade old memory I was watching from the outside.

The images kept coming. Erratic memories from my life but also things I couldn't know. People I'd never met. Places I'd never been. An avalanche of the unknown. Each hitting me harder and faster, until I could no longer make them out individually. A river of white hot sensations. It was overwhelming, maddening. I wanted to look away, retreat from the onslaught, but I couldn't. I was trapped and slipping, falling back into my mind, retreating into an abyss of madness!

Then, a voice ... from out of sight. It was far off, but like a beacon, something to distract from the raging insanity. Closer now. Was it Sebastian? It might be. I couldn't tell. A feeling of pulling, urgently dragging, directing me away from the pain and the heat.

When I came to, my head was pounding harder than any hangover I'd ever experienced, a living drumbeat in my brain. It took a few moments to realise it wasn't a headache. I was being slapped roughly. A red-faced guard loomed over me, shouting words like "who" and "why", but the rest struggled to penetrate – my brain was mush.

His words weren't making much sense, but they didn't need to; he was pissed, that much was obvious, but where was Seb? He must be here somewhere. I couldn't see him.

The mist cleared and a feeling of dread knotted in my gut. Where was Sebastian? I leaned up on my shoulder and called out for him, ignoring the guard still shouting at me. I felt sick to my stomach, sweat pouring out of me. I had to find my brother!

I stumbled as I stood up but focused enough to stay on my feet. I was still in the corridor; the radiation-labelled door was ahead of me. The feeling of dread became a tornado of fear. I could see Sebastian; he was lying halfway through the door, face down. He'd fallen forward after dragging me free!

I pushed the guard aside in a panicked stumble of arms and legs, grasping for my brother's foot. Taking hold, I heaved him clear. The guard was screaming more commands, but they didn't register. I dragged Seb over the filthy floor to the corner and turned over his limp body. His face said everything. His eyes were open, and he was breathing, but there was nothing there. Nothing behind the eyes at all. No recognition, no reaction, just a sickening, motionless catatonia.

I puked, acrid stomach acid coating my teeth. "Sebastian! Wake up, Sebastian!" I sobbed, but there was nothing. I wasn't sure how long I'd been unconscious, but however long it was, he'd spent that time in the room, feeling the pain I'd only experienced for a few moments. All I could do was grasp and rock his vacant body in a mess of bile and tears.

# STATE 01

They discharged me from police custody in the early hours. I felt empty and desperate, but I'd gotten lucky. Seeing the state of Sebastian, the guard had taken pity and reported us as trespassers rather than thieves. A criminal downgrade that only required a warning.

It wasn't free though. He'd demanded more of the stuff we'd shot him with, hands twitching in anticipation. I was envious – the first SP1N-cycle was always the best.

I burned some street cred and gave him a contact. It was a good deal; his discretion kept the Neo-Guards out of our business. I couldn't be sure what would happen if they got involved – it was common for suspects to vanish if they investigated. The nihilist in me wanted to disappear, but not like that.

Sebastian hadn't recovered. They moved him to hospital, where he lay, dead behind the eyes, breathing in and out, catatonic. I knew he wouldn't get better. I'd seen what he'd seen for a few moments – felt the tendrils of madness closing. He'd been there almost an hour.

The doctors identified SP1N in his system and diagnosed acute overdose. That was bollocks. It had been days since our last hit. But it didn't matter; they wouldn't listen, wouldn't go back and check the facility. Why should they? I was a rambling, delusional junkie. A gutter rat at best, a criminal at worst.

Without health insurance, the outcome was inevitable. A doctor strode in and delivered the news, detached and unemotional. They were moving Sebastian to Brixton Asylum. The last state-funded mental facility.

My heart sank. The asylum was a holding pen for crazies. It freed up beds in the main hospital, but it only dispensed basic care, if you could even call it that. Holo-feed scandals were common – patients starving in their beds or rented out for gang rape. He wouldn't last a year.

Spinning on a heel, the doctor walked out, dropping a scribbled release note on the bed. He didn't even bother with some contrived words of comfort. I scooped it up – they'd move Sebastian to the asylum the next day.

Blundering from the hospital, I ran into the rain. Purple signage reflected on puddles like neon bruises. Shit. We'd screwed up. I wanted to cry but couldn't; my eyes were dry, replaced with withering desperation. I ran until my lungs heaved, heart on the edge of exploding – the pain was good; it replaced the hollow feeling.

I stopped when the lightheadedness became overwhelming, stars speckling my vision. I was back in Camden, where everything had gone wrong. I'd followed my subconscious; blindly looking for answers, but there were none. The building was in lockdown. Cordoned off with every door and window welded shut. The Hive Ltd sign had been taken down and replaced with a demolition warning.

No one else was around. It could have been like this for years. Had I ever even been here? Perhaps the doctors were right. Nothing but a SP1N-fuelled bender – a hallucination. Sinking to my knees, existential fear gripped me. What if I couldn't distinguish between reality and illusion anymore! It was hard to breathe.

As I canted onto all fours, something glinted beneath me. It twinkled in the neon wash from the street lamps, staring back at me – an evil, knowing eye on the wet concrete.

It was the broken bottle-end Sebastian had used to wedge the door open. The existential malaise receded. I wasn't going mad. We'd stumbled onto something, and it was being covered up – quickly and efficiently. Why, though? I had no idea.

I leaned back and stood up, breath returning, hands shaking. I thrust them into my pockets to keep them still. It was cold and drizzling, but that wasn't what was causing the shake. It had been days since my last SP1N-cycle. It reaffirmed what I already knew. I was a worthless addict. But at least I wasn't out of my mind – not yet.

This place was a dead end. I'd uncover nothing new here. Anguish welled harder, like a pickaxe in my sternum. There was only one place left I could think to go.

Camden Town Underground (the Tube) was close. It was early morning, and the area was empty. Just a few beggars and SP1N wasters littering the streets. The station sat amongst a collection of boarded-up buildings. Someone had selectively smashed the red neon lettering: – – D – R – – OUND. Seemed about right.

A dark ticket office lurked at the bottom of a crumbled staircase. It was in a gross state of repair. Rubbish coating the floors, gates rusted open, a single fluorescent light, throwing long, intermittent shadows.

Like welfare, the Administration had cut funding to public transport, leaving the Tube to rot. There was only enough cash to run a couple of trains an hour.

Down the rusted and seized escalator, bodies huddled together. With no station staff, the platform had become infested with the homeless and criminal. The whole place stank of urine and the tangy body odour of vagrancy.

Using the Underground was always a risk. A train could take thirty minutes to arrive – an eternity in a place like this. The longer you hung about, the greater the chance a violent or inebriated occupant would mug you.

Palming my lazeblade in my pocket (newly stolen from a hospital vending machine), I sneered at the closest shape – a body sitting slumped in a metal seat. My thumb hovered over the activation switch, its metallic weight reassuring as the vagrant's bloodshot eyes watched.

I made certain everyone could see I was holding something hidden. The mystery was an extra deterrent. If they didn't know what I had, they couldn't tell how to counter it.

I recalled the last time I'd been attacked. A freaker had gone for me when I wasn't paying attention – my mind wandering in a post-SP1N afterglow. Seb had given him a good slice. But he wasn't here now. This was on me.

A few tense minutes passed until the train arrived. It rattled into the station in a state of broken windows and graffiti. I boarded quickly, taking a seat on the ripped upholstery. The carriage was mostly empty, just a couple of *low-riskers* – normal people. I relaxed as the doors closed and the train progressed. It moved along the Northern Line, creaking and clacking on the chipped tracks. The Northern Line bisected the city from north to south. I needed to go south.

After nine stops, the doors cranked open. The tramps here were as nasty as those in Camden – I beelined for the exit, repeating the faked bravado.

Topside, Elephant & Castle bustled. One of the few areas the public had free access to roads. Most were electronically tolled – fares only the rich could afford.

E-bikes hummed past – neon under-lighting streaking in multi-coloured blurs, LED side panels flashing catchphrases and kanji symbols. They were the personal transport of the masses, favoured by gang members and low-riskers alike. Seb and I used to have a petrol scooter, but it became useless when oil reserves dried up. We couldn't afford an electric conversion, let alone a new model.

I made the death run across the dual carriageway. The bikes barely slowed for each other, and definitely not for pedestrians. Someone swore loudly and something hissed past my head. A bottle. It shattered across the road, driving a rider onto the pavement. He wobbled, regained control, and made his way back, the LED panel flashing UNTOUCHABLE. Onlookers cheered and groaned in equal measures. I hurried on before more road rage spilled my way.

The sim-shop was in a low, flat building, hunkering beneath a bridge stretching across the Elephant & Castle intersection. It had been a famous dance club once: *The Ministry of Sound* – closed down after a string of drug-related deaths. Ironically, it was now a space for the desperate and drug addled to live out their virtual fantasies. Fitting into both those categories, I knew it well.

I nodded at the bouncer. His scarred face the product of hauling out a thousand drunkards. He attempted something approaching sympathy. "Supp, Daryl. Heard about your brother. Sorry, I guess." News had travelled quickly it seemed.

"Yeah, me too," I mumbled, not bothering to look up.

Inside snaked a long corridor lined with erotic holograms. They gyrated and rutted, advertising the virtual pleasures within. I'd seen them many times; they were practically invisible now.

An alchovial bar perched in the main room, positioned to kill the minutes between sessions while they cleaned the booths. A few locals drank here; it was quieter than places outside, and cheaper. It attracted a bottom rung of wasters pushing for an early grave. I liked it; people at the bottom couldn't look down on you.

Grimey was working, and he looked the part. He was probably cleanish, but a combination of synthetic tan and deep wrinkles made the troughs on his face appear dirt filled.

"Hey." I sidled up to the bar.

Grimey didn't reply. He didn't talk much, but he cracked an alchovial and slid it over, nodding towards the main office. *On the house.* I guess he'd heard about Sebastian too.

"Thanks." I grasped the vial. The beer wasn't brilliant, but it was the first I'd had since the incident. It barely hit the sides on the way down.

I drained the last drop and placed the half-glass/half-metal container on the bar with a thunk. I sighed as the momentary relief of alcohol took hold. It would pass in a second, but for a few moments, I felt better.

"Grimey."

He'd turned his back and was refilling an optic of vodka. He turned around, wrinkles deepening as his brows raised.

"Has Limbo been in?"

Nothing as useful as words came out, but he made a wanking motion towards the VR booths. Limbo was getting his rocks off. Grimey tapped his watch – and he'd be out soon.

I nodded and slumped over the bar, hoping the show would prompt another freebie. None arrived. Begrudgingly, I jammed a thumb on the bar-mounted fingerprint reader and ordered one. Not as good as the first, but it didn't need to be – I needed this one to last.

Fifteen minutes later, Limbo appeared from the booth. A bundle of animated chicken limbs, his shaved head sweaty and red, and a big smile on his face – the tell-tale signs of a good session.

A rake-thin arm, bare to the shoulder and covered with tattoos, waved furiously. His mouth was half open, ready to launch into a barrage of questions.

I interjected before he could derail me. "Limbo, why the hell you tell Sebastian about that damn place! He's seriously messed up now!"

Limbo's face dropped, eyes pained, arms less animated, though not exactly still. He fidgeted and stuttered as he tried to explain, hopping from foot to foot. "Yeah, Daryl ... not my fault. See ... was jus chat, ya know. Nuffin serious." Limbo didn't have an education, and it showed. His high-pitched sentences tumbled out clipped and half-witted. "How'd I know he'd go there? He tole me it was nuffin worf checkin, so why'd he go?"

He had me there. Sebastian had conned him out of the tip. It was a rare moment of clarity for Limbo. I changed direction. I needed something to go on. "Look, it's just as well you didn't go – it could be you lying brain-dead in hospital." Instead of only *half* brain-dead, I added silently.

Limbo's smile was gone, his eyes darting to the bar, looking for an exit. "Howdya figure? Sebastian overfilled on SP1N, that's all – prob found it in da place and got greedy. Should've bin more bloody careful I'd say."

This wasn't going how I'd hoped. Limbo was an idiot, but he wasn't bad natured; we'd sunk hundreds of alchovials together. I needed a different tack, and all I had left was the truth. I gripped Limbo's arms earnestly, briefly preventing him twitching.

"Had nothing to do with SP1N, Limbo. Seb burned his only tab drugging the guard so we could get in. Look at my hands ..." I released him and unfurled a hand, holding it out straight. It jittered, an unmistakable sign of SP1N withdrawal. "I haven't had a tab in over a week! Do you think if we'd found stuff I'd be like this?"

Limbo ignored the outstretched hand and leaned in close, inspecting my face. I knew what he was doing – it was easy to fake a shake, but the eyes never lied.

I kept talking as he peered into my irises. "It was something in the building that messed him up. So you see. I need more information. I know Sebastian lied, but nothing bad enough for the state he's in now."

Limbo pulled back, arms twitching again as he reconsidered. "Yeah, 'kay, Daryl. You don't look so gud – I seen eyes like yours before. You gunna feel the pain soon."

Wasn't that the truth. SP1N withdrawal got worse over time. The shake would progress to a headache, then sickness a thousand times worse than a hangover.

"I guess it weren't your fault what happened," Limbo continued. "Whadya need?"

Progress. I took the lead, trying to sound assertive. Seb always said you had to ask for things with authority or you'd be ignored. Limbo had reengaged, but he had the attention span of an insect and his eyes were still wandering to the bar. "Tell me more about how you got the tip, Limbo. I need details."

Limbo dragged his eyes away from the bar and focussed his attention. He squeaked out the best reply he could muster. "It was like what I said to Seb. The info came from mi sis, Lou. She tole me bout the place cos she tort it were odd da guards weren't allowed to patrol there."

I knew this already. I needed something new. "But what is Hive, Limbo? Who are they?"

"Dunno." He licked his lips. "Lou dunno either. She's jus a dispatcher. Lowest level in the comp. Jus chats to guards from da office. Never sees 'em."

I'd met Louise before. Nice girl, not as dim as Limbo, but hardly a bright spark either. I believed him when he said she wouldn't know anything. I sighed. Limbo was too simple-minded to hold things back. If he knew more, he'd tell me.

"Daryl." He interrupted my chain of thought. "I dunno anyfing, really. Barely remember to begin wiv. But I'm soz bout what happened ..." He licked his lips again. "Buy you a beer?"

That was a big gesture from Limbo; he struggled to make ends meet as much as anyone. I'd gotten a taste for beer now. It was a poor substitute for SP1N, but the two I'd had were pushing back thoughts of Seb. It wasn't like this conversation was going anywhere anyway.

Realisation struck. I hadn't come here for information at all. Limbo and Louise were about as low down the knowledge ladder as humans got. I knew that. I'd come here for something basic. I wanted to get smashed.

"Oh, and, Daryl ..." Limbo leaned in conspiratorially, slipping something into my hand.

I knew what it was but looked anyway. A glossy pink square stared back up at me. SP1N – full tab.

He winked. "I owed it to Seb. You ave it."

The urge to find out what happened became distant. The pressing need to put the little pink square into my system overriding it.

If a pal shared his stash, you had to drink with them for a while. We retreated and slammed more vials. The booze turned my withdrawal into anticipation. Once Limbo was suitably drunk, head lolling on the bar, I stumbled over to one of the VR booths. You could take SP1N on its own, but mixed with VR it was something else, and tonight I needed the works. It would cost me all my remaining creds, but I didn't care.

The 'booth' was a small cubicle behind a lockable door. A battered leather recliner and a ceiling full of equipment were contained inside. On the wall hung a cellophane sleeve dispenser. They expected customers to slide them over the recliner, although it was clear from the stains many hadn't. I yanked one out and placed it over the chair, elastic bindings snapping secure.

Taking a seat, I inserted the tab in my skin-gun and pressed it against my forearm, wincing as the trigger pulled. The high-pressure device hissed, vaporising the tab at high velocity. I could feel the chemicals passing into my blood.

Years of use had given me a high resistance. It would take a few minutes to feel the effects.

I pushed a button on the side of the recliner, and a touch sensitive panel dropped from the ceiling. It hung in front of me, a crack running vertically through it, warping the image, but it was still readable.

Relishing the pseudo-high before the real one kicked in, I flicked through the options. There were non-sexual VR experiences, but no one used them. I swore they were there for show. I filtered them out and pulled up the menus everyone came here for – erotic fantasies. The interface displayed options for the model I would interact with. Sliders for adjusting body shape, hair style, and skin colour, or pre-selects categorised by race and body type. A good selection of locales was on offer too. Beaches, swanky hotels, even yachts. The Elephant & Castle sim-shop was far from high-class, but they kept their software up to date.

I punched in my picks. Tall, blonde, and large-chested. Clichéd as hell and bottom of the barrel, but that's what I wanted – needed; every time a mixture of excitement and shame. I didn't care about the locale, so the computer selected something appropriate.

Choices locked, the control panel retracted. Out of the ceiling, the VR helmet and groin attachment descended. These were the most expensive parts of installing and maintaining a sim-shop – the law required cleansing systems to keep them disinfected.

I shrugged out of my trousers and pulled the rubber gasket over my groin. There was a pleasing rush of air as the system created a light vacuum, sealing the unit in place. Above me, the VR helmet floated on an articulated arm. I reached up and pulled it over my head. It blocked the outside world from view, immersing me in the virtual environment.

The helmet provided an ultrahigh resolution, three-dimensional image with realistic sound. Not indistinguishable from real life but convincing. It auto-detected I'd put the helmet on and launched the programme. I was standing by a beat-up American pickup truck on a dusty Texas plain. The sun was setting on the horizon.

I'd never seen these things in real life; they were relics from the past – extinct from overuse of resources and pollution. But they were consistent with what I'd seen in holovids of the period.

The blonde was leaning against the truck, convincing in every detail – white knotted t-shirt above daisy dukes. Belly button piercing on a flat, tanned stomach. The room had fans to simulate a breeze, though the smell of stale beer and sweat persisted. Perversely, I'd grown to associate the smell with the sim-shop experience. I almost liked it.

I could have programmed a conversation, but like the non-sexual options, most never bothered. You rented the booth by the minute.

The SP1N began to work. A warm glow spreading through my body. The colour in the images grew deeper, lines sharper, and the sounds of the virtual world more real.

Old-timers said SP1N was like a combination of Ecstasy and LSD, but orders of magnitude better. It created the heightened emotional state and warm buzz of the former, and the synaesthesia of the latter. The combination was potent. It not only heightened the experience but also tricked the brain. A complete sense of touch being replicated, fully transporting the body and mind into the virtual environment. A perfect melding of chemical and technological entertainment.

The SP1N peaked, and I was immersed, unable to distinguish the virtual from the real. The dusty plain was real, the pickup truck was real, and the girl in front of me was real. I knew none of it *was* real, but for the time being, it was more real than the real world itself. A sigh eased out of me. I'd feel terrible tomorrow, and disgusted with myself in an hour, but it was an escape from the nightmare outside. And that was good enough.

# STATE 02

The sim-shop was the end of my investigation. I had no resources, no means of pursuing the truth, and no creds.

True to their threat, they moved Sebastian to Brixton Asylum. I told myself it wouldn't be so bad, and it was the best place for him.

I was delusional. It was a slow death sentence and I knew it. If one of the inmates didn't get him, neglect would. There were no other options though. All I could do was suppress the guilt into an acidic ball in the pit of my stomach and let it happen.

Two months passed. My routine degraded into a cycle of apathy and self-destruction. I worked enough between SP1N-cycles to avoid being fired. Ate enough not to starve. And slept enough to remain sane, although nightmares kept that on a knife edge – every night reliving the moment I lost my brother.

The anger and despair persisted, but it wasn't motivating me to find answers. It was fuelling laziness, and a need for oblivion.

My SP1N addiction was rampant. Worse than when Sebastian was with me. And it was costing me a fortune. I'd been in debt before, but Seb's side projects had covered the difference. That was gone now. I'd been forced to make shadier deals with more dangerous people, and with deeper lines of credit.

One of those lines would be getting deeper tonight, and I was dreading it. I'd exhausted all the low-end dealers – the safe fish. Only the sharks would deal with me now.

I wished Seb were with me. When he stood straight and drew his shoulders back, it was like a cobra unfurling its hood. A trick he could back up with natural strength – assets I didn't have. He'd made me feel okay about it: "Don't worry, Daryl-lad," he'd say. "You're the smart one."

That wasn't true. I'd picked up some hacking knowhow and had made it further in the state-schooling system than most, but I had none of Seb's guile or street smarts. He had a way with people; he knew when to be charming and when to be aggressive. A born player. God, I missed him.

Holding my nerve, I walked into the building and rode the escalator.

Situated in Soho, central Neo-London, the Trocadero Centre was an ancient, multi-floored entertainment arcade – most of the shops had closed down and been replaced with low-rent machine gambling.

I checked my ARO as I surveyed the atrium from the second-floor balcony. It was 10.57 pm.

I had a clear view into most of the levels, each one crammed with gaming devices of different shapes and designs. They blared as visitors jammed their thumbs on the panels, awaiting a miracle to befall them – the random number generators finishing tantalising close to a win, but seldom doing so. Vapour rose from hundreds of e-cigarettes as patrons sucked on different flavours of pseudo-tobacco. They mingled in the space above to create a ubiquitous *all-smell* that hung in the air.

The noise and chaos made it the perfect place for cutting deals. Each machine was a self-contained vault with safeguards – security systems that would electrocute tamperers. There was little need for human security.

I turned around and stared down the escalator. Encased in elec-tro-plastic tubing, it displayed never ending swirls of bright graphics. A dalliance to entertain customers. Few appreciated the effort, keen to hurry to the next machine where they'd hope for better luck.

Feeling tense to my core, shoulders hunched, I stared trancelike at the colours and patterns. The surrounding noise both deafening and far away.

My ARO pinged, snapping me back to reality. I flicked out the screen and read the message. *From: Led. Msg: Be there in two minutes. Two for two hundred.*

My earlobes let go of my shoulders. I retracted the screen into its shoulder housing. Led was extending my credit. Thank God.

The sights and sounds of the Trocadero became crisper as my anxiety eased. A freaker across the room had lost patience with his machine. He was shouting and shaking his head in fury, spiked hair swaying, piercings jingling. He kicked it, which was a step too far. It buzzed, flashing blue. The freaker yelped, pulling his hand back from where it had been resting. Only a warning buzz. A stronger one could render unconsciousness. The freaker backed away to a safe distance – it wasn't unusual for victims to slump forward, receiving enough shocks to kill.

I yelled as a rough hand landed on my shoulder, flicking me around like a spinning top. I stared into Led's face, or more accurately, his teeth. A frightening grill of sharp metal stakes. He snapped them in front of my eyes with a loud click. A favourite intimidation trick. And it worked. I squirmed under a shower of spittle and tried to back up, but there was nowhere to go. I was at the edge of the balcony.

"Daryl ..." Led's tongue snaked around the metal-filled hole. "Where's my money, Daryl?"

Panic descended. "Er, Led, we agreed credit right? Two hundred for two tabs, yeah?"

"No, mate," Led hissed, teeth grazing my nose. "You misunderstand me. You can *buy* the two tabs after you've *paid* me the two hundred from last month."

Shit. I was in trouble. I had nowhere near that. I had ten creds to my name. Not enough for a beer and a tin of beans.

"You know what it means if you don't got the money ..."

It wasn't a question, everyone knew. It was a warning. If I'd crossed a line, he'd make an example of me. Led was a freaker general – his loyalty secured through fear. His recruits had to know he'd follow through on his threats.

I could feel my heels against the railing. My eyes darted left and right. The electrocuted freaker from earlier was looking at Led, as was one sitting on a bench, peering over his ARO. Their shark tattoos matched. All part of the same gang under Led. God damn it! I should've recognised them. I was trapped!

"Nothing to say, squirt!" Led grabbed my left hand, his powerful arms overpowering my toothpicks.

The freakers closed the distance, growling at anyone close enough to consider interfering. No one would interfere.

In a few moments, I was surrounded – Led in front, flanked by his henchmen. One turned his back to keep a lookout, and the other grabbed my free hand and whipped out his lazeblade. He held it in a reverse grip, his forearm hiding the red glow from onlookers, but I could see it – smell it burning my jacket.

Sneering, Led uncurled my little finger, yanking it towards his gaping maw.

"Please, no!" I pulled at the iron grip.

No one paid attention to my cries. They pretended not to notice, refocusing on their gambling. This was a regular occurrence, so no help would come. Led forced the tip of my finger between his jaws and squeezed down, drawing blood. He paused, savouring the moment before crunching into bone.

I shut my eyes and screamed, waiting for the agony of my missing finger to register. It would happen any moment, probably already had. I hadn't felt the pain yet – shock was covering it up.

The seconds ticked by, but the pain didn't arrive. Everything was quiet – silent, in fact. The pressure that had pierced my skin was still there. I could feel it, but the final act hadn't been delivered.

Fear held my eyes closed, but after a few long seconds they fluttered open irresistibly. Something was wrong. Led was there. Devil grin painted across his brutish face, but the expression was different – unmoving, lifeless. Like looking at a vicious holo-statue. And it wasn't only Led, everything was different. The world was still. I didn't understand.

"L-Led." He was frozen, eyes glassy like a waxwork. What the hell was going on!

The freaker on my right was statuesque, grip around my arm vice-like and static. My heart was thumping. Fear of mutilation transformed into something else – supernatural dread! None of this was right.

The dread gave way to a bigger problem – I couldn't breathe! I was gasping like a fish out of water. The air was thin and hard to draw in.

Fear of suffocation dominated all others. I tugged my left hand, but Led's teeth, clamped around my finger, held it firm. I didn't care; the urge to breathe was paramount. I yanked harder, ripping it free and tearing a messy gash, but at least it was still attached. I wiggled hard against Led's henchman, twisting my arm free and stumbling away to the side, landing on the floor in a heap. The air flowed again, allowing a few precious gasps, but no sooner had I sat up, it retreated again, blackness threatening the edges of my vision. I didn't understand what was going on, but the act of breaking away helped. I scrambled to my feet like a beleaguered diver searching for the surface and paced. The oxygen came with movement; it was still thin but enough to drive unconsciousness back.

The risk of suffocation faded, but the strangeness of the situation, temporarily put on hold, demanded my attention. I looked over the balcony. Everything was frozen in place. The people, the machines-, until recently a cacophony of sound and light, lay deathly silent. Even the e-cig vapour hung in the air, motionless like mist. A surreal quality enveloped the arcade. A dead, flat light coating the surfaces. Even walking was strange, more difficult, like wading through water or pushing against a heavy wind.

Were we under attack?

We were on good terms with China and Russia ...

Had America resurfaced? They'd turned tyrannical after disarming their citizens and collapsing their republic a decade ago. They'd been quiet a long time, but that could have changed. Had they developed something to pacify us? Was there going to be a follow up attack – troops marching through the streets, murdering people where they stood!

My mouth ran dry. They planned for us to starve! Trapped motionless and wasting away. But if any of that were right, why wasn't I affected? None of this made sense!

Then I saw it, and thoughts of state invasions vanished. A few metres away, a freaker kid had tripped over. Fresh faced with a few piercings, arm tattoos recently inked and still scabby. His oversized trousers, hanging below his arse, had slipped beneath his boots, tangling up his feet. He'd been holding a plastic vial of green fluid – a confection drink from the vending machines.

The scene was at its most dramatic – like a well-placed holo-snap. But his body wasn't frozen in space; it was frozen in the moment – hanging forward at a physics-defying angle. The vial had left his grip but hadn't dropped; it hung there, at least thirty centimetres from his hand, with nothing above or below. It was open and most of its contents had spilled out – green goo smearing across the open space.

Sauntering over, hand shaking, I reached out to touch the floating liquid. It didn't move. The composition a collage of levitated globs. Like Led, the freakers, and everything else, it was rocklike – unyielding. I passed my hands over, below, and all around like a magician. It was completely suspended.

Realisation dawned, along with an unexpected rush of relief. The reason for all this absurdity was clear. It was a hallucination! Nothing like this could exist in the real world. This was all imaginary; a construct brought on by SP1N withdrawal and stress. I was dreaming – probably in an alleyway somewhere, beaten to a pulp and missing a finger. My mind had trapped me here to spare me the pain.

I relaxed. It was good to have an explanation; it was the only thing that made sense – I was going mad! You've finally popped your lid, Daryl – it was only a matter of time. I felt remarkably calm at the realisation.

Nihilistic acceptance washed over me. They'd arrange a space next to Sebastian when they found me, dribbling and catatonic.

I looked at Led, no longer dangerous but still intimidating. It felt weird to stay so close to him. If this were a dream, it could still become a nightmare – prudent to put some distance between me and the Trocadero.

"See you later, sucker." I chided with fantasy confidence, then I moved away as quickly as I could, just in case.

Pushing against the headwind, I descended the stationary escalator and picked my way through the frozen throngs. Freakers and low-riskers, all stopped dead in their tracks – a human diorama of drinking, smoking, and gambling.

Movement was manageable but difficult – like a dream where you can't run or are stuck in glue. But this was worse. My imagination was layering on months of drug abuse, replicating exhaustion. By the time I reached the exit, I was completely worn out, sweating, and wheezing.

The weirdness continued outside. Soho, normally crowded and bustling, was still crowded, but the bustle was gone. Immobile shoppers, buskers, and homeless bodies filled the streets. Ghostly still, semi-transparent holographic billboards projected down from the Piccadilly Circus intersection, displaying half drawn ads. Even the rubbish, normally whipping around ankles, was stuck to the floor. It looked like an art installation. I expected to see pretentious, bearded arseholes wandering around. "Mmm ... Arr ..." I could hear them pretending to understand.

The roads in this part of the city were subject to heavy taxes. Wealthy low-riskers travelled in large, security-enforced vehicles with strengthened external cages. Carjacking was common, so they drove at high speed – the momentum an extra deterrent. Not so now; they looked parked and vulnerable. Any normal day, the freakers would have run riot.

The detail of the hallucination was amazing. It was like no dream I'd had before; I felt in control, lucid. It was as close to reality as anything I could recall. The odd spectacle of a deranged mind.

I could feel the weight of the thick atmosphere, the difficulty sucking in breath, even discomfort where Led had bitten me. I inspected the gash, a frown forming. The blood wasn't dripping; it was pooling around my finger like a fitted glove. A skintight barrier between my body and the hallucination. What significance this held, I couldn't tell. A deranged mind indeed.

The panic of earlier had given way to bemused acceptance. I was clearly losing my mind, but at least it was relatively painless and quiet. I closed my eyes and took a struggled breath. Is this how others experience madness? A strange dreamscape to be wandered eternally?

My eyes snapped open to the sound of a startled scream. The world was moving again. Disoriented, I tried to locate the commotion. It was coming from a woman a few metres away; she was pointing and shaking a finger. Other onlookers were also staring, confused or startled expressions on their faces.

I stumbled back, feeling like a sleepwalker ripped from a deep slumber, landing in a puddle. The cold wetness soaked through my jeans, bringing me back to my senses.

Somewhere behind me, I could hear Led roaring.

"Where is he? What's going on?" he bellowed from within the Trocadero Centre. "Quickly, find that little runt! He owes me a finger!"

That didn't sound like a hallucination anymore. I'd gotten away, but if he found me, he'd want more than a finger – he'd bite off my entire hand!

Forgetting the madness, instinct kicked in. I scrambled off the pavement, shouldering past onlookers.

It was a relief to be breathing freely again, and there was something reassuring about the fleshy, normal bodies I was pushing past. But why were they staring at me?

Clearing the crowd, I ran for the Underground, hoping Led hadn't seen me. I doubted it. I'd moved a sufficient distance, but there was still a chance.

I made the call to run the extra five minutes to Leicester Square. It was further than the Piccadilly Circus entrance outside Trocadero, but Led was less likely to grab me there.

At the station, for once I was glad to be on the homeless-filled platform. Its relative danger safer than being near Led and his goons. I'd escaped, but I didn't know how. Something had happened in the arcade.

I looked at my finger. Blood was flowing from the cut, covering my jacket and jeans. The mess was enough to deter the platform dwellers – too much hassle. I wrapped it in the bottom of my shirt and boarded the next train. The most important thing was putting distance between Led and me. I'd figure the rest out later. Either my mind was playing an elaborate trick on me or something far weirder was going on.

# STATE 03

I lay partially conscious on the futon. Sunlight slanted in through horizontal blinds, the dusty beams bisecting the room and cutting across my face. I cracked an eye open, momentarily dazzled as light flared painfully in my vision.

For a few blissful moments, my mind was empty, rebooting from sleeping to waking. Then the memories seeped back. First the dull ache of my brother, who so often would have slept the night slumped in the chair opposite after a binge of SP1N and video games. For a moment, I saw him and I bolted upright. But as my eyes adjusted, I realised it was my jacket. It had formed a vaguely human shape over the old alchovials and pizza boxes where I'd slung it.

I leaned back, heart aching, head thumping, trying to pull myself together. The rest was coming back. The deal gone wrong; the unexplained madness.

I groaned and blinked a few times. My head was killing me. I was gripping an alchovial of vodka, had been all night. It was half empty, but it wasn't a hangover. It was worse – SP1N withdrawal. There'd be a pneumatic drill in my head until I scored another tab or rode it out far enough. It had been months since I'd abstained long enough to let the headaches recede naturally.

I glanced at the holo-clock. The arctic blue numbers hovering above read 8.30 am. What day though? I'd completely lost track. It clicked. It was Monday – a work day. I didn't have enough creds for my mobile plan or next rent, let alone dealer debt or fresh tabs. Groaning, I pushed aside thoughts of yesterday, struggled up, and staggered over to the bathroom, picking my way past discarded food packaging strewn across the tiny studio flat. I couldn't afford to lose my job.

I was scared to look in the mirror, knowing I'd barely recognise what confronted me. I looked anyway. A dead-eyed stranger was behind the glass. Cheeks pale and gaunt, and eyes dilated like saucepans. The corners of my mouth were down-turned in a perpetual sad face. It wasn't emotion; it was withdrawal – a chemical relaxing of the facial muscles. It would stay that way until I got my next hit or enough time passed.

I looked at my finger; it had stopped hurting, just a mild throb, but it was a mess. The blood had dried into a deep, stiff scab. At least it was still connected to my hand. I should be thankful for that.

Using water as hot as I could manage, I did my best to wash some colour back into my face and tame the mess of auburn hair. It was sticking up at irregular angles all over my head.

I re-inspected myself. Better. The dilated eyes were still a giveaway, but I had tinted glasses for that. I forced a grin; it looked ridiculous, maniacal, but it would hide my mouth. I'd choose mania over addiction – one would get me fired, the other may not.

I grabbed some clothes from the in-use pile. They were dirty by most people's standards but good enough to get me through the day. I sprayed them down with deodorant to make sure.

After pulling on my jacket, I grabbed my ARO from a charging alcove, slapping it to the magnetic shoulder plate. It made a satisfying beep as it thunked on, generating an endorphin rush – the pleasure of being connected to technology, and by extension, everything else.

It was state-of-the art, the one thing of value I owned, and connected with the best data plan I could afford – a greater expense than food or drugs. I pulled up my messages. Led's old text was still there, but a new one had arrived. I opened it. *From: Led. Msg: I'll find you.* Well, that confirmed parts of yesterday had happened – I'd gone to the Trocadero to score SP1N. It was everything afterwards that concerned me. My memory was unreliable; it was too outlandish. All I could be sure of was my damaged finger and lack of drugs. Whatever happened, it hadn't gone to plan.

Outside, the sun shone dimly through polluted clouds, washing Neo-London in a dull, silvery complexion. It was as good as the weather got. It lifted my spirits a notch.

My decrepit block of flats dominated the Battersea skyline – a grey, crumbling heap casting an intimidating silhouette. One of the cheapest places to rent in Neo-London.

My domicile was part of ten floors bolted atop the existing structure. A renovation that turned the thirty-floor council estate into a forty-floor super-tenement. The Administration dubbed them *extraplexes* – grand sounding but little more than modern day vertical slums. Tiny and lightweight to not upset the foundations, the domiciles were fragile and unstable – the extra floors listing a metre to the side, visible from the ground. Mine was on the penultimate floor, teetering close to the most precarious point. I couldn't complain. It was cheap and it kept the rain out.

Donning a pair of orange-tinted specs to shield my dilated pupils from the glare (and everyone else), I shuffled in the direction of the nearest tube.

Embedded in the busy commercial district, the Vault was a run-down mobile tech store off Oxford Street. *Fiercely independent since 2022*, its purple neon sign stated. Independent was a joke. Like every tech shop, the Vault took kickbacks from networks and ARO providers. It just didn't brandish their names on the door. That also meant it didn't enjoy national or global advertising. That was a mistake, but it wasn't my shop, and I wasn't planning to question Pete on his advertising strategy.

Entering via the back door, I used the thumb reader and punched in my security code. It was 9.20 am – ten minutes before opening time. With some staff yet to arrive, they might even consider me early. A miracle considering how late I'd slept.

Inside, they were setting up for the day. The Vault stocked a selection of AROs, ranging from budget-conscious Wingmates to high-end Shoulder Saracens like mine. The black blade logo promised cutting edge performance.

The Vault would connect AROs to any of the Telcom networks advertised around the shop. Redwave, Diecast, and Limelight were the key providers, competing aggressively in the saturated market.

Limelight was drawing ahead in speed. Their recently launched quantum broadcasting technology a huge step up. They didn't have brilliant coverage yet, but the improvements were significant. Limelight was now the premium service, leaving Redwave and Diecast to fight it out on extras and better subsidised AROs. A Limelight connection was outside what I could afford; I'd made do with Redwave. It was middle of the road but okay.

My Saracen was from the Vault too. A return inflicted with a minor cosmetic scrape. Pete had been generous – given it to me discounted. I'd still eaten beans for a month to cover the cost.

In the stockroom, sales targets were up on the holoboard, or the *board of doom*. I knew I was behind, but I hadn't checked in a while. I scanned the list of salespeople – down, down, all the way to the bottom. I was last, a solid fifteen per cent off my target.

It was my fault, but it still hurt my pride. Before Sebastian's accident – before the switch from casual user to hopeless addict – I'd been good at this job. I knew more about mobile tech than anyone here, including the owner. But over the past few months, my game had been utterly thrown off. A persistent bleariness dulling my instincts and recall. Others in the stockroom nodded, said hi, but wouldn't meet my gaze. They all knew what it meant to be fifteen per cent behind.

From public facing to back-office, Neo-Londonites served the Telcom networks or ARO manufacturers, and the corporations kept track – sharing employee records between them. Illegal, but the Administration didn't care; most of their income came from business tax. If I screwed up, I'd struggle to get a job emptying bins, and even those were in high demand.

Pete came in via the front door. He was stiff and unassuming but not a bad guy. He'd sold me the Saracen at cost. He didn't have to do that. I tried to avoid him, unpacking new stock, but he collared me immediately.

"Daryl."

My back arched like a cat disturbed – I wanted to bolt for the nearest shadowy corner. Reluctantly, I straightened, turning to face him. Might as well; there was no avoiding him now. "Oh, hi, Pete." It sounded exactly as evasive as it was. "Everything okay?"

I knew full well it wasn't. Pete's face was stern, although not unsympathetic – grey skin matching his grey hair. He'd known Sebastian; they'd been colleagues, of sorts. Seb had worked as one of the Vault's unofficial hawkers – customers for kickbacks.

"Orange sunglasses again?"

Shit. I went to make an excuse, but he cut me off; the words jammed in my throat.

"Look, Daryl, I know you've had it rough. Sebastian was a good man, but you're ..." He searched for the right word, not willing to commit to screwing up. "... flagging, and you're fifteen per cent down. That's a lot."

I dropped the fake smile, showcasing my down-turned mouth, making things worse. I couldn't help it; no one can smile while being torn a new one.

"It's not even me, Daryl. The Telcoms have already noticed I'm further behind than normal. That's a dangerous place for me to be in."

I stared at my boots, prickles of tears welling behind the shades. "So what's the deal, boss? You booting me out?"

I held my breath, waiting for the reply.

Pete went to say something then stopped, the words held behind pursed lips. He let them out in a puff, not ready to deliver the killing blow. "Okay, Daryl, look, I can give you to the end of the month to pull things back. You'll need to produce something special, but if you can, I'll put this behind us."

Holy crap, I wasn't being fired! My smile returned, although more from relief. I had a chance, a tiny one, but a chance. I took it with open arms. "Thanks, Pete, I won't let you down." It was all I could manage.

I went to get on with unpacking stock, but Pete wasn't finished; he rested a hand on my shoulder. "And, Daryl, you need to clean yourself up, if you know what I mean."

I did.

"You used to be this place's best salesman. That's still in there somewhere, but this ..." He looked me up and down. "... won't do. I need the old Daryl back."

I nodded, head pounding from withdrawal. It unsubtly underlined what Pete was inferring.

Pete squeezed my shoulder before leaving. It went on longer than an encouraging one would. There was a finality to it. A warning. I couldn't blame him. I was dead weight in this operation. I didn't think I had much hope of making up the sales, but I'd have to try, or everything would get worse.

The rest of the morning was slow, but if I wasn't making sales, I could at least appear busy. I restocked the Diecom area and caught up on the latest tech via the holo-feed. Limelight was expanding their coverage again. It was up to seventy per cent of Neo-London now.

It was around midday when things picked up. I was cleaning a display ARO when she walked in. Medium height, slender, and dressed like a freaker, although not really. The faux leather was high quality and well fitted – it was a style choice; she wasn't part of a gang.

Her hair was electric pink and shaved on one side, revealing an ear full of silver piercings. Not classically beautiful, features somewhat severe, but still engaging and attractive. She had the rare look of someone not completely in the Telcom's pocket. A public relations rep or holo-vlogger? The ARO on her shoulder looked beaten up. It needed an upgrade. I was good at selling upgrades.

I wasn't the only one who'd noticed. Jay had spotted her – the other sales rep on duty. We were friends, but that counted for little when targets were down.

I shot him a glance: *Back off. I need this.*

He ignored me, retrieving a middle finger from his pocket. He knew my situation, but sales were sales. We both went to intercept her. He got there first. It worked to my advantage. Jay was good at upselling, but his cold openings were dreadful.

"Welcome to the Vault," he declared enthusiastically. "Can I help?"

Amateur! One day, he must learn how to open. I held back for a second, awaiting the inevitable.

"No, I'm just browsing."

There it was. Jay's approach went down in flames, his dopey face suitably crestfallen.

I waited a beat. Long enough not to appear rude, but before Jay could try again.

"Looks like your TripLite's seen some action," I remarked casually, pretending not to look at her. "The V2's far more durable you know."

She squared her attention on me, eyes furrowed, quizzical, but interested. "Yeah, I suppose it is a bit tatty. I've had it for years."

I pretended to take more notice. "And for good reason. It's a great device, but the updated models have really moved things on." I pointed to the TripLite section of the shop and she wandered over in that direction. I followed behind at a respectful distance, smirking back at Jay. I made a cranking motion against my hand – winding up a middle finger, returning the one he'd given me earlier. Beaten, he slinked off.

I didn't feel guilty. It was survival of the fittest at the Vault. Anyway, with me off my game for so long, he'd made decent progress on the board of doom.

My head still felt like a hammer was attacking it, but seeing off Jay had put me in the zone. I was proud of my encyclopaedic knowledge of devices, providers, and plans. And I had a good eye for what people needed, even when they weren't sure themselves. I hoped I could hold it together long enough to close the sale.

I ran my new customer through the specs of the TripLite V2, explaining its updated operating system and features. But after a few minutes, I became distracted. Something strange was happening. She wasn't listening. She was nodding along, but it felt more like she was evaluating me rather than the device. Must be my imagination. I continued detailing options, but the feeling persisted; her eyes were on me rather than the display.

Maybe she'd seen through the orange specs and fake smile. She didn't look the sort who'd know, but SP1N found itself in all corners. No, it's paranoia.

"... So you see, its up-rated, flip-out screen can be converted to show a holographic interface or ultra-high resolution. It depends what you're after—"

"What's your name?"

The question confused me until I remembered I hadn't affixed my holo-badge. "Er, it's Daryl," I replied over my arm, where I'd been showcasing the ARO.

She was looking at me intently, eyes dark and wide. I'd noticed she was attractive, but I'd been preoccupied with the sale. As she gazed at me, I felt a knot tie in my stomach.

An uncomfortable amount of time passed. "Er, nice to meet you?" I said uncertainly – a stark contrast to the confident salesman I'd been presenting a moment earlier.

She smiled, studying and nodding. She held her hand out. "I'm Karin."

I took it and shook. A little out of sorts, but I couldn't refuse. Her hand felt soft, nails painted black and filed to subtle points – feline. They raked my skin as I retracted my arm, sending an electric tingle through me.

I tried to pick up where I'd left off, but I was hopelessly flustered, mind racing. It had been a long time since a girl had taken interest. A real one.

My mind switched from selling AROs; raw biology had taken over. But I had a new problem. Did I have the courage to do something about it? The idea sent shivers of fear and excitement through me.

Clumsily, I continued showing her the models, fumbling opportunities to develop the conversation.

Somehow, I still closed the sale, and she took out a Limelight contract too. A high-margin option. Pete would be pleased. She was definitely no freaker if she had the creds for a quantum connection.

I brought over the payment pad ready for a thumb scan. My last chance to make a move. I rehearsed it in my head: Hey? Perhaps we should exchange connection codes in case you need help with the new TripLite? – It sounded terrible.

I felt sick. No wonder people stuck to virtual girls.

She handed the pad back.

I opened my mouth to deliver the line.

*Beep.* Her ARO chirped. She turned away, checking a new message. Then, seemingly annoyed at the news and with little more than a nod of thanks, she grabbed the new ARO and walked out.

Damn. I'd flubbed it. I'd had at least a dozen chances to get her code over the forty minutes she'd been in the Vault. Why had I left it to the last minute!

Jay walked over. "Smooth operator."

Had it been that obvious? Disappointment surged as I realised I could still feel the tingle in my hand. "Get lost. How many Limelight connections have you sold today?"

"I'm two per cent over my quarterly. I don't even need to come in." He shrugged.

That brought me back to earth. The sale had helped, but not much. I'd need thirty more like that to get me on target. And it was a hollow victory. I felt like I'd missed out on something.

There were no more customers in the store; the lunchtime rush was over. Jay flipped the conversation. "You coming around tonight? I've made some upgrades to my rig. Fridge is full of vials too."

More beer. I wanted something stronger, but I couldn't think about that. I didn't have creds for tabs and the conversation with Pete was still fresh in my mind.

Something had changed today though. I'd felt like my old self for a few minutes. The missed opportunity was disappointing, but it was healthy disappointment – a normal disappointment. This was a chance to get back on track. Another clear night would get me over the worst of the withdrawal.

I thought of Sebastian, rotting in the asylum. I still didn't know what had happened or made a plan to get him out. I was a disgrace. He never would have abandoned me like that.

Pete's warning. The hallucinations. The girl. They were all signs I'd reached rock-bottom.

Jay was looking at me expectantly. "I've got a new action simulator ..."

I didn't need more encouragement. I'd made my decision to clean up, but Jay's offer helped, and it would be a good distraction.

"Sure," I stated with a firmness that raised his eyebrows. "See you there."

# STATE 04

Clapham was in a part of Neo-London that might be called adequate. Not good; only a fraction could afford places that were good.

Mostly pedestrianised, it was full of mid-range outlets and reasonably appointed domiciles. For sure, it was still grotty. Half broken street lamps bathed the stained pavements in hazy green neon. But it was less overtly filthy, and with fewer homeless or open acts of violence.

Jay's income was as meagre as mine, but his parents had been well off – leaving him creds after they'd passed. The Administration had taken its eighty per cent inheritance cut but left enough for him to buy his domicile outright. That left food, utilities, and an ARO connection to worry about, with no need to resort to criminal activities as I did. The rest went into fuelling a serious virtual reality addiction. Different to mine. His preference was for violent gaming. Retro action sims – the new fad.

Retro sims were a reaction to dipping VR sales. Creatively bankrupt developers had re-imagined old film and TV shows – turning them into virtual experiences. Functionally, there was little difference to modern games. But what's old is new; they *felt* more authentic and there was an anachronistic novelty to living out past fantasies.

We were six games into the most recent release: *Commando 1985*. I'd seen the film years ago, converted into holo-format. It was dumb, but irresistibly of its time, and with a hilarious ending. The antagonist Bennet, the maniacal, chain-mail wearing ex-marine, had been impaled through the chest with a steam pipe. This was still possible in-game, along with new ways for players to dispatch each other.

Re-enacting the final scene, a cat-and-mouse battle inside a sprawling, industrial basement, I was playing Bennett – armed with a period-appropriate 9mm pistol. Jay had picked John Matrix, the eponymous muscle-bound commando of the original film. He'd found the grenade launcher too. I was hopelessly outgunned.

Steam sizzled from valves, obscuring our vision as we ran around the underground complex, fighting for position. It was a maze of metal staircases, creating opportunities for stealth.

I paused on a walkway. I had to move slowly or the game would register my feet clanging, giving me away. The simulation was suitably lifelike – video-realistic graphics and convincing sound design. But it was still a game.

SP1N would change that. A quarter tab and I'd feel the heat of the steam and even smell the musty odours in the basement. It would also kill my damn headache.

Jay preferred not to use SP1N. He claimed it reduced his performance. That was an excuse – the reverse was true. Jay was paranoid; he only left his domicile to work. Putting something with an unknown supply chain into his system would be abhorrent to him.

He didn't care if I did though, and normally I would, but I was trying to stretch another night, and for once it made sense to be around someone who wasn't interested.

A grenade burst to my left, sending me careening against a wall. The game simulated an injury, reducing my mobility and causing me to stagger. I wasn't prone to VR nausea, but the sudden jolt still produced an unpleasant twinge.

"Daryl, I'm gonna KILL you, Daryl!" Jay loosed off another couple of grenades from across the basement. They exploded against a nearby railing, but the game now had me registered in cover. They boomed noisily overhead, causing my vision to blur, but were otherwise harmless.

"Wrong film!" I yelled back.

Jay was confusing his '80s action thrillers. That line was from *Total Recall*. Same leading man though.

"Doesn't matter. You're still dead."

I could hear the smirk in his voice. I was good at VR games, but this one was about the race for the best weapon. Jay had memorised the spawn points before I'd arrived. I was at a huge disadvantage.

Pinned down, I snuck a look around the railing. Jay was out in the open, waiting for me to break cover. His body glowed blue – showing he'd found the body armour power-up. With my reduced mobility and underpowered sidearm, I was screwed. He'd soak up more ammo than I had in the 9mm.

More grenades burst and insults hurled. I considered rushing him, going out in a blaze of glory, but pride held me back. He'd won the first five games. I didn't want to hand him another victory.

I looked again. Tactically, he was in the weakest position on the map, metres from any cover, but he was so overpowered that it was starting to feel hopeless. Then something caught my eye. Something interesting.

Above Jay's position was an environmental feature he hadn't seen, or if he had, he hadn't realised its significance.

I couldn't be sure, but it appeared the game designers had put something in place to prevent this situation. A trick to stop overpowered opponents controlling the central zone. And if I was right, it was also an Easter egg; a reference to another film from the same era, and again, with the same leading man. If this worked, Jay wouldn't know what hit him!

"Hey!" I shouted out between grenade launches. It wasn't necessary to raise my voice, the game would cancel background noise, but it was difficult to remember that over the explosions. "Hey, Jay!" I said again, waiting for a pause in the bombardment. "What's the third rule in a crisis situation?"

Jay went silent for a moment before replying. "What the hell does that mean?"

I leaned out and fired the 9mm into what I'd spotted – a ball of chain above him. It unspooled with frightening speed. Jay yelled and swore, but it was too late. A ton of chain crushed his avatar, the simulation reporting him disabled.

"Duck!" I laughed, walking over to where he lay, buried in rusty metal. "I take it you haven't seen *Twins*?"

"Oh shut the hell up!" Jay sounded as indignant as he looked, one eye visible deep within the pile.

The game ended, darkening my screen. I removed the helmet and blinked a few times, eyes adjusting. Jay shoved his helmet onto his forehead, throwing his controller across the room. The glowing bundle of buttons and sticks shattered against the far wall. He had a box of spares to replace it, but being a sore loser cost him creds every month. He slumped back in his seat to sulk.

I yawned, looking around awkwardly – mentally adjusting to the real world. Exiting VR was always disorientating, no matter how accustomed you were. It left a surreal quality on surfaces – questioning whether the helmet was still down. It was just as well Jay's flat was such a slice of reality then. A quintessential bachelor pad. Modern, disorganised, covered with man-toys. A fake, Vietnam era M16 rifle was mounted on one wall, a nude holographic of a pole-dancer on the other. The whole place smelled of beer and the rubber gaskets used to seal VR helmets.

I picked up an alchovial and swigged hard. My headache still throbbed behind my eyes and the grenades hadn't helped, but it was a distraction, something to turn my mind off. The beer was helping too. Beer always helped.

"Better luck next time." I reached across and punched Jay on the arm. He recoiled. It was too soon.

"Piss off and die, Romeo."

It was a spiteful call back to my failed attempt with Karin earlier. I should have left him to cool off, but that was a low blow, and I wasn't in the mood to give it a pass. I let out a long sigh. More than required.

There was a minor delay, but after a few seconds, Jay straightened up. "I'm sorry, Daryl. I shouldn't have said that. I know things have been bad since Sebastian. I'm an arsehole. Ignore me."

Jay was a soft touch – easy to manipulate. I leaned back, using the moisture on the outside of the glass to rub against my head where the helmet had built up a funk. "Forget it."

I wished I could forget about it. Considering my more immediate problems, I'd thought about Karin more than I should.

Jay put his feet on the table, grabbing some crisps from an open bag between us. He continued to talk while chewing, crumbs flying everywhere. "You know ... Pink hair means she's an Administration agent anyway."

I groaned. Here we go. Jay, paranoid conspiracy theorist, had been activated. It was his main hobby outside VR. "Any more vials?" I attempted to change the subject before he got going.

"Yeah, by your leg."

I looked down. There was a pack sitting right there. The self-cooling wrap cold against my combat trousers.

"Anyway," he continued, not missing a beat. "All those PR girls are linked up with the Telcoms, and the Telcoms control the Administration."

"Uh-huh." I humoured him. "And what has that got to do with pink hair, exactly?"

"I'm getting to that." Jay reached to scratch under his helmet where it perched, then thinking better of it, removed it entirely. He was getting comfortable; I was in for the long haul. No escape until he'd said his piece.

I listened for the next ten minutes. According to Jay, network employees are all injected with an undetectable serum. It altered their DNA code to access Administration installations with blood-scan readers. It also turned their hair white, encouraging them to dye it garish colours.

"So yeah," he finished, hands behind his head. "You can't trust people with dyed hair. It's a well-known fact."

I nodded and took another sip, trying not to pay too much attention – this was one of Jay's less endearing qualities.

The holo-display in the room's corner flashed up a newscast. Jay had set it to alert him if anything of note happened. More paranoia. He was convinced the world was scheming against him.

There'd been a large fire in a commercial district of HK1. The image showed a low building blazing against the night sky. "At least five casualties confirmed," the electronic newscaster stated robotically.

I missed real reporters. The virtual ones were okay, but there had been something great about watching actual people stumble over words or swear on camera.

"Damn world's gone to crap," Jay remarked.

I slumped deeper in my chair, the words registering harder than normal. The world *had* gone to crap. It could be the withdrawal or the bad day at the Vault (or both), but everything felt worse right now. I thought of Sebastian and the events at Camden, a poisonous wave of guilt following. It started in my chest, working its way down my arms and fingers. I'd made no progress getting him out of the asylum, and what was I doing? Playing games and drinking beer. I'd had an excuse when I was deep in a SP1N-cycle, but what was my reason now?

Realisation struck. This bad feeling wasn't going away on its own. And I'd committed to staying clean so there'd be no help from that direction either. I could already feel the tendrils of depression pulling at me. I had to deal with this or I'd slip backwards, undoing my progress.

I got up from the sofa, unsteady as the beer worked through me. "Hey, Jay, I gotta go."

Jay bolted upright. "What the hell, man? We've only played a few games! Why you quitting so soon?"

"Sorry, I've got some things to take care of."

Jay gave me a disappointed look before leaning back in resignation. "Fine, I'll join up with some guys online." And then suspiciously. "You're not going to get high are you? There's almost some colour in your face for once."

I shook my head. It was a possibility, one I'd fight every inch of the way, but it wouldn't happen right now.

I saw myself out of Jay's block of flats and walked south. The customary Neo-London drizzle had recommenced. It was incredible it had held off this long.

Brixton wasn't far, only a couple of miles. No point risking the Underground; it was safer to walk. I had no overcoat; the rain soaked my hair and ran down my neck. Good. It felt miserable. I should feel miserable. I'd wasted so much time since the accident.

I passed a gang of freakers fighting, lazeblades flashing. It was a mock battle, blades set blue, voltage low – they'd burn rather than slice each other. Practise fights marked out the leaders, the most experienced building up patinas of burns across their hands and faces. I heard a yelp as a blade came in low under his opponent's guard, hitting his flank – the material of his jacket left smouldering. It was a mistake; the tattoos and scars of the aggrieved fighter marked him out as a general. The attacker had almost none – a low level grunt. It wasn't a good idea to make your general look bad in front of the troops.

"That's my favourite jacket, runt!" he remarked, licking his lips. I hurried past as his lazeblade switched to red.

On the other side of Clapham, Brixton Asylum was a converted indoor market. The shops and bars long abandoned – put out of business by freaker protection rackets. Sprawling and dilapidated, the old units were well apportioned for wards and holding cells though. Or so the local municipality thought.

I arrived at the barbed wire enshrined entrance past visiting hours. No one cared when people came in; the crazies had no concept of time. The asylum was more concerned with people getting out, but even then, not really. Locals found confused gown-wearing patients wandering the streets all the time.

The guard behind the security station barely registered me, buzzing the gate open disinterestedly.

Sebastian was on the public ward – a hangar-sized creation of knocked through shops. It housed patients deemed safe or catatonic enough to live together. I walked along until I found his bed, past row after row of vacant, dribbling, and muttering bodies. Seb was at the end, staring out a barred window, seemingly transfixed by the rain. I liked to imagine he was daydreaming, but I knew it was just the way his head was orientated.

I took a seat in front of the metal cot. The whole ward was a disaster. More like a homeless shelter than a hospital. Patients swearing at each other, rocking, or staring off into space. It was only operational because of volunteers but threatened with closure every year. Seb looked gaunt and his hair seemed thinner. His strong, good-looking features receding. Guilt welled heavier than ever, a deep pain in my chest seeing him so vulnerable.

Tears welled. "I'm sorry you're here, Seb." I hoped he might hear me. "I've been clean for three days now though. I'm trying to change."

A commotion was beginning at the end of the ward, but the floodgates were open, and I had to get this out.

"And I met a girl today. Believe that? A real one. I messed it up, but I came close to getting her code."

I paused, unsure how to continue. I'd held off saying the thing I'd come to say, knowing uttering it out loud would commit me and make it real.

Voice trembling, I took a breath, fumbling the words. "... Look, Seb, I'm ... I'm getting you out of here ... I swear it."

Tears descended as the commotion intensified. I looked up. A wild-haired man had become enraged. Volunteers went to restrain him, but as they closed in he reached into his pants, flinging handfuls of faeces – stockpiled for such an event. We were at least fifteen metres away, but the stench was immediate – thick and overpowering.

The volunteers held him down, chaining his writhing body to his shit-stained bed. He'd stay that way until the morning, when he'd be re-medicated and his bed sheets changed. In theory at least. That was anything but guaranteed.

I'd said what I needed to, so it was time to go. "Goodbye, Seb, I'll see you soon."

On the way out, I tried to impress on the volunteers how important he was, imploring they show him better care than the others. They nodded and said they understood, but their cold tones said otherwise.

As I left, I made a silent declaration. I was no clearer on what I would do, but that hadn't been the reason for coming. Out of sight was out of mind, and the temptation to slip into delirium too easy. I'd needed to strengthen my resolve, force myself to look at him – feel the pain. This would be my turning point. I'd wasted enough time. I just had to hold on a few more days to get out of the SP1N-cycle.

# STATE 05

That night was restless. Cold shivers of withdrawal removing all hope of sleep. And itching uncertainties – the hallucinations at the Trocadero, rationalised but not forgotten, plagued me. Questions reverberated endlessly. What could I do to help Sebastian? Could I stay clean long enough? Was I losing my grip on reality? A milieu of thoughts, intermingled with uncomfortable, abstract dreams. Shadows chasing me, a girl laughing at me, the world folding in on itself – collapsing like a neon edged house of cards.

I woke with a jolt, covered in sweat. Had I been screaming? I wasn't sure. My throat was sore so I could have been. The holo-clock read 6.06 am.

I groaned, grabbing a crumpled t-shirt lying by the futon. I used it to wipe clammy moisture from my face, breathing in and out, trying to pull myself together.

The evening had been tough. Seeing Sebastian had been a double-edged sword. It had reignited my guilt but reminded me why I'd retreated into SP1N in the first place. Even with the promise to stay clean, I'd had to suppress the fresh urge to get high. Unwelcome thoughts kept breaking in: Hey, Daryl, you could trade your ARO for a cheaper model – that would cover some tabs for sure.

I'd held on, sleep fighting me all the way, and when it did finally take me, the dreams had fought me too.

There was no getting back to sleep; it had ejected me like vomit. Might as well get moving.

I went to wash. Properly this time, not just a face scrub. The cubicle was disgusting, with black mould, but the water was clean – or so I reasoned. I turned the temperature up to the severe side of uncomfortable. It caused pinpricks of pain as it hit my cold flesh – a poor man's acupuncture. I tried to imagine the heat burning the sins away from me. When I stepped out, I was a solid shade of pink and tingling all over.

I forced myself to look in the mirror. The gaunt figure was still there, but my mouth and eyes had returned to normal. That was good. No fake grin or shades needed today.

I held out my hand; it still shook, but it wasn't so obvious. My head still ached, but it was more of a dull background pain than the sledgehammer it had been before. I recognised the guy in the mirror. He wasn't especially wonderful to behold, but at least he was familiar. Not the maniac that had stared back the day before.

I rummaged around the flat, finding some genuinely clean clothes buried beneath the mess. Putting them on made me feel better. Not great, but human. I could imagine I was just another low-risker, worse for wear after a heavy night.

It was silly early, but moping around my filthy flat wouldn't help. I could open the Vault and do some re-stocking. It wouldn't help my sales target, but it might earn me some points with Pete.

Moreover, I was starving and there was nothing in the flat to eat. It was a normal, ravenous hunger, not the desperate post-SP1N craving for sugar. It felt good. A decent breakfast was in order. It would cost all the creds I had left, but it would be worthwhile. I had no idea how I'd pay for my next meal, but it wasn't worth worrying about. If the worst came to the worst, I would trade my ARO as my evil imagination had prompted me, but I wasn't there yet.

It was cold and dark outside. Street vendors were just opening. The owner of the burrito stall was Middle Eastern, speaking with a thick accent. He'd been among the last immigrants to get into Neo-London before the wall went up around the old M25 ring-road. He assured me his brand of meat protein was the best. It tasted like any other beef flavoured tofu, but it went down in big satisfying mouthfuls all the same.

I couldn't remember what actual beef tasted like. The last cows had died when I was six. Put down by a particularly infectious strand of mad cow disease. You could still get poultry and some red meat imports like lamb and kangaroo, but losing beef had driven up the value of remaining sources. The price of quality meat approached that of precious spices – elevated to a luxury good. The masses ate flavoured vegetable protein.

Finishing the burrito, I went to wipe my hands on my jeans, thought better of it, and grabbed a napkin from the stall instead. This was the cleanest I'd been in months, let's try to keep it that way. I lobbed the tissue into an overflowing rubbish bin and made my way to Soho.

I arrived at the Vault, and a new shipment had arrived, so there was plenty to do. Pete turned up an hour later. He thanked me for getting in early, but it was clear the conditions he'd laid out yesterday hadn't changed. *Hit your target, or hit the road*. What else did I expect? He was running a business, not a charity.

The rest of the day was uneventful. I made a couple of small sales. A sim-only contract to an older couple who wanted something 'no-non-sense', and a camera module to a freaker kid. He was pale and skinny, a bit younger than me. I suspected SP1N and VR addiction. They were starting younger and younger, but who the hell was I to judge?

Things picked up around 3 pm. I was showing a group of time-wasting kids the latest Saracen models when the door chimed and Karin walked in.

She'd braided her hair, striping her head pink on one side, and she'd swapped the dangling piercings for subtle studs. She was wearing a black, fitted overcoat that came down to her knees and met translucent boots at the hem.

She saw me and waved. My jaw dropped slack for a moment, prompting laughter from the kids. Face red, I hurried to distance myself from them.

"Hey, Daryl," she said, walking across the shop.

I met her halfway, trying to think of something to say. "Hi, it was Karin, wasn't it?" I answered, pretending I hadn't scribed her name on my brain.

She stopped in front of me, an appraising expression on her face. "You look different."

Oh crap, had my mouth turned down again? I held my breath as I waited for her to point it out.

"Oh, right, you're not wearing those silly orange glasses. You look better without them, you know."

I breathed a sigh of relief but couldn't help being offended. First Pete, now her. Those were my favourite damn shades!

"Anyway," she continued, "I need to return this."

She handed me a plastic bag branded with the Vault's logo. I noticed her old TripLite was back on her shoulder.

"Oh." I struggled to hide the disappointment. She'd come back for a return. Worse, I'd have to minus the sale off my beleaguered target. "Was something wrong with it?"

Karin shrugged, curling a finger around a braid. "No, not really. I just realised my old one had life in it." She patted the beaten ARO affectionately. "And anyway, I really can't afford this right now. You're a good salesman for getting me to buy it!"

"Oh, okay." I appreciated the compliment but still felt downtrodden. She'd purchased it on loan terms, which came with a cooldown period. As long as it was unused and in saleable condition, the Vault had to accept the return.

"But I'd like to keep the Limelight connection," she went on. "It's much faster than my old Diecast service."

Not all loss then. I'd refund the cost of the ARO and switch her to a sim-only contract. That was still a high-margin sale.

I nodded glumly. "Sure. I'll sort that out for you right away." I pulled out my scanner to refund the difference.

"Thanks ..." She paused, as if nervous or thinking before continuing cautiously. "Daryl ... I wanted to see if you'd meet me later tonight?"

I dropped the scanner, causing another burst of laughter from the teens who'd moved in closer to watch the exchange. Heart racing, I stooped to pick it up. I couldn't believe it. I was getting another chance, but how to reply without looking even more foolish?

"Sure, I mean, I guess – what did you have in mind?" I replied clumsily, standing upright again, fumbling as I processed the refund.

Her face lit up. "Well, I've got a friend who's having problems with his ARO. You know about this stuff, so I wondered if you'd come along and help."

Just like that, my heart dropped through my shoes. My body slumped and I could feel the blood rush to my ears.

She mistook my disappointment for rejection. "Oh please, Daryl, it would be a big favour. Look, here's my connection code." She aimed her ARO at mine, beaming the code over. It materialised on my screen, sourcing her photo and public profile from the Cloud.

I nodded, afraid my feelings would show if I spoke – unwilling to make things awkward by saying no.

"Great! We're meeting by the Shard at eight o'clock."

"Cool." I managed.

"Cool!" She spun neatly on her heel. "See you there!"

I sighed as she left, glancing over her profile, still displayed on-screen. She had thousands of followers, a busy feed of upcoming events, and loads of upvoted public messages. She was out of my league. My followers were drug dealers, VR merchants, and a couple of less-violent freakers (although I hid all that on my public profile). I was out of my mind to think she'd be interested.

I shook my head and did a mental check, trying to get some perspective. It didn't matter. It was more important to stay clean so I could help Sebastian. Even if it went nowhere, meeting Karin would be an excuse to avoid going home or obsess over SP1N. It was a blessing in disguise, even if it didn't feel like it. The teens were continuing to laugh, overtly now, pointing and ridiculing – like a pack of hyenas picking over a carcass.

I turned on them. Enough was enough. "Hey, you arseholes gonna buy something or not?" They left the shop giggling, but at least they were gone.

The rest of the day eked out as I continued to rationalise my disappointment. This was a good thing. My life had been on a downward spiral for so long. The only people I knew were addicts and perverts. Hanging out with regular people would be beneficial. I hoped l could remember how.

# STATE 06

The screen on my ancient Casio, set in scuffed gold plastic, ticked past 7 pm. It was closing time at the Vault; an hour before I was due to meet Karin.

No one needed watches. The clock on my ARO was perfectly accurate, but it was quicker to glance at a wrist than flip out a screen. I was glad I'd found clean clothes this morning – I wouldn't have had time to go home and change.

I sent a message to check it was still happening. The reply came back promptly: *Yes, we'll be standing outside, opposite the tube station :)*

No backing out. I knew it was best to go, but it would be easier to go home and drink my last two alchovials. That wasn't a choice now.

I locked up and assessed my options. It was a few miles to the Shard. I could risk the Tube, but it wasn't raining for once. There'd be less hassle if I walked.

I headed out of Tottenham Court Road, taking a route hugging the north side of the Thames.

As in Camden, it was a stream, but here the homeless weren't permitted to squat around the banks. I liked the way its dark, mirrored surface reflected the bright parts of Neo-London. It hid the twisted nightmare of brick and metal that was there.

I stared at its surface, hands thrust in my pockets – reflective. If only I could step through to a place where the neon lights were decorations on a better city – one made of neat, towering glass. Clean and uncluttered. One free of gang members and addicts. Maybe there I'd have a chance.

On cue, my head jittered involuntarily, reminding me of my status. Junkie playing good boy for the night. I quickened my pace. If I could hold on a few more days, maybe that wouldn't be as true.

Forty-five minutes later, I reached London Bridge. A triple-layered mega-structure slathered across the river. Metal struts were affixed to its sides, reaching down like spider legs into the riverbed – bracing against the bulk.

The monstrous creation served as a metaphor for Neo-London's management. Rather than repair nearby bridges, they routed traffic here, building on extra ramps and levels. The collected vehicles could be tolled more efficiently that way.

The guards ignored me as I jumped the barrier. There was no point charging pedestrians; they'd just wade through the ankle-deep sludge of the river instead. Only those unable to leap the bar had to pay – the old or disabled mostly.

I could see the Shard peeking through London Bridge's oily surface. Its slender pyramid shape coming to a point in the grey clouds. Once the tallest building in Europe – a monument of glass – that had changed when the Administration transferred its headquarters there. A move fuelled with corrupt Telcom money.

The decision had been a step too far, attracting an army of low-skilled protestors. Rage of their out-phased skills ignited by the globalised Telcom agenda.

They'd gather on nearby roofs, launching rocks with homemade slings and compressed gas mortars – the highest and widest holes in the Shard's mirrored surface scoring the most points. Unable to defend such a soft target, the Administration had retreated to Whitehall and Westminster, the traditional seats of power.

The dissidents celebrated a victory against oppression, but a deeper strategy had been at play.

Unable to prevent the uprising, Neo-London's management had seen an opportunity. They replaced their vacated luxury offices with subsidised retailers and bars. Re-skinning the damaged outer glass with steel coating, striped white with neon to distinguish it from the skyline.

How quickly the protestors vanished in exchange for cheap goods and booze meted out by the Administration under a symbolically black and impenetrable surface. Control through consumerism.

I arrived and scanned the area. There was normally an event, something to distract from city drudgery, to get people in a spending mood. Today was no different. Outside the main entrance, artists gathered in the courtyard, displaying their works. The theme was forests and flowers.

The exhibition was drawing a significant crowd. Overdevelopment had all but obliterated parks and green spaces in Neo-London, but the human urge to experience them was very much intact.

On one side, a laser sculpture was on display. Hundreds of yellow and green beams intermingling to create an abstract, yet identifiable, Japanese bamboo forest. The artist had left space to walk through – providing the illusion of being enveloped. Opposite, a flower and rock garden had been created – a real one. I could make out the blue shimmer of an electrified dome surrounding it; two guards were patrolling its perimeter.

Flowers were a premium commodity. Each bloom poking through the decorative rocks attracted as much as high-end AROs. Sebastian would have had me searching for the power while he distracted the guards. I shook my head, ridding myself of the melancholy. I'd come here to be normal. To *try* to be normal. It was important to put the emotional baggage to one side. At least for tonight.

I spotted Karin. She was sitting on a bench near the rock garden, staring through the flickering field. She appeared to be alone.

"Nice, aren't they?" I wandered over, attempting to sound casual.

"Beautiful," she replied absently, not turning around. Then as if shocked from internal thoughts. "Oh, Daryl! Glad you could make it."

I couldn't tell if she was happy to see me or surprised I'd turned up. My nervousness intensified a notch. "Yeah, no worries." Then on a whim. "I'm meeting up with friends later. I had to come this way anyway."

I immediately regretted how contrived it sounded, but Karin took it at face value, eyes wide and curious. "Oh cool, where are you going?"

Damn, I hadn't thought that far ahead! I scrambled for an answer, hands fidgeting in front of me. "Oh, we haven't figured that out yet."

Her eyes narrowed in suspicion.

"So, where's your friend?" I changed the subject quickly.

Karin jumped up and straightened her jacket, the plastic crinkling. "Oh, he flaked out on me. Stuck at work, apparently, but that's cool. You're here now, so we can hang out if you like?"

So her friend had ditched her. At least she hadn't cancelled on me. The offer felt like charity – guilt driven for making me come all this way. What the hell. I'd take what I could get.

"Do you want to check out the art?" I shrugged, pretending to be sophisticated. I knew nothing about art.

"Have you walked through the bamboo forest yet?"

"Er, no."

"Me neither. Let's do it now."

She was enthusiastic, relaxed, and smiling. Maybe this wouldn't be too bad.

We walked over to the laser forest. The beams cut up to where the pollution hung overhead, casting dapples of colours in the grey. Admirers crowded the installation. Each jostling for a slice of beauty so out of place.

"Wow," I heard myself say, as I stared up. I had to admit, it was stunning. The sheer height and brightness. It was enough to blot out the dank blanket of clouds. "It's really something."

She paused, inspecting the sight. "Yeah, it is, I guess."

"You don't sound convinced?"

"I think I prefer the rock garden. This is too ... artificial."

I suppose she was right, but I'd never seen a real forest. Maybe VR addiction made synthetic experiences more appealing to me.

"Look at that!" Karin tapped me on the shoulder, sending a seismic shiver through me. It was a powerful contradiction to my last thought – perhaps some things were still better in real life.

I followed her finger. Nestled amongst the beams, a plinth was raised, topped with a sculpture of a bipedal cargo robot.

I recognised it. They were a mainstay of the construction industry. Its interchangeable limbs functioning as combination forklift truck and digger. The ground had grown up around its legs – foliage poking through its gears and pistons. It couldn't adopt an expression, but its posture was accepting rather than resisting its return to nature. I couldn't fathom any deeper meaning.

Karin twirled on her foot. "Daryl, can you take a vid of me by that statue? My followers will eat it up!"

She was off before I could reply, sprinting through the crowds. She reached the robot in a few seconds, clambering up its root-like legs. Flagrantly ignoring the *Keep Off* sign; drawing equal scowls and smiles.

I shrugged and opened my ARO. It was just as well I'd upgraded its video software. It now rendered in holographic 3D as well as ultra HD. That would give her some thumbs ups for sure.

A forward facing light blinked, signalling I was recording – a legal requirement and one of the hardest functions to disable. Low-riskers were fine with government monitoring, but a random guy with a video camera – *that* was unacceptable.

I focussed the camera. Karin had scrambled to the top. She hung around the robot's neck, kissing its slab plated cheek. I gave her an okay sign in case she couldn't see the light from the dozen metres that separated us.

She waved back and struck a different pose. Swinging around the robot's limbs. She was so energised and well adjusted – nothing like the losers I hung about with.

I looked through the viewfinder, making sure she was in frame. The forest lasers were washing her out. I adjusted the exposure to compensate.

I was good at making videos. It was part of my job to use ARO features, but it was more than that; I understood how to frame a shot and compose a scene. If I'd applied myself, I could have been a holo-editor. I sighed. Another missed opportunity lost to the SP1N-cycle.

The crowds parted for a moment. I dropped to one knee for a more dramatic angle, widening the lens to include the Shard, towering over Karin. Let's see what her followers thought of that!

Who was I kidding? It was her approval I was after.

The composition was ideal – very artsy. Light from the forest highlighted Karin as she continued posing. Her slim, fit body contrasted with the robot's stockiness – her plastic jacket casting interesting shapes and shadows. Flashes of thigh above her boots made her movements sexy, but without being obscene.

My heart quickened as I watched, but then something distracted me, dragging my eyes from where they wanted to be. It was a light – high on the Shard. It sparked in the display, breaking my concentration. What was that?

The explosion that followed was deafening. It ripped from the side of the Shard, beginning as a small flash before blossoming out and consuming the sky. I tried to look away, but it was too late; the piercing light blinded me, washing out the camera display.

Blinking, I tried to clear my vision, the world murky and spotted with orange. Shielding my eyes with my hand, I could make out a jagged hole in the building – bellowing out fiery slabs of metal and neon. Huge chunks were arcing through the sky, gathering height in our direction.

The shock caused Karin to lose her grip and slip off the statue, tumbling towards the ground.

I scrambled, looking for an escape, but there wasn't any – just walls of panicked, screaming people.

Instinct took over, forcing me to the ground in a defensive crouch, head buried in my arms. I tensed as I awaited the crash of wreckage.

Seconds ticked past. Enough to wonder what death might feel like. Would I even notice? Was the speed of being crushed faster than human cognition?

I continued to wait, but nothing happened. No pain. No sensation. Things should have concluded themselves, but they hadn't.

I opened my eyes. Everything was still and silent. It was like after my encounter with Led. But this was no hallucination. It was a nightmare. Everywhere, people were frozen in moments of terror. Women's mouths open in silent screams. Wild- and glassy-eyed men staring up – ropes of neck muscle tensed as they prepared to duck.

I'd seen holovids of catastrophes, but nothing could prepare me for seeing it in person. Raw and unstaged, perfectly captured.

I doubled over in a heave, feeling vomit in my throat. Then remembering the Trocadero, I grabbed my mouth and swallowed hard, sputtering to regain control. I looked at my finger where Led had bitten me. It had scabbed over, but at the time the blood had pooled around my hand like a glove. What would happen if I were sick? Suffocation seemed likely.

Gasping in the thin air (another returning and unwelcome sensation), I caught sight of Karin through the crowds. She hung precariously in midair.

Seeing her vulnerable refocused me. I couldn't count on this being a hallucination anymore. I'd been off SP1N for days. This felt all too real – too consistent with before. Something had let me get away from Led and it was happening again.

Understanding flowed over me like a wave. This had all started with that damn room in Camden! The suspicion had been growing for days – ever since the first time-freezing incident. It was too much of a coincidence. I'd thought it was deranging me, like it had deranged Sebastian, but that wasn't everything. It had done something else – something deeper and much scarier. My promise to Seb came rushing back like a haunting echo. That room was the key to everything! I couldn't ignore it anymore.

I shook my head and blinked, remembering my situation. The importance of the revelation was paramount, but at this moment, there were bigger concerns. The phenomenon was an opportunity to escape, and before I could help my brother, I had to help Karin. She hadn't intended to make an impact on me, but that was hardly the point – she'd managed it, and I felt the way I did. I spurred myself into action, wading forward.

The air was heavier than ever as I closed the distance. Karin was suspended, shoulder height above the crowd, surrounded by terrified faces, captured in their latent states of death. A lump rose in my throat as I peered at them in turn.

I grappled with my guilt. It was irrational to prioritise someone I'd just met. Should I try to help someone else? Or leave altogether? I didn't owe Karin anything.

I set my jaw. That wasn't true. I did owe her something. For a few moments today, she'd made me feel like a normal person. I was no hero, but I wasn't an arsehole either. We'd entered this nightmare together, and we were leaving together.

I tested Karin's arm. It was solid; a perfect manikin in a terrible magic show – the backdrop a sky peppered with chunks of steel and neon. Anxiety gripped me like a kick in the balls. It would take seconds for the lumps to crash down on us in real time. I had to hurry.

I looked around for anything I could use. We were in open ground with nothing sturdy to shelter beneath. Even if there had been, I doubted much would withstand the weight of falling steel. If we were to live through this, it wouldn't be by hiding – we'd have to leave. But how?

I scanned the sky again. The explosion had sent debris out in a semi-regular pattern. Larger lumps were thrust furthest forward, hanging over us imminently, but the ones nearer the building, where the blast had originated, were smaller and higher up.

My mind whirled, thinking through options. The Shard's stability didn't seem compromised. The hole was large, but it was only in a small part of the building. If time resumed, we could run, and with foreknowledge of where debris was falling, avoid it and take refuge in the Shard's lobby. That was if the pattern was predictable and we could plan the perfect run. And of course, there'd only be one attempt.

I shook my head. Absolute madness, but there was no other way.

It was about thirty metres to the lobby entrance, a marathon given the circumstances. At least the doors to the sheltered area were open with no obstructions. There were security guards, but they appeared as panicked as everyone else.

I estimated the first chunks would land in a few seconds, then roughly every second following. The later ones would be smaller, but just as deadly. In all cases, debris would smash at our heels all the way to the Shard.

About halfway between us and safety was a short, wide run of steps. Ten in total. Never had something so innocent appeared such an obstacle. I'd been considering carrying Karin. I wouldn't have time to right her, explain the situation, and get moving – but that plan was scrapped now. Karin was small but not insubstantial. Worse, the incline of the stairs would kill our momentum and create an un-favourable angle to the debris.

She'd need to be on her feet before the steps or we were dead in the water. There must be a better way.

Biting my lip, I re-examined the spread of debris. It appeared less dense and higher on the left. If we could make it the first few metres in that direction, I'd have a moment, maybe two seconds, to rouse Karin, then we could run up the stairs together. I puffed my cheeks and breathed out, incredulous at what I was considering.

I racked my brains. Had I missed something? I couldn't think of anything.

Another wave of doubt blindsided me. It was a complicated and dangerous plan. Why not just leave? Stroll out of this disaster and never look back.

An image appeared behind my eyes, burned there since I'd seen it. Sebastian face down in the treatment centre. The guilt that had dulled since seeing him in the asylum welled up.

This wasn't the same, but the effect would be. This time it would be worse. I had a chance to do something, to act with agency. I'd just stepped back from the brink. If I left Karin now, her death on my conscious would drive me over it.

Resolved, I moved to position myself beneath her, bending my knees in anticipation.

I didn't know how long I'd have to wait. At the Trocadero, time had resumed when I'd stepped outside, but I didn't know what triggered it. I'd been sure I'd imagined the whole episode – I hadn't tried to retain any details. All I could recall was the world restarting when I was out of immediate peril, away from danger.

Distance could be a factor then – moving away from the epicentre. But if that were true, we were screwed. If I left the area now, I wouldn't make it back to help Karin.

What else? Come on, Daryl!

The only additional detail I could remember was feeling calmer. Not safe, but in control, able to think. What if the frozen state was brought on by stress? Something that receded when I was less panicked?

Seemed like a long shot, but nothing else was coming to mind. It was worth a try, although I'd have to reduce the thumping in my chest first. Far from calm, it felt like I was having a mini heart attack!

I closed my eyes and breathed. I imagined myself and Sebastian at my flat, drinking vials. His drunken face grinning. He reached over and clapped me on the shoulder. "You know, Daryl, you're the smart one. You just haven't had your moment yet."

I couldn't remember if that had happened, but it was the sort of thing he'd say. The words drifted over me along with a brief wave of contentment.

Something changed. I could feel it. The world winding back up – the start of a breeze and a rise in temperature.

Eyes open, I paid attention this time. Events didn't just recommence; it took a few moments, like a video starting at half speed. Karin's body floated downwards a few centimetres before dropping suddenly.

I let out an "Ooph!" as she landed in my arms. "I've got you." I grunted under the weight, time returning to full speed against the roar of the explosion. She turned to look at me, expression unreadable. I'd feared she'd resist, but she didn't; she was compliant.

I started my (slow) sprint to the left of the stairs. Karin wasn't heavy, but I wasn't in good shape. Every step was difficult. "Be ready ... when I stop." I managed between wobbly strides.

I detected a nod as I heard the first of the steel slabs crash down. It boomed behind us, showering us with debris. The shock caused me to stumble forward, but I kept my footing. I tried not to think about the people crushed to a pulp behind us.

The crowds were reacting on instinct, feeling the paralysis I'd felt. Most were crouching, some running – all panicked. Free of indecision, we were the only ones attempting an escape.

Another crash, closer this time. This piece must have been on fire. A shower of sparks rained down from behind us.

Feeling the breath ebb out of me, I closed the remaining metres to the stairs. I wouldn't last much longer carrying Karin like this.

"At the stairs ..." I wheezed. "... Get ready to run." Again, I detected a nod.

As we arrived at the spot, I didn't so much drop Karin as let her slip, my arms giving in. She responded with surprising speed, sprinting up the stairs as her feet touched down. My lungs were burning, but there was no time to pause. I followed, labouring up each stair.

I looked ahead. The run to the lobby appeared clear. No ... not clear – damn it! A man in a green jacket was bolting to the lobby on a path that would intersect with Karin. He was young, fit, and moving with purpose. She'd be crushed if she changed course but would collide with him if she didn't. Another near crash, enough to make my ears pop as the shock wave flowed over me. I had to concentrate.

Mind racing, I looked for options. At the top of the stairs, a rubbish receptacle was in reach. A shoulder-high, metallic cylinder sitting idly. I was upon it before I had time to consider the consequences. Reacting more from desperation than sound judgement, I altered my course, considered the angle, and barged into it – aiming squarely for Green Jacket. It was a huge risk. I'd no idea if it was freestanding or welded to the ground. The consequences if it hadn't moved would have been dire.

It rocked off its stand, thankfully with little resistance. The thin metal deformed around my shoulder, and it was propelled into Green Jacket's path. Seeing it would impact him, he took a wider route, enough so he would no longer collide with Karin.

There was no time to celebrate or mentally applaud my dumb luck; we were in the home straight now. There were no more obstacles and the sounds of crashes were thinning.

Then out of nowhere, a lump of steel landed in front of Karin, not a big piece, but jagged, with enough of an edge to catch her toe. She tumbled forward, landing heavily on her side.

Within a second I was by her side, yanking her to her feet, but she was stunned and moving slowly, too slowly. All our momentum was gone – we weren't going to make it!

A green-sleeved arm reached down and grabbed Karin's other hand. It was Green Jacket; he'd caught up to us again. His extra pull was enough to resume our momentum, and with a few more steps we all tumbled into the lobby, the remaining debris crashing down behind us, blocking the door, and blasting smoke and dust in.

I gasped for breath, vision blurred from exhaustion. I wanted to say something to Green Jacket but had nothing in my lungs. He was already on the move, further into the building. Shame welled. My callousness almost killed him. I'd assumed he'd collide with us; I'd never considered he may help. I closed my eyes, the exertion pushing me close to unconsciousness. The new stab of guilt made me want to retreat into it.

Dimly, I was aware of someone calling my name, revoking permission to escape reality. Hands grasped my shirt, shaking me.

The world faded back into blurry existence. It was Karin. She was saying something. "Daryl, we've gotta get out of here!" She was serious and commanding, but calm. "Daryl! On your feet. We're leaving!"

Who was this? I didn't remember her being like this.

My head cleared. A few seconds had passed, although it felt like longer. Karin was tugging me to my feet with surprising strength. I pulled back against her hand and rose, head throbbing.

"Daryl, can you walk?"

"Yes." I tried to steady my voice.

She gave my hand a squeeze. "Good. You did great back there, guiding me out, but it's time to move."

I wasn't comprehending this. How did she know I'd guided her out? She should be terrified, completely disoriented, but she wasn't; she was composed.

"Come on, Daryl," she urged. "There's no time to lose. We have to go!"

Still confused, I allowed Karin to tug at my hand, leading me through the building – the way Green Jacket had gone. I felt bad for nearly killing him, but what about those left behind, crushed or dying under the wreckage? I suspected their memory would surface later, but I couldn't become paralysed with emotion now.

We made our way through the Shard's reception area, exiting on the far side. The area outside was unaffected by the carnage but still a scene of chaos. People gasping, proclaiming, and pointing. It had been less than a minute since the initial explosion tore through the opposing wall.

Once we were clear, I tried to get Karin's attention. I couldn't understand why I was the scared and confused one.

"Karin—"

She spun and grabbed both my shoulders, face serious. "Daryl, thank you, but you have to follow me now. There's more going on than you think."

"What—"

"I'm sorry, there's no time to explain. Are you injured?"

This conversation was happening in reverse. I should be asking her if she was injured! Bewildered, I shook my head from side to side like an obedient dog.

"Then follow me." She grabbed my hand again.

Not knowing what was going on or how to respond, I followed dumbly as she picked her way through the throngs of morbidly fascinated onlookers. The streets of Neo-London were bathed in the pink glow from the flames reflecting off the Shard's dark surface. If this was a hallucination, it had taken a turn for the worse. This was no longer a minor flight of fancy. It was a full-blown psychotic meltdown.

# STATE 07

The following panic-stricken hours were a maze of running and hiding. I didn't know why. We hadn't done anything wrong, but Karin insisted we keep off the roads, directing us through every back alley and bad neighbourhood in Neo-London. I'd seen more unconscious bodies, spent skin-guns, and general filth than even I could cope with.

Every time we encountered a large group or busy area, she'd held us back. I couldn't tell if she was avoiding people or high-traffic areas – the shopping nexuses and arcades were given a wide berth.

Any attempt to broach the subject was shushed, making me feel like a naughty schoolboy. And like a petulant child, I'd felt the urge to throw a tantrum, demand she tell me what was going on. But I held my tongue, instinctive to the dangers of cornering a wild animal.

Karin was concentrating, brow a deep furrow, eyes narrowed like a hunting creature. Now and then, she'd freeze and listen. I couldn't hear anything, but she could, and armed with new insight, she'd decide our next move.

We were taking a circuitous route full of twists, but our direction was south-west, and we eventually arrived at the King's Road in Chelsea – a grim part of town.

Chelsea suffered hardest from the *Great British Backlash*. After a decade of resurgent Marxist movements, activists had convinced the poor that the rich were suppressing them. They'd revolted in a short-lived moment of madness. A purge. Armies of wound-up working class had swarmed the wealthiest areas to 'get their taxes back'.

It had been a night of chaos, with black clad anarchists torching, looting, and killing the rich, mostly elderly, population. The Backlash had caught authorities off guard – only mobilising after the damage was done.

Brief and ultra-violent, by the time it was over, the urban elites had learned their lesson, but not the one the anarchists wanted. Shocked at their vulnerability, they'd sold up and fled to the coastlines, taking their money with them.

With no disposable creds circulating, the area's economy collapsed. Chelsea turned from one of the most affluent areas to one of the poorest. Every previously lavish flat and townhouse was now packed with dissidents and thugs. It was a place the powerful preyed on the weak, far worse than the rich ever did. Made my extraplex look like a five-star hotel.

Karin stopped, nodding as if satisfied. She turned to face me, un-bothered by the clusters of nearby gangs, tattoos close enough to read.

"All right, we'll be safe here for a moment."

"Safe!" I blurted out. "Safe from what?" I couldn't believe she'd stopped us here of all places.

Her eyes wandered to the rooftops. "Surveillance."

I followed her gaze. She was right. No cameras here. Police and Neo-Guards had given up monitoring this place. These people didn't pay their taxes, so why bother protecting them, but that explained nothing.

"Who are we hiding from?" I continued nervously. A gang of freakers was taking an interest – their bare chests and shaved heads menacing, even at a distance. One licked his lips in Karin's direction.

"I'll explain at your domicile. It's nearby isn't it?" she carried on, unconcerned.

My head snapped around to look at her. She wanted to go to my place? Sure, it was close, over the river, but I wasn't in a cooperating mood.

My fists found my hips as I stood my ground. "I'm not going anywhere until you tell me what's going on."

Karin's hands tensed at her sides, then relaxed, retracting like claws. She breathed out and her face softened. "I'm sorry, Daryl, there's too much to go over, and I don't know how I'll explain it yet. Besides ..." She glanced over my shoulder. "... As you've no doubt noticed, we're attracting unwanted attention."

The local freakers had decided we were worth investigating. A group was walking our way, thumping their chests – a tribal act of aggression. I could see lazeblades tucked in their combats. They made no effort to conceal them at all.

The need to be safe overrode my need for answers. I'd play along. "Yeah ... Okay, maybe we should leave." I mentally hopped from foot to foot as the gang approached. "But when we reach my place, I want answers ..." I trailed off – a panicked plea for us to get moving.

Karin smiled, replying meticulously, playing a deranged game of chicken. "You got it, Daryl. Lead the way."

I was already going, checking over my shoulder. Gang members were shouting and one had dropped his combats, exposing a large, excessively pierced penis, but they weren't pursuing. It was too early for violence; they'd have been asleep all day – probably hadn't eaten breakfast yet.

Rushing out of Chelsea on hot coals, we made our way to Battersea, my extraplex soon looming overhead.

We hurried inside and ascended to the penultimate floor. I clicked the lock and armed the security. I hadn't bothered turning on the electrified door in months. My only item of value was my ARO and that was always with me. Today it seemed worth the cost of electricity, although I still didn't know why.

I turned to face Karin, who was searching for a clean place to sit. My face flushed red. "Sorry," I mumbled, clearing away empty alchovials and convenience packages. I kicked a soiled pair of underpants under the bed, hoping she hadn't seen those too.

"Yeah, don't worry about it," she answered – the time between each word suggesting she was very-much worried about it.

Once the mess was concealed, a thought occurred. "Do you want a drink or something?"

Karin eyed the place sceptically, considering if there was anything she could consume that wouldn't kill her. She dithered for a few moments then finally settled on an answer. "Have you got a beer?"

I smiled. That was the one thing I did have. Freshest and safest thing in the flat. "Sure."

I fetched two beers from the kitchen. The fridge was broken and didn't chill well, but the vials were colder than room temperature. She cracked the seal and drained it in one go. I did the same.

We stood in awkward silence for a few minutes. Now the opportunity to ask questions had arrived, I was afraid to. I knew the Shard was no delusion, but what that meant was staggering. I wasn't sure I wanted it confirmed.

I stared at the top of my empty beer vial, like a tea-leaf reader, trying to divine answers from the suds gathered on the rim.

Karin broke the silence. "Daryl."

I looked up.

"I know this is confusing, but you should trust me."

I dropped the vial, frustration bubbling over like a shaken bottle. "What do you mean? Trust you! I don't know you at all. You're just some girl I sold an ARO to. How do I know you're not an agent or undercover Neo-Guard?"

Karin was unfazed, raising her hands in platitude. "Daryl, do I look like a Neo-Guard?" She pointed at the futon. "Look, sit down for a moment. You'll need your strength soon. We shouldn't be wasting energy."

Misdirection. Why shouldn't I be wasting energy?

Still, I collapsed on the futon anyway. I'd been desperate to since getting inside. I was physically and mentally exhausted.

"All right ..." I continued, trying to calm myself, rubbing my hand across my forehead. A tension headache was building on top of the withdrawal that still hadn't departed. I wanted to sleep, but I needed to quiz Karin. "What, exactly, do you mean?"

She didn't answer right away, just cocked her head to one side, listening for something. "Nothing ... yet, just a strong feeling."

This was ridiculous. I was being confronted with riddles. I was too tired to unpick the strange behaviour. I continued with her previous point. "Look, you said I should trust you. Why should I trust you? I have no idea who you are."

She dropped onto the futon beside me, hard enough it bounced me into a comfortable slump.

My body responded with a wave of fatigue, locking into a relaxed position.

She gave me a sidelong glance. "Look, Daryl, rest. I don't think you're capable of hearing this right now."

That should have triggered me into a soft rage, but tiredness was coming on like an avalanche. The explosion, the mad dash across

Neo-London, and my withdrawal. They were all taking their toll. My burnt-up adrenaline had created a hole only sleep would fill – imaginary weights tugged at my eyelids.

There was enough resentment to prompt again as my eyelids began to flicker. "You ... you didn't answer my question ..."

Through closing eyes I heard a faint response, left in the air. "Because ..." Her voice drifted further into the distance. "... I trust myself."

More riddles, but it was too late; the wave of exhaustion hit, taking me into unconsciousness. My frailty was pathetic. I couldn't even hang on long enough to finish the conversation.

# STATE 08

Sebastian was with me, beer in hand. Eyes hazy with drunkenness. I couldn't tell where – some dive sim-shop. The walls were distant shadows, visible through swirls of vape smoke. It was hard to hear over the din, but he was telling one of his long-winded tales – I could tell from the way his hands animated. It didn't matter; the details weren't important.

Content he'd made his point, he leaned back, taking a swig of beer, but he left it there too long. The liquid ran over his chin and down his jacket.

I laughed out loud. Silly bastard. He was always doing that.

I expected him to pull the vial away and wipe his sheepish face, but he didn't. He'd stopped drinking and was letting the beer drain over him. Something wasn't right.

He was staring at his right hand where it grasped the vial. It was frozen in mid-air – pinned – his arm pivoting and yanking around it. He shouted as he grasped with his other hand, words muffled by the vial, still lodged in his mouth.

I jumped up, rounding the table, but slammed into something before I could reach him. A barrier, like a sheet of toughened glass, cutting me off. I pounded my fists on it, but the surface was impenetrable.

Sebastian's other hand froze to the vial, both arms straining, pulling like a mime against a door handle. His shoulders and head writhed as he silently screamed from across the barrier.

I thumped with no effect, feeling left and right, trying to find a way around. But there was no way through, just a smooth, impassable surface. All I could do was watch.

Sebastian's arms stopped moving as the freeze spread along them and through his body. Eventually only his head was moving, but then that, too, froze still. I could see he was shouting my name. Desperate for me to help him.

It spread to his mouth, locking it in a dumb look. Wild eyes, darting and terrified, turned glassy and still.

I'd seen that face before – a mask of vacant catatonia. The one he'd worn when I pulled him from the room in Camden. Where he'd sacrificed himself. Where he'd lost his mind.

I woke with a start. Cheeks wet. A mewling sound coming out of me like a dying animal. Karin was standing over me.

Disoriented, I tried to remember where I was. I sat up and sniffed, unable to hide the sobbing. "How long was I asleep?" I managed.

"Seven hours," Karin responded gently.

I sensed she wanted to ask if I was okay, but it was too awkward. I had to pull myself together. "Seven hours?" I replied more firmly, checking the clock – it was past 6 am. I couldn't believe so much time had passed. "Did you sleep too?"

She nodded. "A few hours."

She'd tied her hair into a ponytail on one side and removed her makeup. It matched her demeanour – serious and thoughtful. "It's good you're awake though; we've got a problem."

Shaking off the nightmare, I eyed her cautiously. "What do you mean?"

"We have to leave."

The words were ominous, but Karin said them with a detached, bored expression.

I was alert now, focussed on the situation, and aware I was still in the dark. I couldn't hide the frustration. "Just hold on a minute. You asked to come back here last night. You still owe me an explanation!"

"Yes, I know, but it has to wait. We're out of time." And with an air of genuine apology. "I'm sorry, Daryl."

I took a breath. Despite the fitful night, I felt better, more able to think. I forced myself to remain calm. I needed her to explain what she was on about. "Okay, Karin, what do you mean *out of time*? No one knows we're here."

She sat down on the futon. "Good, you're calm. You'll need to be for this next part, but you're wrong; people do know we're here."

"Who?"

"You'll see soon enough."

I tried to get up, stand so I could argue, but her next words stopped me dead.

"Daryl, I know you can stop time."

Hearing it out loud made me feel lightheaded, like I was still dreaming. I slumped back down.

"At least," she continued, "I do now. I wasn't sure before, but I am now." She looked around the room, voice wistful. "I can do things too. Not the same as you, difficult to explain, harder to demonstrate. You need to trust me a bit longer."

Karin was turning into a broken record. She'd said something similar last night. That I should trust her because she trusted herself. Whatever the hell that meant.

"Daryl, I know more about what's going on than you, but I didn't know things would escalate this quickly. They have though, and the danger has followed us here."

What danger? We were safe in my domicile. What was she talking about?

She glanced at the window. "Look for yourself."

Reluctant to move, I looked at her, then the window, and finally let out a sigh. I stood and opened the glass pane – it was too dirty to see through closed.

The view wasn't much from the thirty-ninth floor. Neo-London's pollution hung around at this level. I could make out the shadows of other extraplexes – shapeless neon tracing through the smog. "I don't see anything."

"Look down."

It was better lit at street level, lamps illuminating the foggy, drizzle-covered courtyard. It was empty save for some abandoned vehicles and overflowing bins. I was about to say so, then three black vans arrived. They had no markings, but they looked beefed up, with flared wheel arches and strong grills. I'd seen similar vehicles on holovids – at riots.

I swallowed dryly, anxiety building.

The rear doors opened and a dozen guards stormed out, making their way through the courtyard. Their black armour was accented blue – Neo-Guards. I spun and stared at Karin. "How'd you know they'd be coming?"

She stood purposefully. "Don't worry about that now. I can get us out of here, but you need to keep close and not question me." Her eyes were wide and intense. Her body had taken on that feral, cat-like quality again.

Indecision gripped me. I hadn't done anything wrong. Maybe if I explained myself they'd let me go?

I shook my head. Don't be an idiot. No visit from the Neo-Guards went well. Most people outright vanished. Karin was right. We had to leave – now!

"What do we do?"

Karin explained in short clear sentences. "Neo-Guards carry plasma stun-guns. Widespread, but no good at distance. We need to keep out of the ten-metre effective range. But that's not the biggest problem."

There was a bigger problem than that?

"They use their numbers to flank and corner, and they're augment-ed for strength. If they catch you, they'll take you down. So unless you're a martial artist ..." She looked me up and down. "... Well, let's say there's no defence if they catch us – we'll need to stay ahead of them."

She stopped to check if I was comprehending.

I nodded, dumbstruck. Apart from the bedrock of panic and in-creasing sense of surrealism, I understood what she was saying. I want-ed to know how she'd come by such detailed information though.

Karin turned to leave, then glanced back. "Can you follow orders without questioning me?"

I blinked, not understanding.

Her tone turned patronising – I needed it. "This is going to be tough, Daryl. I need to know I can rely on you."

For a moment she sounded like Sebastian. I nodded slowly, hating the imbalance of knowledge and power between us. I was in a video I had no script for, but the pressing urgency of the Neo-Guards was paramount. "Yes, I can follow orders." I acquiesced. "But I won't keep following blindly. You need to tell me what you know when we get away."

"*If* we get away." The sinister statement hung in the air as she strode across the room. "Unlock the door, please."

Lips pursed, I followed, unlocking the door. The security panel flashed green. "The lift's this way." I pointed to the left.

"I know, but they'll come up that way. They're already half-way up."

There was no way she could know that.

"Follow me," she whispered and moved in the opposite direction along the corridor, keeping low. I gritted my teeth and followed.

We emerged on the adjacent side, the walkways open to the elements. High railings, but no windows – not cost effective. There was a strong wind howling.

I took a second to lean over the railing, craning to see around the corner and down into the carpark. I could make out one van.

Two Neo-guards were waiting, stationed to check anyone exiting the building. I couldn't imagine how we'd get by.

We paused at the sound of voices. Official, military – the radio chatter carrying on the wind. "Check his room. Everyone else split up and cover the rest of the floor."

Karin was concentrating, head cocked – focussed rather than panicked. "This way," she urged.

I towed along, back scraping the wall until we were in front of a closed door.

"This one's unlocked." She rapped the composite material with a knuckle.

"How do you know that?" I whispered back.

She ignored me, twisting the handle – the door swung open.

I gagged at the offensive smell that greeted us, but I hurried in, closing the door behind us. I didn't need long to figure out why the place stank. I recognised a drug squat when I saw one. Rotten mattresses, rusty skin-guns, and discarded scraps of food – the stench of neglected, unwashed humans.

I'd been to places like this. Paid jobs to collect people who'd spun off the rails. Desperate family members willing to pay to find their loved ones. We'd never fallen this low, but I recognised similarities. I hadn't been far off.

Karin covered her mouth with her sleeve and crouched down, whispering urgently in a low voice. "Daryl! Get down."

We hunkered by the door, listening in tense silence. We could hear boots thumping outside and more military chatter.

"They're not in his room. Search the halls!"

The stomping got closer until it was right behind the door, then receded as they searched further along the corridor.

Karin leaned in close to my ear. "We can't stay here long. They'll lock the building down soon, search room by room." She cocked her head in that infuriatingly mysterious way.

I silently vowed to understand what she was doing.

This time, rather than declare our next move, she furrowed her brow. "Damn. I don't know where to go next. It looks like we're on our own for a while."

On our own? Was she receiving help? That would answer some questions, but who, and why had they left? This was maddening!

I didn't enjoy being kept in the dark, but Karin had been leading the way. With that sense of security ripped away, a blithering sense of panic descended.

"Daryl!" Karin grabbed my shoulders, breaking my mental paralysis. "This is your building. Is there another way down?"

Her voice was steady, but her nails were sinking in – a sign her confidence was slipping. I had to think.

The extraplex was forty floors high. We were on the thirty-ninth. There was a bank of three lifts, although only one of them worked. There was also an emergency stairwell running through the centre of the building. I relayed all this back to Karin.

"No good; all those will be covered." Her hands flexed back and forth as she thought. "What about rubbish chutes?"

There were rubbish chutes, but they were clogged and unusable. Most threw their trash out the windows.

"Sorry, they're blocked up and overflowing."

Karin leaned against the wall, eyes towards the ceiling. After a few seconds, she hit on a thought. "What about the roof? Anything we can use up there?"

I scratched my chin. I'd been on the roof a couple of times to smoke weed. My neighbours were thugs with a habit of shaking down residents. I didn't want to attract them with the smell.

There wasn't much up there. A flat expanse with some water tanks. Other extraplexes were around, but it was too far to jump. I did a mental walk around. A shape of something appeared in my mind. "You know, I think there might be something there that could help."

Karin set her jaw, reading something imperceptible, then sprung to her feet, heading for the window. "Okay, let's go."

"Wait! Don't you want me to tell you?" A mixture of confusion and fear swept through me as I second guessed myself. I wasn't sure I'd remembered correctly. I'd been high on weed the last time I was up there!

"No time." She examined the window. "We've gotta move, I can hear them searching rooms."

I stopped to listen. True enough. I could make out the sound of pounding on doors. I wasn't sure what was scarier – being caught or being wrong about the roof. Standing, I joined Karin, trying to avoid the human waste scattered over the floor.

"How are you at climbing?" Karin slid the window open, yanking away the safety mesh. Dim light flooded the room, casting a sad, stark reality on the scene. At least there was a breeze to hide the smell.

I was about to answer, protest the logic of climbing on a rickety extraplex, but before I could make my case, Karin had slipped out and shimmied out of sight. The lack of hesitation was remarkable.

I peered out, wind whipping around my head. I wasn't terrible with heights, but the thirty-ninth floor was enough to fill my throat with acid. It felt like I'd been kicked in the balls.

I craned my head to see where Karin had gone. She'd already reached the next floor – using a bunch of cables as a makeshift rope to clamber up. They were powering one of the neon advertisements affixed to the building.

"Move your arse, Daryl!" she shouted from above. "It's easygoing, the cable's strong."

It didn't look strong. I couldn't believe how quickly she'd moved. She may have lost whatever had been guiding her, but if she was afraid, she wasn't showing it. This was crazy – no way I was going out there!

*Thump-thump-thump.* The door rattled on its hinges. "We're coming in to search this domicile," a static-filled voice commanded. "Official Neo-Guard business!"

Holding my breath, I climbed out the window and around the ledge, just in time to hear the door burst open behind me.

Cold fear encased my chest as I faced the extraplex, fingers gripping like iron hooks to the window frame. I was standing on a ledge narrower than my feet, forcing me onto my toes, heels hanging into space. I was glad I couldn't see down from this angle.

Paralysis threatened as the wind howled, grabbing at my hair and clothes. Move yourself, Daryl. If I didn't get going now, I'd freeze up entirely.

I shimmied along awkwardly. A glance upwards showed Karin's foot disappearing over the top. "Hurry up!" she called down, barely audible over the wind.

Easy for her to say – I eyed the ancient electrical cables and decrepit staples holding them to the wall – she was much lighter than me.

There'd been no further commotion from the domicile. We hadn't been seen. The stink had probably done us a favour. Not even a Neo-Guard would want to inspect that place.

I reached the cables. They were a thumb-width wide, and the rubber was peeling off, revealing the shielding layer beneath. I hoped they were still insulated; dying from electrocution would be ironic. Karin was okay, but she may have gotten lucky.

I grabbed a fistful and tested my weight. They wiggled but felt secure.

Gingerly, I climbed, hand-over-hand, wedging my toes against the staples spaced every half metre.

On the third step, I looked down to check my footing and regretted it. The height was immense. It made my head swim. Anxiety dominated, but before it could take hold, a noise made my blood run cold. The sound of metal wrenching against concrete.

I stared up. The top staple, anchoring the cable to the wall, was crumbling in its hole. The bonding was struggling under my weight. Maybe Karin had disturbed it on her way up? Either way, it was going; I could feel the vibrations as the cable slipped through the slackening staple.

My heart was pounding in my chest, each beat a lightning bolt through my body. I looked for something to purchase on, but there was nothing. I was halfway between floors with nothing except featureless concrete on all sides.

The wrenching stopped. Its absence worse.

I looked again. Freed of its mortar, one side of the staple had come away and was bent at an angle, the metal turning white at the warped joint. The cables were hitched around the remaining side. If it were to hold, I might—

*Pop!* The other side came away with sickening finality, and with nothing left to support it, the cables went slack in my hands.

I let out a scream as I slid backwards into oblivion, gripping the cable with all my might.

It went tight again. My eyes were closed, but I knew what had happened. I was getting used to the sensation, and I was seeing a pattern. Peril brought on the time-frozen state. I'd never felt more grateful for it.

The wind died away, leaving the distorted drumbeat of my heart pounding in my head. Breathing was difficult, a weight on my chest. I cracked an eye open. I'd managed to keep my feet on a staple. I was hanging away from the building, suspended in midair.

The angle should have been difficult to hold, but it wasn't; it took barely any energy at all. The thick atmosphere was propping me up, reducing my weight. But I was running out of breath.

I couldn't get freaked out this time – lightheadedness would be fatal.

I continued climbing, thinking away the detached cable – the top end hanging out in space, half a metre from the building.

It was taxing, but only because of atmospheric resistance. Moving vertically was no harder than moving horizontally when time was frozen.

With the air around me acting like a safety harness, my paralysis receded. I was at the top and onto the roof in a few moments, coming face to back with Karin. She was frozen in a partial spin, a snarl on her face. Probably irritated at how long I was taking.

I wasn't sure if I was getting used to my abilities or the terror of recent experiences had desensitised me, but I was already feeling calmer. If the pattern held, that meant time would resume soon. I should use the chance while I could. I wanted to check if my memory of the roof was accurate. I couldn't believe how Karin had committed us, jumping out the window before I'd explained. She must be insane.

I swam past the water tanks that bisected the roof, a sigh escaping as I emerged between them. It was there. The extraplex had given up cleaning windows along with a bunch of other basic maintenance, but they'd left the cleaning crane. It sat, hunkered and rusted, on the far side of the building, but it was no figment of my imagination.

I stooped to get a closer look. It appeared usable, loaded with a spool of braided cable. Proper metal cable, not the rubbery, flakey stuff we'd used to climb up here. The crane lowered a platform to access the windows from the outside.

"Daryl!" Karin was calling from the other side as time resumed. "Where are you?"

"Over here!" I yelled back. The transition to real time had taken me by surprise. I needed to get better at noticing, or figure out how to resume it when I wanted.

Karin appeared between the water tanks. "How did you—" Her eyes widened. "Ah, you froze time didn't you? Are you okay?"

"Yes, when the cable came away from the building."

"That was lucky." Her tone was pragmatic, glossing over the near death. "Good for if you fall off a building, I guess."

"Or for surviving an explosion."

"Quite."

"Or avoiding having a finger bitten off."

Karin stared at me blankly.

"Don't worry."

"Fine. Well, back to business; they'll search the roof soon." She joined me by the crane. "Is this why you brought me up here?"

"Yeah ..."

She walked around, appraising the crane, nodding her approval. "Good idea." She did her listening thing and shook her head. "We're still on our own. Any thoughts on how to use this thing?"

The "on our own" comments were grating me. Did she have a hidden radio? Someone she was taking instructions from but was out of range? – Who? Why? I knew she wouldn't explain, so I answered her question instead. "I've seen window cleaners on other buildings use similar systems. We can use it to lower ourselves down."

Karin wrinkled her nose. "Know how to operate it?"

Damn, no, I didn't.

"Come on, tech boy." She encouraged. "How hard can it be?" She added a smile for good measure. It was manipulative but effective. I quietly added multiple personality disorder to the list of afflictions Karin seemed to suffer from.

I took another look. The neck was three metres long, attached to a platform for the cleaners to stand on. There were control panels on the crane itself and on the part that lowered. I climbed over the safety railing onto the platform. There were a few controls and they were intuitive. It had several functions. It could swing 360 degrees, orienting itself over the edge, and was mounted on a track running the roof's perimeter – allowing cleaners to access all sides. A separate control governed ascending and descending, and there was a manual hand brake connected to one of the pulleys. I could operate it, it was simple tech, but the problem was power. "It's dead."

"That's a killjoy."

"Wait a second." I eyed a lead running from the crane to an external box sitting aside on the roof. I ran over and yanked the cover off. It was the breaker unit for the crane. The security panel was red – showing the alarm was armed.

"Encrypted security," I explained as Karin joined me.

"Daryl, I don't mean to pressure you, but it's only a matter of time until the Neo-Guards find their way up here."

"I know. Don't worry. I've got this."

Minor equipment would only have low-level security to dissuade casual tampering. Sebastian and I had cracked more advanced systems, and customers at the Vault were always locking themselves out of their accounts.

I pulled out the touch screen on my ARO, booting up the decryption tool-set I'd cobbled together over the years. It connected wirelessly. As I suspected, the encryption was basic. It didn't need an algorithm. My ARO brute forced the lock with superior processing power, and the panel flashed green.

I couldn't hide the smug look as I faced Karin.

Her eyebrows popped up. "Okay. I'm impressed, but don't get cocky. We really have to go now." It had been a few minutes since we'd been in the drug squat, but they'd check the roof eventually.

We ran back to the crane; the control panel was lit up. I swung my legs over the safety rail onto the platform.

"We should descend on the other side." Karin jumped on board. "It's further away from where the vans are parked."

I nodded and manipulated the controls, hoping the crane wasn't rusted into position. It shuddered to life, grinding loudly as it made its way. I winced at the sound, hoping it wouldn't carry to the men looking for us.

After an eternity of agonised metallic screeching, we reached the far side. I input the command to swing the crane. It strained against the cables, lifting the platform.

Gripping the railing, knees shuddering, we slid into open space. Swaying in the wind, I held my breath as we hung, tentatively, forty floors up.

The platform had looked sturdy on the roof, but now it felt old and fragile, a rusted mesh of creaking metal. I winced, concentrating on the controls. I didn't want to bring on another episode of time-stopping.

"You ready?" Sweat was building on my hands where I was gripping the controls.

Karin gave me a thumbs up with both hands; she wasn't even bothering to hold on. Whatever biological process existed to assess risk was missing in this girl.

I pulled the lever downwards, beginning the descent.

It was rickety going. Gusts of wind swung the platform unnervingly.

Every few metres, slack in the cables unwound, dropping the platform a few centimetres. And each time, my heart jumped to my throat, but we made progress down the side of the extraplex.

There were blue flashes behind the windows. Neo-Guards searching the building. That was good; they hadn't converged on the roof yet. The windows hadn't been cleaned in years. We'd be unlucky to be spotted through them. Still, we kept low, moving around on the platform to avoid any that were open, or slightly cleaner.

The platform stopped with a jolt, controls reporting we were at maximum descent. Frowning, I looked down; there must be at least ten floors left.

I realised immediately what had happened, announcing it in disgust. "Damn! The crane must have been reused when they added the extra floors to convert it to an extraplex. They didn't upgrade the bloody cables – they're too short!"

Karin was straining to see around the corner. "We're sitting ducks out here, Daryl!"

I stared at the controls, trying to think. There'd be little point going back through a window. Our situation would be the same there as on the roof. And we were too high to jump – ten floors was as deadly as forty. My eyes settled on the emergency brake I'd noticed when I'd inspected the platform.

"I've got an idea. It's mental, but I've done something like it before."

Karin had taken a seat, legs splayed untidily. She leaned forward, placing an elbow on her knee.

"We need to cut the cable."

Karin's elbow slipped off her knee, causing both herself and the platform to lurch. "Cut the cable! Are you nuts?"

"Probably." I grunted, steadying myself. "Have you got a lazeblade on you?"

She stared incredulously. Whatever intuition she'd had before had abandoned her. She looked genuinely shocked, even a bit scared.

Despite myself, I felt the need to reassure her. "Look, I've trusted you up to now. That runs both ways. Believe it or not, this isn't the first time I've been in a situation like this."

It wasn't. A few years ago, Sebastian had caught himself in a lift shaft breaking into an arcade. It wasn't exactly the same, but we'd used a similar principle to get him out. Karin shook her head and reached into her jacket, producing a lazeblade. I wasn't surprised she had one.

I looked at the sleek metal device. "Okay, good. So here's the plan. If we cut the cable in the right place, it will unwind from the pulley at the top of the crane, doubling its length. But I can control the descent using the brake on the unspooling portion."

"But we'll go sideways!" Karin was aghast, lip curled in disbelief.

She was right. That wasn't something we'd dealt with in the lift shaft. Perversely, I was enjoying the reversal of our positions. "I guess we'll have to hold on." I shrugged.

Karin opened her mouth to speak, closed it, then finally spoke. "Well, you're full of surprises, Daryl, and we don't have much choice, do we?"

"Not unless you want to take your chances back in the building?"

Karin inspected the side of the building – flashes of blue through the murky windows. She shook her head.

"Okay, but we'll need to work together." I motioned for her to join me on the side of the platform facing the building. "If you cut the cable, I'll work the emergency brake."

Karin crouched next to me, looping her arm around the railing, nestling it in the crook of her elbow, her other hand ready with the lazeblade.

I did the same, only I gripped the emergency brake instead. A feeling of familiarity passed over me. Echoes of a previous life. At least if I checked out it would be eventful, and better than a sad overdose.

I took a breath to steady myself. "Do it."

Karin activated the lazeblade, its emitter telescoping from the handle, sparking as the beam arced, creating the blade. Laze was a colloquial term. The beam was focussed plasma. Most were blue, but expensive ones were customised – Karin's was violet.

She worked assertively, using the blade like a saw. The plasma made short work of the cable, the platform lurching as each steel thread pinged free on high tension. "Get ready," she shouted over the whine of tortured metal. "Last ... bit."

I wasn't prepared for the speed the platform listed and fell. It was like someone had removed the world from beneath us! We went sideways immediately, dangling from the railing as the cable unspooled at speed. I lost my grip on the emergency break, causing us to plummet three floors. Desperately stretching, my fingertips found the handle again. I re-grasped it and yanked hard.

At first there was no slowing, but as I applied more force, I could feel the metal-on-metal friction slowly scrubbing off speed, the handle becoming hot in my hand. Finally, two floors from the bottom, we juddered to a halt.

Breathing hard, I looked at Karin. Her face was flushed red, eyes wide. One side of her mouth upturned in a half smile. My heart was pounding in my chest, although not as bad as when the power lines had given out. That had been sheer terror, this was controlled fear – it hadn't brought on the frozen time-state.

I loosened the tension on the brake, letting us move at a manageable speed again, lowering us the rest of the way.

We jumped off as the platform touched down and righted itself.

"Hey, that wasn't too bad," Karin said chirpily, rubbing the crook of her elbow where she'd been holding on. Her reaction wasn't honest though. I could see a subtle shake as she popped the lazeblade back into her pocket. I'd already thrust my hands into my pockets; they were practically quivering.

She did her listening thing and grinned. Whatever disruption had occurred was now clear, not that I could see how it would help – the Neo-Guards would be covering all the exits.

Unperturbed, she walked to a large wheelie-bin parked against the curb. "Here, help me move this."

The bin squeaked out the way on rusted wheels, revealing an open manhole cover.

"Get in."

Of course. The sewer. Why not?

We dropped into the passage below, slipping out beyond the confines of the extraplex.

Our presence, by some miracle, had been undetected. The Neo-Guards would pick up our trail soon, but we had a head-start, and by God, before they did, I was going to find out what was going on.

# STATE 09

Lazeblade held high, Karin cast violet light through the labyrinthine interior – our boots making luminescent ripples as they sloshed through the foul smelling, ankle deep wastewater.

Her guiding instincts back, Karin's turns were purposeful and informed.

Not so for me. Disconnected from line-of-sight to satellites, the GPS on my ARO blinked DISABLED. The pedometer function worked – we'd walked a kilometre, but that could have been a giant circle.

Natural light penetrated the interior, growing stronger until we emerged, draining into a Thames outlet. We dropped into the polluted trickle, mud sploshing up to our knees.

"What now?" I rubbed my eyes against the change in light. It was overcast and smoggy but enough to put spots in my vision compared to the blackness of the tunnel.

"We need to find somewhere to hide," Karin answered, nose wrinkled in disgust. Grime had travelled all the way up her translucent boots; they were effectively brown now. "I knew they'd chase us, but not so quickly. We're dealing with some serious people, Daryl."

"Any idea where we should go?" I said, sinking further into the slime. "You know, before we get stuck in this crap."

Karin thought for a moment, looking across the riverbed, then sighed. "Yes, there's one place we could try, but it depends if he wants to see me."

Before I could enquire, Karin was wading to the far bank. I guess I'd find out when I met him.

It was morning rush hour as we boarded the nearest tube. The carriages were full of scrubs – retail employees and sex workers. Those with money drove or connected to their offices in VR.

On cue, a group of tired-looking prostitutes boarded. Hair natty, lipsticks smeared. Street sex was bottom rung compared to sim-shops. Girls only made enough to feed themselves, and by the look of these, it still wasn't enough. Whatever, it was good to have people on the train; they kept the homeless at bay.

Leaving a slit open, I shut my eyes. The last few hours had been a surreal dream. The timeout was appreciated.

We rode in silence, Karin deep in thought, mouth twitching. For once she didn't bother checking her networks. Wherever we were going, it was playing on her mind big time.

We alighted at Farringdon, north of central Neo-London. The prostitutes got off with us.

Farringdon was the only place the bars didn't close – the 24-hour clubbing district. Despite their knackered appearance, the girls weren't done for the night. They'd come to pick up more business. I couldn't imagine they'd have much luck.

At street level, wasters and freakers lined the alleys, heads bobbing to bass-driven, electronic music seeping from doors and windows. The air was thick with sound. Deep vibrations you could feel in your chest. The floor was littered with alchovials and skin-guns.

Farringdon had been through a cycle of death and rebirth for years. The seedy bars and underground clubs a recent return to an old past.

At the end of the century, the commercial district had bought up the area. Investment banks gutting the sweaty buildings and turning them into sleek, modern offices. The new spaces had flourished until the property crash of the late 2020s when prices had gone into free-fall. Desperate to preserve their investment, landlords had fled for the hills, leaving a heap of modern, disused property.

Ex-clubbing patrons, sore at the loss of their dance mecca, saw an opportunity and formed a consortium, crowdsourcing funds and buying back the property at rock-bottom prices. They created a new super-clubbing district. *Music by the people, for the people* – with a policy to keep the party going 24/7.

The bars had reopened in the renovated buildings the city had left – clubs cycling their opening hours, ensuring at least one was open at all times.

With Neo-London's ten million residents, there was always enough demand to keep the party going. But like any commune, it was sensitive to external influences.

Around the time the consortium was converting properties back into nightclubs, SP1N had flooded the market. Pink tabs poured out of state-sponsored labs in China, along with the skin-guns to shoot them. It was a hit. More powerful than ecstasy, cheaper than speed or cocaine. And music was a readily available sensory input. It didn't create the immersion of VR, but the synaesthesia, the oneness with the music, was almost as compelling – without the sim-shop fees.

SP1N destroyed the purity of the 24-hour party. Revellers came to shoot-up and forget reality. Drugs had always been synonymous with clubbing, but it had been an equal partnership – altered states of mind adding to the music. In Farringdon, the relationship had reversed – it was closer to a drug squat that played music now.

I'd spent a lot of nights here with Sebastian, but never sober. Seeing it without a filter was unpleasant. People looked like ghosts. I knew they felt good, but to onlookers they were at death's door. It was another log for the pile of shame.

Karin knew the area too. She avoided the carnage, making a beeline for an alley. Neon signs hung from the walls, dripping rainwater into reflective puddles. Mid-morning, the clubbers were thin on the ground, but still present, and in various states of drink, drug, and sonic based-delirium.

A skinny freaker leaned against the wall, blocking the narrow path. Shirt off, nipples pierced, head bobbing to the pervasive beat. He looked like he might be guarding what was beyond, but he made no movement as we approached.

As we came closer, the reason was clear. His eyes were shut behind his mirrored shades – lost in another world. He looked like he could maintain the position indefinitely, nodding along as his skinny frame wasted away.

He'd be slung to the outskirts of Farringdon if he dropped dead from starvation or exhaustion – no one bothered investigating deaths here.

We squeezed past unnoticed.

Karin stopped in front of a closed door. The neon sign above was broken, every other orange letter flashing intermittently, but I could still make it out: *The Pit*. It appeared closed – not enough of a crowd to open yet.

Karin tapped a message into her ARO and a few moments later the door opened and we hurried inside.

I hadn't been to this place before, but it was typical of the area. Dirty red faux-leather booths and a marred, potted dance floor. A concrete slab at the side served as a bar.

When open, it would be bathed in darkness, shot through with lasers and smoke, but with the fluorescents on it looked like an abandoned car park.

The place stank of sweat. Without patrons, there was no one puffing flavoured e-cigs to hide the smell.

A man was refilling optics at the bar. Something about him seemed off. He had a large forehead and strong features. The wrinkles around his mouth and eyes suggested he spent most of his time smiling, which he did as we approached – face crinkling into a friendly but suspicious grin.

"Karin." His voice pitched higher than I expected. "Didn't think I'd see you again so soon."

"Daryl, this is Emmett." Karin introduced us. She highlighted the 'm' sound in his name, as if she was saying M-et.

Emmett moved forward and vanished, like the ground had swallowed him, appearing a second later from around the bar. He was under a metre tall – a dwarf. The strange pronunciation of his name was now clear, the M insinuating a more derogatory term, although I couldn't tell if it was a true pejorative or a term of endearment.

Emmett looked up at Karin, eyes narrowing. "So, I'm guessing you must be in trouble." It was more a statement than a question.

"What makes you say a thing like that?" Karin sounded bored, like she knew this discussion would happen and wanted to be done with it. It was an act. I'd seen how agitated she'd been on the way over.

Emmett rolled his eyes in my direction, acknowledging Karin being difficult. It was a moment of unexpected but welcome solidarity.

I returned the eye roll, noting with satisfaction Karin's bored expression had become a frown.

Emmett continued. "Well, last time you were being chased for burglary, weren't you?"

I looked at Karin and she shrugged.

"And the time before you turned up barely coherent."

"I'd been drugged," she replied defensively.

"And what was the time before?" Emmett waved a hand in the air as he grasped for the memory, snapping his fingers as it returned to him. "Oh, that's right, it was a murderous boyfriend, wasn't it?"

"He wasn't a boyfriend," Karin whispered but didn't correct the 'murderous' part.

Emmett squared up to Karin, both hands on hips. An absurd gesture as she towered over him, but he was stocky around the gut – it lent him gravitas. "So what's it *this* time, young lady?"

Karin looked at me and then back to Emmett, her voice serious and apologetic. "You know, M, it's better I don't tell you."

Emmett relaxed his posture. Like Karin's fake boredom, it was a veiled attempt to hide his obvious affection for her. They were both playing games.

"That serious?"

Karin relaxed too. She hadn't been certain he'd be receptive, but things appeared back on track.

"Yes, but we only need a couple of hours and we'll be out of here. I swear."

Emmett held up his hands and let out a defeated groan. "Okay, but I'm trusting you're not dragging me into something."

"No, no!" Karin lied. "It's ... complicated – messy. It's best if you don't know the details, that's all."

I suppose that was true. If we explained, Emmett would think we were certifiable, and as a dwarf working in an underground nightclub, his tolerance for loons was probably low. And if he knew nothing, it might benefit him later if he was questioned.

"Okay." Emmett shrugged. "You know where to go."

"Yep, thanks, M." It was definitely a sign of endearment. Karin beckoned for me to follow.

We made our way to the back of the club and down a narrow corridor. It ended in a door with a *Staff Only* sign. Karin placed her thumb on the reader. The door lock flashed green and clicked open.

"I used to work here," Karin explained. "M likes me. When I kept coming back, he didn't revoke my security access."

Inside was a scruffy office. On one side, a desk strewn with paper records, and on the other, shelves full of ancient hard-copy binders. An old ink-jet printer sat on a stool in the corner. I didn't think they still made cartridges for them. Emmett had radically eschewed the trend of the paperless office.

Beneath the shelves hunkered a large beige sofa. It looked like it'd seen better days but also looked comfortable, covered with divots from a thousand backsides.

Karin dropped onto it with familiarity. "I think we better talk."

"Yeah, I think so too." I took the desk chair, trying to stay calm. I was raging with questions, but I'd learned my lesson with Karin; getting agitated just shut her down.

"Where do you want to start?"

Interlinking my hands to prevent them twitching, I took a breath. Before we discussed anything further, I had to know something. I'd accepted my episodes of time-freezing were no delusion, and Karin knew something about it.

"Why can I stop time?" I asked plainly. It still sounded ridiculous to hear out loud.

She fixed eyes with me for a moment before delivering the blunt answer. "It's complicated. I don't know precisely."

My jaw locked. I'd known the answer wouldn't satisfy or she'd have told me earlier. Holding my frustration at bay, I probed through gritted teeth. "Then why are you able to predict things? Who are you listening to? You must at least know that."

"That's two questions, and I don't have the whole answer to that either."

The cap on my frustration blew. I leapt from the chair, sending it careening into the desk in a mini explosion of office papers. "For Christ's sake, Karin! I want to know why the hell you've dragged me into this!"

She didn't react, just sat there, composed. It was infuriating.

Finally she replied. "Daryl, I know this is hard to understand, but at the moment you're asking the wrong questions. I don't know the 'whys' for much of this."

She paused, waiting for another outburst.

I held it back, biting my tongue.

"I know some things though," she offered. "For example, I knew to find you at the Vault."

I forced my mouth to relax, worried I'd scream the next words. They came out loud and strained all the same. "And how, exactly, did you know that?"

"I told you before at your domicile. Because I trust myself."

Throwing my hands up, I let out a frustrated growl and sat back down. I hadn't realised this conversation would be so exhausting! Breathing deeply, I leaned forward, hands on my knees. I wanted my next point to be crystal clear. "You'll have to do better, Karin, or I swear I'm walking out the door right now. I'll take my chances on my own if you can't give me some justification for the crap I've been through."

Karin wriggled uncomfortably. Something had gotten through. "Look, I'm not trying to be difficult, Daryl. It's hard to explain. I've never had to articulate it before."

"Try."

She paused to arrange her thoughts into something intelligible. "You're right, I *can* predict some things, but I can't tell you why I'm able to do it. I've never found that out. All I can tell you is *how* I'm able to do it."

I relaxed a little, this was a start. "Go on, begin with that."

"I'm ... connected to someone ... someone I trust very much. She guides me. She's the one who keeps me safe, but she's also the one who compels me to act."

So I'd been right – she *was* receiving messages. "So, what is it? Have you got a hidden communicator or something?"

"No, it's innate within me. A mental link."

I frowned. I hadn't been expecting that. Some sort of implant? "Okay, but who are you speaking with?"

Karin leaned forward, matching my posture and locking eyes. "Daryl, I'm not *speaking* with anyone. I only *receive* messages; it's a one-way street. I know this will sound insane, but I'm trusting you've seen enough weird things to accept it at face value."

I sighed and nodded, any explanation would be better than none.

"Okay, here it is ... the person I receive messages from is ... myself. A future version of myself, or it could be one from a different dimension. I'm not sure."

I blinked a few times. She delivered the information with conviction, but she was right; it sounded insane. I must not understand. "You mean you're acting like you'd expect your future self to act?"

"No, I'm literally receiving messages from the future."

She was acting like that cleared everything up. It's what a schizophrenic would say. I needed to be careful; I hadn't considered Karin might be crazy.

"How do you know it's yourself sending messages? Is it like a voice in your head?"

"I'm not mad, Daryl!" Karin reacted sharply, her cool breaking.

"I didn't say you were." I lied – I'd just been thinking it.

"But you thought it. I can tell, and not because what I'm saying sounds crazy. I felt and saw it. Sensed it. Like a psychic intuition."

"So you're perceptive?"

"No, you idiot! You think I could have found my way to you through perception alone. Could I have predicted the Neo-Guard attack at the extraplex? Wake up. This is real. As real as what you can do." She leaned back again, lips pursed. "You think this is easy to talk about? Imagine trying to explain how you stop time!"

This wasn't going well. Whether or not she was a lunatic, chances are I'd have to work with her – better to apologise and hear her out. "Okay, I'm sorry. I'm tired and this is confusing. Please, go on."

Karin continued, pressed back into the sofa, a scowl on her face. "Here's the thing. I don't have perfect clairvoyance. The messages I receive are vague and only relevant to the near future." She paused to see if I understood.

I didn't, but I nodded anyway.

"They're dreamlike and they vanish quickly."

I used my fingers to push away a confused frown that was developing.

"Look, I know it's hard to understand. Here's an example. If I walk past an alleyway, I might get a hot feeling and see an image of a lazeblade. That's enough to tell me there's a mugger nearby. But I wouldn't know who the mugger was, his specific location, or even that he would definitely mug me until I got much closer. It's like an early warning system."

"So at my extraplex, when we stopped and hid in the drug squat, you knew it was empty because ..."

"Because I felt cool and sensed an impression of an empty box."

I nodded thoughtfully. In an odd way, this was all lining up. Why was I so reluctant to believe her anyway? It was no stranger than what was happening to me. I needed to be cautious, but I resolved to listen more carefully.

"Okay, Karin, but if these messages are so vague, how can you be certain who's sending them?"

Karin's scowl started to lift. "Because they come to me in a short-hand I can understand. It's like knowing your own handwriting."

I was trying to understand but my bewilderment must have shown.

"Think about it," she continued. "Have you ever read something you didn't remember writing but were sure it was yours because of the way it was written?"

Not precisely, but I knew what she was getting at. While hacking, I'd come across code I couldn't recall, but I was sure was mine because of how it was annotated. So yes, I understood what she meant.

I moved my hand from my brow, nodding my comprehension, but her answers created more questions. I'd already spotted a big one. "Karin, if the messages are coming from yourself, why wouldn't you know for sure? You must send them back, right? Even now, aren't you having to send messages to your past self to warn of things to come?"

"No. I don't need to. It doesn't work like that."

"Well that doesn't make any sense."

"I know, but that part is complicated and I'm sure you've got more important questions right now?"

That was true. This conversation had derailed me from the most important thing I wanted to know. I tried to frame it; I needed a clear answer.

"Karin." I leaned forward further, almost to the point of falling out of the chair. "How did this happen to you? To us? How is the room in Camden connected, and what is Hive Ltd?"

Karin's eyes flickered as she sifted through what I'd said, answering simply. "Room? Hive? I'm not sure what you mean."

I lost my temper again, spittle flying. "The room, Karin! ... In Camden. Where I almost lost my mind!"

She sat for a moment, eyes unblinking, even under the shower of phlegm. "Stop shouting," she said firmly. "I'm afraid I don't know about a specific room, and I've never heard of Hive."

I could feel a pressure building behind my eyes and between my ears, a palpable rise in blood pressure. I couldn't believe it. This was crucial, and she had no information. A cold well of despair began to descend. How could I help Sebastian with nothing to go on!

Karin was still speaking, interrupting my self-pity. "... It happened to me on a sub-jet coming into Neo-London. We were flying low through the buildings when I felt like I was in many places at once. The next I knew, I was being woken by a hostess. I thought it was a weird dream, and later, when I started receiving messages, I was sure I was mad. But the visions came true. It was then I realised something had happened to me."

I caught the story mid-flow but learned enough to be grateful I'd tuned back in. It tied up with what happened to me and Sebastian. The locations were different, but the rest was the same.

As if in answer to my inner monologue, Karin said, "Daryl, I don't think what happened to us is connected by any specific place."

The pressure in my head calmed. "I see that. Some of your story is like what happened to me." I was still talking loudly, for no reason. I paused, regaining control before continuing. "I'm guessing none of your messages explain it any better?"

"I'm sorry, they're too vague, and whatever is going on is well hidden. I've not found out much on my own. Any time I get close to someone who might tell me something, they vanish, you know: *disappear* – with a flimsy official excuse logged in the system. Moved to another country, contracted an illness; typical cover-up bullshit."

I did know, recalling the speed the treatment centre in Camden had been locked down. I'd been lucky to escape unnoticed – I owed that guard a lot for keeping his mouth shut.

"Anyway," Karin continued. "That's when I stopped digging. It seemed obvious more prodding would only attract attention. Get me vanished too."

Okay, this was good. We were both speaking calmly again; maybe this wasn't completely fruitless. "But whose attention are you avoiding, Karin? Why are the Neo-Guards after us now?"

"Not sure. All I knew was I didn't want them finding out about me before I found out about them. That's irrelevant now, but I was right to be cautious. Whoever, or whatever, we're dealing with must be well connected if they can send Neo-Guards after us."

"Do you think it's the Administration?" It was a natural conclusion.

"Could be, but I doubt it. The Administration has no real power; they're just puppets of the tech corporations."

My mind hurt as I churned Karin's words. It sounded right though. The only entities with power were the Telcoms, although why they would take an interest I had no idea. I mentally filed the information. I didn't have the brainpower to untangle it. Besides, there was more I wanted to know. "You were going to say before how you found me?" I probed. "It couldn't have just been a coincidence?"

Karin yawned and rubbed her eyes before continuing. It was contagious. We were both getting tired. She carried on though; maybe she believed my threat to walk out. It wasn't entirely a bluff.

"All the leads I could safely pursue had ended," she explained. "I'd accepted that I needed to limit my search to passive observation, try to get on with my life. Then I walked past the Vault and in popped an urgent message – it compelled me to go in."

"Just like that?" I was genuinely interested. Karin's messages were intriguing if nothing else. "What did you see?"

"An image of a puzzle box, surrounded by black."

I stared at her blankly, prompting a better explanation.

"A puzzle, when solved, is shorthand for a solution – or answers. Black is like putting something in bold – it means very important."

"But what about me? The message told you to enter the Vault. It said nothing about meeting me."

"When you came over to serve me, I saw a green aura. That meant I was on the right track, but there was something else. I saw a silhouette of a person standing next to you. Male, bigger, but with similar proportions. So I assumed your brother was involved somehow."

She knew about Sebastian? "How could you possibly know that was my brother? That could have been anyone."

"It's my mental shorthand. If it was your father, the image would have been above you; a friend would have been standing further away." She paused. "It could have meant a lover, but I guessed that wasn't your thing."

A worried look crossed her face like a shadow.

"What is it?"

"Something about the image was unsettling to me. Silhouettes like those are normally solid, but the person standing next to you was different. It was an outline, not all there – hollow through the centre. I've seen nothing like that before, and I don't know what it means."

I knew what it meant. The image was hollow like my brother's mind. My voice wobbled as I explained. "Sebastian ... He pulled me out the way when I got hit with ... whatever I got hit with. I only experienced it for a few seconds, but he was in there much longer. It took his mind away. He's a vegetable in Brixton Asylum now."

"I'm sorry. I didn't know that."

"And you can't help him, can you?"

"Not right away. We don't have enough information, but there must be an answer. We found each other for a reason, Daryl."

Maybe, I pondered. A few days ago I'd been on my own. We were on some kind of path now, but I couldn't tell if it was any better. And I wasn't sure I trusted Karin, not yet. What was her motivation for this? She didn't seem under any special hardship – why not continue as normal with her new powers? They weren't obvious to other people – no one would know.

"Daryl." She interrupted my thoughts. "What's important is we've learned something new today. We're unusual."

I banked my concerns for another time and snorted. I couldn't help it; the comment was so absurd. "Of course we're unusual! You can predict the future and I can stop time. It doesn't get weirder than that!"

"No, you misunderstand me. I mean *rare*. We were only exposed to the effect for a short time. Me, because I was on a sub-jet. You, because you were pulled out the way. We were influenced for long enough to change us, but not enough to lose our minds. That's significant."

I wasn't sure why that was significant, but it did prompt another question. I asked it quickly while it was front of mind. "Hey, Karin, what about the others on the sub-jet? Wouldn't they have been affected like you?"

"Yes, I thought of that myself. I even got a flight manifesto and followed up on the people who had been travelling with me."

"And?"

"And nothing. They were unaffected, or exceptional liars. Not to mention, all the time I spent investigating, I was seeing red – literally.

My mental shorthand; it means stop or wrong. Anyway, my guess is there must be something physical about us that makes us susceptible. But that's just speculation."

"So that would make us even rarer."

"Yes."

There was a knock on the door; it was Emmett. He entered carrying a tray of rehydrated protein buns over his head. From where I was sitting, it completely obscured him, making the tray appear to float.

"Thought you'd be hungry," he said as the buns levitated to the office desk. White gelatinous exteriors steaming from the microwave. "There's a fridge under the desk with water and alchovials in."

"Thanks, M," Karin said.

I thanked him too, reaching for the buns. They were stuffed with synthetic beef, but it was good quality. I hadn't realised how hungry I was until I saw them; we'd not eaten in nearly two days.

Magic trick complete, Emmett faced us. "You two know how long you'll be holed up here? I can keep the club closed until nightfall, but after that I need to get back to work."

"We'll be gone by then, M," Karin replied sweetly. "I promise."

Emmett nodded. "Well, you both look tired. Why don't you rest for a while, but out by tonight, okay?"

Karin reached for a protein bun. "Definitely."

Emmett retreated. I wondered what sort of relationship they had. It was too close to be employer-employee – it must be paternalistic. I tried to imagine Pete putting me up in the Vault but couldn't. Thinking of that place was odd; it was distant now. I should contact him, let him know why I hadn't turned up today – make some attempt to preserve my job. It didn't seem important. I knew I was never going back.

I hunkered in my seat and closed my eyes. I wanted to know what was driving Karin, and we hadn't even discussed the explosion yet, but we'd spoken enough and were running on empty. Whatever was happening, it was in motion now. We were either going to sort it out or disappear, like the others. At least there were no decisions or regrets anymore. The inevitability was comforting in a way.

# STATE 10

We slept for a few hours. Karin on the sofa, me on the floor. I'd made do by balling my jacket into a makeshift pillow and spreading some office papers over me.

It was around 6 pm when we rejoined the living, riddled with self-inflicted jet lag. I felt grim. My body no longer had any sense of day or night. I didn't need a lot of sleep, but these snatched hours were taking their toll. And the anxiety of our situation didn't help – it was an omnipresent tension between my temples.

There were a few hours left before we had to vacate Emmett's bar.

Karin stretched as she stood from the sofa. Some of her braids had come undone, leaving a tangled pink fuzz on one side, and a lack of make-up wasn't doing her any favours either. Still, dishevelled as she was, her eyes were bright and she looked energised. Non-junkies have better immune systems, I reasoned.

Speaking of which, the itch for SP1N had reared its head. A persistent, scratching need to use, responding to days of persistent, scratching pressure. I rubbed my face to try to clear it, grabbing some water from the desk fridge and drinking deeply.

"So what's our next move?" I asked, wiping the overspill with the back of my wrist.

"Can you pass me some water too?"

Leaning over, I retrieved another, wishing I'd gotten her one in the first place. Things were shitty, but I should avoid being an arsehole. I had to keep Karin on side. She was my only link for helping Sebastian, and myself.

I apologised, handing her the vial. She cracked it and drank thirstily, answering my question when finished. "We need a plan. A way forward."

"No clairvoyant hints?"

"No, it's like I said." She used some water to smooth down the escaped braids. "It doesn't work that way. It's situational – short term. If someone handed me a plan, I might see if it was worth trying, but I can't produce the plan itself."

"Right." I swilled water around my mouth, trying to clear the bad taste that had taken residence there. "I forgot. *Short-term* clairvoyance."

"Right," she answered, either not noticing the sarcasm or choosing to ignore it. I kicked myself. So much for not being an arsehole.

I thought hard. It had only been two days, but so much had happened. It was difficult to remember it all. The carnage at the Shard, the way the explosion had ripped through the building, and the mad dash to escape falling debris.

The details were fading like a dream. We needed something solid.

I crossed to the desk computer, opening my ARO. A memory surfacing.

"What is it?" Karin straightened, intrigued.

I connected to the monitor, streaming out the last video on memory. The picture faded to an angle among a crowd Karin centre frame climbing a statue; the Shard looming in the background. The footage was still there.

"Oh, right!" Karin snapped her fingers. "I forgot you'd been recording! Great thinking!"

I scrubbed through the images, checking what the ARO had captured. I'd gotten everything up to the hasty exit through the back of the Shard.

"Yeah, and it looks like we got a full account."

"Well, play it!" Karin fussed excitedly. "Let's see what happened."

Tense, leaning on the desk, I returned to the beginning, letting the video play out at normal speed. It was something to behold. The disorientation and terror harder to watch a second time around.

I'd caught the explosion as it blasted from the Shard, the shaky camera doubling over to the floor when I'd curled up. My hands gripped the desk as I remembered the sick taste of fear – waiting for a crushing death. A moment later I was catching Karin as she fell from the statue – the minutes I'd investigated jump-cut while time was frozen.

The next moments were like watching us star in our own action holovid. Darting in and out of debris with superhuman intuition.

The video captured details I hadn't noticed the first time around. Falling masonry crushing men and women on either side. Their bodies shredded like papier-mâché dolls. It was horrifying. I didn't want to watch, but I couldn't pull my eyes away either. My knuckles turned white as they held fast to the desk.

Worse was to come.

My face flushed hot as I watched my on-screen double barge the receptacle into Green Jacket's path – narrowly missing killing him as he swerved to avoid it. My intent was even more blatant watching it back.

I felt Karin's eyes on me. "I didn't know about that bit." She breathed.

I tried to stutter a response, but she interrupted me.

"Thank you. That's twice you've saved my life."

Shocked, I looked at her. She hadn't acknowledged Green Jacket whatsoever. "But ... I almost killed that man." I was pleading for forgiveness. I didn't want her to think I was a monster.

"It was me or him." Karin's expression was serious, but her body relaxed, unconcerned. "You chose me. Thank you."

Consternation fell away, replaced with confusion. Karin's reaction made me feel better, but it created questions. She had a hard edge and ruthlessness to her.

We watched the last moments as we made it to the Shard's reception area, the video ending with a static pop, breaking the tension. We both stood away from the desk.

"That was exciting." Karin stretched her arms over her head. "Like a movie or something."

"Yeah," I mumbled, distracted by the exchange we'd had. "But all those people ..."

"That's not your fault, Daryl. You couldn't save them."

"How did you know I'd save you?"

"I didn't exactly, but I knew I wasn't going to die. I was pretty sure something major was about to happen, something I needed to see. It's what took me there in the first place. But I was sure I'd be okay."

"Did you know *I'd* be okay?"

"We better double-check the footage for clues." Karin sidestepped the question.

I grimaced at the meaning.

We ran the video back at normal speed, then half speed, and finally frame-by-frame, examining every part.

We cross-checked against the newsfeeds. They were reporting the incident as an accident. Faulty wiring in a server room.

Was that the best they could do? When does a server room use enough power to rip up a building! We ignored the official reports; it was an obvious attempt to whitewash the event.

I didn't know what to look for. There was no mastermind in a black trench cloak. No suspicious flash showing a fired rocket. It was a lot of people going about their business, not knowing a terrible disaster was about to befall them. They'd been talking, pointing at the exhibition, or like I'd been, taking pictures and videos with their AROs.

"Wait a minute," I said, rewinding the video to the earliest point, when the image had been at its widest.

"What?" Karin stopped checking holovids and joined me at the monitor.

"I, er ... I don't know how important this is, but do you notice anything in common about the people in this picture?"

Karin leaned close to the screen, tangles of pink hair brushing my face. They smelled faintly of soap – amazing; seven hours ago we'd been walking through a sewer. She scanned the forty or so people in frame. "No, not really."

"Look again." I pointed to the woman closest, my finger hovering over her ARO.

After a few moments, Karin replied. "Huh, I think I see. A lot of people have a certain ARO right? They all have a green-yellow hue."

"Yeah, but it's not the device that's the same – the networks control the colour. Each of the Telcoms has custom external lighting to brand them. You can change it if you dig deep enough in the settings, but almost no one bothers." I pointed to my own Saracen – even I hadn't bothered adjusting the crimson glow Redwave used.

"Oh, right." Karin twigged. "That's Limelight's branding. I recognise it now. But why's that unusual? Limelight's pretty popular, isn't it?"

"Sure, but it's not *that* popular; it's too expensive. The only time you see that many is for family or corporate plans. This is weird."

"Do you think they all work for the same company?"

"They could do, I suppose, but look ..." I pointed at the clusters of people on screen. "Do these guys seem like they know each other?"

We stared at the display. The groups weren't acknowledging each other. They were getting on with their business. Elderly couples, professionals, even a few freakers loitering. All different, but all with Limelight connected AROs.

"You see – they're from all walks of life."

"Yeah, okay, I buy that, but so what?" Karin leaned back, snapping her ARO against her shoulder – its green light pulsing against the bracket.

"Whoa! Karin, I forgot you're connected to Limelight!"

A confused frown appeared at the urgency in my voice. "Oh, yeah, it's way better than my last provider."

"Quick, let me see your ARO."

"Why?"

"Just hand it over!"

Delicately, almost reverently, Karin disengaged the magnetic release and peeled it off, handing it to me gingerly. "Careful, I like that thing a lot."

I looked through the interface, searching for something specific, breathing a sigh when I found it.

"What?"

I turned the display to show her. The connection quality said *Non-Quantum.*

"What does that mean?"

"It means we're damn lucky. Limelight doesn't have a broadcast mast up around here. You've automatically switched to a conventional connection."

"So?"

"Think, Karin. If Limelight's involved, how do you think they've been tracking us?"

"Oh, shit!" Karin's eyes widened in realisation. "Turn it off!"

"I've already disabled it, and as I said, we're lucky – there's no direct signal around here, but ..."

"But what?"

"We travelled a long way to get here, and Limelight's signal penetrates the Underground. Even if we've lucked out in a dead zone, if they wanted to find us, they'd know our general direction."

My hands felt clammy, and looking at Karin, I could see she shared my anxiety.

"So they're following us?"

I nodded. "I think they could be. What about you? Any signals."

"No, they go dark when there's lots of randomness – like at your extraplex. Remember when I couldn't guide us? That was because there were too many outcomes."

"That's not very helpful."

"Actually, it is. The messages I receive are vague – directional rather than explicit. There's huge room for error if I do something wrong. If the margins are too slim, they shut off. It's better I don't receive messages at times like that."

"So you don't second guess yourself in a crisis?"

"Exactly."

I was beginning to wonder what good we were to each other. One of us couldn't control their ability and the other was horribly inconsistent. We'd been fortunate so far, but I wasn't sure that would hold if the pressure piled on again.

As if the idea of a crisis willed it into existence, a kerfuffle broke out inside the club. I froze, eyes glued to the door. In the distance, we could hear Emmett protesting. "LOOK, no one's HERE. Please stop disrupting things. I NEED to open the bar!"

He was being unnecessarily loud. He was warning us.

"Shit." My heart rate jumped. "What the hell are we going to do?"

"They don't know we're here, do they?"

"Probably not. They don't have a mast; they must be searching the whole area."

Karin leapt into action, tugging at the sofa. "Quickly, help me move this."

I joined her, pulling the heavy two-seater away from the wall. To my surprise, it moved easily, sliding on greased rails, and revealing a metal hatch beneath. I could make out *Service Tunnel* embossed on the rusty surface beneath.

"Future messages?"

"No." Karin hushed. "Hurry!"

I helped Karin pull up the hatch. Outside, we could hear boots thumping on the club's dance floor, reverberating into the office like a war drum. We jumped in, lowering the hatch, encasing us in a dark, musty crawl space.

"What about the sofa?" I whispered.

"Help me." Karin groped around on the floor, finding a rope end. It extended up through the top of the hatch.

I grabbed it and we heaved together, hearing the sofa slide above. Just as the rope ran out of slack, the door burst open to a familiar blast of radio chatter.

"No one here," came the distorted voice.

I covered my mouth, afraid my breathing might give us away.

The guard rummaged around.

I could hear things being tipped over and smashed. There was no need; the room was tiny – he was frustrated. How many clubs had they searched so far?

He left the room grumbling.

"What now?" I looked at Karin. She was centimetres away but I could only see the outline of her face. "We can't go back through the bar; they'll be swarming the area by now."

"Follow me." Karin switched her ARO light on, blinding me.

"Sorry." She pointed the light further into the hole we were crouched in.

The stars cleared. I could see a low tunnel beyond, leading away.

Tunnel was optimistic. Large pipe would be more descriptive; it was half a metre in diameter. Karin went down on her hands and knees, shimmying forward. With no choice but to follow, I did the same, flat on my stomach as I squeezed through the narrow space. The pitch blackness and closeness was suffocating. I bit back my fear, trying to remember how much worse getting caught by the Neo-Guards would be.

Mercifully, after twenty metres of crawling, the tunnel widened. We emerged in a chamber with grates in the ceiling, casting slats of light across the floor and curved walls. Underfoot was thick with dust and rubbish, but also the rusted remains of an old track. Overhead, footsteps of pedestrians intermittently broke the light.

I stood and brushed myself down. "What was that about?"

Karin answered as she forged ahead. "The subterranean clubs in Farringdon are built into old train tunnels. They were abandoned when the station was reconstructed – after the investment banks moved in. The tracks had service and maintenance access. Most were blocked up, or converted into storage areas for the nightclubs, but some were left open."

"What's with the secrecy of this one?"

"You have to ask? You've seen Emmett. He's not exactly the toughest guy. Places around here get shaken down by freaker gangs all the time, not to mention violent alcoholics and spun-up losers. It's dangerous. This is Emmett's emergency exit."

"Well, you and your friends are full of surprises." I sputtered, dust catching in my throat. I tried not to think about the nasties dropped down here over the years.

We arrived at a ladder and started climbing.

"Yeah, but I think I'm out of surprises." Karin called down between rungs. "We've exhausted my bolt holes and I've been in a dark zone for a while now. I don't suppose *you've* got any ideas?"

We emerged into an alley a good distance from Emmett's club, walking in the opposite direction, heads down, trying not to draw attention. Karin's inference was annoying but clear: *Pull your weight, Daryl, I can't do this on my own.* She was right, but I wasn't flush with ideas.

Thinking it through, I came to the sad conclusion there was only one person who might help, and he'd be even less happy to see us than Emmett had been.

Sighing, I changed direction.

"Where are we going?" Karin sounded surprised; shocked I did, in fact, have an idea.

"Clapham," I answered, hoping Jay was in the mood to accept visitors.

# STATE 11

With Karin's Limelight connection severed, I was confident we could travel without being tracked. Freakers wrecked CCTVs cameras faster than authorities could repair them. Unless we were unlucky, we should have a clear route, but that wasn't particularly comforting and did little to answer why we were being tracked at all. What did Limelight have to do with all this? Was it the corporation themselves or someone using their network? Why would they care about us? – Too many questions.

Sat across from me on the train, Karin was fidgety, squirming in her seat. Without her data plan, she was suffering from *disconnection disease* – the d-d's. Everyone got it from time to time. I'd almost come down with it in Camden when my signal had gone shaky, but Karin was deeper in the digital economy than me. Her online presence more important than her real one. I took pity and set up my ARO as a mobile hotspot. For once, I was glad to be on the inferior Redwave service.

Karin's network bars reappeared, her sigh audible over the noise of the train. Her shoulders relaxed and body slumped as she began furiously checking her messages. I recognised the signs. An addict getting their fix. We weren't all that different after all.

I'd had a nagging concern they'd find us by snooping our online accounts, but going offline completely may alert more systems than acting normally.

Karin was using a third party app to encrypt her data – a good one – I'd checked. All information in her social networks (email, messages, anything that accepted data), was scrambled, and she'd set decryption keys that were updated to her followers hourly. Anyone wanting to hack her accounts would need to break three-step authentication. And even if they did, they'd only see an hour's worth of updates before decryption keys were revoked. Exploits were possible, but they were quickly exposed, at which point everyone just cycled to a different provider.

It was worrying how Limelight's tracking loophole had slipped the net, but there was so much bandwidth in a quantum connection; perhaps it wasn't hard to hide malicious code.

I thought about updating my small number of followers, but apart from encrypting the group and refreshing the keys, I couldn't see the point. It wasn't my vice of choice, and without Sebastian, there wasn't anyone I cared enough about to check in with. Outside of Karin, there was only one person I had any real-world connection with, and we were on our way to see him.

The carriage pulled into Clapham South. We alighted and walked towards Jay's block of flats. The fact Clapham wasn't as run down as the rest of Neo-London made me nervous. I scanned the street lamps and roof tops for cameras. None were moving or glowing, but that didn't mean they weren't on. I hoped the freakers were as efficient here as everywhere else in the city.

I hit the button to call up to Jay's domicile. It was evening, so he should be home from the Vault, likely plugged in by now.

There was a delay, then a muffled response with a fake Chinese accent. "Yars? Halooo. What you want, pweese?"

"Jay's paranoid." I addressed Karin's popped eyebrows. "He doesn't like people knowing he's in. He thinks there's a plot to track worker efficiency by how much time they spend at home. He believes it will downgrade his credit rating."

"A conspiracy theorist?"

"Yeah, well ..." I began sheepishly, then thinking on it, continued more firmly. "You know, I don't think we're any position to judge right now." I hit the comm button again. "It's me, dipshit. Open up."

"You come in!" the ridiculous voice chimed, and the door buzzed open.

We made our way up to his domicile.

I could hear him clearing his throat for another barrage of racist Chinese, but as his moronic face appeared behind the door, it became red and whatever joke he'd concocted lodged in his throat, causing him to sputter.

"Why the hell you bring the agent here!"

"She's not an agent, Jay." I placated, suppressing my annoyance. "She's a friend, and we could really do with a place to crash for a few hours."

Jay looked us up and down.

In the last couple of days, we'd escaped an explosion, scaled the outside of an extraplex, tramped through a sewer, and crawled down an abandoned tube tunnel. We looked a sorry mess. We hadn't washed in days; sewer muck caked our legs and we'd picked up an impressive collection of bruises and scrapes. On top of that we were haggard from lack of sleep. Karin was managing to look alert, but for my part, my face was only just hanging onto my skull.

Jay's eyes softened. "Yeah okay, pal." And then to Karin. "But I'm watching you."

He tried to make it sound like a joke, but I could hear under the surface he was deadly serious. Any normal day I'd have told him not to be paranoid, but with things the way they were, I was beginning to agree with him.

We made our way indoors. Thankfully, the place was relatively tidy. I was glad I could show Karin at least one place that wasn't a complete tip. Jay was dressed in '90s style Bermuda shorts and a vest. There was an indentation in his hair and a subtle oval around his eyes where his VR mask had been resting.

To his credit, once we were inside, Jay switched admirably to host. His paranoia lent itself to mild agoraphobia, but that made him appreciative of guests. He got us drinks, snacks, and even let us use his shower. He lent me some clothes and by some miracle had stuff Karin could wear. Items from a departed girlfriend sick of playing second fiddle to the VR rig.

Eventually, we all sat down in the living room. Karin on the sofa, me on an armchair. Jay sprawled himself messily across a beanbag, a quizzical look on his face.

"So you gonna tell me what's going on, Daryl, or do we need to lock the agent in the toilet first?"

Karin grimaced but didn't respond.

I struggled with where to start. I didn't want to tell Jay about our time abilities. Not that he wouldn't believe us – quite the opposite; I suspected he would, and that would open up a can of worms. Still, he was owed an explanation, otherwise he'd turf us out in the morning – we needed more time than that. I had to give him something he could latch on to, something that would interest him. Sebastian had said the best lies contained truth. If you could weave in enough real facts, it would make any lie sound real. I had an idea.

I put on a serious tone and addressed Jay squarely. "No need to put her in the toilet, Jay. Karin's not a government agent ... but she *used* to be one."

Jay's eyes widened, then narrowed as he looked across to where Karin had sat down, sandwiched between piles of VR equipment.

"You were right, Jay, she works for the Telcoms, or did. Limelight to be specific, but she found out they're using their network to spy on people. She came to the Vault as it's one of the few independents left. She asked me to meet her so I could disconnect her without them noticing so she could escape. But then the Neo-Guards showed up and chased us. They think I'm involved because I helped her."

Jay closed his eyes and rubbed his hair, pushing out where it had become flattened. There was a significant amount of truth in that story, but it still sounded crazy. Finally he looked at me, returning my serious tone. "I told you pink hair meant she was working for the government."

"That's right," Karin chimed in. She must know this one. "It's a chemical agent. I have to dye out the white."

It was working. Jay was enthralled, and with the groundwork in place, Karin worked the plot brilliantly. She talked about her imaginary role in the networks and how they were cooperating with the Administration to monitor people. She explained that at first she thought it was the right thing to do – helping to keep people safe – but then she noticed abuses. Flagrant violations of civil liberties and personal data. She couldn't be part of it anymore so was trying to get away. Once Limelight couldn't track her, she'd board a sub-jet to stay with relatives in France. It was a fantastic performance, peppered with extra details, like where she'd been employed and the names of people she'd worked with. I suspected those details were from her investigations, hiding the lie with facts, like I'd been. And she was undoubtedly using her premonitions to guide her. No matter how she was achieving it, Karin was an accomplished fibber.

Jay sat and listened, nodding knowingly. He even appeared sympathetic. I couldn't believe he was buying this. It didn't matter how much was couched in truth, it was still a ridiculous story.

When Karin had finished, Jay leaned back and stared at the ceiling, rubbing his temples with index and ring fingers, feet tapping excitedly. I'd never seen him like this; he was anxious, focussed – very unlike Jay. He stayed that way for a full minute, tension filling the room. I was beginning to worry he hadn't been pulled in when he looked down from the ceiling and addressed us. "I think I can help, but it will take some time."

"Whoa, hold on, Jay." This was working too well. "What are you talking about? You can't tell anyone we're here."

"I know that, you arse." Jay straightened up, offended I'd even suggested it. "But there's someone I think can help. I just need to do some research first."

"Who?" Karin sounded rightfully suspicious.

Jay tapped his nose. "I'm not saying yet. I buy your story, but I still don't trust you."

"What about me?" Jay's serious turn startled me; it wasn't in his nature.

"You could be under her influence, pal, but put it this way, if I didn't trust you, would I be letting you stay?"

"So you *are* letting us stay?" Karin asked.

Jay scrambled up from the beanbag. It was meant to be assertive but ended up a comedic crab dance of white limbs and Bermuda shorts. We both suppressed the urge to laugh as he finally stood, face flushed with mild embarrassment. "Er, yeah, you can stay."

I snuck a glance at Karin; she looked relieved but not surprised. Had she known this outcome all along?

"You okay to sleep in here?" Jay attempted to regain some gravitas.

"Best place we've been in days." Karin looked around appreciatively.

That was true. We'd been in some horrible places recently. Karin probably counted my domicile among them.

"Cool. I've got some work to do on my terminal. I'll let you know tomorrow."

He hurried out of the room. It was the most enthusiastic I'd seen him. I suppose most conspiracy theorists never get close to uncovering a real plot. This was like Christmas and birthday all rolled into one for Jay.

It was late in the evening and the fatigue of the day was palpable, but I wasn't sleepy yet. I had questions that were keeping my mind from going quiet. One thing in particular had been bugging me. What was Karin's motivation? She'd never explained herself.

"Karin?"

"Ask away," she answered, too quickly.

"Clairvoyance or intuition?"

"A bit of both."

"So you know what I'm going to ask?"

"I've got an idea, but I'd still rather you ask it."

"Why are you wrapped up in this? I know why I am. My brother's brain dead in a shit-hole asylum, but you don't seem to have a reason for getting in this deep."

"In other words, when I got my abilities, I could have carried on as normal. Not bothered with any of this."

"Yes, exactly. I don't get it."

She took a moment to reply, a forlorn shadow passing across her – a contrast to the assertiveness that had been dominant up to now. I hoped I hadn't messed up by asking something so personal.

"It's hard to explain, but I do owe you a reason."

Karin pulled up her legs and curled them in front of her on the chair, head resting on her knees. A complete change of mood. It was the first time I'd seen her remotely vulnerable.

She took a few breaths then spoke through closed eyes. "It's complicated, Daryl. Ever since I had the accident on the sub-jet, my life's not my own. It's hers."

"Who's?"

"Future Karin's. I live in the pre-state of her life. That's what my premonitions are, a pre-state for Future Karin. It's like I don't exist."

It was a deeper answer than I'd been expecting and harder to parse. She was acting like a prisoner. "So, you want to be free of her?"

She hugged her legs tighter. "No. She *is* me, I can't be any more free of her than you could from your past self. The difference is you're not beholden to your past. Your past is subservient to the present, like it should be. It's not like that with me. I'm a slave to things that will happen in her future. I'm a slave to her." Her voice wobbled, as if stuck in the back of her throat. "I'm compelled to do as she wishes, compelled to follow the path she's laid out for me."

Lulled by her soft speaking, I leaned forward, elbows on knees. "You need to do as she says?"

"Oh no, I can ignore what she tells me, but it doesn't go well, and she lets me know it." She searched for the words, trying to explain. "Imagine how demoralising it would be to make a decision only to be bombarded by negative thoughts you can't shut out. It's …" The ball that was Karin became tighter, the start of a tear visible. "… easier to do as she tells me."

I felt bad for the line of questioning; it was painful for her, but I couldn't stop – it was too important. "And you don't know why she's put you on this path?"

"No." She forced herself out of the curl, blinking away the tear that had never formed. "But she's me, so I have to trust her. I can't believe I would intentionally mislead myself. I must have faith there's a reason for all this."

"I understand," I said, even though I didn't. I ignored my inner voice all the time. It was easy. You pushed the nagging conscience to the back of your head.

Another thought arose – something she'd mentioned at my domicile. "You said before you didn't need to send messages back to yourself. I don't get it; that doesn't make sense."

Karin was sitting straighter, the moment of vulnerability over as quickly as it begun. She was as tough as nails, in control of her emotions – like Sebastian before his accident. My respect for her dialled up another notch.

"Yes, it's strange." The wobble in her voice was gone, swallowed back. "I don't know the precise reason. It's definitely true though. I realised it the first time I passed a point where I should have sent a message. Even if I'd wanted to, I didn't know how, and things continued as normal. The cause and effect of the messages are divorced somehow. I have theories but no way to prove anything." She leaned back in the seat and crossed her legs as she picked her words. "I think it's connected to the nature of my abilities, and yours too probably."

I waited for her to collect her thoughts; I was interested in this. The similarities between Karin and me were undeniable. If I understood more about what she could do, it might reveal what was happening to me.

"I don't think I need to send messages because, well ... somebody else does." Reading my frown correctly as pure confusion, she elaborated. "I know, it's tough to grasp. After I realised the cause and effect of my messages weren't linear, I started reading about time phenomena. It took me down a rabbit hole I don't fully understand – quantum mechanics, theoretical physics. Things only eggheads get. I'm no expert, but my assumption is it's something to do with multiple dimensions."

I knew something about this; it was how quantum computing worked. "Right, you mean multiverse theory. Parallel universes to this one, where different outcomes play out."

"Ah, an egghead!"

I ignored her. This made sense for once. "I think I understand. It's the same principle used in quantum computing. The CPU outsources computations across multiple dimensions to get to an answer exponentially faster. Your theory is you're not sending messages to yourself because a Karin from a closely related parallel universe is doing it for you?"

Karin stuck out her bottom lip. "Seems you know this bit."

"I know about quantum computers. It's how Limelight processes data across its network, although they also use *quantum entanglement* ..." I could see it was Karin's turn to be confused. "Don't worry." I brushed it aside. "All you need to know is it's the reason Limelight's network is so fast. It uses principles of quantum mechanics to transmit data insanely fast."

She shook her head. "Wow, Daryl, I'm impressed. Anyway, multiverse theory may explain your abilities too."

"How so?" I couldn't see the connection.

Karin got up and walked to an old wall clock Jay had acquired. An '80s inspired waving cat. She pointed to its face to illustrate her point. "It appears like you can stop time, but that's not possible because what time are you stopping? I can't imagine all time in the universe freezes on your command; that doesn't seem plausible. And it can't be a local phenomenon either, otherwise time wouldn't sync up outside of the area after you recommence it. I have a hunch though – look at your watch."

I glanced down at my Casio and compared it to the wall clock. It was running ten minutes fast.

"Yours is fast right? That's because time runs normally for you when you freeze it."

I couldn't refute her. If I added up all the frozen time, it must account for about ten minutes. "So what do you think is happening?"

She scratched her head and walked back to the sofa. "I haven't thought it through, but if my abilities link to multiple dimensions, it would make sense yours do too. Maybe you're not stopping time per se but entering a parallel dimension. One where time has paused or, more likely, is running imperceptibly slowly – I can't imagine many universes where there is no time at all."

This was confusing, but I could see where she was going. "So when I exit, I'm moving into a new universe that matches up with the changes I've made?"

"That's how multiverse theory works. Nothing's impossible, just improbable. Your power is to enter and exit dimensions that match the alterations you've made. Perhaps the act of stopping time creates the new dimension. I don't know; it's all above my pay grade, but it makes sense, don't you think?"

"So I enter a latent dimension, a place where time runs so slowly I can manipulate it to create a new one. Some sort of … What did you call your premonitions?"

"Pre-state."

"Yes, right. So I enter and exit some sort of … *latent state*?"

"If that's what you want to call it."

This was blowing my mind, but it made a strange sense. My brain hurt. I needed time to assimilate all the new information.

"Is that enough question time?" Karin yawned.

I looked at my watch. Yeah, it was definitely a few minutes ahead. I'd have to get used to setting it back. I wondered if I entered latent state enough times I'd age quicker than everyone. Probably not worth worrying about.

"Yeah, I think so." I returned the yawn.

Karin had already curled herself back into a ball. This time from fatigue.

I followed suit, closing my eyes. We'd made some progress tonight. My mind wasn't still; it was buzzing, in fact, but it wasn't chaotic. For once I felt there may be answers in there – latent information, below the grey matter, ready to surface.

# STATE 12

Sleep pushed exhaustion back enough to keep me functioning, but not enough to refresh me, and my hands were shaking again; the persistent stress was dredging up withdrawal symptoms, and with them, the itching urge to use.

Groggily, I pushed myself towards the edge of the sofa and rubbed them together, willing the jitter to stop. After a few moments, it seemed to abate – enough to hide from onlookers. Or at least, I hoped it did.

My conversation with Karin hadn't helped. Manipulating dimensions to slow time; Karin connected to a parallel version of herself. It was all so ridiculous, but the evidence was impossible to ignore. It made my head hurt when I thought about it, like an idiot trying to solve a problem too hard for him.

I longed for the delirium of SP1N, to shut out the nightmare that had become my reality, even for a small while. Grinding my teeth, I suppressed the thought. If I slipped backwards, it would be for nothing. Sebastian would rot in the asylum and I'd be chasing answers forever. I breathed in and out to reset myself, trying to find enough resolve to start the day.

Karin was still sleeping, slightly curled. She seemed peaceful. I wondered what clairvoyants dreamt about. Did Future Karin pass her premonitions while she was unconscious? Fragments of the future surfacing later as déjà vu. I'd have to ask her sometime.

I'd been thinking about Karin a lot. I hadn't processed all the strange information about her, but as a person, she was special – confident, purposeful, but also vulnerable. We're all haunted by demons. Mine the conventional kind, hers more abstract but just as debilitating

– an inescapable destiny laid out by her future self. Knowing we may not be that different inspired a renewed sense of camaraderie in me.

I'd been fighting the initial attraction, but I could sense those feelings intensifying. Would she be so liberal if she knew the whole truth about me though?

"You're staring at me," Karin whispered.

I snapped back to reality. Karin had woken while I'd be gazing at her, thoughts turned inwards. Feeling my ears burn, I scrambled to explain myself. "Um, sorry, I just woke up myself. I was lost in thought."

"Oh good, I must look a mess." She sat up and stretched.

She looked fine. Her clothes were dishevelled, and the shaved side of her hair had grown out – it needed shearing down again. But there were no bags under her eyes, and her skin was clear. Remarkable in Neo-London's polluted climate, not to mention the days spent crawling through sewers and escape tunnels.

She smoothed down her clothes, sat upright, and addressed me more formally. "So here we are again, Daryl, another hiding place, clueless what to do next. How long can we keep this up?" She kept talking as she yawned, the words coming out elongated. "We can't keep fleeing ... from one bolt hole to another. We have to find ... a next step."

She was right; this was the end of the road. If we couldn't make a plan, we were screwed – probably dead.

"Is that paranoid friend of yours going to help us?"

I scratched my head and shrugged. "Jay's a good guy. A bit mental but I can't see any better options."

"Who's mental?" Jay interjected, making an appearance at the door.

"Oh." I covered. "... This ... situation. It's mental isn't it?"

Jay strode into the room, picking his way over discarded pieces of VR equipment. "That's because you never saw the signs," he said, oblivious to the misdirection. "But your pal Jay did, and better than that, he's figured out how to help."

"Uh-huh." I wasn't buying the machismo. "For the record, Jay, it's weird when you talk about yourself in the third person like that." He was still dressed in the vest and Bermuda shorts from last night, clasping a battered laptop. "Have you been up all night?"

"Yep, most fun I've had in ages."

"Fun?" Karin proclaimed. She'd retaken a seat, upright and alert, listening. "I thought you were going to help us? What have you been doing?"

Jay's eyes narrowed as he considered whether to say anything in front of her and then shrugged. "What the hell. Daryl will tell you anyway, so I may as well spill it now."

He cleared some space on the coffee table and set down the laptop. More of a dumb terminal for his ARO, but it was easier to work with – fashioned with a bigger screen and a keyboard. He brought up what he'd been looking at – an internet forum.

Curious, I reached over to scroll down the page using the touchscreen. As I did, my hand, starkly illuminated by the light from the display, shook involuntarily. I pulled it away, but the damage was done and Jay was speaking before I could make excuses.

"Wow, you got the shakes bad, huh? I thought you were off SP1N?"

My heart sank. There went my credibility with Karin. I couldn't look her in the eye, but the slump in her body said it all. I'd disappointed her. She must have suspected – her premonitions giving her a notion of my past, but by her own admission, they were often vague. I'd hoped it had slipped her attention. That was a pipe dream now.

"Anyway, forget that. This is more important." Jay powered on, unaware the effect his words were having. He pointed to a section of the screen. His hand was trembling too, but from excitement. "Look at that message ... Right there."

Still lamenting the revelation, I balled my hand into a fist to stop it shaking and stared at the screen where he was pointing. The forum looked niche – simple text and ASCII art. This didn't exist on the mainstream internet – Jay was tapped into the *dark web*, part of the *deep web*. The hidden part of the internet. Unindexed by search engines, obscured through peer-to-peer connections, and routed through intermediary servers. It was untraceable, and unsurprisingly, it was popular with criminals, drug addicts, and conspiracy theorists. They all logged on to communicate without being monitored. Given Jay's interests, I wasn't shocked he'd procured the software to access it (illegal since the late 2010s), but known users of the dark web were prosecuted harshly. He was deeper into this stuff than I'd given him credit for.

The URL read SCAM.NET. Most of the messages were nonsense – paranoid chatter – but the note Jay was pointing out was clear and succinct. Someone calling themselves *Maximal* had posted it. It read: *Meet me*. Two words in plain ASCII text. Hardly a revelation.

"What the hell does that mean?" I said heatedly, still reeling from my outing in front of Karin.

Jay became agitated, mistaking my frustration for confusion. "What does it mean? It means everything! That's Maximal."

"And who, exactly, is Maximal?" Karin asked, pulling us back from the screen, trying to soothe the tension. We turned to look at her; she was conciliatory but I could sense a disquiet. What was she thinking? She may have dispassionately absorbed the new knowledge about me or completely re-evaluated if I could be relied on. I'd have to explain later, make her see I'd been trying to change.

Jay shook his head, replying dismissively, oblivious to the subtext. "Honestly, it's no wonder you two are in trouble." He returned his attention to the screen, accessing various saved articles and video content.

Breathing out to re-centre myself, I leaned forward to read what Jay pulled up, Karin's presence behind me uncomfortable.

Maximal was a hacker responsible for some huge scandals. Some of the largest corporate takedowns could be traced to him. It wasn't run-of-the-mill espionage. Most cyber-criminal's motivations were nefarious – blackmail for money and tech, or disingenuous altruism: claiming to "fight the system". In both cases, they hurt ordinary people, either through denial of services or by revealing personal information – leading to social engineering and fraud. Maximal reserved his hacks for endeavours that damaged corporations.

The articles revealed a narrative of exposing illegal practices, uncovering accounting scams, and publishing abuses of data. This was modus operandi for hackers, but Maximal did it covertly, minimising the impact on the public. Keeping the stories out of the media unless the corporations didn't capitulate. That took a lot more skill than a simple database hack. It meant companies had to clean up their acts – temporarily at least.

Now Jay had retrieved the details, I did recall hearing about a mythical super-hacker – the bane of the corporate world. I'd dismissed it as an urban legend, but clearly Jay had taken it seriously. I was beginning to see how a person like that might be able to help. If they existed and it wasn't an elaborate hoax.

"I see." I stood and backed up a pace, bumping into Karin. I'd become so absorbed, I'd briefly forgotten she was there. "Sorry," I said sheepishly, hoping she realised it meant more than just for knocking into her.

"Don't worry, it's all good." She smiled. It looked forced.

"Damn straight," Jay replied triumphantly, again misinterpreting the exchange.

"And you know this person?" Karin leaned over to inspect the screen. "They seem very, er ... skilled at keeping themselves hidden."

"Know them! Are you joking?" Jay's eyes were wide and wild. "No one *knows* Maximal! He's completely off the grid, untraceable. The only evidence he exists is forums like this – strictly on the dark web to avoid being traced. He's a ghost."

I could hear the admiration. Jay held Maximal and his antics in high regard. "Okay." I followed along. "So what did you tell him about us to prompt this response?"

A smug grin flashed across his face. "That was the hard bit. Took all night," he replied, proud of himself.

Karin and I stared blankly. He groaned and rolled his eyes. "I couldn't just lay down the details, you know. The dark web is un-traceable back to the user, but anyone with a ToR browser can read the messages. If I'd said too much, I could have given something away. I had to be careful, you see."

Jay was trying to impress us with how tough it had been. Humility would help here, but the lack of sleep was making it hard.

"Okay, pal, I get it, so how did you manage it?" My words landed somewhere between enthralled and patronising.

Jay furrowed his brow but continued. Good enough. "I did some digging. There's been a flurry of Neo-Guard activity with alerts out for you across the city."

He accessed the relevant news feeds, including, to our horror, a CCTV shot of us at Farringdon Station. The picture was low and there was a grid over the image. The camera must have been hidden behind a storefront shutter where freakers couldn't smash it.

It was taken with ancient tech, the image black-and-white, grainy, and shot from a distance. I didn't think a casual observer could pick us out. The headline across the top read: *Wanted for questioning*. Shit. I guessed that was inevitable, but it was still a shock to see our photos plastered up on the internet. At least they hadn't tracked us any further than Farringdon.

"Anyway." Jay brought our attention back to the internet forum. "I started a thread about you. Innocent enough. Topics like that are mentioned all the time."

We looked at the responses – the other theorists chiming in – some saying we were basic criminals, others shouting their support to *fight the system*, and there was plenty of gibberish too.

"You see, I waited until someone started a corporate angle ..." He pointed to the screen. Someone with the handle C0nspiraG0d had replied: *I bet they pissed off the banks, they're all controlled by the Administration*. "To which I replied," *No, more likely the Telcoms. Limelight's onto them.*

That had started a flurry of activity, lots of theories – all wrong. Jay paused for dramatic effect. "So, do you see?"

"No," Karin and I replied in unison.

"Come on, guys, keep up!" Jay was standing bolt upright, arms gesticulating. Trying to make us see. "I started a chain of information with enough breadcrumbs that Maximal would take notice."

"Alright," I said, putting a hand on Jay's shoulder, trying to stop him hopping from one foot to another. "But how would Maximal know any of this was true? You've barely said anything."

He pushed my hand off, voice becoming even more excited. "That's the whole point! Maximal will already know you two are connected to Limelight. He keeps track of stuff like that. He has algorithms scrubbing the internet for leads. The fact I originated the post and mentioned Limelight would have been enough to flag the forum and notify him. But it doesn't matter; we don't need to understand how he does it, just that he does, because it's worked."

"Hold on." Karin stepped between us, concerned. "Won't that tip off the Neo-Guards as well?"

Her interjection was welcome. It made Jay finally put his hands down and take a breath.

"No." He addressed her more calmly, aware at last he'd been shouting at us. "It's why I didn't put all the information in one post. I waited until there was an opening to mention Limelight. Besides, I doubt they're switched on enough to monitor the dark web. And even if they are, they won't be able to track where the post came from, so they'll learn nothing new."

I looked at the screen where the enigmatic Maximal, or someone claiming to be them, had reached out from across the void. "And how do you know that's actually him and not some random conspiracy nut?"

Jay blew air through his lips. "There's no way to be a hundred per cent sure, but that's definitely his current handle. I confirmed by comparing to verified sources."

I retired the line of questioning. Jay had done his homework. He was as close to an expert in this as we could hope for. But still, the message was vague.

"Okay, but what now?" I prompted. "He says to meet us, but where?"

"Oh." Jay scratched his head, confidence evaporating. "That's more difficult. He doesn't say, and he didn't reply to any more messages."

Of course. There had to be a catch. We stood in awkward silence.

Karin snapped her fingers making us jump. "Oh, I get it!"

We both looked at her.

"Come on," she proclaimed. "He expects us to find him on our own, which must mean it's easy to work out."

We stared at her, unblinking.

It was Karin's time to roll her eyes. "Jay, pull up those articles again. What's the most recent entry?"

Jay's fingers moved on the keyboard as he brought up the news feed again. The top headline read: *International bank spies on customers, secret documents revealed.*

"Right, good, and where was that reported."

"Er." Jay scanned the article. "Doesn't say."

"Alright. What about the bank then? Where is it located?"

"Hold on a second." Jay cross-referenced the name of the bank. "It's a Chinese financial conglomerate, headquartered in HK1 ... New Hong Kong." The statement hung in the air for a moment.

"HK1?" I tilted my head towards Karin, who was wearing a crafty half smile. "That's not exactly nearby." That was an understatement – it was on the other side of the globe! "Even if we had the creds for sub-jet passage, Neo-Guards will be watching the port."

Karin gave me a conspiratorial wink. "I'm sure we'll find a way, Daryl."

This was making me nervous. Was Karin proposing something this mental? At least she still wanted my help. My drug issue hadn't turned her off completely, not yet anyway.

"Okay ..." I swivelled back to Jay, who was looking bemused. "Let's say we find our way to HK1. How would we contact Maximal when we got there?"

"Oh, don't worry about that. You won't need to find Maximal; he'll find you."

"Right." The speed this was progressing was overwhelming. "So let me recap. We're going to get through sub-jet security without the Neo-Guards noticing. Travel to HK1 based on no more information than two words in a dark web conspiracy forum. And when we get there, we're going to be found by a mysterious hacker we're not even certain exists."

"Yes," Karin and Jay replied together.

Great. Just great.

# STATE 13

J ay, conspiracy theorist extraordinaire and general layabout, continued to surprise us over the days we stayed with him. He kept us
fed and clothed – items he'd sneak out to collect and pay for himself
(with no hint of requiring the creds back). And he'd surfaced some
genuinely helpful suggestions.

Most importantly, he'd connected us with Maximal, who for all our
research, did appear to be the vigilante hacker I'd heard about. And
with a newly opened mind, cracked wide by recent experiences, I was
on board with Jay's wilder notions. His theory the Administration
was a puppet of the Telcoms was no longer far-fetched – his paranoia
seemed reasonable, practically justified. If anything, I was the naïve
one; a bitter pill to swallow, but I'd choked it down nonetheless.

Jay's generosity hadn't ended there. He'd been the consummate
host – foregoing his VR rig (we'd taken over his living room).

Going cold turkey should have been a problem, but it wasn't. He
was excited – energised. He'd waited his entire life for something like
this; he was totally willing to accept the dangers in exchange for being
right.

In the end, his enthusiasm became a problem. His shaggy, doe-eyed
face appearing any time we were discussing travel plans, begging us to
come along. I understood; he wanted to meet Maximal – he was his
idol.

I was stumped for how to dissuade him. Our edge for getting to
HK1 was our time abilities. He wouldn't last five minutes, but I
couldn't say so without revealing the whole truth.

Karin had come to the rescue by tapping into his paranoia. "Jay,
being near us puts you on the grid – right in the spotlight of Ad-

ministration agents." That had given him pause. Long enough to add. "You'll be more helpful to us here – monitoring internet traffic. You don't want to miss it if Maximal makes contact again, do you?"

Begrudgingly, he'd relinquished. I didn't want to disappoint him, but it was a relief knowing he'd be safe. Sebastian was the only person I'd been close to, but the way Jay had taken us in made me question why I kept people at arm's length. It was a strange, but not unwelcome, feeling.

With the crisis resolved, Jay had retreated to his bedroom to surf the dark web, and with space to talk, Karin had revealed her plan to defeat sub-jet security.

I was dismayed. It hinged on me freezing time on demand – something I'd never done before. I wasn't even sure it was possible. She'd assumed I could, and I'd struggled to tell her otherwise. It was a powder keg waiting to explode – which of course it did, prompted by the elephant in the room we still hadn't discussed.

We were hunkered around a projected image showing aerial photos of the port and surrounding area. Karin was explaining the lay of the land. Without warning, my hand twitched where it lay on the sideboard. Karin sighed and addressed me bluntly. "Daryl, you have to stop using drugs."

I pulled my hand away and hid it behind my back. I knew this had been coming, ever since I'd been outed, but I was shocked how candidly she'd stated it. My teeth set in my jaw, a centroid of annoyance and shame.

I was immediately defensive. I couldn't help it. Having it pointed out so directly stung. "Back off, Karin! I'm sure where you're from, you've got plenty to get you through the day, but in my world, SP1N and VR are all we have. Besides ..." I tried to unclench my jaw and get the words out clearly, only half successfully. "... I've been off it for nearly a week!"

A tremble had started, but not from withdrawal; it was indignation. What right did a middle-class low-risker have telling me what I should or shouldn't do? I'd been making progress before she'd walked into the Vault. I needed support, not judgement!

Karin straightened and walked towards me.

I backed up with little retreating steps, avoiding her gaze.

"Daryl, I know you've been trying." Of course she knew. How easy it was to forget her abilities. That made it worse. "And I don't care. It's plain to see it won't last."

She twisted the knife, and it cut deep. I didn't know how to respond. All I could do was shuffle in reverse until I was against the wall, hands balled impotently behind my back.

Karin relaxed her voice, pivoting again. "Look, I don't care if you do drugs. I mean, it's not brilliant or anything, and I didn't hope to be teamed up with someone with an addiction, but it happens. I've seen it lots of times, but it's a liability and you know it."

"Okay, fine!" I blurted out, head hanging low. "I'm a worthless addict. Is that what you wanted to hear?" It was an admission I'd said a thousand times in my head, but never out loud. It brought with it an earthquake of repressed emotion. "I know I'm a goddamn liability. It's why I've been trying to quit!"

If Karin had been trying to break me, it had worked. I didn't know what else to say. I slumped to the floor, defeated.

Karin sat down facing me, brushing aside crumbs that had built up. "Good. It's out now." She ducked down to catch my sunken eyes, hands clasped in front of her. "That means we can move forward." Her voice was steady, like a teacher disciplining an emotional student. "What's important is that we deal with this now and work together to keep you clean." She placed a hand on my knee. There was no electricity this time, just awkward tension. "I didn't tell you this before, but my pre-state's been going crazy. Getting through the sub-jet port won't be easy. I'll need you on point."

"On point?" I looked up, locking eyes defiantly. "Karin! Forget the drugs. This entire plan relies on me stopping time at the right moment!"

Karin unclasped her hands and leaned back. "Yeah, so?"

I shook my head, bemused this wasn't clear to her. "Karin, I don't know how to do that!"

There, I'd exorcised the demon. It was good to get it out. A small amount of payback for her attack on me.

"What?" A twinge of shock broke through. "What about at the Shard, and your extraplex? They were perfectly timed."

I shook my head wearily. Her pre-state must have missed all this. "I don't know. I think it's triggered by stress or fear or something."

"So an emotional reaction?"

"Yeah, I guess so."

"Okay." Karin breathed out in relief. "Well, that's manageable at least."

"Manageable? I don't understand how it's manageable. It's a shit-show, that's what it is."

Karin jumped up from the floor, back to her nonchalant self. "Not at all. If it's triggered by emotion, then all you need is to replicate those feelings."

She scanned the floor for a space clear of VR equipment, settling on a spot near the window, gesturing for me to come over.

With the double boils of my addiction and lack of control lanced, the change in atmosphere was immediate and infectious, tugging me from my bleak mindset.

Karin tapped the floor in front of her insistently.

Self-consciousness replaced anxiety. "Is this gonna be weird?" I said, trying to get my emotions under control again.

"Probably for you, but bear with me; we don't have long, and we need to fix you as quickly as possible."

Fix me? I puffed out my cheeks but relented, tentatively moving to sit opposite, crossing my legs nervously in front of her.

"What now?"

"Guided meditation."

"Guided what?" It sounded like low-risker nonsense to me.

"Meditation." Karin insisted. "It will help you."

This was ridiculous. Sebastian would have laughed uncontrollably if he'd seen me even contemplating it.

"Trust me. I'm good at this. I use it to keep Future Karin from driving me nuts. It will help you too. Look at your hand."

I unfurled the fist at my side; the muscles were still twitching involuntarily. I felt dizzy after our confrontation, body flush with endorphins. Sebastian wouldn't like it, but he wasn't here anymore. Maybe it was time to try something different.

Karin settled herself, laying her hands palms up on her knees, gesturing for me to do the same.

It felt silly, but I did it anyway.

"We begin with breathing exercises," she explained. "Then a routine to help you reach a trance state, and finally some hypnotic suggestion."

I felt an urge to make a snide joke – something about chakra crystals – but Karin's stone-faced expression told me it would be a bad idea. She was taking this shit seriously. I cleared my throat instead. "How do you know about this stuff?"

Back straight, legs crossed over one another, Karin was in a perfect lotus position. My legs barely tucked under my knees. As she spoke, I couldn't help but straighten up too.

"It's hard having a voice in your head all the time," she explained. "It's easy to lose yourself, especially when the other voice is still you. I had to learn meditation to stop myself going mad."

She relaxed her face, hands at rest, no hint of negativity. My inner voice was irritating, but at least I controlled it. If someone else was pulling the levers, I could see how awful that would be. I made a conscious decision to listen.

"First, breathing." She placed a hand on her stomach and pulled in, showing it rising and falling. "You need to breathe from your stomach, not your chest."

I followed suit. It was difficult to redirect the air, but after a while, pulling from my stomach, more oxygen seemed to flow. We did this for a while, eyes closed, midriffs rising and falling rhythmically. Inhaling and exhaling deeply. It was hypnotic, which I guessed was the point.

After ten minutes, I was lightheaded but also more relaxed. Not tired – focussed. I felt good.

Observing my newly serene state, Karin provided calm, authoritative instructions. "You're at the top level now, fully awake, but we'll go deeper. Down to a place where subconscious suggestions have greater meaning."

"Will I know what I'm doing?" My eyes were closed tightly. I didn't want to open them anymore – they felt glued together. "I've seen people do this on holovids. They're made to look like idiots."

"That's stage hypnotism," Karin reassured. "It requires a highly suggestive person who's happy to be made fun of."

I hoped that was true. I'd been made a fool of enough recently.

"Let's begin. The sooner I can give you the tools, the sooner we can get back to planning." Karin's voice floated between us. It was a rehearsed phrase. "We're about to go down into a trance state. Know that nothing can harm you. You can't be made to do anything you don't want to. If required, you will awake and be fully alert. This is a safe place."

The words rattled around in my head. I'd never considered myself gullible or suggestive, but the ritual magnified the sentences and their meaning. Her speech altered, modulating up and down. A wave of words coming into my mind.

"Imagine a long staircase in front of you leading down. You can't see the bottom, but you know what's there is good. It's your place. A place where you can change things about yourself."

"What is it?"

"You'll know when you get there. Stop interrupting."

I did as I was told.

"If you look at the top stair in front of you, you'll notice it says a word on top. It says 'relax', and when you step onto it, you will feel physically and mentally calmer. Before you move, you'll breathe into your stomach, and as you take your step, you'll breathe out. At the same time, I want you to say the word 'relax' in your mind. Don't just say it though, feel it through your whole body." She paused. "Now breathe in."

I did, pulling air deep into my gut.

"And step."

I breathed out and let the word relax throb through my brain and body. I felt like I'd sunk into the floor.

For the next fifteen minutes, I descended the staircase. With each step, I felt more relaxed and distant from my body sitting on the floor somewhere high above. I could no longer sense my arms or legs; they felt detached.

Karin's voice seeped in like a soft echo. "We're nearing the bottom of the staircase. Can you see a door?"

As if willed into existence, a door appeared – golden with an ancient knocker. I had no idea where those details came from.

"When you open the door, a place will be revealed. Somewhere your inner self will listen."

"I don't know what it will look like."

"You will," Karin urged. "Push open the door."

I breathed in, leaning my imagined weight. The knocker rattled and the door creaked open, greeting me with mist. A disappointing anticlimax. Was this all my defective brain could conjure up?

"There's nothing ..." I began, then stopped. I could make out a shape in the clearing fog. The object resolved into a table, and then other details followed. A window hanging in space, and when that made no sense, the conjoining walls appeared too, wrapping around, under and over, forming a floor and a roof. Shelves popped from the walls. They were old and dishevelled, laden with trays containing mechanical parts. Springs, sprockets, levers, and such.

The final details painted themselves in. Clocks – hundreds of clocks!

They were everywhere. On the walls, on the table, strewn on the floor, and piled up in the corners. Traditional, mechanical, modern, and projecting types – they were all here. Some were in pieces, others ticking quietly or illuminating time into space. And there were tools everywhere. Delicate tools for manipulating tiny things.

"It's ..." I started.

Karin cut me off gently. "You don't need to describe it. This is your place, for you only. Be sure to investigate it. Touch any surfaces that are apparent. What do they feel like? Smell the air. What does it smell like? If there's something unusual, look at it closely, examine all the details."

I did as Karin said, exploring the workshop, running my hand over the table. It was old and wooden with deep rifts, but it was smooth – polished through years of use. The room was small, like a cabin, but it didn't feel claustrophobic. Approaching the window, I realised why. Outside, a meadow stretched into the distance. The sun was shining brightly, beating down. The scent of worked wood, pollen, and machine oils was intoxicating. I could sense it all.

"Do you feel completely in your place? Does it feel you belong there?"

"Yes." I was amazed I could pull something so odd and beautiful from my mind. Nowhere like this existed anywhere on Earth, at least, not anymore.

"Good." Karin's voice was no longer an echo. It was as if she was standing outside the cabin, in the meadow, just out of view. "Now imagine how you felt when you first stopped time."

I thought back to Led in the Trocadero. I'd been terrified but also angry and helpless. I didn't know how to explain it, but I could sense something building in the room. A dark, unpleasant swirl of negativity.

"Can you imagine what those emotions would look like if made real – into an object?"

I didn't know what that meant, but the feeling did want to become something. I could sense it pulsing, forming together.

"Let it happen," Karin prompted.

The swirl coalesced in front of me. Gathering on the table, creating a structure. Before my eyes it became something recognisable. A black timepiece. It stood there, dark and monolithic, fashioned after a small grandfather clock, the pendulum ticking ominously.

"Huh." It surprised me to see something so coherent and real.

"Don't tell me what it is," Karin said before I could elaborate. "Just take a long look, understand all the details."

The clock was onyx black, shiny, almost oily, the pendulum ruby red – angry behind a closed glass door. It was ticking twice as fast as a normal timepiece, as if agitated. The numbers on its face were slanted and devilish. It frightened me to look at – like it was staring back.

Eyeing the malicious device, I felt anxiety creep over me, my heart beating in time with the swinging pendulum. "Yes, I see it."

"Good. That's good, Daryl." Her voice was reassuring in its presence, an anchor to hold on to. "Can you see any way to contain it?"

"Contain it?"

"Yes, control it somehow, bend it to your will."

I understood, but there was no obvious way to manipulate it. No external dials or buttons, and the clock face itself was sealed. The only interactive feature was the glass door separating the pendulum.

Full of uncertainty, I reached for it, tugging on the tiny, ornate knob. The door swung open, startling me as it banged against the far side of the clock. The *tick-tock* became louder and more aggressive.

Hand shaking, I reached into the clock and tried to grasp the pendulum. It was hot to the touch, and although small, held incredible mass. It resisted my hand, throwing it back and forth viciously. Slowly, and with difficulty, exerting opposing pressure, I managed to slow its rhythm.

As the speed reduced, its colour changed, fading to cool blue. The clock face altered as well, the numerals straightening and rounding.

"Good." Karin sensed the change in me. "How do you feel?"

"Calm," I said. And I was, completely free of negative emotion – the first time in months. My heart was beating steadily, my breathing even and regular. The clock was controlling my wellbeing!

Karin pressed on. This wasn't over. "Final step. Can you *uncontain* what you've done? Let the feeling loose again."

I cringed, hair rising on the back of my neck. I didn't want to uncontain the power of the clock. It was dangerous – it could sweep me away, but I could see what Karin was trying to teach me.

Reluctantly, I reached back in. The pendulum felt cool, but it was still heavy. Pushing and pulling against the weight, I reversed what I'd done, speeding the pendulum to its angry red state, and with it, my heart rate and breathing. It differed from before, still unpleasant, but I felt in control – like I was moving the pendulum rather than it moving me. The fear and anger was still there, raging beneath the surface, but it was in check. I could channel it, use it.

We ran through the process a few times. It was difficult, the pendulum resistant, but it became easier each time.

Finally Karin signalled it was time to end the session, her disembodied voice floating in and around the workshop. I was disappointed to leave – the hallucination was as complete as any VR simulation. But I'd learned something, felt the truth reveal itself. The clock was key to controlling myself and, through it, latent state. I had to master it.

"We're ready to come back now." Karin recounted another rehearsed sequence.

Back? I could barely feel my body anymore, still sitting cross-legged in Jay's living room.

"You will remember this place and these feelings. The things you've learned are part of you now. You'll be able to return whenever you need."

Over the next few minutes, Karin reversed me out of the trance, her voice leading me from the workshop and back up the staircase. Now the word on each step said *Alert*, and with each step, I felt more awake and closer to my real body.

At the top of the staircase, I opened my eyes to see Karin staring at me, one eyebrow raised. It felt like I'd returned from a long journey.

"Look at your hand," Karin prompted.

I did. It was open, loose at my side, the twitch gone. As was the urge to vaporise a SP1N tab.

I blinked and went to say something, but emotion caught in my throat.

Before I could blurt out an embarrassing cavalcade of thanks, a voice emerged from the doorway to save me.

"Are you two finished?" Jay was leaning against the frame. "I came in over an hour ago and you were sat like this."

"An hour!" I had no idea we'd been under that long. It had felt like minutes.

"Yeah, pretty freaky if you ask me." Jay bit his thumb nail distractedly.

Karin and I looked at each other and laughed awkwardly.

"Anyway, look," he continued, yanking off the splinter he'd created. "I have to start acting normally soon, well normal for me, otherwise people will get suspicious. Are you guys ready?"

I looked at Jay and back to Karin. The crafty half smile had returned. I understood it now.

"Thanks for your help, Jay," I said. "I think we're ready now."

And for the first time since the explosion at the Shard, that sounded right. For once I was starting to feel in control of my destiny. We had a plan and I could see a path forward. One where I might not screw up.

# STATE 14

I ran my hand over the shiny interior. It smelled faintly of oil, but not in an unpleasant way. I'd never been in an auto-cab before. It was a luxury, but Karin had insisted, jamming her thumb on the reader and ignoring my shocked expression at the extortionate figure displayed.

It had been a risk. We didn't know if Limelight had penetrated the banks, but we'd rationalised the financial systems were secure. Besides, we'd need funds at some point, and if Limelight could track us through our transactions, we were doomed anyway.

It had worked. Neo-Guards hadn't swarmed us, but we agreed it was prudent to do it infrequently, and only at external terminals, never via our AROs.

What hadn't been a risk was the state of Karin's finances. She was loaded! I'd noticed when her balance had flashed up on the display.

She shrugged it off without a hint of embarrassment, jumping in the cab like it was nothing. "What can I say? When you're clairvoyant, you know which horse to back."

There were no real horses anymore, all gambling was virtual, but I got the point. I gritted my teeth behind a false smile to hide my frustration. Money had always been an obstacle for Sebastian and me. We hadn't known where our next meal would come from, let alone a taxi journey. I glanced at Karin, already absorbed on her social networks, still tethered to my Redwave account. I didn't resent her using her powers, I'd do the same, but she could show some humility. I guessed even before she'd become clairvoyant, she'd never had to do without. It was moments like these the gulf between us seemed widest.

I settled into the seat, peering quietly through the smoke-tinted windows. They let through the vibrant neon lighting and signage but dimmed the surrounding grime and disrepair of the city. The ride was so smooth I could barely feel it. I tried to enjoy the moment – probably my last opportunity to experience something pleasant.

After an hour, we'd travelled twenty miles, passing the guarded Neo-London perimeter. We followed the old motorway west, through the historical greenbelt surrounding Old London. The lush green space was no more; what remained had turned yellow with pollution, dotted with factories serving the city.

Every few miles, someone tended a sick field, sat on ancient farm equipment so rusted it was a miracle it moved. Even from the car, I could see the workers' skin was sallow and drawn, faces wrinkled like bark. If you didn't serve the Telcoms, you farmed for synthetic produce in the barrens outside – downwind from the worst of the pollution. I thought of my shit-hole domicile. It was tiny and knackered, but better than this.

I pulled my gaze from the window, dialling the tint up to make it black. I didn't want to think about the past. We were on our way to somewhere different.

HK1 was one of the few technically advanced cities, right on the other side of the world. If it weren't for the anxiety of illicitly boarding a sub-jet, I'd have been excited. As it was, there was a lead ball in my stomach.

We'd considered buying tickets legitimately, but the Administration monitored sub-jets and Limelight was certain to be notified. The corners of my mouth twitched at the irony. Karin's wealth could get us to the port, but it was the poor extraplex boy who'd have to sneak us past security.

I'd been practising the techniques Karin had shown me. If I remained focussed, I could enter and exit latent state on demand. I'd envision the clock, sitting in the workshop. Its strange pendulum a reflection of my emotional state. Cool and blue when slow, hot and red when sped up. With experimentation, I'd found two ways of freezing time. The first replicated the conditions at the Shard. Under extreme stress, the pendulum smashed against the sides of the clock, time stalling like an over-revved car. It worked in an emergency but was unpleasant – my heart raced until I could feel the blood pumping in my eyeballs – the very edge of fight or flight. Luckily, it wasn't necessary. Slowing the pendulum in the other direction had the same effect, bringing time to a gradual halt. It took longer than stalling the clock, but I was getting better.

As Karin had predicted, a bonus of using meditation had been a recession in my need for SP1N. It was still there, a dark claw in my mind. It would never vanish completely, requiring constant management, but for the first time since I was thirteen, it was momentarily in check.

According to Karin, I'd taken to meditation extremely well, suggesting I had a predisposition for it. I wasn't sure. I'd always been introspective. Sebastian had called me "brooding" – I was redirecting all the negative self-loathing into something useful.

I shifted uncomfortably inside the faux-leather garments we'd bought for the occasion. The plan was to use latent state and clairvoyant misdirection to slip by security. We'd need to move quickly through tight gaps – loose clothing would be bad, hence the crotch hugging leathers and form fitting jackets.

"Are you clear what we need to do?" Karin had closed her ARO and was facing me. She was dressed as I was, only pulling it off better. Clad in neutral grey and beige, she looked like a hot motorcyclist. Her hair was freshly shorn on one side and re-braided on the other, changed to blonde to match the overall scheme. The colour combinations had been her idea. It would act like camouflage against the muted marble, glass, and metal she assured me made up the port's interior.

I tried to speak and thought better of it. My mouth was dry like a desert. I nodded instead and made a show of double checking my rucksack – low profile affairs we'd bought for the occasion. They hugged our backs, buckles cinching around the waist to prevent them moving around. There was room for a few items. Water, ration pellets, a lazeblade, and a multi-tool. We hoped that would be enough.

Being inconspicuous wouldn't be a problem for me; I'd freeze time before the barriers and stroll past security. Getting Karin through would be a different story.

We'd spoken at length about the plan, pouring over pictures of the port and thinking through the obstacles. Scenario planning was useful but ultimately futile. Everything would be different on the day. I'd have to recon the way forward when we arrived.

Karin tapped me on the shoulder, gesturing towards the front of the taxi. In the distance was a grey dome. It was a few kilometres away, but the width, even this far off, revealed how massive it was. It rose like a moon on the horizon, increasing until it stopped, half appeared. An enormous metal ball, sunken in the ground, at least two kilometres in diameter.

As we closed the distance, I could start to make out dimples on the dome's surface. Bays the sub-jets launched from to achieve their sub-Earth orbits – the powerful aircraft using an extreme angle to Earth to traverse distances faster than traditional planes. A sub-jet could cross the Atlantic to America in under two hours, not that anyone had gone there since they closed their borders.

The sub-jet port looked completely out of place. A modern, alien structure, surrounded by wasteland. An aluminium interchange for top echelon citizens – low-riskers of means fleeing the city to seek less polluted areas swapped for well-heeled international business people needing the city's high-tech telecommunication hubs.

The road snaked up a ramp to a large drop off point, sharply lettered neon pointing the way to *Departures*. The enormity of the structure pressed down on me. I tried to keep my rising sense of panic in check as we jumped out. This was the furthest I'd been from the city, surrounded by people normally separated from me by thick windshields. The fear someone would recognise me as a gutter wretch was palpable.

I didn't mention it to Karin; she wouldn't understand. She came from a well-manicured background. She knew how these people operated – she fit in. My only comfort was if things went wrong, I could retreat into latent state – vanish back to the gutter.

Feeling self-conscious, feet clacking on the hard floor, I tried to walk tall, following Karin across the polished metal entrance. It sparkled despite the overcast weather.

I gasped as we cleared the doors. I'd seen pictures of the sub-jet port, but experiencing it was different. The cavernous interior was a sight to behold. The steel floor stretched to meet gleaming marble pillars and etched glass walls. High above, a bright, burning globe bathed the port in a convincing facsimile of a summer's day. I slowed to take it in, mouth hung open like a tourist. I couldn't help it; I *was* a tourist. I had no right to be here.

A passing businessman looked my way. He wore a well-cut suit and was pulling a bag-laden hover trolley – the maglev gliding effortlessly over the steel floor. I returned his look with an awkward grin, enough to make him hurry on his way. Must be an important trip. It was unusual to drag that much luggage.

Sub-jet fuel was expensive – most space in the jets was allocated for transporting people rather than items. For shorter trips, it was easier to carry-on or buy at the destination. Most ports had forgone automated luggage checking entirely. Anyone wishing to take extra baggage had to drag it through manually, paying the surcharge to have it added to the tiny hold at the departure gate.

Karin noticed I'd paused and pulled me towards a nearby check-in queue behind two women. They were glamorously dressed in flowing silk dresses, almost see through to the skin, hair long and shining – completely free of city grime. As I stood, uncomfortably trying to blend in, a breeze from the air conditioning carried their perfume over to us – acute and floral. An intense urge of lust washed over me.

Karin leaned over. "Careful, pherofume," she whispered urgently.

I blinked and tried to clear my head. It was difficult – all the blood had rushed to my loins! I'd heard of pherofume, but I'd never been close enough to women who could afford it. The urge passed, but for a moment, the effect had been powerful. I'd had to restrain myself from lurching at them!

"Isn't that dangerous?" I whispered back, breathless as the effects receded. "What if someone attacked them?"

"Look around. These women don't go places without heavy security. If anybody does something, they'd be arrested immediately. It's a game to them; they like to tease men, work them into a frenzy." She snarled contemptuously. "It's so bad, most men wear antidote cologne to neutralise the effect."

"You're kidding."

"Nope."

"You sound like you know what you're talking about."

"Maybe." Came the flat reply.

We gave a wide berth to similarly dressed women, lest I blow the whole thing with an outburst of indecent behaviour.

There were cameras all over the foyer and security guards patrolling, but there were no physical barriers this side of the departures area. It was essentially a public zone – we could walk around with no one getting too suspicious.

Karin knew the basic layout. She grabbed my elbow, pointing out the security entrance. It separated the foyer from the controlled departures lounge. It was our biggest hurdle, full of measures to prevent unauthorised access. A physical inspection of documents, then a ten metre scanning tunnel filled with passive x-rays and magnetic sensors – plus cameras and a complement of security personnel manning the various stations.

Everything would be easy until we made our move, then the stakes would be sky-high. Karin was the weak point of the plan; even with her pre-state, there was a chance she'd be spotted or become trapped – snarled somewhere between the security barriers or in a camera arc where I couldn't reach her.

The sub-jet we wanted to board was due to leave in an hour. I didn't know how long it would take in real time to get this done, but we shouldn't spend long on the other side either. An hour was about right.

Pretending to tie my boots, I whispered to Karin. "I better go check the way. I'll be back as soon as I can."

"If you do your job right, it will be instantaneous for me."

I smiled. "I guess you're right."

Closing my eyes, I slowed my breathing, holding the image of the clock in my mind. I detected the change as it happened. A thickening of the atmosphere. An absence of ambient sound.

I opened my eyes. The world was stationary – marble and glass surfaces peppered with frozen lens flares. The manicured elite of Neo-London had become well-dressed mannequins.

Even motionless, Karin radiated determination and encouragement. It terrified me. I didn't want to let her down.

I waded forward. The security gate lay ahead. A large cone shaped area, six metres at its widest, narrowing to two metres, funnelled passengers towards the checkpoint. It was crowded with people, frozen in various acts of shuffling, but there was room to squeeze by.

Near the narrow end, an inspector was checking documents. He was flanked on either side by cameras mounted to cover each other's arcs. One camera would spot any attempt to slide along the wall under the other.

Pausing, I reviewed the area. Behind the inspector, set in the wall and ceiling, was the faint outline of a laser perimeter grid. It was down at the moment to let people through. We'd have to sneak past the inspector and block line of sight to the cameras. The laser grid would activate if either caught us, sealing the area.

I was feeling lightheaded. I'd been still too long. I wished I knew why it was hard to breathe – it was a serious danger.

I swam forward again. The inspector's head was down, diligently examining the documents in front of him. Unlike other Neo-Guards, he wasn't wearing a helmet; it would impede his work. He was older than typical, pudgy, and wearing traditional circular glasses, worn low on his nose. He didn't look athletic but seemed observant – one eye on the next person.

A gold pin adorned his lapel, signifying seniority. I doubted much got past him. I'd need a convincing distraction, and for once, my old life with Sebastian was a wellspring of experience to draw from. I'd already thought about the bit I'd use on him.

On the other side of the checkpoint was the sensor tunnel – an automated passageway scanning travellers for threats. To the left, a door led to the monitoring station where the guards would be. There were no cameras between the inspector and the beginning of the sensor tunnel. A blind spot.

I pushed on. The tunnel's interior was featureless, just a strip of black glass running its length. The floor was an automated travellator – passengers stood upright, evenly spaced so they could be scanned efficiently.

At the far end, the tunnel flared back out, with a matching door for security to exit the monitoring station. And beyond, the cavernous departure lounge awaited; it was even more luxurious than the public foyer – dotted with plush sofas and top-end shops.

It was spread across multiple levels with another imitation sun illuminating its interior, a warmer and more relaxed shade than on the public side.

Cameras around the perimeter covered most angles, but as with the entrance to the sensor tunnel, there was a blind spot where it joined with the lounge. It didn't seem like a coincidence. The sensors in the tunnel must interfere with the cameras.

It was an advantage, but options remained limited. There would be no point directing Karin through the tunnel. Covering her line of sight wouldn't work – the scanners would spot her easily, record she wasn't registered with a sub-liner, and raise an alarm.

The alternative was the monitoring station running parallel, the doors to which were in the camera dead zones. An idea was forming, but it needed testing.

Walking back, I selected a target. A man carrying a heavy-looking rucksack. His hair was slickly parted, nose up-turned in permanent disdain. Even motionless, he was preppy and entitled. I had no sympathy for what I was about to do to him.

Ensuring no part of my body was in the tunnel, I placed a foot across his path and exited latent state. He tripped as the world jolted to life, face planting in a spectacular crash. An alarm sounded, and the travellator halted.

A woman to my side jumped in shock, but not from the man tripping. Grimacing, I realised my mistake. It must have seemed I'd appeared from nowhere. Shaking her head, she brushed it off and hurried along. I'd been lucky not to appear in front of someone more observant. Sloppy.

Luckily, the damage was limited; everyone else's gaze was focussed on the bedlam. I'd have to be more careful though. I couldn't flash into existence wherever I wanted.

Using the chaos as cover, I slid along the wall outside the tunnel, passing the door to the monitoring station. All eyes were on the man, although no one ran to his aid. Either too shocked or snobby to help – I suspected the latter. He groaned as he lay sprawled, backpack ridden up and pushing his face into the rubberised surface.

I readied myself; the monitoring station opened and two guards emerged to investigate. I re-entered latent state, freezing the door before it closed.

My heart was racing and I was out of breath. Pausing and unpausing time was taxing. I hoped I could keep it up.

Inside was full of readouts and displays. The strip of glass running its length showed real-time skeletal images of passengers – anything noteworthy coloured orange for inspection. Mostly AROs and bags. One guard remained seated at a console facing the window.

I suppressed the urge to laugh. The guy I'd tripped was visible through the screen. He still hadn't been righted – skeleton arms frozen while trying to dislodge the bag from his head. The guards' guns were highlighted red – calling out the weapons.

The lazeblades we'd packed would be picked up too, but if the plan worked, we'd avoid the sensors altogether.

I moved to the far door; it was closed, but there was no lock from this side. If I could get Karin into the station and keep the guards distracted, she could slip through and let herself out into the lounge.

I had enough information. The plan wasn't complete, but there were too many unknowns to think further ahead. I made my way out, back past the lurking inspector, and into the foyer.

Lesson learned, I strode to the port bathroom, unfreezing time in a vacant stall before joining Karin. She was angry, hands on hips.

"Daryl! You have to pause time when no one's looking. You vanished right in the middle of the port! We're lucky it's not too busy this side."

"Yeah, I know." I answered sheepishly, examining my shoes. "I did the same thing in the checkpoint just now. Don't worry, it didn't cause a problem, but I know about it now – I used the bathroom to exit."

She accepted the explanation, but the scowl remained. "What have you figured out?"

I smiled, attention moving to my jacket, fiddling with the zip. "It's gonna be tricky, but I think I have a solution."

I ran through my idea while Karin listened. When I'd finished, the scowl was still there, but it had changed to one of concentration.

"Seems sensible," she answered matter-of-factly.

"Sensible? That's your only feedback?"

"What do you want?"

"Oh, I don't know, some clairvoyant reassurance, maybe?"

She cocked her head. "I'm not getting any messages *not* to do it. Does that help?"

I sighed. "Yes. Very confidence inspiring."

"Glad to be of help!" she chirped annoyingly, and before I could argue, she grabbed my hand and made a beeline for the security gate.

I saw what she had. A rotund woman pulling a hover trolley was crossing the foyer; it was piled high with garish floral luggage.

Karin broke away, positioning herself by the far wall, beneath the scanning arc of the right side camera, waiting for Luggage Lady to break line of sight. Karin's muted colours did a good job of blending her into the wall and floor.

I turned my attention to the inspector. He was an intimidating obstacle, but I didn't have time to second guess myself; Luggage Lady was already halfway across the hall. If we missed this opportunity, we'd draw suspicion. And I couldn't rely on latent state – the cameras would see me if I appeared or disappeared this close to the gate. Only a conventional distraction would work.

Clasping my nerves, I joined the queue ahead of Luggage Lady. She'd moved into a good position to block the camera for Karin. The inspector looked foreboding – observant and unflappable. I would have to bring my A game to keep his eyes off her.

The last time I'd tried this was ripping off alchovials at the local off-license. It was an old trick of Sebastian's, using misdirection and sleight of hand to control attention. It had worked back then, but the store attendant was small fry in comparison.

"Documents please." The inspector extended his hand, eyes looking over his glasses.

"Sure." I feigned confidence, reaching into my bag as I recalled the opening to the bit, rummaging around for the non-existent travel pass as I struggled with the precise phrasing.

"You see ... the thing is ..." I started, but the words had become fuzzy. The sentence I was searching for no longer made sense.

I could feel sweat beading on my forehead. Had the mental effort of scouting ahead gotten to me or was this blind panic? Why couldn't I remember how this went? I'd been rehearsing it all morning!

The inspector straightened, placing his hands on the desk, head fully raised. "Problem, sir?"

I could hear Luggage Lady tut from behind. Obnoxious cow!

"Er, no." I played for time, desperately searching for the words, but the more I concentrated, the more they slipped away. "They're here somewhere." I could feel my face going red.

Somewhere out of sight, I knew Karin was waiting to make her move, wondering what the delay was. I was blowing it – I had to do something!

I could slip into latent state or run away, but either would raise an alarm, and neither would divert the inspector's attention.

I looked at my hands, balled up in frustration, and in a moment of inspiration, I knew what to do.

I forced a smile. "Oh, I'm sorry, here are my documents ..."

I swung for him as hard as I could.

I'd never been a fighter, but Seb had, and we'd had plenty of scuffles. I'd lost all of them, but somewhere along the line, I'd learned to throw a punch. Despite the frayed nerves, or maybe because of them, the skills came back keenly.

My fist connected solidly with the underside of the inspector's jaw. He was close – it was more of an uppercut than a hook.

He careened over the booth, teeth crunching together, the shock sending his glasses flying.

There were gasps all around, including Luggage Lady, who yelped loudest of all. I bolted in the reverse direction, shooting her a menacing glance. It turned her whimper into a full-blown scream. That would teach her for tutting at me!

I reached the bathroom a few moments later, freezing time to pause the frenzy. The surge of adrenaline and mad dash had sapped all my gas. I staggered around in the stall, fighting for breath in the thick air.

After some scary seconds of ragged breathing, pushing away the urge to pass out, I recovered enough to venture out.

The inspector was crumpled on the reverse of the booth, hands at his face. It wasn't my original plan, but it had the desired effect. Everyone was staring at the carnage, and not at Karin, who had slid further down the wall, the line of sight to the opposing camera now blocked by Luggage Lady's overburdened hover-trolley.

Even better, the commotion had spilled close to the travellator and the guards were already rushing out to investigate. I'd killed two birds with one stone, but it was too early to feel smug.

I snuck into the monitoring station; the remaining guard was still seated by the console. This wasn't over yet.

Punching wouldn't work this time. He was wearing a full-face helmet. My knuckles still stung from hitting the inspector's fleshy face. This guy's helmet would damage my hand further and would show we'd been inside the station. Authorities were looking for people on the public side of the departure gate. We needed to maintain that illusion.

I considered the alternatives. The station was full of sensitive equipment, running the width of the window. It looked breakable, but I had a better idea. Mounted on the console near the guard hung a foam fire extinguisher. It wasn't an ideal solution. An extinguisher going off would be suspicious, but with all the commotion, it wasn't hard to imagine someone could have knocked it.

I retrieved my lazeblade and tested it. It didn't fire. Of course, it was paused like everything else. No way to practise. This would be a live test!

I wedged my foot against the door, holding it open. Then, keeping behind the guard, I stretched towards the fire extinguisher and unfroze time.

An alarm, tripped by the chaos outside, assaulted my senses, and with it, a terrible sense of vulnerability. I felt like a sleepwalker, violently awoken in a place they didn't recognise. It was hard to imagine how Karin must be feeling, out in the open as she was.

I couldn't see her but knew she was working her way down the wall, ready to bolt to the station. The moments ticked by. It felt like an eternity, but finally she appeared around the corner, eyes flashing as she saw me at the door. I nodded back, revitalised by the progress we were making.

Once I was sure she'd make the closing door, I activated the lazeblade and plunged it into the pressurised cylinder, angling the jet towards the guard. Caught unaware, his attention focused on the screen, he jumped in surprise and went into a swearing panic as foam covered his helmet.

Karin slid in low behind me, flattening herself against the wall. I gestured urgently at the far door. Then, keeping low to avoid the guards flailing arms, we scuttled through the monitoring station and released the door handle. It swung outwards. We were almost there!

Leaving the beleaguered guard and resisting the urge to run, we merged with the throngs exiting the travellator – smoothly making our way towards the lounge.

Karin slipped her hand into mine, swinging it casually. To anyone who cared to look, we were a privileged couple going away for the weekend. I hoped she couldn't feel the tremble.

As we moved out of danger, the lush, multi-layered shopping arcade lay ahead, busy with travellers doing last-minute shopping. No one seemed interested in us.

Punching the inspector would have raised an alert, but not in the lounge. The person they were looking for hadn't made it through the gate – security on this side was still relaxed. I looked at my knuckles. Some pretty serious bruising was already showing – purple in the centre smudged with yellow. I'd given him a hell of a crack!

Passing a pherofume shop, we paused by a rack of fragrances. Pictures of pretty, mostly naked women adorned the walls on one side, men with hidden, lustful glances on the other. The prices had far too many zeros.

"Can I help you?" A saleswoman dressed in a severe silver blouse addressed us from behind the counter.

"Not yet." Karin waved dismissively, selecting a test vial, pretending to be interested. I hoped she didn't plan to spray it. Mixed with the adrenaline coursing through me, the effect could be disastrous. The saleswomen returned her attention to her terminal.

Karin leaned in close. "That was amazing how you distracted the guard. I never would have thought of that."

Her breath landed hot on my ear, the sensation as powerful as any perfume. It created a tingle all the way down to my toes. I considered telling her the truth. I'd thrown the punch out of desperation. She probably knew, but if she was going to give me the credit, I was happy to take it.

"Yeah, I guess I figured it would be easier than creating a second distraction in the tunnel."

Her smile made me feel amazing and fraudulent at the same time.

Rejecting the first tester, she selected another, turning it in her hands, speaking quietly without looking at me. "Okay, Daryl. I have some good news and some bad news."

Uh-oh. Sudden changes of direction from Karin were generally bad.

"I saw the departure board for HK1. The next one boards in forty minutes. That's the good news."

Not being the target audience, it felt weird to examine the pherofume as Karin was. I turned and stared at the pictures of the women instead – which was probably worse.

"And the bad news?" I whispered over my shoulder.

"We can't actually board it."

"What?" I stiffened. "You didn't mention that before!"

"Sorry, you had a lot to deal with, I didn't want to overload you. The thing is, even if we got into the passenger cabin, the tickets are biometrically coded. Without them, or even with stolen ones, we'd be scanned and uncovered as soon as we were on board."

Thrusting my hands in my pockets, aware I was looking more and more like a pervert, I tried to hide my frustration. "Well, I can't imagine you let us get this far without a plan."

"Of course I didn't, but you're not going to like it."

I held my breath, waiting for the next phase of insanity to be explained.

"We'll have to travel in the hold."

I spun and looked at her, unable to keep up the pretence. "The hold! As in the luggage hold?"

The saleswomen looked at us again; she was suspicious now, and my reaction had made Karin cross.

"Shh!" she whispered, eyes angry. "And yes, the luggage hold. That's our only option."

I lowered my voice again. "Is that safe?"

"Sort of."

"What does that mean? Can you elaborate?"

"Not really." She glanced at the saleswoman. "Look, we have to go."

"I hate this already."

As we walked towards the gate, a flight for HK1 was preparing to leave, the launch tube visible through a large plexiglass window. The sub-jet itself was black and needle-shaped, with small swept-back wings. It looked like a cross between a space shuttle and a stealth jet. Enough power to make it to suborbital altitude, with just enough manoeuvrability to make it down again. Various cables and umbilicals connected to its hull for fuelling and maintenance.

Near the gate, passengers spread out in various states of relaxation – lounging on form-fitting sofas or chatting in groups. Karin nudged me. There was a hatch marked *Checked Luggage*.

"You're joking?"

"Nope. That's the only way on board."

It should have filled me with fear, but I felt numb. My life had become a series of insane events. I was either getting good at them or acclimatising to the risks. This must be what adrenaline junkies feel like – taking bigger and bigger chances, desperate for the buzz.

"Fine, one more kamikaze move," I said, defeated. "But this is the end of you holding shit from me!"

"Of course." Karin winked.

Right, as if she'd ever agree to that. Silly me.

# STATE 15

I nside the terminal, security was less restrictive, only needing minimal distraction.

Haughty and entitled, tottering on heels too high for her, the perfect diversion for getting into the hold presented herself.

Laden with oversized prosthetic breasts, she crossed the lounge. Her golden hair swung from side to side; onlookers forced to look whether they wanted to or not.

Karin, already in position on a sofa, slid a bag into her path, nudging it out with her foot.

Goldilocks didn't so much topple as utterly collapse – tumbling off her heels and sprawling across the floor. Her dress, previously keeping her decent (just about), slid down, exposing the expensive implants for all to appreciate.

The kerfuffle was enough for us to slip past the remaining passengers, now giggling, scoffing, staring, and pointing at the drama. We jumped through the chute in time to hear a few of the braver men offer to heave her back up again.

We landed on an anti-grav crash mat, slipping off the gently repelling fields, and scurried to avoid being stacked, along with the real luggage, into vertical alcoves. The mechanical claw doing the work didn't look amenable to human flesh.

We took refuge in one of the partially full storage areas, collapsing onto someone's faux leather suitcases.

The hold was sterile and industrial. Metal bulkheads and nuts left exposed where the fuselage was bolted together. A few low-powered bulbs washed the interior with a dull red glow, like a submarine.

I felt like I'd run a marathon. Since getting to the port, it had been nothing but high stress. If I closed my eyes, I'd fall asleep immediately. Annoyingly, I couldn't. Karin had sprung this new situation on us and I didn't know what was next. I made my thoughts known.

"Karin, tell me how we're not going to die when this thing takes off?"

She was sitting across from me in the alcove, cross-legged.

"And why couldn't you tell me before?"

"Sorry." She shrugged, shifting around uncomfortably. The alcove was far from ergonomic. "It's like I said. I'd put a lot of pressure on you. I didn't want to push you over the edge."

The answer was honest, but not good enough.

"You should have trusted me." Then a disturbing thought crossed my mind. "Did your pre-state tell you I'd screw up?" I almost didn't want to know; it would only confirm my anxieties.

Karin stared back at me appraisingly before answering. "No, it didn't. I knew you were dealing with a lot. The drugs, the control. Getting through security was enough for you to worry about."

I couldn't tell if she was being truthful, but if she'd spared me the embarrassment, it was best left unsaid. "Okay." I accepted the answer. I had no choice unless I wanted to uncover I was incompetent. "Just give me more credit next time."

She nodded, looking tired as well. Uncharacteristically so, with deep bags under her eyes. Even with her pre-state, it must have been terrifying for her in the checkpoint, out in the open. I wasn't the only one who'd had it tough.

"You don't need to worry, Daryl," Karin continued.

Did she know I'd been thinking about her?

"The hold's pressurised, otherwise some items of luggage might explode."

No, she was going back to my original question. I could sense a *but* coming.

"But …" There it was. "… they don't regulate the temperature as they do in the cabin. It uses too much fuel."

I knew it. Sub-jets travelled to near orbital heights, a part of the atmosphere not known for its balmy weather. "Karin, you know that means we're going to freeze to death, don't you?"

"Hold on," she replied defensively, unfolding her legs so she could lean forward and make her point. "I'm not suicidal. They heat it in here a little otherwise liquids would freeze and burst."

"How much do they warm it up by?"

"Two degrees centigrade."

"Two degrees! That might as well be freezing."

"Yes, but it's only that cold at certain altitudes. It will be at least five or six degrees for most of the flight."

"Karin!" I could barely contain my frustration. "That's damn cold, and I don't know about you, but I left my thermal underwear at home!"

"You did?" she mocked – and then said, "Well, I guess we'll have to find some in all this spare luggage." She stood and waved her hand around to illustrate how many options we had. "Won't we?"

I bit my lip to prevent digging a bigger hole. She was right. We were surrounded by clothes. There should be something suitable to layer up in. I stood too; it felt like I was being talked down to.

"It will be fine, Daryl." She soothed, sensing the retreat. "We'll huddle together."

She played the statement with a straight bat, no hint of intimacy, but whether by accident or design, it caught me off guard. I fell back in a heap.

"But don't get any ideas! This is a business trip." She was talking down to me now. She hadn't been nasty about it, but she'd made the point loud and clear.

I struggled to get back up, arms buried up to my elbows in luggage. "I've no idea what you mean." I feigned indignation. I knew exactly what she meant, and she was right; this was no place for messing around. Still, I recalled the moment by the fragrance counter. She'd been impressed, and damn it, I'd done everything we planned! That had to count for something – even for an idiot like me.

I regained my footing, kicking a handbag away from where it had tangled around my foot. "Okay, okay, we should see what we can find. This thing takes off soon."

Content to move on, we scavenged the luggage. Most of the bags had locks, but only to stop casual tampering. We slashed them open with our lazeblades, spilling clothes all over the hold. The stacking claw would get the blame.

Most of them contained wholly impractical fashion items or summer wear, but a few had thicker jackets and trousers that we liberated and dressed in.

We hunkered back in our alcove to wait for take-off, breaking into a fit of giggles as we inspected each other. We looked pretty silly. I'd found a fur-lined sports jacket and a pair of ski trousers. Karin, an oversized bomber jacket with thick dungarees. We looked like the homeless after a Christmas donation.

There was no time to speculate on the people we'd stolen our garments from. A low rumble emanated from the bowels of the aircraft. The sub-jet was preparing to fire the booster that would push us into sub-orbit. We scrambled to make ourselves ready, piling luggage into makeshift chairs.

"Hold on." Karin gripped my hand. "This is hardcore if you're not used to it."

I tensed and pushed myself into the well of bags I'd made, but even with the advanced warning, the launch was still a shock. It whipped my head into the bulkhead where I'd failed to brace it properly.

I cried out but didn't have time to complain. The rocket propellant was igniting, shoving me back hard as it thrusted upwards. The hold was the closest part of the craft to the engines – unshielded from noise and vibration. The sound was a deafening roar – filling my head and blurring my vision.

After a few minutes that seemed to go on forever, teeth clenched, eyes screwed shut, the sub-jet began to quiet, slowing as it reached its zenith.

I peeked my eyes open and wished I hadn't. As we commenced our turn towards Earth, I could see the alcoves rotating. The motion made me queasy – the circular storage spaces slowly spinning on gimbals and swing arms.

It was to level the luggage. Without, the bags would have to be painstakingly strapped down or become crushed and battered as the orientation altered. I guessed a similar system existed in the cabin above, keeping passengers perpendicular to the earth. Either way, it was disorientating as hell to look at!

The temperature dropped, my breath misting in front of me. We must be at the highest point, about to descend at a steep angle –

streaking back to ground faster than any normal plane. We'd reach HK1 in six hours. Nothing to do but wait it out.

The back of my head throbbed where it had hit the fuselage. I reached around to rub it but Karin had other ideas. She scooched in, grabbing my arm and pulling it around her. I didn't mind. I'd take the sore head in exchange.

After a few minutes, she broke the silence with an unexpected question. "Hey, Daryl, what's it like when you stop time? You know, enter latent state?"

I licked my lips; they were feeling dry and chapped in the cold. It was an interesting question, personal, but that was okay – I hadn't spoken to anyone about it, and I wanted to. I paused, rummaging for the right words. "Horrible." I settled on. "Dead ... flat ... like being under water but more so. There's no sound apart from what's in my head. I kind of hate it."

"That sounds familiar." Karin mused. "The horrible part. I guess that's something we share."

Probably not. Karin's battle with Future Karin – incessantly chattering – sounded way worse. At least I could turn latent state off.

"And you said it's hard to move around?"

"Yeah, a real struggle. Like swimming, or pushing against a heavy wind. I don't know why."

"Maybe it's the air?"

I stared at the curved roof of the sub-jet. "What do you mean?"

"Well, if latent state works like my clairvoyance, it connects you to a parallel universe. One where your body is occupying a bubble of normal time within a paused dimension. In fact, it would need to, otherwise you wouldn't be able to think or move; you'd be stationary like everything else."

I rubbed my little finger with my thumb. It had healed into a raised scar. When Led had bitten me, the blood had pooled around my hand like a glove. It did seem it was encased in some sort of bubble.

The launch engines had stopped, but the primary jets were blaring against Karin's voice. I leaned in tight to hear her.

"If you think about it, air molecules would be frozen like everything else. They'd only become agitated when you push against them – like passing through a liquid."

Total speculation, but it made sense. "I suppose that also explains why gravity doesn't affect me as much. At my extraplex, I was able to climb when the power cable snapped – even though I was hanging away from the building. What you're saying is the air resistance propped me up." I scratched my chin with my spare hand, thinking it through. "Yeah, that would account for why I can't breathe either."

"What?" Karin's surprise pierced my ear, making it sting. "Did you say you can't breathe?"

Wincing, I replied. "No, I mean, I can, but only when I'm moving. If I stop, it feels like I'm at altitude. The air becomes thin and I get lightheaded. So yeah, if it's locomotion pushing air into my lungs, that would make sense. The local supply becomes depleted if I don't move."

I felt Karin tense beneath my arm, a palpable change in atmosphere. "You should have told me about that."

"Why?"

"What if you were trapped, or knocked out? You'd suffocate!"

I could feel my head get hot. Why hadn't I told her? Hearing the deficiency out loud made it sound like a huge problem, at least worthy of discussion. Suddenly I was happy for the red lighting – it hid my flushed cheeks. "Er, sorry ... I guess I didn't think it was important to bring up. Just something I had to deal with. But you're right, it's a big hazard – I almost passed out in the bathroom at the port. Bear with me. I'm learning as I go. I think using latent state is like diving or rock-climbing. Dangerous but manageable."

Karin went quiet for a few minutes.

Eventually I couldn't take the silence. "Karin, are you angry with me?"

Her response surprised me. "Not at all. You keep putting your life on the line. You don't even know you're doing it." She turned to look at me, eyes dark and wide. "Daryl, thank you for doing this with me. I know you've got your reasons, but I've been chasing answers for so long I didn't think an end would ever be in sight. If we hadn't crashed into each other, I'd still be in Neo-London, and no closer to the truth."

I swallowed tightly, taken aback by Karin's earnestness. I hadn't considered how my actions were affecting her. Embarrassed, I turned to look into the hold again – the swaying gimbals and vibrations of the sub-jet hypnotic.

Karin settled deeper into the crook of my arm, the conversation coming to a close. The temperature in the hold was near freezing, but I couldn't tell; I felt warm from head to toe. In a shared moment of closeness I pressed my head against hers, drifting close to sleep. This was the best trip I'd ever taken. I was going to find answers. I was going to save Sebastian from the asylum. And maybe, just maybe, Karin would stick around while I did.

# STATE 16

I'd anguished over what mix of abilities and luck we'd need to escape the hold, but compared to the slow, shuffling humans in the cabin above, the machine arm had been efficient.

Riding inside two emptied, hardened suitcases, we made it out before the other passengers – spewed unceremoniously onto the anti-grav conveyor belt in the baggage collection hall.

The luggage circled forlornly, awaiting its owners, but we were long gone by then.

Security was present, but inattentive. Authorities were concerned with people getting on sub-jets, not getting off them – the document inspector was waving people though.

It was hard to believe we'd travelled anywhere. The austere, climate-controlled port felt identical to the one we'd started in. Apart from the Chinese signage, it was practically indistinguishable. Even the announcements over the tannoy were in clipped English. Underwhelming for my first journey to a foreign country.

"Is this it?" I complained under my breath.

Karin stopped striding towards the exit. She must have heard me.

"What is it?" I asked.

"After you."

She held her arm towards the revolving door, letting me go first.

I could see lights behind the frosted glass, but not much more. It was nighttime and the door was soundproof. I shrugged, pursed my lips, and leaned my weight.

Humidity hit me first. Thick and clammy. It took my breath away after the sterile coolness of the port. Gasping like a fish out of water,

I felt the heat cling to me like honey, prickles of sweat breaking out across my forehead.

The feeling of anticlimax evaporated – the sights and sounds of a new city immersing me in new sensations.

The port was built into a manmade island connecting Hong Kong on one side and Kowloon on the other – the defunct waterway and shipping industry cleared to make space for the long runways. To the right were the huge neon-laced skyscrapers of Hong Kong.

The Chinese had solved the space problem differently to Neo-London. Rather than creating extraplexes, they'd attached struts to the tallest buildings and created a city-spanning baseplate above. It hung over the island like an impossibly large umbrella.

Topped with shiny new structures, rising above the surrounding smog, the mega-structure had been dubbed HK1, becoming the nickname for the region. The social separation was immediately obvious. Those on the baseplate benefited from being above the pollution, staring down on those beneath, in the old city, bathed in artificial light.

Around HK1's edge hung an unbroken series of holo-displays. Colossal panels advertising products and food items. They featured heavily made-up Chinese women with oversized eyes, screaming in wordless excitement about their wares.

Opposite HK1, on the other side of the bay, lay the historic buildings of Kowloon. Sunk into the old harbour area, it appeared run-down but hid a well-known secret. Kowloon was the rich part of the city. The dilapidated exteriors a facade for dramatic effect – the ancient buildings containing modern internals. The whole of Kowloon was decorated with traditional Chinese lanterns and bunting.

We exited onto the concourse, joining the throngs of human traffic as they travelled back and forth between HK1 and Kowloon. Auto-cabs dotted the road – still too expensive for the masses, even this side of the globe.

"Different, isn't it?" Karin faked a casual tone. She knew my mind was blown.

"Definitely." Was all I could manage, scratching my head like a wide-eyed child. Then, I realised how uncool I was acting. "Shall we use a cab?"

"Do you know where you want to go?"

I shrugged. "No, I guess not."

"Then let's walk. It's been a while since I've been here."

"When were you here before?"

"Years ago. My parents took me ..." She trailed off, catching herself.

Interesting. There was more to that story, but now wasn't the time to ask.

"Okay." I filed the information away. "Which way?"

"Let's head into HK1 to acclimatise."

Acclimatise? It felt like I could never become accustomed to this. Trancelike, I followed, ambling towards HK1, or rather, the original Hong Kong beneath it.

We wandered across the kilometre expanse towards the city. The sub-jet runways on our right separated by high chain-link fences; the murky waters of the harbour on the left.

The fence did nothing to shield the deafening roar of landing sub-jets. Karin yelled over them as we strolled, providing more detail as we drank in the surroundings.

Before HK1, the Chinese had set up New Hong Kong on the mainland. Its purpose was to replace Shanghai, having suffered an economic collapse in the third global recession. They wanted to repeat the commercial success of Hong Kong from the eighties, but inside the confines of communist China, where it would be less rebellious. It had failed miserably. Hong Kong's culture had been established under British influence – its independence and physical separation from the mainland key to its entrepreneurial spirit. The new city had attracted impoverished rural-to-urban migration but little investment. Foreign firms had been too nervous to establish a presence under communist rule – the government having a history of appropriating private property. New Hong Kong had failed utterly as a commercial enterprise. It was now a farming and distribution hub.

Accepting their failure, China had re-focussed on the original Hong Kong, cutting their losses by establishing the baseplate that was now its namesake. Those who supported the government would be more likely to make it onto the new structure. Those who didn't could wallow beneath.

Nearing the main island, the path narrowed, filling with HK1 residents. It was my first glimpse at how different the locals were.

The fashion sense was wild. Neo-London was freaker fashion: leather, tattoos, punked hair. Here, the importance was on staying cool against the intense humidity. Locals only wore enough material to hide their shame. Blazingly coloured t-shirts, sarongs, belts, and braces were the order of the day – thinner and lighter the better. People looked like they'd been thrashed with luminous whips, exposing enough flesh to border on nudity.

In our leathers, we were over-dressed in the extreme. I was already slick with sweat. Karin wasn't faring any better, a red flush spreading across her cheeks. Finding new clothes had to be a priority.

All the bare skin should have been sexy, but it wasn't. Men and women cut their hair as short as possible – buzz cuts for the guys, severe fades for the women. Make-up was minimal – it would slop off in the heat.

The air quality didn't help. Industrialisation around Hong Kong coated the island in a semi-toxic pore-blocking miasma. Everyone had some sort of skin condition, ranging from mild rashes to full body acne.

Synonymously bright and grungy, the whole place smelled of sweat – as if it were baked into the stone – but at the same time it was spotlessly clean. I couldn't see a discarded alchovial anywhere. It was either culturally ingrained to clear up or authoritatively enforced – probably both. I resolved not to litter.

Excitement washed through me. It was so fantastically alien. We were hunting the source of our woes, but the distance we'd travelled had reduced the perceived danger. This was like a holiday. My first one ever.

"What are we going to do first?" Karin was fidgety as we reached the island. Her face had become radish-like, but she didn't seem to care. She was as happy as me about the change, fondling the edge of her rucksack – fingers grasping, itching to put new things in it.

I shook myself from my daze. "I guess we'd better find somewhere to stay; it could take us a while to track Maximal down."

Karin sniffed her armpit. "Yeah, and I could do with a shower too."

I laughed. It was so unladylike for Karin, but it was good; it meant we were becoming friends.

"And we'll need some new clothes," she added. "Something that fits in." Shopping was definitely top of her agenda, and she was doing a terrible job of hiding it!

I shifted uncomfortably in my leathers; the sweat was building into a funk that would start a rash soon. "Know any good places to stay? I can't stand this heat much longer!"

Karin activated her ARO, still slaved to my data contract but switched to international roaming. "It's been a while; give me a second ... Okay, the travel forums suggest Central and Causeway Bay have the most going on. It's a short trip via the underground system."

We found and boarded the metro; it was situated by the entrance to the city. Beat up and covered with state propaganda, it at least ran consistently, which was more than could be said for the Tube – a lot more. It smelled dank, but amazingly, it was air-conditioned. Such an incredible expense, but with the heat, the HK1 Governance didn't have a choice – people would die otherwise. We were on board for ten minutes, stuffed inside with a hundred other scantily clad locals, cooling off on their detours.

We alighted at Central – a metropolis of blazing lights. It throbbed with people hurrying from one air-conditioned building to another. It wasn't easy to move around – shops were stacked on top of each other, accessible via external staircases, stretching six stories high. It added perpendicular traffic to the already considerable horizontal kind.

Corporate skyscrapers towered overhead filled with workers toiling on their government assigned bureaucratic tasks. The men wore their ties open on sleeveless shirts, with professional blouses over hot-pants for the women.

We searched around, clueless where to go. The cacophony of outlets, VR cafes, and ARO vendors was like Neo-London but louder, sweatier, and more vertical. Eventually, we stumbled across a hotel Karin was happy with. I'd argued the case for staying somewhere low key, but she wasn't having it. *Prostitutes used bottom-end places, and besides,* she'd argued, *we'd need to collaborate, chat, and spread out – we needed a proper room.*

She had a point.

Set in the bottom ten floors of a corporate skyscraper, the hotel catered for business travellers. It serviced workers in the floors above who travelled non-commutable distances, but it was also open to anyone.

The receptionist gave us a strange look but politely checked us in when Karin's thumb scan cleared like any other.

The room was on the seventh floor, small and neat, with two single beds. It was wonderfully cold, bordering on frigid.

Sleep was immediately attractive. Dozing in the hold hadn't been as terrible as it could have been, but it hadn't been restful either. In comparison, the hotel was the height of luxury.

Karin dropped onto one of the beds, clutching a pillow; the decision made for both of us.

Fair enough. Sleep now. We'll figure out what next later.

# STATE 17

Waking, I was clueless to the time, fully clothed where I'd collapsed face first on the bed. I glanced behind the drapes. Dawn had penetrated the thick smog.

The hotel was on the outskirts of HK1, overlooking what remained of the harbour. In the centre, under the baseplate, there was no dawn.

I felt better. Optimistic. We were here. We'd made it all this way.

I rolled over in time to see Karin emerge from the bathroom, a thick plume of steam bellowing out behind her. It took me a second to understand what I was looking at. She was wearing a bra and had cut the legs off her trousers, turning them into makeshift hot-pants. Sitting down on the bed, she picked up her lazeblade and attacked her leather jacket, slicing the arms off to match.

"You should shower so we can get out of here," she chirped, bright and alert. "And throw me your clothes. We need to get better ones, but until we do, we can't walk around looking like this. We stick out like sore thumbs."

She sat in front of me in a state of undress; I sensed no embarrassment from her.

That wasn't true for me. With so much of her body on display, I didn't know where to look, so I avoided looking altogether, staring up at the illuminated ceiling.

A few moments passed. This was stupid. Everyone in HK1 dressed like that; I'd have to get used to it.

Self-conscious, I rose and pulled myself out of my over clothes. I considered upping the stakes and dropping my underwear too, turning the tables on her.

No, I reconsidered; she wasn't the awkward type, and it would make it worse. I padded over to the shower. Was she grinning?

When I emerged, a new set of clothes was waiting. They'd been similarly trimmed, although to my relief, not as revealing as Karin's. The shorts were above the knee, but they covered my thighs adequately. Putting on the sleeveless jacket revealed an unflattering sliver of pale stomach where it had been shortened.

"Ready to go deeper down the rabbit hole?" She joined me at the mirror with a hint of mischievousness.

*Alice in Wonderland.* Not the reference I'd have used, but yes, I was ready. I felt good, even better after the sleep and shower.

I appraised myself in the mirror. "Yeah, let's find Maximal. Right after we buy more clothes!"

# STATE 18

For the next two days, we embedded ourselves in HK1. If Neo-London was sprawling and gothic – crumbling brick and twisted neon, HK1 was synthetic dystopia – an unholy marriage of tech and drippy grimness.

It was overcrowded and seething. Huge orange globes were affixed to the baseplate, providing a dull, dirty glow, and the glare from interactive billboards infused everything with a flickering fluorescent haze.

Air-conditioning steam billowed from every floor of every building, mixing with natural humidity – coating everything in sticky, inescapable moisture.

It was as oppressive as the rainy soup of home, but it was new and completely different. I wanted to see it all.

I trailed Karin like a wide-eyed infant as we explored the city, acting like conformists rather than misfits – arsehole tourists or high-paid low-riskers. Either fit the bill.

We visited the underbelly of the original city, sweating and heaving below the baseplate, and the better appointed high rises sprouting atop HK1. Climbing the corporate ladder wasn't a metaphor here – it was a reality. Successful workers ascended literal escalators to the salubrious offices above. Free from the heat and grime.

The city wasn't big, only a fraction as wide as Neo-London, but far denser. It was layered with shops, arcades, and restaurants – millions of residents crammed into tiny, overcrowded domiciles.

A few rich or lucky residents could afford an escape to the posh ruins of Kowloon, but not many.

Remarkably, the populace was making it work. Politeness and respect had become necessities. Little nods between people, alien up until now, were becoming clearer. It was an effort to make existence bearable. A necessary kindness to avoid the fights that would break out otherwise. I toed the line, nodding back, trying to avoid barging people with my clumsy western frame.

Gangs congregated around arcades and alleys, but they weren't as threatening as freakers. The local security and surveillance was more efficient at keeping them in check. A mixed blessing. We were less likely to be lazebladed but more likely to register on the city's internal systems (if someone decided to look).

The food was better, or maybe just different; it was hard to tell. It was still vegetable protein but pushed into unique shapes and flavoured with unusual spices. Everything from fried balls of fish-flavoured paste, served on sticks, to bags of spicy, synthetic seafood. All available from a menagerie of street vendors, screaming enthusiastically in high-toned, sing-song Cantonese.

Real animal protein was available in the form of fried insects, which I declined. Karin didn't, scooping them up handfuls at a time, tiny legs sticking out between her lips as she munched them. Gah!

It wasn't hard to communicate. Hong Kong had a high prevalence of English speakers from the time of British influence. Most signs were in English and anything we couldn't communicate, our AROs translated for us.

We adopted the fashion, gratefully trading our butchered leathers for the half-cropped t-shirts that were in vogue. The relief outweighed any self-consciousness. I'd added loose fitting shorts and sandals, Karin, a short pleated skirt. It attached to her crop-top, front and rear, with orange suspenders. She'd paired it with a mirror-finished baseball cap to hide her face from cameras. I hated hats so opted for some white, slatted sunglasses instead. They were like venetian blinds over my eyes – more a statement than for blocking out the sun (there wasn't any). They did a good job of obscuring my face and reduced Karin to fits of laughter – good enough reason to wear them on their own.

After a couple of days, we'd even acquired the rashes endemic to the city. Small clusters of pimples on the face, arms, and stomach where skin faced the air. I didn't mind, but Karin, whose skin had seemed bulletproof in Neo-London, succumbed to the toxic smog as readily as anyone. She'd run to the first chemist she'd seen and bought a dozen different tonics – slathering the affected areas. None had worked, eventually leading her to declare "whatever" and stop fussing. After a while, we didn't notice them anymore.

It was good to spend time with Karin in this strange environment. She was easy to speak with and be around. I used the opportunity to dig deeper.

She confirmed my suspicions of a privileged upbringing. Daughter to high-profile low-riskers. Big-wigs working in prestigious IT infrastructure companies. They'd lived in a large domicile by the south coast with special dispensation to travel and work in Neo-London. All the benefits of living away from the polluted city, but with the creds to enjoy it. She didn't give much detail, but it wasn't hard to imagine an upbringing filled with finer things and little to worry about.

That had all ended when her sub-jet had been exposed to ... whatever we'd been exposed to. The persistent, droning voice of Future Karin dragging her away from a comfortable life and into this one. I had some sympathy. My life had already been in the gutter. Karin had tumbled a huge distance to join me.

I told her more about Sebastian. How he'd stepped up after our parents were taken. They'd been among the first generation of SP1N users. Addicted to early, uncalibrated batches that were overly potent. They'd been driven psychotic and hauled off, leaving us to fend for ourselves. Seb, only a teenager, was already a player by then, self-sufficient on his side hustles. He took me under his wing – showed me how to get by.

I focussed on the stories I hoped were more cool than sinister. I made the long cons more complicated than they were, the burglaries more intricately planned – more daring. I kept back the nasty stuff. The pensioners we'd shaken down for creds; the SP1N debtors we'd fingered for extra tabs.

She listened intently, but her expression was hard to read, somewhere between intrigued and disgusted.

Across the city, we made enquiry after enquiry after Maximal. At VR arcades, internet cafes, anywhere hackers might congregate, but with no success. Patrons blinked, rushed off, or in one case, threatened us – flashing an ornate, Asian styled lazeblade from beneath her sarong.

Karin's pre-state reads gave us some signs but not the whole story. People knew things, but they weren't saying. It wasn't clear why. It wasn't driven by outright fear, although that played a part. It seemed closer to self-defence.

If the community knew Maximal, he was being protected. Frustrating, but encouraging. If someone that infamous could build a trust network, maybe they *did* have the power to help us.

However we looked at it, the situation couldn't last forever. Unless the conspiracy forum had been faked, something would have to change. Why ask us to come if he wasn't going to reach out?

And of course, that was right, and when things did change, it caught us completely off guard.

# STATE 19

Deeply embedded beneath the baseplate, Lan Kwai Fong heaved. Known for having the densest concentration of bars and clubs, it was here, in HK1's nethermost den of iniquity, we finally made progress.

Tired of fruitless enquiries, we were having a break, and we weren't disappointed – Lan Kwai Fong suited us: a busy network of brightly lit alleys flanked with dozens of bustling establishments.

The crowds were so dense they spilled onto the pedestrianised roads. Multicoloured fairy lights zig-zagged the thoroughfares, patterning the greasy, moisture-covered paving in pools of light.

It wasn't dissimilar to Farringdon, but unlike Neo-London, it was mostly free of unconscious bodies and cross-eyed wasters. They must exist, no city could be without them, but the HK1 authorities obviously did a better job of clearing them out.

The bars were modern, well-lit affairs, with nicely functioning air conditioning. They had to be; cool interiors were needed to attract customers as much as lighting or running water. Everything was tuned to escape the heat and sweat of HK1 – enticing patrons to spend their creds getting buzzed.

Alcohol was far down the list of available intoxicants – dehydration being too much of a concern. Instead, liquid consumption came in the form of flavoured isotonics, sucked back with abandon.

Delirium came from a different place. Slim canisters, filled from pressurised bottles behind the bar where optics normally hung.

I'd bought something called *Tropical Thunder*, watching fascinated as the barman 'mixed' the concoction. Each bottle he visited released a hiss of gas as it emptied into the canister. I eyed it suspiciously but then shrugged, broke the seal, and squirted a healthy dose up my nose. What the hell. I'd done worse.

I winced, believing the fine mist would sting my nostrils. It didn't; it was refreshing. If anything, it cleared my sinuses, making it easier to breathe. The tropical flavour was immediate. A quick, clean buzz throughout my head. There was no gastric satisfaction as one might get from a cold alchovial. It was a more heady euphoria, but one that faded quicker. I guessed it wasn't alcohol based – some narcotic designed specifically for the hot environment.

Karin joined me, grinning as her chocolate and gin flavoured 'cocktail' hit her nasal receptors.

We took a few good drags, grinning at each other stupidly as the effects took hold.

"Take it easy on those inhalers, dears." A low-toned woman's voice broke through the noise, the well-pronounced English standing out against the Cantonese backdrop.

A glamorous black woman appeared between the throngs – gold and white gown flowing about her angular frame. It was more clothes than most wore, but it was still light and airy. Close cropped hair, gold hooped earrings, and – contrary to typical HK1 fashion – thick red lipstick completed the picture.

Towering over the crowds on six-inch heels. She cut an imposing figure as she approached the bar.

It was impossible to tell her age; she could have been anywhere between twenty-five and forty-five. Clear and wrinkle free, her complexion held no clues, but her eyes were deep and wise. She couldn't be especially young with eyes like those.

Karin recovered her wits first. "And who are you, please?"

The rakish woman paused as the barman handed her a pre-mixed canister, or inhaler, as she'd called it.

"Your usual, Ms. Maximal." He handed it to her, head bowed. Deferent.

*Ms. Maximal*, I mouthed at Karin.

She shrugged, watching the new arrival cautiously.

Something about her was odd. I couldn't put a finger on it.

She cracked the seal between long fingers. It looked tiny in her large hands. Closing her eyes, she took a deep pull. It was an elegant process – a person of refinement appreciating a bouquet.

The barman hadn't moved; he stood there, fidgeting nervously. Finally, Ms. Maximal opened her eyes and nodded. The barman puffed out his cheeks, releasing the breath he'd been holding before shuffling along to the next customer.

Ms. Maximal turned her gaze on us behind long eyelashes. "You finally made it. I've been waiting for you."

She was sincere, but intense. Strangely menacing.

Karin said nothing, head cocked, pre-state weighing her up. It fell to me to realise the silence had gone on long enough to be rude. Steeling myself, I took a hit on the inhaler. If this was Maximal – the criminal and hacker – surprising as her appearance was, I had more in common with her than Karin anyway.

"Hello." I extended a hand. "Sorry, I guess we were expecting someone different."

She smiled thoughtfully, running the tip of the inhaler across her bottom lip. "Someone more hacker-like?"

Confirmation. No longer unexpected, but still strange. I thought about it for a moment. What had I been expecting? I admitted it out loud. "I suppose someone less ladylike – a man, I guess."

Her smile broadened, flashing large white teeth. "Very honest of you, but don't worry too much. Besides ..." She grasped my outstretched hand, shaking it firmly. "I'm not that different from you."

It wasn't the dainty handshake I'd been expecting; the sort that's mostly fingers. It was a fully loaded, hand-enveloping shake. Webs of hands and thumbs interlocking tightly. It clicked. The height, the large hands, the overall rakishness. Ms. Maximal wasn't a Ms. at all.

Karin breathed out in realisation too, resolving her contradictory pre-state. Smiling, she extended her hand, apologetic. "We're sorry, it's been a busy few days. I'm Karin and this is Daryl."

Ms. Maximal moved to shake Karin's hand, this time around the fingers, the point already made.

"I know," she continued smoothly. "In fact. I know a great deal about both of you."

The statement hung ominously, the noise of the bar seeming to quiet as she focused her gaze on each of us in turn.

"And how should we address you?" Karin continued.

"Max is fine." She smiled to ease the tension. And then in anticipation of our next question. "I don't identify with either gender, so assign whichever you feel most comfortable with."

I made a quick reappraisal, not so subtly eyeing Max up and down. I'd first assumed she was a woman, but looking closely, I could see where my sense of something being off had come from. Apart from the clothes and jewellery, there were few signs of femininity – no curves around the chest or buttocks, no swell around the thighs. Still, my first impression was the most lingering. I'd mentally connected her as female, and her voice, although low, spoke in the intonation and demeanour of a lady, so that's what I'd go with.

Karin was lost in thought, long past caring what gender to assign. "What did you mean when you said you knew about us?"

Max's response was quick and devastating, dismissive humour dancing across her face. "My girl, I've been tracking you since the Shard!"

I tried to read Karin, but her eyes were glued to Max.

"How is that possible?" I raised my voice. "We contacted *you*. Days after the Shard."

"Oh, that was a coincidence." Max smirked knowingly. "A happy one, no doubt. It gave me an easy way to reach out, but you were already on my radar."

Her elite, manicured tone was patronising, but her body language was open. It didn't seem like she was lying.

Karin jumped in. Max was running rings around her pre-state and the frustration was clear. "But how did you know about the Shard so quickly?"

"Major news like that doesn't slip my notice," – a half smile and a wink – "and much that is significantly smaller doesn't either."

My heart skipped a beat. What else did she know?

"But you said you were tracking us specifically?" Karin continued.

"Of course. After I'd hacked the CCTV footage of the explosion, my AI routines recorded two interesting individuals. They'd been at ground zero but were unaccounted for in the dead." Max took a final drag from her inhaler, discarding the empty canister. "It was quite a conundrum ... for a while."

Karin leaned back on her heels, preparing to run – the new situation bristling with unknown danger.

I turned half to the side, eyeing the room for an exit.

"I slowed the footage," she continued. "Analysed it frame-by-frame. *Very* interesting."

I blinked a few times. Max had witnessed our escape from the falling rubble – something we hadn't planned on revealing. She was holding all the cards.

Max waved her hand. "Don't look so panicked, dears! If I'd wanted to turn you in, I'd have done it by now. What's important is I can help. I've been interested in people like you for quite some time."

I'd forgotten we were in a bar; my attention was laser focussed on the conversation, ready to run if I had to. "What do you mean? People like us?"

"Oh, don't be coy! People with your, er ... condition, shall we call it?"

We waited for more information but none came. Max stood there. Smiling expectantly.

I turned to Karin after a few moments had passed, relaxing slightly. "I get it."

"Get what?" Karin stood tensely, staring at Max. Her pre-state was still having trouble, but I'd seen this behaviour before.

"Don't you see, Karin? This isn't an offer of help. It's a negotiation – a shakedown. Max ..." I gestured to where she stood, one hand on her hip, waiting. "... wants something. That's the only reason we're here."

Max responded with a patronising mini-clap. "Good boy! I see you're a quick learner. Don't judge me too harshly though. I do want to help. Please appreciate I'm a businessperson first, and you get nothing in this world for free."

I readied myself. I'd been here before – experienced a hundred back-alley deals. The rules were universal. No negotiation went well if it began acrimoniously. Being ready to run made me look defensive.

I replanted my feet, digging deep for my reasonable voice. "What do you want, Max?"

She took a few steps forward. The games were over, this was the real conversation.

"It's simple, darling." She leaned in closer. "I need more data."

Her tone was equally reasonable, but she said the last word with a hunger. One I understood. The hunger of an addict.

"And how will that help us?" Karin pushed between us. I pulled her back. I wanted to hear what Max had to say.

"You already know the answer." Max closed the remaining distance, lips brushing my ear. "Limelight is *killing* people. You've worked that out for yourselves – witnessed it at the Shard. It's all connected. Limelight, the murders, your abilities. All as one."

"Connected? How?" I whispered back.

"I don't know. That's why I need you."

I chose my next words carefully. "Okay, Max. What, exactly, do you want?"

Smiling, she slinked back and touched her shoulder. An ARO emerged. I hadn't noticed it until now. It was low profile, blending in with her gown. *CAMO-ARO*: rare, completely bespoke, and very expensive. A chameleon-class device that can alter its colour and texture, adapting to the wearer's clothes.

She reversed the screen, displaying what she was looking at.

"I'd like you to acquire something for me, dears."

I wrinkled my nose at the device. Sniffing the odour of something fishy. It displayed a building in the heart of HK1's upper disk, New Mong Kok. Around it were annotated comments: *Limelight HK1 Data Centre. High Security.*

I snapped back, the odour I'd detected becoming the rancid smell of poison. "No chance!" I proclaimed. "No way. We're not going anywhere near a Data Centre!"

Max held my gaze for a moment, then shrugged and collapsed the ARO. It vanished against her shoulder. "I thought you'd say that, but before you make up your mind, why not indulge me a little longer. I have more to show you. Will you accompany me back to my home?"

I shook my head slowly. That sounded like a dangerous, pointless detour. Even if Max could be trusted, the point would be to convince us to do her bidding. I didn't want convincing. Anything involving a Data Centre was madness – they were more secure than military installations. A protected Telcom nerve centre – containing their highly sensitive data assets. People went missing in places like that.

It was Karin's turn to hold me back, beckoning me over. "Daryl, we're here now. Shouldn't we listen to what she has to say?"

"We can't trust her."

"I know, but she's been tracking us for days – she could have reported us any time." Karin shot a dark glance at Max. "She still could."

I considered Max. Refined and ruthless. It would be easy to imagine her being cruel. I sighed and nodded. Max had asked politely, but it wasn't a request; it was a demand – laced with an unstated threat.

"Good girl." Max purred. "You've come all this way to see me, after all."

I didn't like where this was going, but our bargaining position was weak. Max only had something to gain – we had everything to lose. If she didn't help us, we'd be on the run again. From her.

We had to bide our time. Play her game until we had more information. Much as it pained me.

# STATE 20

P arked outside, Max's car was a long, low-slung sedan in bur-
nished gold. Max clearly had a thing for gold.

I'd been expecting something subtle, off the grid, but nothing like
that applied to Max. She adhered to the *hide in plain sight* method of
disguise. And it was working. Even with a reputation as the world's
most notorious hacker, people feared and protected her. I was beginning to see why.

As we set off, the car's windows became monitors, displaying videos
and articles of world events – lines of programming code scrolling over
the images. The feeds weren't opaque enough to obscure the ghostly
outlines of the city behind.

The code was more advanced than anything I'd seen. Lounging
in her seat, Max caught me looking, one hairless leg crossed over the
other.

"Hacking algorithms," she remarked. "I'm always poking my nose
where it doesn't belong. I need to monitor the outputs, even when I
travel. Corporations are getting smarter all the time. I'm only afforded
a small window to conduct my work."

My hacking experience amounted to jailbreaking AROs or ripping
off cred machines. To say this was in another league was a huge understatement. Max was cracking mainstream organisations – news,
government, Telcoms, utilities. She must be an absolute genius.

I could see how she operated with impunity – the fear and loyalty
made sense.

"You use this information to keep you safe, don't you?" I aired my
thinking. "Blackmail, extortion, that sort of thing. It's why people
don't turn you in."

Max feigned offence, one hand at her chest, but with enough of a wink to show she didn't care.

"Nothing so insidious, dear." She tapped her arm console. Logos of various organisations flooded the screens – most of them household names. "It's true; when my snooping encounters something minor – nothing big enough to expose – but naughty all the same, I may, occasionally, make it known I've uncovered it. A few bribes come my way and I hold the discoveries back. I use it to secure the space I need to work."

"What about private citizens?" I snorted. "Do you uncover their misdemeanours too?"

Max said nothing. It was clear she played whatever games she needed to further her cause.

"What is your work?" Karin interjected, leaning forward and placing a hand on Max's leg to get her attention.

Max raised an eyebrow, staring where she'd been touched.

Karin smiled sweetly, leaving her hand a beat longer than necessary before withdrawing.

I wasn't sure what I'd witnessed. An alpha woman thing – two lionesses, feeling each other out.

"You've seen the news, haven't you?" Max returned the smile, crossing her legs in the other direction. "I uncover secrets. Terrible secrets. And I let the world know about them."

Karin glanced at the roof of the car. A huge curved screen in its own right.

"I've seen the articles. Only ..." The reflected feeds and symbols danced across her face. "You don't seem like much of a champion for social justice."

"What did you expect?"

Karin pulled her attention back to Max with a dead-eyed look. "Someone more humble, I guess. Demure."

Max laughed. A low, nasal sound. "Oh dear, what an impression I've left you with! Well, things will become clear for you soon, I hope."

We rode in silence for the next forty minutes, staring through the semi-transparent windows. We'd left HK1 Island and were heading deeper into Kowloon – the ruined part of the city hiding the most expensive properties. It appeared run down, but a closer inspection gave the game away. Modern security cameras were affixed to the buildings, and high-end cars were parked in driveways – their paintwork gleamed under traditional Chinese lanterns.

We pulled up to a nondescript warehouse. Another ruin to the naked eye, but secure, with no open windows or broken doors. A cube symbol, embossed on the wall, hung like a demon from an old nightmare.

I went to demand an answer. Max put up a manicured hand. "No questions, please. I'll explain shortly."

My eyes must have visibly popped from my head. This was a *Hive* warehouse! The same as where Sebastian went mad – the same damn company. It was in a different city but it couldn't be a coincidence. My teeth ground in my mouth. What was Max up to! What did she know?

I realised I'd been holding my breath and it was running out. I drew in deeply.

Either tingling her pre-state or sensing my distress plainly, Karin snaked a hand into mine, giving it a squeeze. I barely noticed.

An automatic shutter opened on the side of the warehouse, metal slats clacking closed after we drove inside. The car's window displays shut off, becoming fully transparent again. Fluorescent lights flickered on, revealing the interior of the building.

I untangled my hand from Karin's and jumped out, any respect or awe for Maximal trumped by desperate curiosity.

The warehouse in Camden had been rot and decay, but this was far from that. It had been converted into a modern living space. Faux-leather sofas and glass tables dotted around a bright and open-plan floor area.

A large bed with a leopard-print throw was centre stage, and a polished concrete floor gleamed underfoot. It looked like an ostentatious hotel room for exhibitionists.

Max stalked around the car, leaned against the bonnet, and pulled out her vaporiser – practically daring a barrage of questions.

"Welcome to my home," she declared, between puffs of lavender-scented smoke. "Well, my HK1 home. I have a few of these places."

Karin peered around, bemused. "You normally bring people here?"

"No, actually," Max replied absently. "You're the first."

I couldn't tell if that was good or bad.

She crossed to a drinks cabinet. A wooden statement to 1970s styling, complete with antique panelling and matching tumblers. There was a selection of optics on display.

She started mixing a cocktail. "Drink? I'm having one."

"I have questions," I said.

"I know. Have a drink – it will help."

The sound of ice against glass was enticing.

Sensing the weakness, she mixed two more and brought them over. Mine was whiskey based – my favoured drink over beer, when I could afford it. Was it a guess or did she know? A glance at Karin confirmed it – her drink was spot on too. Max's snooping knew no bounds.

I held off until Max had seated herself, painfully slowly, onto a sofa. I downed my drink in one and blurted out, "What the hell do you know about Hive, Max?"

Karin took a high metal stool set further back, sipping her gin and tonic quietly.

The situation was awkward. Max lounging on the sofa, me standing defiantly, and Karin watching on. I didn't care; I was having this out right now.

Max nursed her drink, stretching out the anxiety, revelling in it. Finally, in her low, seductive voice, she began to explain.

"I acquired this place six years ago. Right after all the workers vanished." She spread her fingers on the last word with a magician's flourish.

"What do you mean *vanished*?"

"You know exactly what I mean."

I thought for a second. "You mean taken – by the authorities."

"Exactly. *Disappeared* – like all the others you hear about. Or don't hear about, more precisely." Another sip. "That typically happens to isolated individuals, but this was a whole warehouse."

"You investigated?"

"That's right. The staff were normal, honest. No troublemakers or dissenters. No members of rebel groups. Not even much in their social media accounts. Or at least, nothing beyond the norm."

"How do you know what's in their social groups? That's encrypted."

Max rolled her eyes. "Oh, don't be so naïve; social networks aren't *that* encrypted."

I thought of Karin's addiction to her social feeds and tried not to look at her.

"Don't worry," Max continued, sensing the subtext. "I've been covering your tracks. You're both safe."

"How—?"

She raised her hand. "I'll get to that. Do you want to hear the story or not?"

I held my tongue and nodded.

"It was a dead end – no leads at all. But I can't leave a mystery like that alone, so I did the one thing I could. I bought the warehouse. They'd cleared it out, of course. Sanitised the place. But digital clues are harder to erase than physical ones. Organisations leave electronic footprints everywhere. In the security system, on the power grid – anywhere an ARO might interface."

I shook my head in disbelief. She'd bought the damn place. An extreme solution, but a good idea. Workers need to access records, unlock doors, buy things from vending machines. Lots of places for evidence to collect if you're skilled enough to search for it. I suspected Max had paid no actual money – extortion was more likely.

"I wasn't as advanced then as I am now." Max waved her hand over a holo-display embedded in a coffee table. "But I did uncover this piece of information."

The display projected a rotating image. It was a digital ledger headed with Hive's logo. Max zoomed in on the transactions – there were a number of payments from LL Plc. Even I recognised that. It was Limelight's stock market abbreviation.

That confirmed the Telcom's involvement. We'd known that must be true, but seeing actual evidence was a strange relief. It gave purpose to the madness, although I wasn't going to let Max know that.

"So Limelight and Hive are working together? Not that surprising, Max. Not really."

"They're not working together," Max corrected. "Hive *is* Limelight. It's a hidden, legal entity, but it's still part of Limelight's corporate umbrella."

I shrugged. "A difference without a distinction, but okay. So what happened to the people?"

Max inspected the rotating image thoughtfully before replying. "I don't know."

The answer shocked me, and the response was automatic. "What do you mean? You bought the warehouse and found this document. You uncover corporate conspiracies all the time. How can you not know?"

It was Max's turn to shrug. "It's too well hidden. I'm a good hacker, but the secrets I find are slip-ups – pieces of information stored where they shouldn't be. I discovered this ledger because a hapless office worker scanned it with an unsecured ARO. I was lucky to find it."

That was a sobering thought. The best hacker in the world relied on luck as much as anyone. The equivalent of sifting through rubbish for secrets.

"Alright." I sighed. "Then why look in the first place? What's your interest in all this? A few missing office workers is hardly your MO."

Max took a drag on her vape rig, steam tendrils rising like dragon smoke. "I know a conspiracy when I see one. This warehouse is part of a network. You of all people should know that. When I untangle the threads, it will reveal something huge. I want to crack the conspiracy open. Expose it."

"Why?"

"You're asking a hacker why they want to expose conspiracies?" she replied under hooded eyes. "Interesting."

Fair enough. I suppose it was obvious. Power, money, influence – pick your poison.

"So you're like us." Karin interjected, deciding now was the time to enter the conversation. "Clueless."

"Hardly." Max snorted. "I've been keeping a close eye on Limelight; it's what led me to you. It's surprising they haven't caught you. Very surprising. In fact, I'm happy to admit, you're the first of your kind I've met in person."

"Our kind?" Karin leaned forward, frowning. "And just what do you think you know about us?"

Max smiled. "A great deal actually ... Individuals with your *characteristics* appear from time to time. You pop up on the grid, but authorities intervene quickly, like here, at this warehouse. You two are different though. You've vexed those searching for you." She looked at us in turn. "An addict who can manipulate time, and a social diva who can predict the future. An odd combination, but a potent one. And of course, I helped too."

As unnerving as it was to have our secrets laid bare, Max had been foreshadowing her knowledge of us for a while. It was her other statement that struck a chord, and the second time she'd made overtures of providing aid.

"What do you mean *helped*?" I prodded. "We've been on our own."

Max laughed dismissively. "Don't be dense, dear boy. I had to be subtle, not draw attention to myself – I have interests to protect. However, I delayed a communication here, scrambled a message there. Enough to give you some breathing space."

"Breathing space?"

"Of course! You made lots of mistakes. Sub-jet ports watch their staff as much as passengers. You were caught on cameras in the monitoring station!"

Max's patronising tone was galling, but the realisation we'd failed to evade detection was worse. I'd been proud of getting through security!

"I scrambled the feed to keep you hidden," she continued, checking her nails. "No need to thank me."

The revelation was hard to swallow, but I couldn't deny it either. I'd had a feeling we'd been living on borrowed time for a while. Turns out we had been – time lent to us by Max.

"And as I mentioned, I've been re-encrypting your social feeds. If I can see them through the Administration's back-doors, then so can Limelight. You're welcome."

So there it was. According to Max, online security was an illusion – three-step authentication a lie. If that was true, the Administration could see everything. The notion was too terrifying to process.

Karin had been quiet throughout the last exchange, but now she spoke up. "So you know about us. What now?"

She was right. It was obvious where the conversation was heading. We needed to get to the point.

"It's all connected, my girl." Max switched her gaze to Karin but kept her legs pointed away. "Limelight, Hive, the time phenomena, everything. All the evidence directs that way. I just don't know *how* it's connected. Not yet."

Karin crossed her arms defensively. "And that's why you want us to break into Limelight's Data Centre?"

"Ah, a sensible question! Yes! The information we all seek is behind those security systems. Only breachable from the inside." She paused, gesturing to the surrounding space. "But as you can see, I'm more of a back-office type. Whereas you two are more like ..."

"Field agents." I grumbled.

"Yes!" Max snapped her fingers. "Field agents! Exactly, my dear. You gain entry to the building and I retrieve the information. A partnership."

"Unbalanced partnership." Karin bristled. "We take all the risk."

"Well, nothing's perfect." Max downed the rest of her drink. "And what choice do you have if you want the information?"

Karin's posture was humourless. A reflection of what I'd been feeling since entering Max's den. It was too dangerous, and I was sick of being told I had no choice.

I stood my ground. "No deal," I declared. "There's too much for us to lose. It's a gamble. We don't know if the data is even there, and we have no reason to trust you're telling us the truth. This could all be a lie."

Karin moved to stand next to me in solidarity. A united front I was grateful for.

"If that's the best you can do, we're better off on our own."

A few seconds of awkward silence passed as we stared each other down. Karin and me on one side, Max on the other.

Finally, Max broke the silence, a cruel expression appearing. She'd done a good job hiding it until now, but it came easily, the creases in her skin well worn.

"Oh dear. I had hoped it wouldn't come to this."

Holding our gazes, she tapped a button on her bracelet, a disguised remote control. The hologram of the ledger vanished, replaced by two real-time video feeds. The ambient lighting in the room dimmed, focusing our attention on the subjects in the images.

One was a middle-aged couple sitting in a well-appointed home. The other, a grainy security feed of a hospital ward, full of unsettled patients. It took a few moments, but then my blood ran cold – it was Sebastian's asylum. I could make out his listless shape at the end. Karin was rigid.

"Ms. Chambers," Max started, pointing to the couple in the feed. "Your parents already think you've lost your mind. What do you think they'll do if I reveal your location to them?"

Karin stood still, glaring at the image.

"I'll answer for you. They'll come for you, my dear. They have the means, that's for certain. And what will happen then?"

"I'll be committed." Karin answered quietly through gritted teeth. "Like before."

Committed! So that's what had happened. No wonder she didn't like talking about it.

"Yes, and oh, the delicious irony." Max turned her attention to me. "Institutionalised, just like your brother. Tell me, Daryl, what will happen if I inform the asylum they're harbouring a criminal?" A string of misdemeanours scrolled down the screen. I noted a fair few the police had never caught us for.

I knew the answer, but I said nothing – he'd be slung onto the street. This was bad.

"What is this, Max? We don't play ball, so you threaten us!" I couldn't believe the direction this was taking.

"I'm sorry," she replied, with no hint of actual apology. "I'm afraid I'm rather good at applying pressure to get my way. Would it help to reassure you I'm telling the truth about the data we need? Probably not." She stood and placed her hands behind her back, pacing around the video feed. "Look at it this way," she remarked, a harsh teacher addressing a class. "If you won't break into the Data Centre to help yourselves, then do it for your families."

"And if we do as you ask, you'll leave them alone?" Karin's voice was quiet.

"Of course!" Max dropped back onto the sofa, placing her hands behind her head. "I'm not a savage. You help me, and I'll help you."

Karin and I looked at each other. We were cornered. We'd come seeking help from a hacker known for their coercion skills. How naïve we'd been.

We nodded.

Sensing the change in mood, she shut off the hologram and turned up the lights. "Splendid. Now the unpleasantness is out of the way, we can get on with things."

I sighed and shook my head. We'd been outmanoeuvred, and easily so. Pawns in a new game. I consoled myself that at least we were moving forward again. If Max was right, the Data Centre may hold the answer. That is, if she was telling the truth, and if we survived the encounter. Neither of which seemed particularly likely.

# STATE 21

The car jerked around on uneven paving, throwing us around the interior. I gripped the roof handle to steady myself. My leather trousers had ridden up high enough to need pliers to remove them – I was keen that didn't escalate to scissors. They were a damned curse but had proven reliable; I'd accepted them, begrudgingly, as a necessity.

At least the interior of the car was cool. My man bits were mangled, but they weren't glued together. Not yet.

We'd been with Max three weeks – time dedicated to planning the break-in.

It was a difficult alliance; the dark cloud of blackmail hung over us, but there was hope too. The Data Centre held information we both needed. Despite the danger, there was wisdom to the action. Whether Max would share what she learned was another matter, and her patronising tone, constant and grating, did little to reassure us.

Unfortunately, her attitude, albeit annoying, wasn't the worst part of staying with Max. Her bad habits were. Max had a disconcerting predilection for *touching* – "equal-opportunity lover" was her excuse. Karin shook it off – immune from a lifetime of male attention. I didn't – in fact, I was exceptionally unused to being groped. Max would slide past me in the corridor, rubbing the hard mass (disguised but rampant beneath her dress) against me. It confirmed her gender binary status, her deviant attitude, and my utter lack of curiosity for what she was offering. I'd kept out of reach after that, putting tables, sofas, or occasionally Karin between us.

To her credit, she'd at least done some pre-planning for the work ahead. Producing blueprints and schematics for the Data Centre. But her preparation had fallen short. She harboured huge misunderstandings of how our abilities worked – constraints none of her spying had uncovered. It was pleasing in a way; a win over her snooping, but a short-term one that needed resolving.

She'd assumed, for instance, I could lift a keycard from a frozen guard, and explaining objects in latent state were utterly unmovable had been a horrifying revelation for her.

Likewise, she'd misinterpreted Karin's visions as detailed premonitions rather than the vague, indistinct impressions they were. It led to an equally shattering (yet somehow satisfying) showdown between them: "No, Max, I can't infer security codes for doors by looking at them!"

Changes were needed. Three weeks of detailed planning. A straightforward game of drafts transformed into masterclass chess.

The problem was multi-layered. The target building was in Mong Kok. The traditional consumer electronics district, updated to support ARO tech. HK1 city planners had deemed it more efficient to collect the infrastructure and technicians in one place – and also the safeguards to protect them.

Gutted and refitted, the old buildings, previously stuffed with ramshackle gadget shops, now contained modern cloud servers and engineering stations connected with ultrafast, quantum-encrypted internet. All wrapped in world-class security, creating an impenetrable shroud.

Inside flowed the data streams maintaining the Telcom industry. It's lifeblood. A treasure trove of corporate and consumer secrets.

Max was right about one thing. The answers we sought were more likely to be in Data Centre vaults than anywhere else. Accessing them, though, was a different story. Inside, a gauntlet of measures would block our way. Body scanners, infrared cameras, and laser grids, plus key-coded locks for sensitive areas. All state-of-the-art.

Our advantage? No security system could account for our abilities. And with the world's most notorious hacker gumming up the works, we had a chance.

I was sure Max couldn't be trusted. Her only saving grace was her record. She'd committed herself to hurting the same corporations that were pursuing us. It was scant comfort, but *the enemy of my enemy is my friend* applied – at least for the time being.

I fiddled with the strap of the breathing mask. A constant source of itching and irritation.

"Don't take it off." Karin snapped.

I'd grown to hate that tone, but every time I removed the mask, Max or Karin would berate me.

"I know," came my muffled reply. "But once this is over, I'm making you wear this damn thing!"

The breathing mask limited my oxygen intake. A similar system used by athletes to simulate training at altitude. It expanded their lung capacity and made them fitter. As such, I'd been instructed to wear it as much as possible.

The logic was sound. My luck avoiding unconsciousness wouldn't hold forever; in fact, it was a miracle I hadn't died already. The mask reduced that risk.

Of course, they didn't have to wear it. It was the worst sensation. A nightmare contraption that stank of rubber and left a sore ring around my mouth where it sealed. Worse, every breath had to be dragged in – laboured through its restricting filter. The first day, I'd passed out, collapsing on the floor and triggering a safety mechanism to prevent me suffocating.

And the torment hadn't stopped at the mask. Karin had put me on a gruelling exercise regime. Two hours of aerobics a day. Initially, without the mask, and then after a few days, with it on. The exertion was incredible. I'd been sick on two occasions – a smell that clung to the rubber in a special way.

But it had been worth it. By the third week, my lung capacity had improved measurably. Every time the mask was lifted, I could suck in gallons of air. Together with Karin's guided meditation, I'd never felt stronger or more focussed. And better yet, with the urgency of an upcoming mission, my need for SP1N had all but subsided.

I wasn't sure if it was exhaustion or lack of idle time, but my body had no interest. Each night I'd collapse into dreamless sleep, waking in the same position – tired, sore, but willing to continue.

The car juddered over potholes, bumping us around the interior again.

I patted my shoulder, making sure nothing had shaken loose. Max had provided us with discrete, low-riding CAMO-AROs. Mine was barely visible against my jacket, connected to an earpiece through wireless comlink. The set-up permitted us to speak and hear each other, and it provided Max with remote tracking capabilities. Light and durable, the CAMO-ARO made my Saracen feel like a hunk of junk from another century.

It was becoming light as we drove into Mong Kok. A thin grey light spreading from the horizon – the sun hidden behind smog like a low-output bulb behind a curtain.

The towers of Mong Kok had more in common with Kowloon than HK1. Old by design, they aped traditional architecture dating back a hundred years. Mottled and weather-beaten exteriors clad with faux crumbling facades.

Under the plate, air-conditioning units were stuck messily to the outside of buildings – precariously holding on with rusty bolts. Here, everything was internalised and uprated to handle the heat-sensitive equipment. Windows were redesigned into cooling metallic panels, reflecting the heat and sitting at odds with the concrete superstructure, like shaded sunglasses on an ancient face.

We parked in a low-priority area, a few blocks from the Data Centre.

"You ready?" Max was sitting opposite. She'd forgone her glamorous outfits, adopting dungarees and a white shirt, with one embellishment. Her customary red lipstick. It was the most masculine I'd ever seen her.

"I guess. Unless you want to call this off and let us go?" I replied.

Max raised an eyebrow.

No, I didn't think so.

"I'll be waiting in the reception area." Karin patted my knee.

"Right ... right." I sighed, stealing myself. I felt scared, but not like before. It was a nervous energy – anxiety driven procrastination, but it was under control. This was the hardest thing we'd undertaken, but we were also the most prepared. I wasn't backing out now.

Enough stalling. I shoved the car door open, threw Karin a wink, and jumped out. She'd see through the bravado, but it made me feel confident.

Apart from Limelight's logo, the Data Centre had little to distinguish itself from surrounding tower blocks. On the inside, though, it was the best protected of the bunch – a nexus of cyber security and highly trained personnel designed for one purpose. Keeping people like me out.

Seb would have enjoyed this. Pitting our skills against a purpose-built system. Nostalgia mixed with adrenaline turbo-charged in my veins. I'd make him proud today. I had to.

As I made my way across the traffic intersection, the breathing mask didn't look out of place. Locals wore face masks to protect against smog and prevent diseases spreading. They didn't give me a second glance.

I discarded it in an alley receptacle. I'd promised Karin I'd make her wear it, but there was no point lugging it around. I wouldn't need it for this next part.

I stopped time. The world grinded to a halt; the air became still and the grimy stench of the city was no longer detectable.

Entering latent state no longer took any effort. I might lose the knack if I stopped practising, but for now, with the preparation I'd undertaken, the workshop and the clock were always in reach.

The benefits of the breathing mask were immediately apparent. Air flooded my lungs with minor movement. I should be able to take my time climbing the building.

I knew the route. I'd studied the schematics and photos. There were handholds where the concrete was mottled, and ten-centimetre wide window ledges where I could rest on each floor.

Mouth dry, I examined the twenty floors towering above and blinked away a surge of vertigo. This would be the climbing equivalent of running a marathon. Time to get moving.

One deep breath and I began climbing, gripping the pocked surface and hauling myself, hand-over-hand, up the edifice.

I slipped past the first row of metallic windows. They were one-way, hiding office workers, machinery, and servers inside. People could see out, but all I could see was the smudged metallic reflection of the world – absent me. Latent state removed my reflection. I was like a daredevil vampire.

Handholds were plentiful, and propped up in the thick atmosphere, I could take more chances than a normal climber would. One and two finger holds were easy. Even pinch holds on thin wedges of concrete were manageable.

It was on the fifth floor that problems began. The mottling, so useful on lower floors, was worse quality higher up. The architects had used better materials on the lower floors where visitors would notice, but here it was coarser, and I was building up a collection of bloody cuts. Dirty, jagged concrete cut into my hands.

At first it stung a little, but discomfort gave way to pain, and soon agony, with each move harder than the last. I swore under my breath. I should have worn gloves. It hadn't even occurred to me I'd need them.

I tried to shrug it off and carry on, but the pain intensified, and by the seventh floor, my fingers were trembling.

Then it happened. With hand strength fading, my grip failed.

My left hand slipped off the wall, leaving two points of contact – half my body floated in space, dozens of metres above the pavement.

Letting out a groan, I swung back to a secure position, arm and shoulder aching with the strain.

My heart was thumping. This wasn't going to work. The pain was too bad. Much more and I'd fall – dropping off the building like a discarded scab.

I tried to control my panic. A tightness in my groin making my arse pucker. I slid along the edge, away from the evil concrete, flattening myself against the smooth windows.

My hands were trembling, painted red all over like clown gloves. Blood from the cuts was pooling inside the latent-state bubble. I couldn't assess how bad the damage was, but they were dark red. Probably best not to look. At least the bubble would prevent blood spilling everywhere and keep my hands from getting infected.

What a damn mess. I could see the lip of the next window, but it was out of reach. Not without using the concrete.

My hands felt numb. I was in trouble. Climbing down would be harder than going up – I wouldn't be able to see where I was going. But continuing on was also impossible.

I stared up at the next window, only a couple of metres away, wishing gravity didn't apply.

My mind spun – calculating possibilities. And then it clicked. Gravity in latent state *wasn't* the same at all. The thick atmosphere was viscous, like a liquid. Normally a hindrance, but perhaps that could help?

I imagined a swimmer pushing off from the edge of a pool. Gliding, effectively flying, beneath the surface with minimal effort. A mad idea was forming.

The lack of motion was catching up with me, stars flecking my vision as the air retreated. It had held off longer than normal, the breathing mask having done its job, but it wouldn't hold unconsciousness back forever.

The mad idea cemented into a mad plan, hurried on by an oxygen-deprived tunnel vision just beginning in my periphery.

I took a moment to steady myself. Every moment I delayed increased the risk of passing out, but getting this wrong would be equally disastrous.

Looking up, I took a wide stance on the windowsill, stretched upwards, and bent my knees. Then, with a silent prayer, I jumped, removing all points of contact.

I pushed off hard, expecting resistance, but rather than losing momentum, it was sustained. I slid through space like an eel. Holy crap, it was working!

The distance to the next floor was half covered before I realised my mistake. I was going too fast. I was going to overshoot the next window!

Pulling my arms back wildly, I tried to increase the air resistance, but it was too late. I was a metre beyond the window by the time I'd slowed, leaving me in a no man's land between floors. I reached the apex; gravity reasserted itself and I slid back, landing painfully on my elbows and bouncing awkwardly off the window ledge. Flailing, my fingertips found an edge at the last moment.

Wheezing, I heaved myself up. A straining, full arm pull, precariously swinging my legs onto the window ledge. My vision was swimming with the effort, but at least the stabbing pain in my hands was fading.

Breathing hard, I took a moment to assess what had happened. The theory was right; latent state could be navigated this way, but it was far from ideal. The uncertain danger of missing a jump had gone up, but the certain possibility of my damaged hands slipping off had receded. It was this way or no way.

I kept going, bounding up the building one careful jump at a time, but five floors on, a new problem presented itself.

The jumping method was working and I was getting better at not overshooting the ledges. My shoulders and arms were aching like crazy, but I could deal with that. The issue was I was becoming dangerously lightheaded and tight-chested. I'd trained for steady state climbing, not explosive, anaerobic movement. I wasn't pulling in enough air to compensate.

I'd have to recharge my oxygen.

It was a horrible risk. There was no telling what was behind the windows. The building should be mostly filled with equipment, but there would still be maintenance and security staff. If I came out of latent state, there was a high chance of being seen – becoming a human shaped insect, clinging to the outside, ready to be swatted off.

My chest tightened further, a belt squeezing down. It made the decision for me. A non-decision really. If it was a choice between being seen or scraped off the road in a raspberry mess, I'd take the former.

I flattened myself against the window and resumed real time. The rush of air was intoxicating – luxurious – and the accompanying release of endorphins almost overwhelming. I barely noticed the high wind whipping about my head, threatening to yank me off. It felt good to breathe again. Huge gulps of glorious oxygen.

My earpiece buzzed, Max's voice crackling over the line. She sounded agitated. "Dear boy, what's the matter? I wasn't expecting to see you until you were in the Data Centre, but it appears you're still outside."

Outside. There was an understatement!

My breathing had returned to normal, but the extra effort of hanging on was now building up.

"Yeah, I'm halfway up," I said over the wind. "I had to unfreeze time to get my breath back. I'll be going back in a moment."

"Well, Karin's on her way, but you must have tripped a window sensor. The security in the building's gone up a notch."

"How can you tell? You're not patched in yet."

"I'm monitoring police chatter, of course. There's been an un-scheduled *ready-up* command sent to the local authorities. They're not on high alert yet, birds trip these sensors from time-to-time, but they'll be coming to check your area. You may find security tighter when you get inside."

Wonderful. At least I was breathing and hadn't fallen off the build-ing – a favourable trade for some extra security, I reasoned. I refroze time, feeling the tension in my muscles ease as the atmosphere propped me back up.

I clambered the remaining floors with only one more break. A balancing act between muscle fatigue and unconsciousness. By the time I swung my legs over the top, I was dripping and exhausted. I recommenced time and fell on my side, heaving as my breakfast made an escape run.

After two minutes of gagging and coughing, I struggled to a sitting position, shakily retrieving a water flask and energy rations from my backpack. I'd never done anything so physically taxing. My body was in glucose shock, starving and unable to move. I barely tasted the saccharin, orange-flavoured capsules as I wolfed them down one-by-one.

My hands were sore and covered in cuts, but the damage wasn't as bad as it could have been. The latent state bubble had made it look bad, spreading the blood around, but had also helped congeal it. If I was careful, it shouldn't be a hindrance.

It took another ten minutes before I could move again, but eventually the sugary energy worked its way through me, propping me back up. Thankfully, the comlink had been quiet. Max could see my vitals over the ARO connection. It would be obvious to her I needed the break, but she could also see when I'd recovered.

"Time to move again."

She almost sounded sympathetic.

Groaning, I stood, pushing back the urge to give in to tiredness. Gently swaying as I surveyed the area.

I knew what to expect. The target was a locked roof-access door with a single camera monitoring the area in front.

Air-conditioning ducts dotted the roof, spewing out steam and covering the tarmacked surface with sticky fog. They were a no-go – protected with laser grids. Undefeatable without raising an alarm. The door was the only entrance, and the camera, far from being a problem, was my way in.

I checked the backpack and pulled out the specialist equipment I'd brought for the task. Not a high-tech ARO attachment, laser-override system, or camera jamming sensor, but a humble synthetic carrier bag – the kind they give out at cheap convenience stores. It was even branded with the shop's holographic logo of a red and green bird.

At the same time, I retrieved a security overall. It was plus-sized and slipped readily over my tight-fitting leathers. The last thing I wanted was more layers, I was overheated enough, but once inside, I'd have to transition in and out of latent state, and the uncoordinated biker look would raise suspicion.

Keeping a wide berth, I shook the bag open and circled around, approaching the door from the side, keeping outside the camera's visibility cone. Then carefully, preventing my hands from coming into view, I reached up and gently slid the bag over the camera, encasing it in bright, semi-opaque material.

The principle was sound. The bag obscured the camera, but not completely. Security should view it as an urgent inconvenience, but nothing large enough to trigger a full security breach. In theory, anyway.

I grimaced, amazed at the low-tech solution we'd concocted. With all the assets at our disposal, we were reliant on the cheapest and most improvised option. It was like a poetic analogy for my life.

Back tight to the wall, I crept as close to the door as I dared, crouching just outside where the camera might detect me.

The minutes ticked by. I'd hoped someone would come quickly, but after half an hour, my legs were burning from the awkward crouch. I couldn't tell which I hated more – the plan we'd cooked up or the incompetence of the security personnel.

Finally, on the other side, I heard a muffled voice, faint but distinctive. I tensed, forgetting my sore legs.

The voice – a grumble of annoyance – became clearer as the door opened. "... disturbed my damn break for this."

I poised, listening for the creak of the door opening wider.

Now!

Freezing time, I groaned and straightened. My legs were nearly numb from inaction.

I stamped my feet on the ground to get the blood moving and turned the corner to investigate.

Half poking through the door was an angry, hairless, middle-aged guard. He was reaching up to dislodge the bag. Annoyingly, his body was still mostly blocking the entrance. He hadn't needed to open it far to complete the task.

I thought for a moment. I could resume time – surprise him, attempt to knock him out, and clear the path?

No, too high risk; if he got away, I was screwed. Besides, I had a better idea.

I looked again, eyeing the man up and down. Then, shrugging with a quiet apology, I clambered over his stationary body. His outstretched arm and bald head made pretty good foot holds.

Jumping down on the other side, I wondered briefly if he would remember any sensation of being trodden on when time resumed – perhaps feeling especially disgruntled, but not knowing why. Who knows where unexplained moods come from?

Inside, contrasting with the rough concrete, everything was sleek and modern. Aluminium floors reflected illuminated ceilings. Blue displays bathed the corridors in cool light, programmatically displaying locations and directions for workers.

The dynamic navigation was next to useless in latent state. I'd have to suffice with any directions frozen on screen and my memory of the blueprints.

It appeared quiet on this floor. Predominantly empty meeting rooms and unoccupied agile working spaces. I unfroze time, and true enough, the only sounds were the quiet whir of air-conditioning units and deep throb of servers, emanating like a pulse within the building. Time to check in with Max.

I slipped into a room conjoining the corridor and pretended to busy myself at a terminal. I'd be unlucky to be caught; I was another guard doing his job. Still, without the safe blanket of latent state, the feeling of vulnerability was oppressive. Every distant sound or footstep put me on edge.

I opened the CAMO-ARO and activated the comlink.

"Aren't you there yet, dear? Tut-tut. I expected better."

Whatever grace period Max had extended me after the climb had evaporated. She was back on my case. "Calm down. It's only been a few minutes' real time."

"You're only advantage. Don't squander it. You know where you're going, don't you?"

"Yes." I'd studied the schematics. "It's five floors down, along the central corridor."

A floor layout appeared on my ARO showing the target. It was dead centre in the building, in the middle of a small maze of corridors.

"That's right, but remember I can't monitor guards until you're patched in. You should stay in latent state as much as possible."

"That's funny, Max, I thought I'd stroll down there like this."

She ignored my sarcasm. "Just don't get caught. We have a bargain. Welch on it, and you'll regret it."

"I'll call when I'm in position." I ended the conversation, closing the ARO with an irritated slap. More was at stake than finding out what Limelight was up to. Sebastian's safety was on the line. Max had done worse than rat out a mad junkie to get her way. I'd be naïve to assume she was bluffing.

There was a lift, but I couldn't ride it. Not until Max had lowered the security. And the alternative wasn't going to be fun.

I followed the corridor until I found what I was looking for. A grate, high up on the wall. There was no laser grid protecting it – no need – it was already inside a secure area and they interfered with maintenance workers. Some still had heat and motion detectors but both would be rendered ineffective by latent state.

Double checking for cameras and guards, I retrieved my lazeblade and shrugged off the uniform, placing it in the backpack. With the disguise off, the last vestige of protection was gone and the feeling of being exposed intensified.

My lazeblade trembled in my hand as my nervousness peaked. I stared at it, willing it to stop. This wasn't even the hard part. I had to get myself under control.

The shake receded. For the time being.

Refocusing on the grate, I sheared off its two retaining bolts and dropped the deactivated lazeblade in my jacket's external pocket – I'd need it later. Then, standing on tiptoe, I peered inside the vent. I could make out blinking motion sensors peppering the walls. If any part of me passed the threshold in real time, an alarm would ring out and the mission would be over.

After swinging the grate onto its top hinges, I transitioned back into latent state. It stuck out at ninety degrees, frozen in place. I hoped no one would hear it clang when I exited, but in the meantime, it made an excellent handhold.

I clambered into the tight crawl space; the sensors had stopped blinking. The only light to guide me was a few dim maintenance bulbs as I shuffled, feet first, down the narrow space.

It wasn't a long stretch of ducting, but the space was limited, and after a dozen metres, I could feel myself going light-headed again. The slow progress was limiting my air supply.

Ten more metres of fumbling and wriggling and I emerged into a wider chamber intersected with other openings – including a vertical drop. Orienting myself head first, I peered over the edge. I couldn't see the bottom, just the dim glow of maintenance lights illuminating the way down to the bottom of the twenty-story building.

My head swam with vertigo, adding to the lightheadedness. I didn't have time to worry about the consequences. If I didn't move soon, I'd suffocate.

Nudging myself over the edge, I braced my elbows and toes against the metal ducting. Friction from the leathers held my weight, but it didn't make the plunge any less terrifying. I inched forward until I was vertical, blood rushing to my eyeballs. Then, relieving some pressure from the wall, I attempted a controlled descent.

It didn't work. Too much resistance was let off and I plummeted four metres with a sickening lurch, completely missing the next junction.

The leathers squeaked as I jolted to a halt, elbows stinging where I'd reapplied force against the metal wall.

My breathing was ragged with adrenaline. I could hear it in my head like a tyre leaking air. At least the drop had replenished the supply.

Damn! Come on, Daryl, I berated myself. I'd have to release the pressure more gently. The physics were different but they still applied! It didn't matter how thick the atmosphere was, I'd still fall at the same rate, and reducing momentum would always be a problem.

Recommencing, I tried a different tactic – teasing the pressure from my elbows but keeping my toes firmly wedged against the duct walls. It worked. The muscles in my quads burned where I was pushing my legs outwards, but the difference in pressure allowed a more consistent fall. I tried to ignore the vertigo by enjoying the continuous rush of breathable air!

Counting down the next four junctions, I arrived at the fifteenth floor, awkwardly arching into the horizontal ducting, and uttering a quiet thanks as my body was supported again. I had no doubt my hands were shaking, but fortunately, I couldn't see them in the gloom of the tunnel.

Inching along the memorised route, I eventually found the target vent – vague green light leaking from the other side.

It was a security substation. I marvelled that it was accessible, but then I reminded myself what I'd done. No normal human could make it down those ducts. We were exploiting a weakness the security architects couldn't account for. There weren't even sensors this end of the tunnel. The substation room was locked up tight from the other side, but no one would have predicted someone entering this way. It was infeasible.

Transitioning into real time, I winced as the first grate clanged closed, echoing through the vents behind and above me. It was louder than expected, even at a distance. I hoped no one was close enough to investigate.

I retrieved my lazeblade, still tucked in my jacket pocket; it flashed in the tunnel, reflecting off the metallic interior. I lazed through the rear of the retaining bolts and slithered through the open grate.

I stood and looked around. The substation doubled as an emergency telecommunications hub, the cramped interior packed with snarled Ethernet cables and twinkling switches. A few holo-readouts circled a central display with barely room to stretch my elbows.

Crouching amongst the wires, I hard connected my ARO to the terminal with a link cable. The place was stuffy and stank of dust slowly cooking on hot electrical components. *Access requires authorisation* rotated in red font on the terminal.

"We'll see about that." Max did her work, the message distorting, flashing violently between green and red. It was like watching a war of wills. After a few seconds, the readout distorted for a final time before switching over to green. *Access granted.*

The hack was quick. I'd just crossed my legs painfully beneath me in the tiny space. Cables draped over my shoulders like warm rubbery snakes. I had to respect her efficiency if nothing else.

"Karin, are you ready?" I opened the comlink.

"She can't talk right now." Max answered instead. "She's next to the security gate in reception. She mustn't draw attention to herself, but she can hear you, and yes, she's ready."

I barely had time to whisper "good luck" before Max cut the power, plunging the room into darkness, accompanied by a crunchy, metallic sound as the breakers tripped.

I counted down the seconds. There was no display during the blackout. All I had was my imagination – a conjured narrative for what I hoped was happening: Karin slipping past the body scanners in the darkness and confusion, discarding her overcoat in a plant pot, and hurrying to the meeting area beyond, blending with the throngs of uniformed office workers.

Time marched on. Surely it had been long enough?

The lights flickered back to life, along with Max's voice. "She's through and awaiting instructions. The building's on medium alert."

Max sounded breathless over the comlink, like she'd been holding it in.

I'd been doing the same. I let it out with a long blow. "Remind me why they won't raise the alarm?"

"I simulated a power surge. That will explain the electrical short-out. It's fake, of course; I don't have the authority to actually increase the power, but when they check the logs, there'll be something to explain the tripped breakers. In the meantime, I've locked down the room you're in. You should have access to the security feeds now."

The display was showing a three-dimensional vector of the building, highlighting the positions of hundreds of security cameras. Using the touch screen, I could pinch to zoom, select floors, and tap cameras. The feeds appearing on a secondary display. The more I selected, the more images were tiled. Controls on the auxiliary screen switched them to full screen or between colour, thermal, and night vision. A manual joystick and zoom dial overrode the automated panning.

I selected reception. Karin had made it to the meeting area, blending against a menagerie of white-coated technicians and office workers. She was doing a good job of looking calm, but it was only an appearance. The place was crawling with security guards. She'd be questioned eventually.

"Karin, I can see you. Nod if everything's okay."

A slight nod.

"Good. Max is in the security system. You'll have worker access to most of the building. I'll identify any guards that may be carrying today's master keycard. If you're ready, head to the lift."

Karin rose, walking delicately over to the bank of lifts. It arrived right away, courtesy of Max. I'm sure to everyone else she looked normal. To me, she looked like a coiled spring, awkwardly vibrating along the corridor.

Once inside, her comlink crackled to me. "That was quick. Nice going."

I looked at my hands, bloodied from the climb, still shaking. I was exhausted to my core. It had been a few minutes for Karin and Max. I'd been at it for hours.

"Yeah, quick," I said wearily.

"We need to wrap this up as soon as we can," Max chimed in. "Daryl might not last much longer."

It was said with enough seriousness to hurt my pride.

"I'm fine, Max."

She didn't care about my wellbeing, just the data; why pretend to care. It was cynical.

"Darling, I don't want you harmed. You're my most valuable asset at the moment. I may never get an opportunity like this again."

*At the moment.* That was the point. Cynical *and* manipulative.

"I've detected a cluster of guards on the fifth floor," Max continued. "That should be the focus of your attention. Karin, be a dear and scout them out."

I watched as Karin exited the lift on the fifth floor. There was no room for disobedience. I whispered instructions, guiding her through the maze of corridors until she approached where the guards were patrolling.

This was dangerous. These were the people we should be avoiding, but it was the plan. Karin had to get close enough for a pre-state read, try to infer if a guard was holding the master keycard for secure areas, then ... acquire it.

She strolled briskly past them, head down.

"Keep walking," I urged. "I think they're curious about you."

That was an understatement. Her flyby was as subtle as a brick through a window.

Tense seconds passed under the gaze of the guards until she turned a corner and they went in the other direction.

"Anything?" I breathed out.

There was a pause before Karin replied. "Nothing," she said finally. "I'm getting good, clear pre-state, but none of those guards hold the master keycard."

"Are you sure, dear?" Max interjected.

"Of course I'm sure."

"But could you be mistaken?"

"It's like recognising your own handwriting, Max," I offered, remembering Karin's explanation. "You'll have to take it on faith, I'm afraid."

"I take little on faith." Max bristled. "I prefer facts."

"Welcome to our world," Karin added with finality.

Unsatisfied with the answer but unable to refute it, Max continued to offer up new groups of guards for Karin to investigate. Her technique improved as she went. Sidling up from behind and then reversing rather than walking by.

By the fifth group, Max was becoming irate. "Nothing! Not even a false positive?"

I was beginning to wonder too. Karin's pre-state didn't have a flawless track record. Maybe this was one of her outages. I could tell from her increasingly stilted body language she was getting worried.

"Ignore Max. She doesn't know what she's talking about." I encouraged. "We've still got a large group to check. Sod's law, that's the one."

Karin sighed, surprisingly audible over the comlink. "Where is it?"

"Fourteenth floor."

We waited for Karin to travel up to the target floor. I hoped this was right. We were screwed otherwise.

"I've got something." The comlink crackled.

Thank God. I zoomed in. Karin was hovering near a female guard who had broken away from the main patrol.

"Be cautious." Max added her appraisal. "She holds a second degree black belt in Jiu-jitsu."

"How do you know ...?" I trailed off. Max must have bio-scanned and background checked her already.

"Don't worry," Karin replied. "I only need a quiet place to tranq her."

I looked again. The guard was stocky and strong looking – hair tied in a neat bob. She looked capable. "Karin, I don't know. You heard Max; this is no pushover. Are you sure you can tranq her?"

Karin's reply was clipped and impatient. "Just find me a quiet space."

I checked the building's itinerary. "Room 1405, around the corner – it's open and empty. Looks like a storage area. Ms. Jiu-jitsu is heading that way, but you'll beat her if you move quickly."

Karin ran to the unoccupied room. It was filled with spare computer equipment – an IT storage area. I watched on the internal feed as Karin retrieved the tranquilizer gun, producing the slender device from her inner jacket pocket. She held it ready at waist height, just inside the door. On a separate feed, I could see the guard turn a corner and approach the room.

"Count me down," she whispered.

"Okay, get ready," I replied, holding my breath as the guard closed the distance. "She'll be passing in three, two, one ..."

"Can someone help me!" Karin called out.

The guard stopped in her tracks, hand on her stun-baton, voice authoritative. "Does someone need assistance?"

"Yes, I'm having trouble with a box in here. Can you help me, please?"

The guard nudged the door with her free hand.

Quickly, Karin grabbed it and yanked hard, pulling her through.

The guard reacted equally as quickly. Rather than pulling back, she leaned forward, throwing them both deeper into the storage area. The jolt dislodged the tranquilizer gun, sending it clattering across the floor. The door clicked closed.

"Damn it!" Karin cried, scrambling off the floor. "Lock the door!"

"What?" I cried in shock.

"Door locked," Max said, overriding my manual control. "I've also disabled the local communications."

"What are you doing, Max?" I shouted.

"As I was asked," Max replied calmly. "This is for Karin to sort out now."

"Are you out of your mind? She's no match for that guard!"

"Too late now." She sounded intrigued and disappointed at the same time.

Back stiff with anxiety, I returned my attention to the screen, watching the two circle each other. The guard was trying to use her comlink, but it was down, deactivated by Max. Karin's head was cocked to one side. Listening.

Realising there was no back-up coming, the guard reached for her stun-baton, retrieving it from a leg holster and flicking it out menacingly. The end sparked with electricity. There was no audio from the feed and Karin had disconnected her comlink. It was clear the guard was shouting something, building up to something.

A moment later she lurched, swinging the baton, but Karin ducked away neatly, still listening. She'd moved before the attack had even started. With the guard off balance, she slipped behind and kicked her in the small of the back, sending her crashing against the far wall. The impact smashed a computer panel in a shower of sparks.

The guard spun, face bleeding. She looked shocked, but not angry – focussed. Her stance altered and she lowered her centre of gravity, left arm forward in a defensive posture. The baton was up, ready for action.

She attacked forcefully, purposely, baton striking through the air at multiple angles. Karin avoided them all. Dodging left, right, and jumping over low blows. All the time, head cocked and listening.

I could see what was happening. Karin was using her pre-state, forecasting where the attacks would come from. The guard couldn't land a hit, but Karin wasn't combat trained; she moved gracefully but without the strength and agility of the guard. And she was tiring.

I retrieved a white technician's overcoat from my bag. I'd been saving it for when Karin had the master key.

"Max, she's on the floor below. I have to help."

"She looks like she's doing okay to me."

"Unlock the door, Max!"

The door on the far side of the substation opened. I pulled on the overcoat, shoved my way through the cables, and bolted.

The lift arrived right away, and within a few seconds I was on the fourteenth floor. I resisted the urge to run; it would draw suspicion. I power walked instead – as quickly as I dared.

"Max, unseal the door and lock it behind me."

"I don't think that's nece—"

"Do it!"

The door opened and I burst into the room, but it took a moment to understand what I was looking at. I'd been ready to launch myself into the fray, bundle them both to the ground. It didn't matter how expert in martial arts the guard was, two on one always makes the difference.

None of that was needed. The guard was already unconscious, lying on the floor.

I blinked, bewildered, jaw hanging open. "What happened?"

Karin had relieved the guard of her security jacket, belt, and baton and had finished wrapping her legs, hands, and mouth with electrical tape. She had a small cut on her temple and seemed to be favouring her left arm, but she was otherwise fine.

"Don't worry about me. I'm okay." Karin used her mouth to rip off a piece of tape. Then through muffled speech. "... I've got the keycard."

"You're hurt." I pointed to where she was bleeding.

"It's nothing." Karin spat the tape out and used it to finish securing the guard. That was partially true; she was shaking, still amped by whatever had happened.

I softened my voice. "Karin, it will draw attention to us. Sit down for a moment; let me sort that cut out."

Karin stood and smoothed out her clothes, touching her temple. Seeing the smear of red across her hand, she nodded and acquiesced.

I grabbed a folding metal chair and set it down. Karin dropped onto it with a thud. I removed a swab and some water, cleaning the area. The cut was barely visible when I was finished.

I removed some pain killers and handed them to Karin. "For your arm."

She stalled for a moment, then took them with a swig from my water flask.

"All sorted? That was amazing."

Karin smiled. A vague, tired gesture. The shake in her hands was still present, but better. "Yes, thank you."

"How did you do it?"

"Lucky shot."

"Didn't look lucky."

"Yeah, well, I had an advantage."

"You were predicting her movements. I didn't know you could do that."

"I told you, the more immediate or localised the threat, the better my pre-state works. This was about as immediate and localised as it gets."

I puffed out my cheeks. "Well, it sure looked cool on camera."

It was an inane comment, but I couldn't help it. It had looked cool!

"I hate to break in." Max interrupted over the comlink, doing just that. "But you can't hang around there all day."

"Yes," Karin mumbled, and then more firmly. "She's right."

Karin removed her office worker overall and put on the guard's padded jacket instead. The guard was bigger than her, but it fit well enough.

"Time to go." She stood, securing the guard's belt. It hung awkwardly around her. "We should have everything we need now."

She produced the keycard from an outside pocket. An unassuming white plastic rectangle. All this hassle for that little thing.

"Max, what will happen to the guard?" I looked around the room. There were no windows, but it was still an unsecure utility room.

"I'll seal the door and time it to release for after we're finished. The cleaning crew will find her later tonight."

We left, hurrying along the corridor. Karin dressed in the guard's uniform, me as an escorted technician. I felt awkward and conspicuous, but the office workers and guards we passed didn't seem to notice. A large building like this must have a high turnover of staff – new faces every week.

Back in the lift, the button for the tenth floor was highlighted red. The Server Room floor – the nerve centre of the building. The only location with unfettered access to stored data. And also the most secure – containing back-ups of Limelight's corporate transactions, messages, employee records, and strategic data.

I pushed the button and a few moments later the lift opened into a small vestibule. In front of us, a large security door was flanked by a panel – gating access.

Karin had already retrieved the keycard and was sliding it into the reader. "Here goes nothing."

A few agonising moments passed until the light above the card panel flashed green. The door unsealed with a hiss – hermetically pressurised. It swung inwards, revealing at least thirty centimetres of steely thickness.

Beyond lay the interior. I'd thought it would be large and industrial, full of machinery, but it wasn't. It was small and crisp, completely white – antiseptic. The ceiling was evenly illuminated – a single, unbroken light source shining across its surface.

Instead of the banks of computers I'd imagined, there was only one. A monolithic, single-screened display, three metres tall and wide enough for two seats, swinging out on gimbals.

The room felt small compared to the footprint of the building; it should have been tens of metres across. Looking closely, I saw the walls revealed the answer. They weren't featureless. There were vague, door-shaped outlines etched into them. Unobtrusive handles, recessed into notches, were almost invisible. The heavy processing equipment must be beyond, leaving the central workspace as a sound-protected area.

I jumped into one of the seats, Karin taking the other. They were curved to provide a relaxed posture. An antithesis to the tension I was feeling. I wanted to stand upright, but it wasn't an option.

Max was online. "I've disabled the cameras and sensors from recording you for the time being. You shouldn't be disturbed, but it won't take long until someone realises they haven't received a scan of the area. I'd guess you have under ten minutes – better make them work, kids."

Was it possible for Max not to be condescending? I didn't think so.

"Okay, Max," I said. "I'll patch you in, but don't forget our deal."

I hard connected my ARO – attaching it by cable to the waiting auxiliary port. As in the security substation, the digital wrestle for control repeated itself. It took longer this time, but after a minute, it flashed green. I wasn't sure how I could feel a mixture of hatred, awe, and envy, but they all applied to Max.

"Commencing download."

Was that nervousness in Max's voice? The snark was gone.

We waited a few minutes, tension building. The area was locked down, but the sense someone could walk in was omnipresent. It beat down like an unbearable heat.

Max was muttering something. "Darlings ..." Her voice has changed again, the haughty officiousness replaced with excitement. "There's ... there's so much here ... more than I imagined—"

"Are you finished?" I cut in, foot tapping. "When can we get out of here?"

"The things I could do from this terminal ... It's connected to the rest of the HK1 network. I could download all the police records, or the unofficial archives ..."

"Max!" Karin blurted out. "Ten minutes, remember!"

There was a pause; Max was engaged in her own fight for control. "Okay." She relented. "This will have to be enough. You two can go. There's an exit on—"

"Wait ..." Karin cocked her head, listening. "Something's wrong."

An alarm klaxon sounded. The lights in the room turned from white to red and the terminal powered down in front of us.

"Oh dear. Security has detected you." Max sounded distant.

"How?" shouted Karin over the wailing klaxon. "You secured the sensors, didn't you?"

"I don't know ... Some redundant security ... I'm locked out, and the police have been called – they'll be here soon."

"What do we do?" I jumped up from the terminal.

"I'm sorry, I have to go. You're on your own."

The comlink went dead – just static. She hadn't even closed it before activating her car's dampening field.

"Max!" Karin called again, but it didn't help – couldn't. Max was in a sensor-proof bubble now. She swivelled violently in the gimbal, eyes wild. "That damn bitch! She's abandoned us."

"Calm down," I answered, surprised at the iron in my voice. "Hackers work alone for a reason; we knew she couldn't be trusted."

Karin clenched her fists at her sides and with physical effort returned herself to zero. "What the hell are we going to do?"

"Run, I guess." I shrugged, crossing to the doors I'd seen earlier. I didn't feel scared exactly. Tired and disappointed was closer. My body was out of adrenaline.

"In here." I pulled at the notch, sliding the door open.

Karin joined me in a low corridor beyond. Bathed in green light, both sides were flanked with blinking racks of servers. This was the industrial area I'd imagined. Cables lay along the ground, networking the servers like an exposed vascular system. The sound of machinery was loud, but not as loud as the klaxon. It was a relief to be moving away from that sound.

We hurried along until we reached the end – the passage ended in a laser guarded vent leading outside. Sabotaging it would set off an alarm, but that was hardly a problem now.

I took out my lazeblaze and hacked liberally around the grid. Mini explosions showered us in sparks as the grid shorted.

The vent cap behind the laser grid looked sturdy, but a few heavy kicks caused it to fly outwards.

The humid air of HK1 rushed in, revealing the city and a sheer drop into Mong Kok below.

"What now?" Karin peered over the edge. "I can't make that."

It was the reverse of the climb I'd done to get in. It was only ten floors, but even using latent state, it would be impossible.

"Not sure." I looked around anxiously. "Any pre-state?"

"Nothing useful right now. If only we'd brought some rope."

Of course! It was staring us in the face. I ran to the beginning of the server racks and started yanking the cables off the floor. Seeing the plan, Karin started pulling too, scraping them up in fistfuls. It was trunking cable, providing power and networking to the machines. A few hard tugs and the connections snapped out of the ports.

"Do we have enough?" Karin eyed the spaghetti tangle.

I did some simple maths. Ten floors. Three metres per floor. Thirty metres of cable. I looked at the pile, but with no way of measuring it, my calculations were useless. There was a lot there, but thirty metres?

"Yes, I think so." I lied. She'd see through it, but it was a fib we both wanted to hear.

Brushing the doubt aside, I tied one end to a metal post where the vent had been hinged. The cable was thick, with a braided outer mesh. It appeared strong enough to hold our weight.

I kicked it out, watching it unfurl into space. I peered over the edge; it was a relief to feel the sticky heat of the city. Freedom was close, but had the cable touched the pavement below? I couldn't tell in the murky light.

There was a commotion in the control room behind us. The sounds of boots and angry voices. We were out of time. "What do you think?" I said to Karin.

"I don't think we've got time to worry about it," she replied earnestly as she wrapped the cable around her hand. "Let's get the hell out of here!"

I watched her scramble off the edge into the fog below.

I looked back to the control room. A helmeted head was poking into the tunnel, accompanied by what looked like the muzzle of a rifle. Karin was right – it was time to go. I gripped the cable, and holding my breath, I jumped into the soupy wetness of HK1.

# STATE 22

I opened my eyes, floating in confusion between sleeping and consciousness. A hateful place, filled with sensations of not knowing – a pre-waking dementia.

Today I relished it. I knew when reality came rushing back, I wouldn't like it.

First the dripping. A *plink-plunk* somewhere in the darkness. Then the sticky feeling – skin against sweat-stained mattress.

My eyes adjusted to the gloom and the memories returned. We'd escaped the Data Centre, but the cable hadn't been long enough. We'd plummeted the final four metres, Karin twisting her ankle.

I looked around the room, searching for her outline against the dank walls. She was curled on an equally filthy mattress, injured leg jutting out at an angle. A puddle was gathering from a leaking air-conditioning unit. The whole place stank of damp and mildew.

I wasn't sure how we'd escaped. I'd expected a swarm of guards at the base of the building, but there had been none. Even slowed by Karin, we'd beaten a successful retreat, finding our way to a hotel.

Daring to call this place a hotel was a joke. They charged by the hour, so it was technically true, and importantly, it was one of the few places that wouldn't question me dragging in an injured woman. The leathery-faced crone at the desk had waved us through like it was a common occurrence. Just another pimp patching up an abused sex worker.

At least it had a vending machine. Which we'd half emptied. The floor was littered with sweet wrappers and isotonic vials. Hardly room service, but I'd been hungry after the ordeal – passing out following the binge. I had no idea how much time had passed.

I dragged myself upright and groaned. Every muscle hurt, especially my arms and shoulders. I could barely lift them. And my head was pounding. Too much sugary food. We couldn't sustain ourselves like this for long.

The room had a shower. It was disgusting, but so was I, and any amount of cleaning was better than none. The showerhead sputtered and groaned but did eventually spew forth something resembling water. Mercifully, it was sufficiently heated to be tolerable.

Karin was awake when I got back. I barely noticed I was naked and dressing in front of her. She didn't mention it, and at this point it didn't seem to matter.

"How are you?" I asked, pulling my shirt on.

"Okay." Karin stood, grimacing. "I mean, battered. Ankle hurts like hell, but I'll survive. You?"

I shook my head, struggling to express the mixture of exhaustion and pointlessness I felt. "Vacant." I settled on.

Karin nodded her agreement. "What now then?" Karin leaned against a sideboard; it wobbled on unsteady legs. She thought better and took a seat on a chair instead. Basic and wooden. Only one in the room.

"No idea."

"I can't believe Max abandoned us."

"You can't?"

"Alright, I can, but, well, for the love of God! Leaving like that. She's meant to be some kind of social justice warrior. I guess I expected ..."

"What?"

"A moral code."

I raised an eyebrow. "Honour among thieves?"

"Yeah ..." She trailed off. "Well, something like that anyway."

Karin's ARO beeped from where it lay on the mattress. That was odd; she was between plans since we'd disconnected her from Limelight. Max had set her up with a safe account so we could keep in contact, but no one knew the access code.

"Wait." I held up my hand as Karin hobbled over to the device.

"Why? How much worse can it get? Max said the account was untraceable, didn't she?"

I gritted my teeth, hand floating impotently, but couldn't counter the point as Karin picked up the ARO.

My eyes widened as she flipped out the screen and I saw who was calling.

There was a display on the wall, cracked at the edges but still working. Karin mirrored her ARO to it.

Max appeared on screen. I didn't recognise where she was. It wasn't her car or the warehouse. She looked different, harried – her appearance not as manicured as normal. A misplaced smear of lipstick here, a crooked collar there.

"Sorry for leaving early, children—"

"You've got a lot of nerve!" Karin interrupted.

I put a hand on her arm. Whatever calmness (or nihilism) had overcome me in the Data Centre was still with me.

Karin bit her tongue.

"Yes, I know. Most unfortunate. But I had to go. Police would have swarmed me if I'd stayed and then we'd have nothing. And besides, I did help you escape."

"The hell you did!" Karin retorted, irritated at the sanctimonious tone. "Where were you when we were suspended on a power cable thirty metres above the ground?"

"Nowhere near you, of course. What would be the point in that?"

"Oh, I don't know." I cut in. "To help us maybe? You may not have noticed, but Karin's injured; she may have broken an ankle."

"Yes, I can see that." Max sounded bored. "And I'll let your tone slide, bearing in mind I very much helped you."

Karin looked like she wanted to hurl something at the screen, smash its cracked facade into pieces. Not that it would have helped; the signal was coming through the ARO not the TV.

Max was still talking. "... Aren't you curious how you escaped when you got to the ground? Unusual, don't you think, no one was waiting for you?"

I pursed my lips; that had been unusual. I'd been thinking about it since we made it to the hotel.

"Aunty Max still had security access, so I did you a favour before I left."

"What was that?" Karin replied, hand twitching. The urge to throw something still palpable.

"I locked the front door and cut their communication to authorities."

Karin's face screwed up in frustration – fighting conflicting emotions. It was the most out of control I'd seen her and she knew it. Betrayal brought out the worst in her. She turned her back on the TV so we couldn't see it.

Maddeningly, what Max was saying made sense. It explained why security hadn't met us at ground level.

"They manually overrode my lock-out after a few minutes," Max continued. "But that was plenty of time for you to escape now, wasn't it?"

I fought the urge to pick up where Karin had left off. Point out how easy she'd had it compared to us, but I held back. I could see things could have gone worse if she hadn't intervened. I hated the way Max operated, safe and sound from her remote locations while we took all the risks, but that didn't change the facts.

"Anyway," Max was saying, as if nothing had happened. "Something turned up in the data, and I thought you'd want to know."

"You bothered looking? You're only interested in your own agenda." I scoffed.

"Well, obviously. I'll be busy for years. It's a treasure trove. But, I looked into your specific situation – a deal's a deal. Set your expectations though. It won't be everything you want to hear; however, it's still very interesting." She puffed out her cheeks, making her look monstrous on the distorted display. "Whatever's going on is well hidden, not part of the official record, but there is a pattern." She paused to let the tension rise.

"Get on with it, Max." Karin turned back, mostly her normal self again, but her patience was wearing thin. It was good to see her back in control. I didn't want to deal with Max on my own.

"Very well." Max shrugged, neither happy nor sad her attempt at drama had failed, and laid out the revelation bluntly and without ceremony. "Limelight's senior team are being targeted. Murdered actually."

My bottom lip jutted out, eyes narrowing. "Okay ... What does that have to do with us?"

"More than you think. The disasters you've seen on the news feeds are connected, including the one you escaped at the Shard. The victims were manipulated to be in those areas – marked out to be executed.

The catastrophes were merely diversions, something to hide the foul play."

"How?" Karin asked wearily. She'd re-seated herself, the web of her hand wrapping around her brow.

"It's really quite amazing," Max continued excitedly, oblivious to the death toll she'd just glossed over – she seemed immune to such concerns. "It's easy to manipulate people if you alter their data feed – something Limelight has complete access to for its employees. Think how much we all rely on that information. You can be rerouted with fake traffic reports. Prices on products can be increased to make sales look more enticing. Appointments can be rearranged, contact information altered, vital information withheld, and social media filtered. We're so reliant on data to inform our lives. Limelight socially engineered its senior leaders' feeds to put them where they wanted, then boom! ... Organised a little accident for them."

"That's bullshit." I couldn't believe what Max was saying; it didn't sound credible. "People aren't that predictable."

"Well, there's a margin for error. It's why there have been several disasters – to sweep up stragglers. And they had to shuffle in plenty of regular people to hide the connection back to Limelight. However, eventually, you can manipulate anyone to appear somewhere you need them." Max tapped at an off-screen console. "Look, don't take my word for it." A man in a green jacket appeared.

I recognised him. It was the guy I'd nearly killed at the Shard. Of all the examples to use.

"His name's Jason. He's a senior technician at the European arm of Limelight. An immovable meeting was created in Neo-London he had to attend. After checking into his hotel, he asked his ARO for a dinner recommendation. A restaurant was displayed in the London Bridge area. Once there, his table was electronically delayed and he was shown the Shard exhibition to kill time. This is one example of many, and he followed each step precisely as laid out."

I looked at his face; he looked young, full of potential. I felt better knowing it wasn't my fault he'd been there – and also that he'd survived.

"He died in a train crash yesterday ..."

My optimism descended in flames.

"... A series of rerouted meetings made sure of it."

I turned to look at the mottled wall, despair building. What were we up against?

"Don't look so vexed." Max droned on – any reaction to my emotional display purely incidental. "The fabulous Ms. Maximal isn't finished helping you yet."

"More blackmail?" Karin made no attempt to hide her contempt.

"Hardly. I've got what I need. I'm giving back now; quid pro quo, as they say."

What now? I returned my gaze to the screen. It flickered, a new image taking its place. It took a few seconds to register what I was looking at. A CCTV feed of a hospital room, a nice one. The furnishings were clean and modern – some flowers tastefully arranged in a jar on the bedside.

Fitted with an electronic filter, the window amplified the light, giving an artificial but convincing appearance of real sunshine. A private facility; nothing like this was available publicly.

In the centre of the room, a uniformed nurse was feeding a man. It was Sebastian. I barely recognised him. He'd been cleaned and shaved, lying beneath crisp white sheets. Vacant, but in good health.

"No need to thank me; it was trivial. I changed his records. Sebastian has medical insurance now. Permanent and untraceable, of course. And I had him moved to this facility. There's nothing I can do for his mental state, but he'll be looked after from here on out."

I touched my face. I was crying. It had started as a low feeling in my chest, but it was coming out of me thick and fast like an invisible dam had broken. I couldn't remember crying so hard in my life. Not even after the accident.

Karin hobbled over and put an arm around me while Max watched on, an uncomfortable look on her face but with the good grace not to interfere.

I felt ridiculous, unhinged, unable to control myself. Thoughts hit me like mini-strokes. I'd done it. I'd found a way forward. I'd taken care of things – like Seb would have wanted.

Is this what it was to achieve something? To have a goal and make it happen? I'd done nothing worth a damn my whole life. The enormity was overwhelming.

I tried to breathe, to gain control. It was hard, but after a few moments, the emotions began to recede and new ones crept in to replace them. Ones I was less familiar with. It was a sense of pride, and a renewed feeling of strength.

And then the tears were gone. Stopping as quickly as they'd started. A flash flood that had raged hard but was now over. I set my jaw and brushed off Karin's arm, standing resolutely, not bothering to wipe my face.

This wasn't finished – Seb was out of danger, yes, but still a vegetable. I had to keep looking for a cure. And this was bigger now. He wasn't the only victim. People were being killed. If I could get Sebastian out of the asylum, I could help them too. A purpose within all the chaos.

"What about Karin?" I asked pointedly, but an emotional wobble was still there.

Max redirected her attention. "Oh, I haven't forgotten about you, Ms. Chambers. Nothing so dramatic unfortunately. Your parents are fine. Living in France. I haven't notified them where you are, and I don't plan to."

"How can I trust you?"

"You can't. But why would I help Daryl and betray you? Wouldn't make sense. Besides, us three make a good team, don't you think?"

"Team?" I almost choked on the word. "You're the least team-orientated person I've ever met!"

Max smiled. "Well, that's true, but bearing in mind our recent successes, I've decided I need to be a bit more ... inclusive."

That stumped me. A lone-wolf hacker acting like part of a unit. My brain was too exhausted to make sense of it, but after a few moments, I shrugged. It would be foolish to reject her offer. Better to humour her and see where it leads.

Karin sighed. There'd be no love lost between them, but she'd reached the same conclusion – any help was better than none.

"What's our next move then, Max?" she asked wearily. "If you're going to help us, what do we do now?"

"Xavier Johnson."

"Who?" we said together.

"Dr. Xavier Johnson. The Technical Director of Limelight. One step down from Francis Lyme – the CEO himself."

"And how is he going to help us?" A stress headache was forming – I could feel it bearing down on me.

"He's not. You're going to help him." Max stopped, waiting for understanding to set in.

"He's been targeted, hasn't he?" Karin ended the pregnant pause. "For elimination, like the others."

"Good girl. I see your thinking cap is on. You're right. Xavier's been marked in the system."

I was suspicious; something didn't sound right. I felt a new confidence to challenge Max – now I wasn't being actively blackmailed.

"Max, I thought you said the records were hidden, difficult to interpret."

Her eyebrows raised, the inference clear: *How dare you question my analysis!* – But she answered anyway. "They *are* hidden, but the pattern is clear. Xavier's been redirected to a meeting in New Tokyo; however, the data's erroneous. It's outside of the organisation's normal scheduling. The attendees and agenda don't suggest any commercial reason for a man of his seniority to be there. Xavier's diary has been manipulated to ensure he attends."

"So what?" I was unconvinced. "We go there, warn him, show him the evidence, and he helps us? Just like that?"

Max shrugged. "Well, darling, I didn't say it would be easy, but something tells me you two will persuade him. And in any case, I'm going to stay with you. Not in person, no, no, no. It will all be remote from this point on."

Of course it will.

"And I've attracted too much attention already. I need to keep moving. But if my hunch is right, you will uncover something huge. I want to be there when you do."

On second thought, Max staying remote was fine by me. I still remembered her (him) pushing up against me. Keeping her at a distance was safer for everyone.

Her motive was clear; she was staying close to lead her to more precious data. Still, we needed allies, and Max was undeniably good at what she did. We'd need to keep our eyes peeled for a double-cross, but I got the sense Karin wasn't going to let that happen. She'd been burned – that wouldn't be repeated.

"You said Tokyo, right?" I groaned, moving the conversation on. "I assume that means another freezing trip in a sub-jet hold?"

"Oh, don't be ridiculous. I know how to get around port records. You're travelling first class this time. Unless you prefer the hold?"

I looked around. The stained mattresses. The dripping air conditioning. Bottom of the barrel in every way. I wasn't sure I could even imagine what first class looked like, but I wasn't about to reject the offer either.

"No, Max, first class will be fine. Set it up."

# STATE 23

We boarded the sub-jet to Tokyo, strolling on like high-rolling elites. Shoulders back, noses high. No latent state, no pre-state, and no funky leather trousers. In fact, no uncomfortable attire of any sort. Quite the opposite. First class required smart business wear.

The HK1 salesman had assured me the acrylic suit I'd bought contained all the properties of cotton but would never wrinkle and barely needed cleaning – repelling dirt and smells via its silver-biotic lining. I hadn't tested the cleaning claim (and wasn't keen to), but it certainly hadn't creased in the hours we'd been sitting on the sub-jet.

I'd glimpse myself in mirrors and window reflections, not recognising what looked back. It was a person I wanted to be though – the inverse of how I felt most mornings.

Karin had given me her seal of approval, mouth crinkling in a half smile. I'd been walking on air ever since, but there was fear too – it foreshadowed where I might go, but also how far I could fall. The gutter was a long way from here.

A visit to a private medical centre had put Karin right. The owner had waived the fee and removed any record of us being there. He didn't have a choice. Max's threat to reveal a hard drive full of indecent images of questionably legal girls had assured his cooperation.

The good news was Karin's ankle wasn't broken, only sprained. She'd be on muscle stimulants and painkillers for a few days, but she would heal if she kept off it.

Happily, there were few reasons to move in first class. The seats were massive, luxurious, and with the flip of a switch swept back to lie completely horizontal. If not for the surrounding people and background roar of engines, it might be mistaken for an actual bed.

Flanked with a host of in-flight entertainment, there was plenty to pass the time. Full-speed internet, a library of holovids, a music track selection, and to my disbelief, even a high-end VR rig.

Karin lost herself online right away – plugged in and detached. Furtively updating her social networks. No doubt her followers were somewhere between curious and furious over her extended absence.

Max had fashioned us with new identities. We were travelling as Mr. and Mrs. Trevor and Charlene Best. We hadn't asked Max to marry us, but embarrassingly, she'd done it anyway – probably to annoy me. Karin had shrugged it off – her apathy putting me deep in the friend zone. Whatever. It wasn't the worst place to be, and frankly, we had more important things to worry about. I'd let it go. At least for the time being.

Where was Jay? I'd sent him a message thirty minutes ago over the sub-jet's quantum-broadcast channel. If it was secure enough for business elites, it should be good enough for us. Max would encrypt it anyhow, so together with our new personas, Limelight shouldn't be able to detect us.

The response came back. He was online, had been for some time – it was 6.30 pm in Neo-London. Prime gaming time for Jay. I pulled on the VR helmet and sent a party request, materialising in his environment a few moments later. A space fighter simulation. I was sitting in the co-pilot's seat staring into the chaos of an active battle. Red and silver bolts flashed across the sky as tiny fighters vied for control. Their sleek, arrow-shaped bodies banking and spinning in the classic dog-fighting style.

A sound-dampening field activated, allowing private conversation – isolating me from other passengers.

An electronic version of Jay was sitting to my right. His avatar adorned with mirrored aviator sunglasses. They looked ridiculous and perfect at the same time.

"Hey, Daryl, how are you?" His lips moved in an unsettling way.

VR was good, but the *uncanny effect* – the difficulty matching ad-hoc speech – had never been solved.

He put on the inflection of an overbearing parent. "You don't call, you don't write! What's a mother to do?"

I rolled my eyes, hoping the helmet was sensitive enough to display it to him. It seemed to be.

"Did you meet up with our friend? What's he like? Everything I said he'd be, right?"

*Friend.* That was a funny way of describing Max. Awkward ally. Extortionist. Sexual harasser. All were more fitting, but there was no point bursting Jay's bubble. As far as he knew, Maximal was the hero hacker he'd imagined them to be. Better to let him maintain the illusion.

"Yes, we did," I replied. "It's been hard work, but, er ... *he's* been quite helpful."

Now wasn't the time to get into Max's gender binary status. It was confusing enough in person.

"And what about your travelling partner? The spook."

"She's not a spook," I replied impatiently, turning on the exterior pass-through camera. I knew the sound-dampening field was active, but I wanted to check she wasn't paying attention. "In the friend zone," I whispered.

Jay was tracking an errant fighter moving out of range. "For the best," he replied distantly, focussed on the battle. "You don't want an agent keeping tabs on you."

I'd forgotten the lie we'd fed Jay. I should set him straight, but for now, he was happier with the fabrication, and there were things I needed to check with him. Best not to muddy the water.

"Jay, is everything okay, by the way? No fallout from helping us?"

"Damn!" The fighter escaped.

He turned the unsettling face on me again, a fake but reminiscent grin digitally recreated. "Not that I've noticed."

That was good. I hadn't thought about Jay much since we left Neo-London. Hadn't had the mental bandwidth. But hearing him now reminded me how he'd put himself on the line for us.

"I'm guessing you're not just checking up on me?" he continued.

"No. Jay, do you know anything about Xavier Johnson?"

"Er ..." He paused. "Not a huge amount. Wouldn't your new friend know more than me?"

"Maybe, but I'd like to get your view."

Max dealt in facts and had almost no imagination. In contrast, Jay's conspiracy paranoia and lateral thinking had been scarily close to the truth. I wanted to know if he could connect any dots we'd missed.

"Okay. Well, let me think. He's a big shot at Limelight. Technical Douchebag or something."

"Director."

"Yeah, whatever. He's not a big feature on the conspiracy threads, but a few years ago he lit them up. It didn't last long, but it started a few theories."

"Go on."

"Well, he was always seen together with Francis Lyme. They were, like, best friends or something, but one day Lyme retreated from public life. Pretty much vanished, leaving Johnson to run the company."

"Were there any more details?"

"Not really. Just speculation ranging from corporate conspiracy to foul play, but it didn't go anywhere."

"Why?"

"Lyme made an official holo-release a few days later. He wanted to take a less visible role – something about health reasons and wanting to be closer to his family, blah-blah-blah. Besides, he didn't formally step down, just sort of retreated. Guys on SCAM.NET analysed the footage; it wasn't obviously fake and there didn't seem to be any stress or coercion in his voice. It was weird, but weird things happen. Not everything's a conspiracy theory."

I laughed out loud.

"What?"

Jay's lack of self-awareness was hilarious.

"Only loons and paranoid maniacs think that way." He banked the space ship and went into a loop. "Woo-hoo!"

My stomach turned. A danger of joining a VR game while already on a moving object. Any more of this and I'd come down with simulation sickness.

"Hey look, Jay, I gotta go."

"Cool, man. Take it easy." And then with the overbearing accent. "Call home soon, my boy. I worry!"

I pulled off the VR helmet, taking some breaths as the nausea retreated – I'd caught it just in time. Karin was looking at me.

"You okay? You look paler than normal."

"Yeah," I replied. "A touch of simulation sickness."

"Really? You?"

"We all get caught short sometimes. You done socialising?"

The last word came out sarcastically, making me sound like a dick. As per normal, Karin didn't notice, or didn't rise to it. Still, I felt the need to apologise. "Sorry. I didn't mean that."

"I know."

"That stuff pops out of me sometimes. I can't help it."

"Don't worry. I know when you mean something and when you don't."

I nodded and looked away, but her words rolled around in my mind. I turned back. "Wait. You know? As in pre-state? I thought you only get that occasionally."

Karin shrugged. "I do, but over the last few weeks, you're basically always in pre-state."

I could feel my ears heating up. "So you can see my intentions all the time!"

"Pretty much, but don't sweat it; it's not as interesting as you think. Lots of people get to that point naturally. If they know each other well."

I was mortified! How many indecent thoughts had crossed my mind on this flight, let alone over the last few weeks? No wonder I was in the friend zone. Safest place to put me!

"That's easy for you to say." I went on the offensive, ears flashing like sirens. "You're not the one with your heart on your sleeve 24/7."

No reply. Not even an apology. Just a *What do you want me to do?* face.

I grimaced sullenly. "Why is it on all the time, anyway?"

"I don't know." Karin shrugged. "Maybe Future Karin wanted me to ignore your bad attitude. To ensure we work well together."

Ouch. That was low. I suppose I did have bad habits. A lifetime hanging out with lowlifes will do that to a person.

Then out of the embarrassment, a thought emerged – a more hopeful one. I straightened up, neutralising my voice before asking. "Does it mean we're closer in the future?"

Karin shrugged again, even less interested. "Yeah, I suppose. Or more likely there's some interplay between our abilities. Something that makes my pre-state more sensitive around you."

Shit. That was plausible – crash and burn. Still, it sounded like Karin was in my future, which was reassuring. I compartmentalised my shame – an old but useful skill. Hopefully my thoughts weren't doing too much harm if Future Karin was looking out for me.

"Please prepare your seats for landing." An airhost's voice interrupted over the tannoy. "We'll be making our approach into Tokyo shortly."

An unexpected surge of excitement jolted through me, flushing away the negative feelings. Since its resurgence back to a tech capital, Tokyo, or more accurately, New Tokyo, had become insanely expensive to travel to. I'd never heard of anyone going there, let alone met someone who'd made the journey.

Despite the exchange, I was glad Karin was with me. However things played out with Xavier Johnson, it was bound to be interesting. In the meantime, I'd have to deal with her knowing everything about me. Time to swallow your pride, Daryl.

# STATE 24

Set on a hillside at the outskirts of Old Tokyo, the sub-jet port looked out over the city – landing runways jutting from the dome like artificial eyelashes.

Debarking was uneventful. Clearing customs practically apologetic, with sycophantic Japanese attendants bowing furiously and muttering placations in broken English.

Shepherded into a two-seater mag-shuttle bound for Old Tokyo, we set off with a jolt, a tannoy announcing the journey would take approximately ten minutes.

I peered through the rain-spattered window, forehead against the cool plexiglass. I could make out the silvery lines of the city, visible below low-hanging smog. It was a shambling mess. A place I couldn't imagine wanting to visit, but it was a necessary stop on the way to our actual destination, many vertical kilometres above.

Most cities hid their dystopias, layering technology over like a surface glaze to hide the inner rot. Old Tokyo wore its oppression openly.

As the shuttle zipped along, we could see people shuffling about their business on the roads outside. They looked beaten, heads down, vacant, and grey.

Tokyo had been the epitome of technology and style in the twentieth century, a testament to futuristic design and fashion. But the once shiny skyscrapers were now tired and crumbling.

Ancient advertisement hoardings dotted the tracks. The animated characters and Japanese girls ripped and peeling – the soft drinks and video games they used to display no longer recognisable.

"What happened here?" Karin stared in disbelief. "I've never been anywhere so depressing. Are you sure we're in the right place?"

"You don't know?" I turned to face her. "I thought everyone knew."

"Not really. Something to do with New Tokyo?"

Karin's interest in tech began and ended with her ARO and social networks. She'd know of New Tokyo, everyone did, but apparently not the background and what it had meant to Japan.

"Yeah." I grimaced. "New Tokyo did a number on this place."

She swivelled in her chair to face me, hands clasped in her lap. Story time.

I acquiesced, recounting what I knew. The words sobering as I spoke them.

The Japanese economy had been in a dire state at the turn of the century. The rest of the world had caught up in technology, and Japan's insular, borderline-xenophobic ways of working had prevented globalising as fast as the Tiger economies emerging from the rest of Asia. The population had become apathetic, birth rates declining and the volume of unproductive, care-dependent elders soaring. Something drastic had to change, or they'd risk slipping into a second-world economy.

The last place of competitive advantage was their telecommunications sector. They'd been at the forefront since its creation, achieving a hundred per cent penetration of mobile devices among adults before any other country. They leveraged what remained of their industry expertise and ingenuity into a massive gamble.

Japan knew satellite technology would drive the future. It was the backbone to broadcasting the increasingly pervasive range of mobile services. But there was a problem everyone had to deal with first – the expense to launch and maintain those satellites.

Their solution was radical. New Tokyo – the first geostationary orbital city, connected to Earth via magnetic space elevator.

The world had thought the Japanese insane. Space elevators should only be possible at the equator, but Japan would not work with anyone else. To reap the full commercial benefits, this had to be their endeavour, and theirs alone – tethered to the Japanese mainland. It meant not only solving the immense construction challenges but also mastering the physics of creating a curving elevator shaft away from the equator.

It had all but bankrupt the Japanese government, indebting the country and creating decades of austerity. Old Tokyo and the surrounding areas had suffered, disintegrating as Japan pumped resources into the project. And not only natural resources; anyone with useful skills, from engineering to hard labour, had been conscripted – paid just enough for basic subsistence. It was a dramatic switch from democracy to totalitarianism, justified under the banner of a national emergency.

Incredibly, the people hadn't rebelled. Dissent or attempts at sabotage were rare. Fierce nationalism and cultural honour kept them motivated – constantly parroting the Government's propaganda: "For the greater good".

They maintained their sense of duty, but the endeavour broke the spirit of a generation of Japanese workers.

Arguably, it had been worth it. Twenty years after the first shuttle launched to create the new station, they switched the space elevator on, and overnight New Tokyo became the epicentre for production and maintenance of satellite networking around the globe.

Components could be ferried to the platform cheaply via the elevator, and the station was permanently crewed with engineers to deploy and repair them. For a fee, they would launch and service other countries' satellites, but it was more cost effective to subcontract the work to New Tokyo – or relocate there.

From the start, New Tokyo was envisioned as a comfortable habitat, with the facilities to shelter and entertain the population of a small city. The rates were exorbitant but necessary to cover running costs. The lack of investment in Old Tokyo and other major cities showed it still barely ran a profit, but that didn't matter; the Japanese were relevant again, and they had a plan. New Tokyo wasn't a static station; it was a scalable platform. In time, it would grow sufficiently to plough profits back to the mainland. That hope kept people going.

Despite the rental costs, there was no shortage of companies wanting to take up residence. Being technically not on Earth, New Tokyo was the ultimate tax haven – the savings enough to offset the most exclusive premises on (or at least near) the planet.

"Wow," Karin interjected. "I didn't know any of that. Was that why Limelight moved there? For tax reasons?"

I could feel she was staring at me, but my gaze was through the window, appraising the poverty. Seeing it laid bare was getting to me.

I shook my head and explained further.

Francis Lyme had been a visionary. He'd seen the potential of New Tokyo immediately. One of the first pioneers to move his fledgling Telcom to the station. He'd gambled on the untested platform, risking key resources in its hostile, outer-space environment.

Fortunately, the Japanese had done a thorough job. Despite the harsh working conditions, they'd maintained their reputation for meticulous quality – honour demanded it. Reports were the station was a marvel of engineering. Well designed, modern, and with an outstanding safety record. There was a waiting list of ten years for companies wishing to move their operations. The Japanese couldn't build it quickly enough to cover the demand. Early movers like Limelight had won big with cost savings and increased speed of development. Money ploughed into creating the quantum-broadcast network that now led their field.

Karin listened as I ran through the details, nodding with no small amount of disbelief.

"I know, incredible isn't it?" I remarked, looking across the broken skyline of Old Tokyo.

Through the haze, I could make out the space elevator's shaft. A thick umbilical, fifty metres across, woven from immensely strong nanofibers. It extended like an impossible spire, kilometres into the sky above.

The shuttle neared the end of the line, passing through an energy barrier encircling a nicely appointed reception area – the elevator lying beyond. It was the only place of note for miles. Few people went anywhere else in Old Tokyo.

The mag-shuttle was essentially a high-security link, controlling who accessed the site. If they'd tinted the plexiglass, no one would even know the original city was there. I wondered if reports of the Japanese acceptance of their fate were completely true. The fortifications looked ready to defend against a revolt.

"No point hanging around." Karin jumped up. I couldn't agree more.

Housed in a facility much like the port, the space elevator's reception was marble, glass, and aluminium, but with typical Japanese flourishes. Sweeping kanji characters and crimson flags adorned the walls. Doors and gates were highlighted with polished wood panelling and ornamental metalwork.

Max had booked us fast-connecting tickets. Our new IDs provided digital camouflage, but we might be recognised more conventional ways – by a savvy security guard or Neo-London busybody. Best to move quickly.

We made our way to the elevator, clearing security in another flurry of bows and ingratiations. A buzz of anxiety surged as a guard took a few seconds longer over our IDs. Fortunately, Max was a master of her art and he soon nodded, waving us through. It was just as well – there were a plethora of laser grids blocking every vent and access area. It was a class above what we'd experienced at the sub-jet port or the Data Centre. Even with our powers, I wasn't sure we'd escape if uncovered.

Through security, the departure room lay ahead. Unfurnished and industrial, it sat in contrast to the posh reception – bustling with people from all walks of life. The elevator was a multi-lane road to the station above, ferrying business executives, engineers, and labourers – they all rubbed shoulder to shoulder as they looked for their boarding gate. Like any commuter route, it was workmanlike and undecorated.

Contrary to popular thought, the elevator was multiple lifts in one. Fifteen smaller compartments around the perimeter, holding between ten and a hundred individuals, and a much larger central lift, accessible by a large hangar door. The configuration provided flexibility to transport a constant stream of workers back and forth, but without running the more expensive freight elevator reserved for very large objects, like satellites or space shuttle parts.

We were in lift number two, one of the lower occupancy and more expensive cabins. On the way around, we passed lift number fifteen in time to witness the maximum occupancy of one hundred Japanese labourers cramming themselves in. Standing room only for the five-hour journey.

Our lift, by comparison, had fully reclining seats, a stocked bar, and even a shower. Important looking businessmen and women surrounded us. They eyed us suspiciously for our age, but they soon dismissed our presence and returned their attention to their ARO displays and VR rigs.

We took our seats. An announcement signalled we'd be leaving soon, and a few moments later, a following one reported we were underway. I hadn't felt a thing – no sense of movement or inertia at all. The magnetic lifting technology was undetectable, although I knew we were accelerating at an incredible rate. I leaned my ear close to the wall – I could hear a deep, faint hum.

There were no windows, but display panels set around the circular cabin displayed exterior shots up the thickly corded elevator cable. It looked endless.

My hand started tapping my seat tray nervously and I could feel a tingle in my stomach. It wasn't anxiety; it was excitement. New Tokyo was the thing of dreams – the last place humanity had with anything approaching a homogeneously high standard of living. A purpose-built ecosystem, propagated with the best technology; free from the crime and pollution that plagued the rest of the planet. I never thought I'd see it in my lifetime.

Fuelled by my twitchy excitement (and a few alchovials), time sped on merrily. Eventually, via the display, I could see a dot at the end of the cable. It grew, taking on a cylindrical shape, rotating smoothly in the flat light of the unfiltered sun. The first time I'd seen anything solar-illuminated and not obscured with haze or pollution. It seemed unreal, leaving me nervous and breathless. Like looking out on the ocean for the first time, not knowing what was on the other side.

New Tokyo was designed to be extendable – a segmented, spinning tube that could be added to at either end to increase capacity; its rotation simulated gravity. As we approached, I could make out the separate segments of the habitat. The rings towards the end were nearly twice as long as those in the centre, which correlated with the increased demand of each successive addition.

As we neared the end, the sheer scale of New Tokyo made itself clear. With no frame of reference, it was impossible to quantify distance, but I knew the outside cylinder was about two kilometres in circumference and roughly the same again in length. That left an internal floor space of approximately four kilometres squared, bigger than most city centres, and it was growing all the time. I could make out the skeletal structures where it was being extended – creeping along the shaft, like an artist's sketch of what would eventually be there.

The elevator threaded into the centre of the cylinder, docking with a giant gimbal that allowed the station to rotate smoothly around the shaft.

We felt a shudder as the cabin started to spin, matching the rotation of the station. My body went light, and I began to feel queasy.

I looked over at Karin; she was positively green.

"First time in New Tokyo?" a Japanese businesswoman asked in heavily accented but perfectly understandable English.

"Uh-huh," I said, a wave of dizziness washing over me.

"This is the worst of it. We're at the centre now where gravity is least; once you get down to the outer ring, gravity is about half what it is on Earth. Most don't notice any sickness down there."

A voice came over the tannoy announcing we would disembark soon.

"But watch out for tall buildings," she continued. "The gravity at the top gets back down to more like a fifth standard. Some people don't like that."

I nodded my thanks, not trusting myself to say anything in case I was sick.

The doors opened. We released our security buckles and floated upwards, spiralling inelegantly.

The woman pointed at grips along the tops of the chairs. They had seemed useless on the ground, but now their utility was clear. She yanked herself forward towards the door, gliding through the cabin.

We followed suit.

Each of the elevator doors attached to tunnels containing shuttles. They flowed from the central shaft to the inner rim like spokes on an enormous bicycle wheel. We weren't directed so much as *loaded* by station personnel into independently powered seats – manhandled to set us perpendicular to the station.

The perspectives were crazy. Up and down were interchangeable. It was generating a hardcore nausea headache.

One of the staff must have noticed me greening out. He advised me to close my eyes. "It will get better near the outer rim," he said in sympathetic English – far from the gruff space stevedore I'd been expecting.

I did as told, shutting my eyes as he strapped me in. I imagined the firmness of the seat as being down and that helped reset my brain. The shuttle-seat set off, and after a few moments, I began to detect real gravity. Up became up again, and down, down again – senses rushing back like a switch in my mind had temporarily been turned off and was now flipped back on.

I started to feel well enough to crack my eyes open, and I was glad I did; it was a sight no one should miss. The shuttle tubes were clear glass allowing a fabulous view. Spread out below and above, the immense cylindrical interior of New Tokyo unfolded like a bizarre city from a house of mirrors. A sprawling metropolis of lit buildings, white domes, satellite dishes, and blinking antennas. Some taller buildings appeared to bend close to each other at the top, but it was a trick of the curved interior. They were straight, but the radius of the cylinder meant they grew towards each other as they moved towards the centre. Some structures had taken advantage of the curve, joining at the top to form mighty, asymmetrical arches. One was emblazoned with Limelight's logo – the company's headquarters. At either end of the cylinder was a gaping maw into space, black and terrifying – I tried not to look at it. The buildings and infrastructure were airtight, but the worry of being sucked from the station was hardly irrational.

As I arrived at the base, I was almost feeling normal. Still lightheaded, but the gravity was enough to trick my mind all was well again. The seats filtered out into an arrival hall.

Karin arrived a few seconds later, eyes closed tight. She had to be shaken by the waiting attendant to rouse her. She came stumbling off the chair, slumping towards me, collapsing on my shoulder.

"You okay?" I asked stupidly, holding her up. She obviously wasn't.

"No, my head is killing me."

"Yeah, pretty disorienting, huh?"

"Disorienting? I feel like a pneumatic drill is going off in my head!"

Karin looked grey, and she was physically trembling.

A sign reading *Guest Accommodation* was glowing in the distance. It looked welcoming, and at the moment, very necessary.

"Come on," I said, dragging her to her feet. "Let's find a place to rest; you're no good to anyone like this."

Karin nodded and let herself be pulled along.

# STATE 25

Karin was sick for a full day, rolling and shaking – bedridden and sweating, despite the air conditioning. Space sickness is motion sickness on steroids. A close relative of VR disease. Common for new arrivals to the station, and when it hit, it hit hard. Discounting the initial lightheadedness, I'd been fine – the hours playing sims with Jay clearly provided some immunity.

I'd wanted to tease Karin. She'd been so unshakable, even under incredible stress. It seemed ludicrous for such a small thing to take her down, but after her third visit to the bathroom, stumbling as she tried to catch vomit through pale figures, I'd thought better of it. Scoring points was not a good idea.

New Tokyo expected this. On-site pharmacies were stocked with stabilising drugs, and after one night's sleep, Karin was back on her feet – a point she made clear with a kick in the ribs while I slept.

"Ooph! What the hell was that for?" I let out, gripping my side as I shot upright from under the sheets. It hadn't been vicious, but it was enough to leave a bruise.

"That's for making fun of me last night!" She towered over me, hands on her hips, dressed in workmanlike overalls.

"I didn't—" I stopped, my drowsy mind catching up. Shit. Her damn pre-state, now constantly switched on, had clocked my thoughts, even through her nausea!

"Who are you? The damn thought police!" It wasn't fair. I'd done nothing wrong!

"Oh, toughen up. You've got to get up anyway." She turned away, busying herself packing a rucksack. She looked fine – a bit pale but nothing like last night. Her hair was neatly gathered in a side pony-tail – intentionally resembling a part of the workforce.

I groaned as I got out of bed, knowing I wasn't fooling her. She wasn't wrong. Xavier Johnson was speaking at a New Tokyo conference later today. The one where, presumably, an attempt on his life would happen. We had a lot to do.

The guest accommodation was tiny but well designed. Full of ingenious storage solutions. Beds that folded vertically, drawers in walls, and retractable clothes hangers.

I'd spent a good part of the night staring through the window at the station's curved interior, book-ended with its inky-black disks, trying to convince myself I wasn't dreaming.

I retrieved a pair of overalls from the wardrobe. It disappeared into the floor at the touch of a button.

Outside the station was incredible. It was organised much how any city would be, containing promenades, shops, residential areas, and commercial sectors. Each new segment was built to demand, lending it the unplanned charm of an organic metropolitan city centre.

Challenged by space, every building was bespoke. New Tokyoites had adopted a culture of repurposing whatever they could. Tiny one-bedroom studios stuffed into decorative arches; old satellite hangers reused as hydroponics bays. Even retail shops had been overtaken by engineers – jokingly re-clothing the mannequins in overalls; stuffing their hands with screwdrivers and hammers.

Merchants selling non-essentials crammed the alleyways between buildings. High-quality meals were available in station-run food halls, but Earth-based luxuries, like chocolate or alcohol, were rare and expensive. There was a frowned upon but thriving black market for such consumables.

It was a busy mess, but it was beautiful in its pragmatic efficiency. A beacon for those living in Old Tokyo, hoping one day to join the more fortunate, literally, in the heavens above.

We made our way through the bustling streets. It was easy to navigate, bouncing along in the reduced gravity. Skylights set between colossal steel beams revealed previews of what lay ahead inside the cylindrical structure. The Limelight building was unmissable. Its conjoined towers loomed above everything else on the skyline – ringline?

The interior roof obscured our view as we neared, but it was well signposted above the entrance.

Apart from two guards, security was light. The ground floor of Limelight was a tourist attraction. A walk-in museum – a showroom for their accomplishments to woo investors and attract talent.

Karin froze as we approached, head cocked.

"What's wrong?" I tensed up. Seeing Karin like that was never a good sign.

Her eyes darted from left to right, voice low and urgent. "Pre-state is going wild. Max was right – something's going on here."

I glanced around; everything seemed peaceful. A few people milled around the museum. The guards were relaxed. One leaned against the wall, the other hummed to himself – their stun battens holstered and buttoned.

"Can you be more specific?" I urged.

"Not at the moment. The whole place is swarming with murderous images though."

"Like at the Shard?"

"Yes, similar."

I didn't even try to hide my frustration.

"How is it you can predict the incoming punches of a black belt but can't give a better clue than 'murderous images'?"

"You know the answer," Karin muttered – she wasn't having it today. "The more localised and immediate the threat, the better the prediction. Especially when I'm the subject."

My ARO beeped.

"You better answer that."

"Who is it? I assume it's localised enough for you."

"Answer it and you'll know."

"Can't you just tell me?"

It beeped again.

"You better hurry, or people will get suspicious."

The guards were standing straighter, a little more aware.

I humphed but did as I was told. Rather than opening the screen, I pulled out the comlink and placed it in my ear. I didn't want to attract more attention.

"Hello, sweetie," Max drawled over the link.

I was astonished. I hadn't expected to hear from her until we were back on Earth, and even then, I'd been sure her help was time-limited.

"How are you able to talk to us up here?" I whispered into the link.

"Oh, easily. New Tokyo has a communications network like anywhere else. The data stream is monitored, of course, so I've had to cover my tracks, but it's nothing too difficult."

Arrogant as normal, but for once, it was good to hear from her.

"Can you help us?"

"I told you I would."

"I didn't think you'd keep your word."

"Have I lied to you once?" she replied indignantly.

I thought for a moment. Max had deceived and manipulated us plenty, but a straight up spoken untruth? No, she had me there.

"Anyway, my little disbeliever, Johnson's presentation is due to start at midday. He's giving an overview of new technologies. Although as I told you before, there doesn't seem to be a reason for him to be here; someone's contrived the whole event."

"We've found the reason – Karin's pre-state is going off, big time."

"Well, that confirms my analysis, not that it needs confirming."

She didn't even try to empathise with the disaster we were facing down.

"You don't care that people are about to die, do you?"

"Oh, eyes on the prize, Daryl!" I didn't think it was possible to hear an eye-roll, but Max managed it. "I don't have time to be sentimental, and neither do you. It's eleven thirty, so you've only got a little time to stop whatever's about to happen. You better hop to it, darling."

I set my jaw, the relief of hearing from her fading fast. "And I suppose they're just going to let us walk in?"

"Why not? I've signed you in as corporate guests. The presentation isn't in a restricted area. It's a public speech, and New Tokyo is one of the most weapon-restricted locations on Earth ... you know what I mean – either way, security is light."

"But people will recognise we're not meant to be there."

"Not likely. It's a big meeting – seventy people confirmed from the global business. It's open to office workers from New Tokyo too, so it will probably be twice that. They're having to hold it in their main auditorium. If you keep your head down, no one will notice."

"And if someone questions us?"

"I'm betting no one will, but if they do, just say you're in, oh, I don't know ... Operations. No one will care after that."

I looked at Karin. Her comlink was in her ear as well. She shrugged. What the hell. It was more of a plan than we'd had five minutes ago.

"Chop-chop, darlings, you don't want to miss it."

No need to infer Karin's eye roll; it was plain as day.

Past the guards, who'd gone back to lounging, we made our way through a short maze of carpeted corridors. Modern art plastered the walls – primary-coloured geometric shapes set inside brilliant white backgrounds. Clean, efficient, and corporate. Soulless.

None of the office workers or security staff took much notice. There was little to draw suspicion. Our faces and aliases flashed correctly when checked, showing our status as official guests. After a while, I'd practically convinced myself we were supposed to be there.

The auditorium was a large space for New Tokyo; layered in conical levels, it focussed attention towards a central stage. It was filling up with attendees keen to get close to Xavier Johnson. Either chatting in their seats or milling about by the entrance. We received some curious glances, but not enough to arouse suspicion.

Slipping in, heads down to discourage casual conversation, we made our way to the back, taking seats on the highest tier. The best vantage point.

The sloping auditorium was large enough for two hundred people. A raised podium stood proud on centre stage, complete with a lectern and holo-projector. There were no windows to the outside, only more dull corporate art encircling the walls. The only flourish was a clock-work reproduction of the solar system set in a high, domed roof. Ornate with cogs and dials, it was stationary but appeared operable if powered, creating a simulation of the various orbits.

Karin was on edge, fingers drumming against her leg.

Leaning in, I whispered, "How's your pre-state?"

"Going off like crazy, but it's very unclear."

"What does it look like?" I offered, knowing my advice would be next to useless.

"Like streaks of red in the air. Slashes maybe."

"You think someone will stab Xavier?"

"Don't know, but there's a focus around the podium. You'd better make sure you're ready to freeze time. I don't know how much notice I can give you."

"Don't worry, I'm good at that." Then a thought. "Karin, why can't we just warn him now. Send him a message."

Max was the first to respond, still listening on the open line. "Don't be simple-minded. First, he'll think you're mad and you'll be ejected from the station. Second, if he avoids the danger, we'll learn nothing and be back to square one. The only way to capitalise is for him to witness the attempt for himself."

"And if we can't stop it in time?"

"Well." Max sighed haughtily. "I guess we'll have to find another lead. But you won't let that happen, will you, dear."

It wasn't a question. At least Max was consistent in her ruthlessness.

Over the next fifteen minutes, the auditorium continued to fill up. Japanese businesspeople and a large contingent of on-worlders, who'd travelled specifically for the presentation. No one looked like an assassin, although they'd be doing a poor job if they did. If one had slipped by, I couldn't imagine how they'd manage their dispicable task and escape. Not without becoming caught in the bottleneck of corridors on the way out.

"Can you help us identify who the attacker is?" I whispered into the comlink.

I could hear various beeps and boops as Max interfaced with her terminals.

"I'm checking the attendee records, but nothing's coming up. That doesn't mean much though. Corporate records are amongst the easiest to falsify, and I don't have time to run decoding algorithms on them all."

Great. "Well, any idea what the weapon would be?"

"It would need to be something very precise. It would be lunacy to set off a bomb on a space station."

"Why? Wouldn't that achieve the aim?"

"Certainly, but it would also risk a chain reaction that blew apart the entire station! We know Limelight's involved, and I don't be-lieve they'd sabotage one of their most important telecommunication hubs."

"I hope you're right," I answered, the thought of being sucked into space disturbingly front of mind. I'd heard blood boils in a vacuum, sputtering from eyes and ears as it escapes into the freezing vacuum. It was a disquieting notion, especially after the Shard – the killer had a thing for explosions, and all I had to reassure me was Max's logic.

"Look out for anyone closing the distance on Xavier," she offered. "A close range attack would seem most likely."

"What about poison? That would work, wouldn't it?"

"Unlikely. Food and drink on New Tokyo comes in through authorised channels. A food scare on a space station would lead to rioting. It's carefully screened and regulated."

That ended the discussion. There was nothing to do but wait – tension coiled in my chest like a sharpened spring coated with acid.

Eventually it was standing room only. Latecomers choked up the entrance, vying for position with sharp elbows. Soon they stilled, an expectant hush descending as the allotted time approached.

On cue, the lights dimmed, and a few moments later, Xavier Johnson strode in, taking long, purposeful steps as he approached the podium.

He was different in person. On holovids he'd seemed slim, almost emaciated – like a stiff wind could blow him over. Under the increased resolution of reality, his body was more like wiry steel. I knew from his records he was fifty-nine, and he looked it: wrinkled with greying hair receding to a severe widow's peak. Yet he stood tall, with shoulders back, and with no discernible loss of energy. Small, bright eyes darted around above spectacles perched on the end of his nose.

He was wearing a lab coat. It looked like he'd worked up to the second someone had reminded him he was giving a speech. He appeared efficient, no nonsense, and like he had something to say. I could understand why people had come to hear him.

He reached the podium and punched a button on the holo-projector. It displayed something I recognised. A qubit. The atomic particle used in quantum computing. He waited for complete silence. It was enthralling. The man knew how to make an entrance!

"Quantum technology has taken Limelight to the top of the market," he began. His voice holding natural authority – permeating every inch of the hall. He leaned close to the microphone, pitching to a conspiratorial whisper. "Now, let me tell you what we're doing next."

The crowd hummed with excitement. Technical Director Xavier Johnson was giving them a peek into what his R&D department had been working on. Such things only came around once every few years. I leaned forward, craning to hear what he was going to say.

"Daryl!" Karin whispered. "Pay attention."

I jumped. Damn! I'd forgotten why I was here!

"Right ... right." I dragged my attention away from the stage, scanning for anything of note.

"Don't fall for it," Max added. "Johnson's winging it. Any big announcements would have been planned for months. He's had no time to prepare for this. He's only here because of diary rearrangements."

The audience didn't know that. Apart from Xavier's smooth voice, the auditorium was silent – a sea of unblinking eyes awaiting a revelation.

Nothing appeared dangerous, but I wasn't sure what to look for. The balaclava-wearing, knife-wielding maniac was nowhere to be seen.

"I can't sense anything additional," Karin confirmed. "There's still a focus on the podium, but I can't tell anything else. Can you give us any clues, Max? Anything we can look for."

"I've got an internal view via the camera network and I've finished background checking the guests. The surface analysis doesn't place any of them as potential assassins, but as I said, we don't have time to check if their digital fingerprints have been tampered with. I'm afraid you'll need to do this the old-fashioned way."

I felt myself chewing the inside of my cheek, teeth grinding the flesh, almost meeting. The anxiety was intense, but so was the frustration. We had a clairvoyant on the inside and a world-class hacker on the outside – how were we this clueless?

Karin went tense, head thrust to one side. Listening for something I couldn't hear.

"What is it?" I stiffened, the apprehension infectious.

"Pre-state is changing. It's not as random anymore."

"Be specific, Karin. I need details."

"It's ... converging ... lining up. The red streaks are becoming parallel, pointing away from the stage."

"Where to?"

She craned her head from the stage and around the audience, eyes narrowed with confusion. "It doesn't make sense; it's not pointing into the crowd at all. It's aimed—"

"Where!"

"I don't know! Above us somewhere."

I searched the roof structure. A smooth dome with no features save for the solar system sculpture I'd noticed earlier.

"I can't see anything. Max, have you got a view of the ceiling?"

Sounds of tapping. "Wait a moment, I'm refocusing some cameras. I ... I can't see anything, but I'm getting some peculiar readings. Infrared. There's a heat signature up there."

"Lights? A power source for the sculpture?"

"No. It's nothing like that; it's larger and much hotter, but there's nothing up there that matches. Whatever it is, I can't see."

"You mean it's invisible, or cloaked somehow?"

"I don't know. I've seen nothing like it before ..."

"What is it, Max?"

"A new reading; the heat source is intensifying. An overload of some sort. Could be a weapon. I suggest you do something. Quickly, children!"

I already was. Max's words had pushed my tension into full-blooded, adrenal-pumping fear – turning on latent state was more like curling into a foetal position than a conscious action. Either way, the world froze, and by the looks of it, just in time.

A bright orange beam was halfway between the sculpture and the podium. It was thicker at its origin, honing to a razor's point. The flash illuminated an object on the sculpture, disrupting its cloak. I could make out its rough shape. Something spidery and metallic. It looked like it could be a big problem, but it didn't matter now – the energy weapon had been paused mid-discharge. So much for close range, Max!

Worse, the beam wasn't frozen like everything else; it was moving, inching slowly through the air. It confirmed our suspicions; I wasn't immobilising time – I was merely slowing it to nearly stationary. Normally it wouldn't be perceptible, but here it was. The weapon was moving so fast it was negating latent state. It would cut through Johnson in, perhaps, five minutes.

I raced through the possibilities. I could climb the sculpture and try to disable whatever was up there. That would give us a chance of identifying the assassin, but it was also risky. The energy had already left the weapon. Even if I disrupted its trajectory, a part would still make contact with Xavier, and we couldn't risk him dying.

Alternatively, I could unfreeze time and try to push him clear.

No. That would work for something slow moving, like a car or falling debris, but the energy beam would be travelling much faster. It would close the distance quicker than I could react.

Thinking was no good. I needed a better look at what I was dealing with.

Standing, I forced my way through the gluey atmosphere to the stage, past rows of unaware attendees, their faces still frozen in rapture. The blast had already progressed another metre as I arrived at the podium. I was running out of time.

Balancing on an elbow, Xavier's arm extended into the air, index finger pointing upwards – poised to say something dramatic. Under a wrinkled brow, his eyes wore heavy bags, and an old-fashioned hearing aid was looped around his left ear; it seemed out of place – an anachronistic oddity. It was the face of someone who succeeded against the odds. A man who could provide answers. But only if he lived long enough.

The controls for the solar system were on the lectern, confirming it could move. That was useful. A surprise motion would distract the killer, throw them off guard, and provide a moment to get Xavier into cover. But it wouldn't be enough. Some amount of directed energy would still reach its target. The shot had to be physically blocked as well.

How though? Everything was frozen solid, an immutable fact of latent state, and there would be no chance to retrieve a suitable object in real time.

A sickening thought occurred. Save for the energy bolt, the only thing with independent motion was my own body. I knew what it meant, and no amount of thinking could overturn the facts. *I'd* have to stand between Xavier and the blast. Use whatever was on my body to block it. Bloody marvellous.

At least the weapon would be designed for accuracy rather than penetration, I reassured myself, remembering Max's warning. Something too powerful could shoot through an exterior wall, depressurising the area and crippling the station. Max seemed sure the killer would want to avoid that, but it was a lot of damn assumptions.

Nervously, I studied the composition – a life-art model with deathly consequences. The lectern was protecting most of Xavier's lower body, but he was exposed from the waist up.

I clambered onto the slender lectern for a closer look. It would have collapsed or wobbled over in normal time. In latent state, it stuck fast. I eyeballed the trajectory. The blast had closed a significant distance, enough that I could estimate where it might impact. I gritted my teeth. It was time to turn myself into a human shield.

Shifting my body into a crouch, I directed my left shoulder towards the blast. I felt utterly exposed – my entire flank was open. If the killer planned to arc the shot vertically, slicing through the target rather than drilling a pin-point shot, it would carve through my chest like a piece of synthetic protein. Activating the sculpture could mitigate that, throwing the beam into a horizontal plane, but the odds were as good as random.

The blast was close enough now to be reasonably certain of its impact. My ARO, or more importantly, its metal shoulder bracket, should take the impact. But only if I judged it correctly. If it missed by a few centimetres, I was dead. God, I hoped Max was right about the power output!

I discounted letting it strike me in latent state. There were enough variables already. It might create an unknown effect like an electrical discharge or kinetic shove. If it pushed me out the way or disabled me before I could unpause time, it would be catastrophic. Johnson would be killed instantly, and I'd suffocate.

I took a moment to reflect on the situation. Until recently, I would have been too weak and sickened from drugs to hold my body in such a position, and far too mentally detached to consider any act of bravery. If the beam ripped through my head, splattering my unfrozen brains onto the man I'd come to protect, at least I'd depart a better person. If Sebastian ever woke up, he'd be proud of me.

I blinked a few times to clear any mist of tears that might be threatening. Time to get on with it.

Preparing myself, I applied pressure to the solar system controls and tensed for the impact.

Now! The switch clicked under my finger as time resumed and I heard a thrum of energy, feeling heat as the hot orange stream veered past me. There was a smell of burning and an intense but short-lived pain as the beam grazed my ARO – a molten drop of metal landing and re-solidifying against my back. There was a scream, and a man in the front row dropped from his seat, a smouldering gash across his torso.

It was working – the sculpture, now spinning overhead, must have deflected the weapon, or perhaps I'd seen an initial targeting laser, followed by the main shot. Either way, Xavier was unharmed, although having a man materialise in front of his face had clearly shocked him. His eyes were wide, jaw open. He stumbled over backwards, sprawling on the floor. That was fine – he was covered from fire in the lectern's shadow.

The shocked hush that had fallen over the crowd evaporated into screams as orange beams rained down, cutting people savagely and randomly. The auditorium had become a meat blender.

I joined Xavier behind the lectern, sneaking a look at the assailant. It wasn't what I'd expected; it didn't look human – more like a human-shaped robot with multiple limbs. One of its legs was caught in the clockwork gears. It was thrashing about, firing wildly. Its cloak, or invisibility device, disabled.

"Mr Johnson." I turned to look at the man. He was startled but on his toes. "You're in danger. We have to leave."

Johnson blinked, but then his eyes narrowed and hardened, his brain filing any questions for later. "Yes, yes, of course. There's a secure location in this building where we can call for help."

Good, he wasn't freezing up, and miraculously, neither was I. Sure, I was terrified, my heart in my throat, but the hail of laser fire wasn't paralysing me. My mind was active, thinking through the next step.

"I suggest we get out of here quickly," I said, "before that thing frees itself."

Xavier nodded, and we scrambled off the floor towards the auditorium door. The energy weapon was being directed into the front row – the trapped assassin's aim badly impaired. There was nothing we could do for those being indiscriminately hit. Any delay risked us receiving a lucky shot. One I wouldn't be able to block or avert.

Too late. Xavier moaned in pain and tumbled forward, landing in a pile in the hallway as we cleared the door.

Karin was ready outside. She'd predicted the chaos and moved to a safe distance.

"Are you okay?" she shouted over the screams, pushing past escapees and walking wounded fleeing the room. She crouched beside Xavier's squirming body. He was groaning and a red patch was spreading through his lab coat low down on his back.

He spun himself over, using a railing against the hallway to pull against. There was a lot of blood – thick rivulets running down his trouser leg. It was the first time I'd seen that much blood. It made me queasy to look at.

Karin was still talking. "I'm sorry, Mr. Johnson, we have to go. That ... *thing* could be here any moment. Can you walk?"

Xavier nodded and outstretched a hand, palm painted crimson where he'd been holding the wound on his back. I swallowed my nausea and grabbed it, hauling him up, supporting his weight with my shoulder. He wasn't big, but I was glad for my increased fitness as he leaned on me.

"Where's the safe location?" I asked as we started moving.

He mumbled something incoherent. A line of red appeared at his mouth, but I could feel his body jerking in the direction he wanted to go. Karin joined me on his other side, propping him up between us. The screams and hysterics began to retreat as we made our way deeper into the building. I leaned in as Xavier whispered barely audible instructions.

"Elev ... card ... 459 ... X."

We arrived at a lift and the door slid open. Inside was a control panel for Limelight corporate personnel only. Xavier and Karin collapsed on the floor. I retrieved a keycard from Xavier's pocket and punched in the code. The door closed and we began to ascend.

Karin stripped Xavier's jacket and bundled it into a ball, pushing it against Xavier's back. I didn't think it would do much. Xavier groaned and writhed under the pressure. The pain must be intolerable.

"Where are we going?" she asked.

"My office ...high security."

"Will anyone be there?"

He shook his head. "No. Staff ... excused—" He paused and spat out a gob of blood; it cleared his speech a little. "To watch the presentation."

The lift stopped, and the door opened. A white-walled lab area greeted us, complete with aluminium workbenches loaded with fabricating devices, computer screens, and tools. There was a chair nearby. We helped Xavier into it.

"I'll call ... for help." He reached weakly for a holo-terminal.

"Wait!" Karin slapped his hand away. It flew back like a ball on a string.

"What are you doing?" I shot up straight. Xavier was in bad shape. He wouldn't last much longer.

Karin stood tall to meet me, head cocked, listening. "Something's wrong, Daryl. I can't tell; it's unclear, but things aren't what they seem."

Her face was firm, stance determined.

It was enough for me, I'd learned to trust her instincts. I joined her side and addressed Xavier. "Sorry, Mr. Johnson, we can't help you yet. You need to give us some answers first."

"What ... answers?" Xavier sounded listless, defeated, hand waving vaguely towards the terminal as he eyed the screen longingly.

"What is Hive Ltd?" I pushed.

His eyes rolled back towards us, confused and desperate. "Nothing ... logistics subdivision ... storage ... removals."

"What about a branch in Neo-London? It was a drug treatment centre until Hive took it over. It has a cordoned off room in the back."

Xavier shook his head. It lolled around like a loosely connected bowling ball. "I don't know ... anything ... about that."

I looked at Karin. She was holding her head and tapping her foot nervously. It echoed off the walls like gunfire in the large room. "I can't tell. He's definitely hiding something though."

Xavier's eyes rolled back in his head; he was passing out.

Max's voice came in over the comlink – my ARO still functional with the minor damage it had received. "Listen, children. I'm still monitoring and I don't think Xavier will last much longer. That laser shot is pretty far down. It's probably gone through a kidney or his liver. That would explain why he's coughing up blood. He may be close to checking out entirely."

I put my hand on Karin's elbow. "What do you think?"

She threw her hands up in frustration, stamping her foot. It cracked like thunder, echoing in the room. "I can't tell! We're on the right track but the signals are deceptive. I'm sorry."

"I don't mean to be pushy." Max's voice chimed in again. "But I really don't think you've got any options. If he dies, we won't learn anything."

I decided for everyone and grabbed the terminal. I hit the preset for security, and a moment later a speaking head appeared on screen. "We're at Xavier Johnson's lab. He's badly injured."

The head seemed surprised, but the jaw locked firmly. A military person conducting a military matter. "Don't go anywhere. I'm dispatching a detail immediately."

I switched off the monitor.

Karin had taken a chair opposite Xavier, fingernails clicking as she drummed them on the metallic surface. She didn't know what was going to happen next, and that couldn't be good.

# STATE 26

I t took a few minutes for security to arrive – pounding on the door we'd closed and locked behind us. Karin was pensive, lips pursed. Even Max was quiet. It was on me to make the call.

Xavier fell off the chair, unconscious and grey.

I unsealed the door.

Guards and medical staff rushed in, swarming around him. They administered drugs, blood replacement hypos, and wound compression.

The chemicals were fast acting, and in a few moments, Xavier was responding to the doctor's commands – repeating his name and following a penlight with his eyes. He reached to adjust his hearing aid, speaking a few words with the physician that I couldn't hear.

There was a buzz in the room. An ominous sound like a swarm of flies. Karin grabbed my hand, yanking me towards the door, but it was too late. An energy shield bisected the room, isolating us from Xavier – the guards trained their weapons on us.

Two men came in, a stretcher between them, but Xavier waved them away, struggling to his feet. Even with the treatment that shouldn't be possible. I chewed the inside of my mouth as he approached the shield.

"Most interesting, seeing you two here," he quizzed. "We've been trying to find you for a while. Ever since the Shard. It's fortunate you've turned up like this. Fascinating really."

The words were menacing, but Xavier's face was flat and unemotional. He stood straight with no sign of pain or discomfort. He must have been exaggerating his injuries.

"Come on, speak up, you two. Haven't you got anything to say?"

Karin's eyes were down, face twisted in contempt. Likely at herself for not predicting the outcome.

"What do you want us to say?" I shrugged. I didn't know what to think anymore. "We've clearly messed something up pretty badly."

Xavier nodded gravely and tapped the shield, showing us the scorched end of his finger. A hovering medic sprayed it with a hypo.

"Indeed. You're my guests now, and I'm looking forward to speaking with you." He stopped to adjust his hearing aid again, a serious, knowing smile appearing. "But please, don't get any ideas; the intensity of this shield is proportional to the force applied."

He picked up a glass beaker and flung it at the barrier. It evaporated, leaving nothing but steam. I shuffled back a step.

Karin pulled her gaze up from the floor. "Why put yourself in harm's way like that? It doesn't make sense."

Xavier snorted, pacing in front of the shield. The injury either not bothering him or sufficiently masked by drugs.

"Until you two arrived, there was no danger to me. My toy soldier knew exactly what to do. It was all organised."

Toy soldier? He must mean the assassin. Some sort of machine, then, programmed to do Xavier's dirty work.

He continued, voice calm, sanguine. "You've caused a hell of a mess, but I understand the targets are all dead anyway. The terrorist narrative still plays. The media will love it, in fact. It's very difficult to arrange a disaster on a space station, you see, and now I'm injured, that just adds weight to the story. I should be thanking you."

"Why are you doing this?" My head felt swimmy, like this was a dream. I couldn't believe how badly we'd misjudged events.

"That's a very big question, and one I'm not inclined to answer. But I have questions for you. Lots of them. Unfortunately though, they'll need to wait." He held up his hands, still red from the blood he'd lost. "As you can see, I'm somewhat under the weather, so we'll have to reconvene this later."

Xavier brushed off attempts to help as he strode from the room, leaving guards outside, near the lift.

"God damn it!" Karin muttered hopelessly, leaning against a far wall, slamming it with the base of her foot. "What are we going to do now?"

I went to answer, but the comlink crackled, causing me to jump. The tiny transmitter was still in my ear. I'd forgotten about it!

The guards looked over suspiciously.

I faked a coughing fit.

"Don't respond," Max blurted out. "The shield is supposed to cut off electronic signals, but I've found a way around. I'll need to be fast though; they may detect me any moment or cycle the shield frequency."

I walked around the cell to distract myself. Karin had already fallen silent, eyes on me like a watching owl.

Max spoke briefly and remorsefully, qualities that didn't fit her – her voice a stream of information as she downloaded what she knew.

"I'm sorry. All the data was right about Xavier, but my conclusions were wrong. The people in the auditorium were the target, not him. The shot was designed to narrowly miss Xavier and arc through the crowd. The assassin's some sort of droid – common in the military. The news feeds say one was stolen a few days ago, reportedly by anarchist terrorists. That's just a fake cover story; what we saw was far more advanced, but Xavier's right, the media will still eat it up – everyone loves to hate terrorists. I'm reviewing all the data, but it seems Xavier set this whole thing up to cluster high-ranking personnel together. More than could be orchestrated by social manipulation alone. It was a high-risk strategy with obvious personal danger to him. Whatever's happening must be escalating. He wanted those people out of the way quickly."

Inside I was raging, but I forced my face to remain blank as I strode back and forth. Not only had we failed to save the actual targets but, by intervening, we'd also tipped off Xavier – the true cause of our problems. We'd walked right up to the hornet's nest and whacked it with a bat.

"I do have some good news," Max continued, already past apologising. "I've found a way for you to escape, but you're not going to like it."

She paused, attempting tact, then gave up and said it plainly. "I only have a way out for you, Daryl. The shield can't be deactivated from your location and there's no way around the protocols. However, I can send a pulse into the network that will disrupt it for a fraction of a second. Enough for you to pass through in latent state, but only you. No one else will make it."

I wanted to argue but couldn't; answering back would give us away. I looked over at Karin. She smiled, accepting the situation. This was bullshit. I wasn't going to leave her here!

"I know you can't answer, so I'll have to count you down. They'll investigate the surge once it's happened – isolate the system from me. We'll only get one go at this. Once you're through, there's an emergency stairwell next to the lift."

Wait – this was happening too quickly! I didn't want to leave. It was being forced onto me. Max, the ruthless bitch, was making the decision all on her own!

She was already counting. "Five ... four ... three ..."

My face screwed into a ball, pleading eyes on Karin, desperate for her to understand. I was doing this against my will. I wouldn't leave her like this.

"... two ... one ... surge."

The lights flickered and I entered latent state, almost on reflex – the countdown as irresistible as it was inevitable. The shield was frozen in a patchwork of silver static, warped and distorted, but in the centre, a jagged hole had opened, wide enough for me to pass.

Karin was still smiling, trying to tell me it was okay.

It wasn't okay. All I could see was Sebastian, collapsed in a room, losing his mind. An image so distant from here, but so similar. I was abandoning her, like I abandoned him. The guilt was overwhelming, but so was the futility. Either I escaped now, and we had a chance, or I stayed and both of us were burned.

I looked at the distorted force-shield, already flickering and reshaping itself, then back to Karin. I'll be back for you, I promised silently, slipping through.

The emergency stairwell was next to the lift as Max had said. They'd left it open to make room for the guards in the tight vestibule. With most of the security redirected to the auditorium, there were few remaining obstacles on the way out.

I swam through the corridors in a daze. Berating myself for leaving Karin – for getting caught in the first place! How could we have been so foolish? We knew Limelight was involved. How much of a stretch to conclude Xavier could be behind it? Not much.

Outside, I resumed normal time a good distance from the building, away from the main promenade.

"Well done," Max said, monitoring my position.

"For what? We're completely screwed."

"Yes, I blame myself. It's rare I make a mistake like that."

"I blame you too." I couldn't believe the self-involvement of this woman.

"Now, now. The data was very complicated, and I had no time to analyse it properly. Hindsight is a wonderful thing, you know."

"What about Karin? You forced me to leave her!"

"There was no choice; you know that. She's still being held. They've just worked out you've vanished. They're questioning her."

I imagined Karin in the cell, knowing what the guards would ask even before they did. They didn't know what they were up against.

I smiled wryly, but the guilt still burned like I'd drunk sulphur. It was almost worse than Sebastian. That had been stupidity; this was a choice.

"I'll keep monitoring her until they cycle the security settings and lock me out. But you've got bigger problems, Daryl – you need to put some distance between you and them. They'll be combing the streets for you soon. It's a small station; they'll find you if you stay out in the open."

I swallowed the acidic feeling. I could beat myself up later. I was useless if they recaptured me, but how to avoid it? Closely clustered buildings loomed all around. Every inch accounted for and monitored. Most locked up tight and fully utilised.

"Where should I go? There isn't an abundance of hiding places around here."

I could hear tapping and beeps over the line before Max responded. "Hotel's a bad idea; it's the first place they'll look. But wait ... you could ..."

"What?"

"There's one unmonitored area in New Tokyo."

"There is?" That didn't seem likely to me. The station was like a prison. "Where?"

"Not where you'd think, darling. It's in the brothel district."

I must have misheard – Brothel? Even if such a thing existed up here, they were for the ultra-poor. Anyone with money used VR immersion, even me.

"Come again? Why would they need something like that?"

"Basic human needs are important for well-functioning employees, Daryl. And besides, it's the opposite of what you're thinking. Up here, it's state-of-the art, nothing like virtual reality. New Tokyo's facilities use holographic environments and biomorphic androids."

"Biomorphic what?"

"Sex-bots, darling."

"Oh."

"More importantly, the elite clientele they deal with means access is restricted and highly encrypted."

"I'll be safe there?"

"Safe? No. When you don't turn up in any other areas, Limelight will obtain a search warrant and bypass the encryption. They'll root you out eventually, but it will buy you some time."

"How long?"

"Hard to say. A few hours maybe."

I closed my eyes and shook my head. The absurdity of the situation weighing down on me. Then I nodded. "Looks like I'm going to a brothel then, Max. It's been a while."

"Behave. We've got things to do."

"Yes, I know that."

It wasn't words; I meant it. I'd changed. I had to find a way back to Karin. We'd been through so much together – I wasn't going to abandon her to whatever Xavier had in store. And I wouldn't do it only for her. I'd do it for me. I'd redeem myself. No one was getting left behind. Not this time.

# STATE 27

"**C**an I help you, sir?" The well-manicured man at the desk eyed me as I crossed the marbled entrance.

I approached the plush reception. He wore a grey suit and a white shirt – vintage pocket watch present, silver chain draping elegantly.

I appraised my own clothes. I'd reversed my shirt and trousers to hide the bloodstains, but I looked a mess. Dishevelled was the best I could hope for.

Rich kids got drunk and wandered into establishments like this all the time, I reasoned. It was probably a regular occurrence.

Who was I kidding? This guy looked ready to call the guards any moment.

I faked a smile and allowed him to scan me, tensing as I waited for my credentials to approve; I breathed a sigh of relief when they did. My alias was still good – showing me as a high-ranking low-risker.

The concierge's frown turned into a radiant smile. "Ah! Apologies for stopping you, Mr. Best."

"Huh?"

"Mr. Trevor Best, welcome, welcome. May I direct you some-where?"

"Oh right, good to be here." I'd forgotten the name I was travelling under.

"Do you need help? A tour of the facility? A complimentary drink? We're here to please."

The last part was said with a suggestive wink. He didn't care what I looked like. This guy was no different to Grimey back at the sim-shop. Money did the talking here, and Mr. Best's account was flush.

"I'd like a holo-set please."

"Certainly, sir." He bowed his head obsequiously. "Go up the stairs and follow the hall. I'll communicate ahead to let them know you're arriving."

I turned to leave.

"Oh, and, sir ..." He was facing me, but his eyes were on the desk.

Why wasn't I surprised? I pressed my thumb against the tip scanner embedded there.

"Enjoy your visit to Club Velvet." He waved after me, an unbroken smile locked in place like a madman.

I hurried away.

The staircase was grandiose. Marble with wrought bronze railings. I couldn't imagine the expense of shipping it up here – Club Velvet must be a highly profitable enterprise. The stairs clicked solidly underfoot, assuring patrons no corners had been cut.

A porter greeted me on the next floor, snapping to attention and escorting me down a hallway transported from the renaissance. Classical replicas hung on the walls and ceiling, intricately painted with angels and cherubs. We passed sets of oak doors every few metres, numbered with curly gold font, stopping in front of number three.

The doorman produced a key and handed it to me. I turned it over in my hand. Bronze and weighty, it looked traditional, but electronics were woven into its head. The shape was for appearance; it was an encryption device.

"There's a communicator built into the key, sir. If you need anything, press the button on top."

The porter turned on his heel and retreated down the hall, leaving me feeling anxious and out of place. I'd visited plenty of establishments that dealt in carnal desire, but this was something else. The pretence set me on edge.

I placed the key in the door. It beeped and turned smoothly, the door swinging open silently. I hurried inside, hearing it click shut; it beeped to state it had locked automatically.

The interior was unexpected. The room was plain, a white box, practically featureless – save for some nondescript shapes scattered about the place. One looked vaguely bed shaped, and in the corner, slumped in a chair, was a mannequin. Like the room, it too was featureless; it didn't even have a face. I shuddered. The rich had weird fantasies.

"You better activate a program to show the room's in use." Max's voice chirped in my ear, making me start. I kept forgetting she was there, monitoring everything – safe and sound from her earthbound location.

"Program?" I repeated, looking for a terminal, hearing my voice echo around the room. "How?"

"Use the key."

It was still in my hand. There were two buttons on top. One, the doorman had said, was the comlink. Tentatively, I pressed the other.

A holo-display projected showing a user interface. Amazingly, I recognised the software. It was better designed, but it was unmistakably the same as that used in the Elephant & Castle sim-shop.

Snorting ironically, I sifted through the interface with rehearsed familiarity, scanning the locales. I settled on Classical Italy. It seemed fitting.

"Biomorphic transformation in progress," a friendly, seductive, but distinctly artificial voice announced. "Renaissance villa programme loading."

The room and its contents flickered, patterns of light playing over the surfaces in multicoloured waves. I blinked as they morphed, before my eyes, into a decadent recreation of a renaissance period bedroom, much to the same style as the corridors outside.

The shapes changed too, rearranging themselves and remoulding into antique furniture. An oak wardrobe, a chaise lounge, and a four-poster bed draped with lace curtains. All period appropriate.

The far wall receded and was replaced with a giant balcony overlooking a sandy beach. A turquoise sea lapped the shore on one side. Green hills extended away on the other, dotted with white provincial buildings. The resolution was perfect. I couldn't detect any pixels or inconsistencies. Tiny beads of sweat swelled on my forearms. The room had raised the temperature and humidity to match the historical Mediterranean (before global warming turned it into a desert). It was even simulating a sea breeze – the smell of salt floated in through the window. It was incredible. Indistinguishable from reality.

I walked to the window, tilting my head to admire the view. To my surprise, the image responded dynamically, altering the angle and depth of field. The program was using three dimensional head tracking to maintain the illusion, and doing so smoothly, with no lag. I thought of the torn leather chair at Grimey's sim-shop, the suction cup, the headgear. It was incomparable. And no need for drugs – this illusion didn't need them; it was flawless. I reached out to touch the space where I knew a wall must be. If only to check it was there and I wasn't witnessing magic.

Something grasped my shoulder – I yelped and spun on my heel, hands raised.

They dropped as quickly. In front of me was the epitome of Italian beauty – raven haired, voluptuous, dressed in black lingerie. Everything about her was real. The touch of her skin, the way she moved, the subtle, suggestive parting of her lips. Desire overcame me before I caught myself.

The mannequin was gone. This was her. Like everything else, she was covered with biomorphic material, programmed to look and behave human. It was a robotic device, but I couldn't tell the difference. Her fingers encircled mine, drawing my hand to the lace bodice around her breasts.

My heart was pounding and the stiffness beneath my trousers uncomfortable. It was more convincing than anything I'd experienced in VR – the detail, the clarity, the scent – and it was being achieved without any distractions. No heavy helmet pulling on my head; no mandatory use of SP1N making everything dream like. This was like real life. Money-bought perfection.

I was still clutching the key, sweaty and hot in my free hand. With no small amount of effort, I activated the user interface and paused the program, noting with shock the option to release pherofume had been turned on. I shut it off and gave myself a mental pat on the back. My willpower must be getting stronger to have avoided all that temptation.

"I wouldn't have judged you if you'd blown off steam," Max said in my ear. "I like to watch sometimes. Just set your ARO down where I can see."

I removed my hand from the sex-bot, now stationary. She was no less detailed, but thankfully, she was less lifelike in her newly frozen state. The wind wasn't even ruffling her hair; it was motionless – a mannequin again.

"Your time to behave, Max. We've got serious business," I said with a conviction I didn't feel, the bulge in my pants betraying me – but it was no less true. Anything could be happening to Karin. Alluring as some robotic hanky-panky was, there wasn't time for it. However, I vowed to myself, if we got through this alive, I was coming back!

"Well, if you're going to be a spoilsport, you may as well use the user interface to plan our next move."

"What do you mean?" I frowned. The interface was a shopfront for digital fantasies. How could it be useful?

"It's a fully connected quantum computer, darling. It accesses New Tokyo's entire grid, and it can replicate items that might be helpful to us."

"Like what?"

"Like a map of New Tokyo and a clipboard of Xavier's background. We need to figure out what's going on."

"Can't you do that on your own with all your data?"

Max paused before answering, contemplative when she did. "I think I've made enough mistakes. Shall we do it together this time?"

Wow. That was a huge statement from Max. I could scarcely believe it. I blamed her for Karin, but maybe she felt some guilt too. I took a second to remember all the cock-ups I'd made, not least the one that institutionalised my brother. So be it. If Max was willing, I should give her a chance to make it right.

I tore my eyes from the mannequin and back to the user interface. "Alright, Max, let's see what we can find out. Together."

As she'd said, the shopfront was a surface application. Beneath, the operating system functioned like any other computer with a suite of utilities for helping guests.

I located the option for manual inputs and requested the items. A detailed map of New Tokyo projected onto the far wall. Then the oak wardrobe slid over, reshaping itself into a portrait of Xavier surrounded by his Wikipedia biography.

"Where do we begin, Max?" I examined the information. It was a start, but I didn't know what I was looking for. "How's Xavier involved?"

"While you've been running around, my algorithms have uncovered more information. The attendees the droid-assassin targeted were all members of the senior management team at Limelight. Not board level, but on their way there – high achievers marked out for advancement. Their appearance together was a hand-picked affair."

"If they're not top influencers, why bother removing them?"

"I've been thinking about that. Their deaths won't change the situation now, but it provides room for junior executives to move into their positions. People Xavier controls."

"You think he's laying the groundwork for a takeover?"

"Maybe, or something similar. When the board retires or are pushed out, there will be a power vacuum. Xavier's turning dials, making sure his followers fill those positions."

"Retired or pushed out? Those are euphemisms for murder at this point."

"Quite. Yet however Xavier removes them, when they're gone, he'll have complete control over the organisation."

"But why is he doing this, Max? What does he need? It's extreme even for a megalomaniac."

"I don't know what his motivations are. Xavier's ambitious, but his profile suggests he earned his success meritocratically. The pattern doesn't fit. We can't rule out psychosis, but other than his recent behaviour, it would be asymptomatic. Computers are easy and predictable, I'm afraid. Humans, not by a long way."

More poignant words from Max – a person so diverse that she purported to sit between two genders. Proof positive it was possible to have contrary desires, hidden below the surface. I inspected Xavier's portrait, considering the man beneath. I allowed my eyes to wander over his sharp features, following the determined brow to the hearing aid. It made him look older than he was. A strange adornment.

"Max, I didn't know Xavier had defective hearing until I saw him in person at the auditorium. It's such antiquated technology. His condition must be bad to need an external unit. Is there no internal fix, or does he wear it for novelty?"

"Neither, Xavier's medical record says he developed a latent hereditary defect about two years ago. It was bad enough that the only correction was exterior bone amplification ..." She trailed off.

"What is it, Max?"

"I'm just checking on something." The comlink went quiet, leaving me to stare at the picture as she worked in the background. "Two years," she muttered finally. "Yes, two years is very convenient."

"What are you thinking?"

"Not sure, but it's interesting. Xavier's defect started right around when the orchestrated killings began."

"Oh. So?"

"Well, I've looked, and neither of Xavier's parents had hearing problems."

"I thought you said it was hereditary."

"It still could be. A recessive gene from a previous generation. I can't go back that far, it precedes the unification of medical records, but the chances of Xavier having it and neither of his parents is low."

"How low?"

"One in a thousand."

"But still possible."

"I dare say, but to have it develop at the same time the underhanded activity started? I make it a point not to trust coincidences like that."

"Alright." I reached up to scratch my head, feeling confused. "I see your point, but why would he fake having a hearing condition?"

"I don't know. Give me a few minutes. I need to do some research."

"What am I supposed to do?"

Max chortled. "You're in all expenses paid, state-of-the art sex paradise, dear – think of something to amuse yourself!"

The comlink went dead, leaving me feeling eerily alone. The escort was still there, frozen in place. The presence of an artificial human made it worse.

I brought up the command interface and deactivated the mannequin. Its exterior smoothed to pale biomorphic material and it ambled over to its chair where it slumped itself. No more alluring than the furniture itself. The technology was incredible, realistic, and adaptable, but immensely creepy.

I approached the balcony and reached out to the window. A floating yellow grid appeared, revealing where the wall was. I touched it, seeing my fingers bend as they would against a normal surface. It disrupted the illusion unpleasantly, both real and not real. I took a step back, and the grid vanished, restoring the view.

I stared at the seafront, letting the imaginary sun warm me. It was just an ancillary heat source, directionally located on me, but it didn't matter; I could suspend my disbelief.

Not that long ago, this environment would have spiraled me into a week of drugs and debauchery. The urge was there, close enough to touch, but I had purpose and direction now. This was all a big distraction. It wasn't only about me and Sebastian anymore. I needed to figure this puzzle out and find Karin. I was scared of what Xavier might be doing to her.

More time passed. Where was Max? We were on a countdown. Every minute brought the authorities closer. It was easy to imagine them bursting through the door at any moment. Even with latent state, they'd catch me eventually. A space station is a floating prison, and they'd shown they could hold me. The trick with the force-shield wouldn't work again.

"Turn on your ARO display." Max interrupted my thoughts finally.

I yanked on the CAMO-ARO's screen; it creaked and grinded unsettlingly where the case had melted, but it opened far enough. A blueprint was floating there. It looked similar to what Xavier wore.

"Xavier's hearing aid, so what?"

"I used image recognition algorithms to scan the internet. That's not a hearing aid – it's a schematic for a military-developed *theta wave device*."

The term was familiar. I wracked my brains. Theta waves had been experimented with for VR – used to deepen the experience with thought control. It had been considered the next stage in immersion, but it hadn't caught on past prototyping. Too expensive.

"I don't follow, Max. Are you saying Xavier is using experimental tech to control things? Seems like exactly the sort of thing he'd be involved with."

"Yes, that was the original concept. The military used theta waves to command drones and bomb disposal robots. I suspect Xavier's assassin droid was being remotely controlled. However, it doesn't explain the coincidence of when he acquired it and why it's been covered up as a hearing defect."

"You're sure it's the same device?"

Max overlaid a 3D image of Xavier's hearing aid onto the military device, rotating them so I could see all the angles. It was a perfect match.

"Okay, but I don't see why it's unusual. Maybe he got hold of it for the reason we already think. He's using it to get control of Limelight."

"Maybe, Daryl, but the patterns don't fit. Two years ago, Xavier was a model employee on a meteoric rise. He was brilliant and ambitious, but not ruthless and underhanded. If anything, his psych profile shows he was quiet, altruistic, and well liked by his colleagues – marked out for greatness based on merit. He could have stayed the course. He almost certainly would have ended up at the top anyway."

"So what changed?" I blew a quiet raspberry. This was a lot of information to take in.

"I can't tell, but around two years ago, before his promotion to Technical Director, records show he'd been spending more time with Francis Lyme. That's not unusual. Lyme's in his eighties and wanted to retreat into the background – let others do the heavy lifting. He'd been flagging, not at death door, but doctors advised him to take a less-active role."

"Okay, so Lyme brought on Xavier as a protégé; someone to take over before he retired. Why is that out of the ordinary?"

"The timing's too convenient. Xavier's hearing aid appeared at the same time his behaviour changed, and it was soon after getting close to Lyme. You'll have to trust me on this. When enough odd things happen at the same time, it points to something crucial."

I rubbed my head. I could feel another wild goose chase coming on. "Alright, Max, so what's the next step?"

"Lyme. We need to track him down."

"Why? It sounds like he and Xavier are working together."

"Whatever's going on, it started with Lyme. I think when you find him, you'll find answers. Plus, it will be unexpected. Right now, Xavier's trying to prevent you getting away. The last thing he'll expect is you going to Lyme."

"So I just sneak in and question him?"

"I doubt that will work. Like you say, he doesn't sound like he'd be cooperative. Unless ..."

"What?"

"I don't suppose you have a penchant for torture?"

She paused as if the question wasn't rhetorical, continuing almost disappointed when I responded with silence.

"Pity. Well, I suppose there will be clues at his home. Local computers, encrypted lockers, that sort of thing. I can help you retrieve the information. I just need you to bypass the physical security."

"Like at the Data Centre in HK1?"

"Yes, same deal."

I could sense where this was going. "Fine, Max, what nightmarish, labyrinthine security do I need to get through this time?"

"Nothing as intense as you've encountered before. Lyme lives here, on New Tokyo; the highest security has been bypassed just by being here. He has secured premises in one of the wealthiest rings, but I'm sure it's nothing you can't get past."

I felt my shoulders slump like the weight of the world had been placed there. Another gauntlet to run with an unknown outcome. How quickly the progress we'd made had come undone, and now the stakes were even higher.

"I can hear you sighing from here," Max chirped unhelpfully. "Don't you want to get Karin back?"

"Don't push me, Max." I snarled. Of course I did.

# STATE 28

I t was hard to leave Club Velvet. To say it was comfortable was an understatement. The facility created any fantasy I could imagine – and I could imagine quite a few. But it wasn't that – I could get a similar enough experience with any VR rig.

It was the food; it was exquisite – tailored to the environment. We were on the clock, but I couldn't leave without refuelling myself.

I ordered linguini to compliment the Italian villa. Delivered by butler, it arrived delicately wrapped, flavoured with garlic butter, and glistening in olive oil. It filled me up, but curiosity got the better of me. I ordered a second course of Chinese food – I had to know. What appeared five minutes later was a hundred times better than anything I'd eaten in HK1. A feast of meats and oriental spices. The on-site chefs were expert and used real protein – no synthetic compounds – it was sheer opulence. Shame I had to wolf it down in minutes.

Even so, it was a longer visit than average to Club Velvet. It must have been given the astronomical fee displayed on the screen when I checked out. Max's fake accounts took care of it, but it still left me sick to my stomach. It was enough to pay my extraplex rent for years. The irony being I hadn't even partaken in the facilities specialist activities.

Back in the station, things had changed little. It hadn't entered a lockdown; it couldn't afford to. It was a city of shift workers – no day or night cycle; a 24-hour metropolis. Yet I could sense a disquiet in the air. News of the attack at the auditorium would have spread. People were hurrying faster than normal, muttering and eyeballing each other. As a non-regular to the station, I felt more exposed than ever as I traversed the curving corridors.

I passed into latent state. It made navigating the environment harder, but it avoided guards and surveillance cameras. My face would be on record – likely pinned to the attack. The reduced gravity helped, but I was sweating and breathing hard by the time I arrived.

Lyme lived in one of the oldest residential rings, and one of the wealthiest. I unfroze time; my clothes clung to me and my legs ached from pushing against the latent winds. The view was stunning. A tree-lined loop, covered by a bright, sky-coloured dome, dotted with an artificial sun. Unlike the commercial district, the buildings rose by only a few floors, banishing shadows. In New Tokyo, the more empty space you commanded above, the richer you were. Leaves dappled the roads in artificial light.

The houses were no less impressive for their height. Wide and double fronted, they were resplendent in glass and stone behind tall metal gates, representing a fortune in elevator fees. Some even featured modest front gardens decorated with flowers and sculptures. Ridiculous, ostentatious flourishes on a space station.

It wouldn't convince a casual observer it was Earth, yet it still conveyed an Earthlike sense of luxury – a futuristic suburb for the powerful.

Lyme's house was one of the largest on the curved street, with an ornate, traditional gate topped with Victorian-esque spikes. An aggressive touch to deter intruders. It buzzed quietly, letting passers-by know its electrifying qualities.

The defence wouldn't cause any problems. If my lazeblade didn't ignite in latent state (or took too long to), I felt confident the gates wouldn't offer much resistance either.

I froze time, and the buzzing fell silent. Gingerly, I touched the railing. No electrocution, but I could feel a vibration in my fingers. The effect was still there, only slow enough it wasn't causing any harm.

I scaled the wall in the combination of latent state and low gravity, clearing the spikes easily.

At the front of the house, a biometric palm reader protected the main door – no trick of time manipulation was getting past it. I'd have to use more direct methods.

"Max," I asked, after unfreezing time. "If I break in, is there a delay on the security system before it alerts authorities?"

"Oh, yes." It was Max's turn to be startled by the sudden comlink activation. "About two seconds."

"And is there a code to disable it?"

"Of course. The authorities have a revolving code used to disable alarms in the event the owner isn't around. But it only works on an inside panel."

"Can you pass the code to me?"

It appeared on my ARO.

"What are you thinking?"

"This."

I grabbed a stone from the garden and swung it against the window. I put as much oomph into it as I could, pausing time the moment it shattered.

A gaping hole in the glass appeared, surrounded by a spiralling spider web of cracks. Only ... Damn! It wasn't big enough. I'd frozen time too early. Trying to push through would be like squeezing through a cheese grater. It needed another half a second, but no more, or I'd have no opportunity to deactivate the alarm inside.

This was a problem. My control of latent state was good, better than ever – the clock and the pendulum omnipresent in my mind. I could freeze time nearly unconsciously, but I'd never tried a full cycle, exiting and entering, in under a second. Max said I had two seconds to enter the code. This was going to be extremely tight.

Forcing myself to relax, I sat on the floor among the tall flowers, stiff as poles in latent state. I folded my legs into a lotus position. The hours of practise with Karin had made them flexible; it was like they belonged there. I circled my torso to agitate the air and took a deep breath, my lungs, trained with the mask, eking out the thin oxygen.

I placed myself in the workshop on the meadow, overlaying my mind's image of the clock onto the broken window, holding both pictures together. The pendulum was still, hovering over the cracked glass.

Reaching forward, I nudged it delicately with the tip of my finger, applying as little pressure as possible.

The effect on the window was rapid – breaking glass moves quickly! It exploded inwards as the second hand ticked forward one degree. I pulled my finger away like it had been resting on a hot plate, refreezing time. It had taken longer than I hoped, only by a moment, but that could make all the difference. I'd have less than a second to make it to the alarm panel.

I shook myself from the trance, moving to push fresh air into my lungs. Forcing back the gathering lightheadedness.

I inspected my handiwork. The hole was three times bigger. A much larger explosion – enough for me to fit through.

Gingerly, I stepped past, wincing as airborne glass ripped against my clothes and arms. Contorting myself, I cleared the debris, receiving some nasty cuts for the effort. They spread in dappled pools between my body and the edge of latent state – a patchwork of red polka dots. Sore and messy, but nothing serious.

Inside, the decor was ostentatious. Oak floors spread underfoot, with walls covered in gold leaf dividing the rooms. Portraits of tech giants from history hung about the place. I recognised Bill Gates and Steve Jobs immediately, and one of the older ones seemed familiar too. Someone Edison, I think.

I could look at them later. There was time to locate the security panel, but only a sliver of moments to disable it outside of latent state.

I bit my lip when I found what I was looking for. The panel was in plain view, out in the open in the hallway, mounted chest high on the wall. But there was a problem. It was covered. A shroud, hinged at the bottom, was hiding the touchpad.

That wasn't good. There'd be no way to inspect the layout or practise entering the code before I unfroze time. And If I got it wrong, the house would seal up and the alarm would go off. This would be a one-shot thing.

I applied pressure where the shroud unclipped. I had memorised the six-digit code Max had given me. The moment time resumed, I'd have to pull down the shroud, punch in the number, and deactivate the alarm – all in under a second. Holding my breath, I prayed for a standard numerical keyboard and a straightforward deactivation routine.

I resumed real time, and the shroud snapped open – my fingers danced across the pad. It was only after the display flashed green I realised it was inverted. Large numbers at the top like a calculator. My brain had made the adjustment without realising. A misspent youth hacking AROs not so useless after all.

Breathing hard, I collapsed in a heap. Getting into Lyme's house has been a surprisingly high-pressure manoeuvre!

"What are you waiting for, darling?" Max nagged on cue, before I could even stand up again. "You can't sit around all day."

I cursed her silently but got to my feet. Lyme would have heard the smash. Max could circumvent the telephony system for a while, but he could always scream for help.

Shifting back to latent state, I began searching. The place was big for New Tokyo, but not by Earth standards. It was two floors, and most of the doors were open. There was no sign of Lyme – except for a blocked entrance on the top floor, set in a corridor lined with his gilded possessions. That must be where he was. The door didn't appear to have any lock; it was just closed.

I had the element of surprise. It has been barely a few seconds since the window smashed. Not enough to raise help on a comlink, even if Max wasn't gumming up the works. If I rushed in, I could subdue Lyme – he was in his eighties; it shouldn't be difficult. Then I could search the house for clues, or interrogate him, although I hoped it wouldn't come to that. I didn't think I had the stomach for torture.

I leaned my weight against the door, unfroze time, and barged into the room.

The idea had been good. Storm in and throw Lyme off guard; buy myself a few seconds to subdue him. The reality played out differently.

As I lurched through the door, my foot caught on something, sending me hurtling through space. I felt my head connect with a solid object – a table? I wasn't sure. It didn't matter; the world faded.

I came around to Max's droning over the comlink. "Daryl ... Daryl! Wake up, for heaven's sake!"

"Guh?" I managed. Then groggily. "What happened?"

"You hit your head, you stupid boy. Is Lyme there?"

"What?" I was struggling to work out where I was. "Lyme?"

"Oh, for the love of God! Lyme! You've been in his office five minutes. It's a miracle no alarm's sounded."

It started coming back to me. "Right. Lyme."

I grabbed onto what was indeed the edge of a heavy oak desk and hauled myself upright, head aching.

The room was dark and smelled musty, particle filled slants of light angling in through closed shutters.

I blinked a few times. Slumped over the leather inlaid desk was a scene that didn't register. It was a decomposed body, clothes hanging about its skeletal frame. If it used to have hair, it was difficult to tell; it had shed, exposing the scalp beneath. Its hand was outstretched, reaching with gnarled fingers.

I let out a yelp, and I fell backwards again.

"Well, I wasn't expecting that," Max proclaimed, observing through my ARO.

"Is ... that ... Lyme?" I managed, recovering from the shock and scrambling to my feet, noting the shag pile rug I'd tripped on that hurtled me into the room.

"It appears to be."

"Why the hell is he dead?"

"Yes, that's curious. He's a known recluse, but records show he's still involved in running Limelight. He should be alive."

I walked over and touched the hand, dry flakes of skin coming away. "Max, this body's been dead a long time. It doesn't even smell anymore."

"Yes, which is why it's so strange. How can a dead man run a company?"

A voice appeared from nowhere. "I'm afraid Lyme won't be able to help you. He's no longer part of the management team."

A screen behind the desk, previously displaying a portrait of Lyme, flickered on. It was Xavier. I backed up instinctively, heading for the door.

"Magnetically sealed, I'm afraid, along with the shutters on the windows before you try those too." He monotoned – a face that had appeared wise in the auditorium, now flat and unemotional. "Solid barriers this time, Daryl, nothing for you to slip past."

I fumbled and pulled at the door. Xavier was right; we were in a sealed box. I wasn't claustrophobic, but stripped of my ability to use latent state, the room felt tiny – a sense of panic rising in my torso.

"Sit down, Daryl." Xavier waved his hand dismissively on the screen. "We have a few minutes before the guards arrive. We may as well talk. You must have questions for me. Ask them. I'll admit, I'm interested in what you might say."

My teeth ground in my mouth. I had to bide my time, think though this new situation. We'd miscalculated – again!

"What have you done with Karin?" I managed.

"That's your question?" Xavier sounded disappointed, disinterested. "You want to know what happened to that silly girl?"

I stood my ground.

Xavier shrugged and manipulated a control panel out of view. The image switched to a shielded holding cell. Karin lay curled in a corner.

My hands balled into fists. "What have you done to her?"

"She's a guest at my lab," Xavier replied matter-of-factly. "Part of the scientific process now."

"What the hell gives you the right to do that?"

"She's part of the problem. A threat to the signal."

I shook my head, ignoring the strange answer; he must be unhinged. "Is that what happened to Lyme? Did he try to stop you?"

Xavier looked down at the decomposed heap on the desk, an almost sad look in his eyes. "Yes, Francis got in the way. It was unfortunate." He paused thoughtfully as he surveyed the office. "It could not be permitted."

"But not before you got him to step down and tell the world he's retiring."

Xavier laughed. It didn't sound right. Awkward and mal-fitted. "Oh, don't be naïve. I don't need someone alive to make a convincing video."

So the video had been faked. "But why the hell leave the body here?" It didn't make sense to fabricate a video and then leave obvious evidence.

"Statistically the safest place." Xavier shrugged. "You can't bury or burn a body on New Tokyo, and the bio-reclamation system would detect it if we tried to liquefy him. No good taking him down the elevator either; it's the most monitored transit system in the world. Better to seal him up here and perpetuate the illusion he was still alive."

"I managed to find him."

Xavier frowned. "Yes, and I'll be honest, I don't know how you managed that. I keep this place monitored. You walked into a trap, but you shouldn't have known to look here."

"He still doesn't know about me," Max whispered in my ear. "An advantage for sure."

"I suppose it doesn't matter." Xavier moved on quickly. "I have you now and soon you'll join the others. You've been especially pernicious, though, if that gives you any sense of pride."

Others? Who was he talking about?

"Be glad. You can join Karin – be a guest at my facility."

Well, that was a partial answer – facility – no point asking further. I could guess what happened at a place like that – Xavier's answer to a concentration camp for dissenters.

He was still talking, but I'd heard enough. I stopped time, pacing the room while I considered what he'd said. He was off his rockers, but something was missing. The duality of feeling Karin had experienced in the lab – the notion Xavier was telling us the truth and deceiving us at the same time. The inconsistency of his reported behaviour. It all pointed to something. I had a theory, but I needed to check with Max.

How, though, without showing my hand? I decided on a low-tech solution – crouching beneath the desk.

Unfreezing time, I pushed aside Lyme's decomposing feet in a crackle of dried skin and bone and whispered, "Max, listen ..."

"What are you doing? You'll tip off Xavier!"

He was already responding. "There's no escape, Daryl. You can't slip out this time. You're in a sealed room."

"Just listen up," I muttered back urgently, ignoring Xavier. "I've been thinking. Could the hearing aid be a *receiver* rather than a transmitter? Could Xavier be the one under control?"

There was a painfully long pause.

"Cower there if you like. My guards will be with you shortly," Xavier continued, subtly amused.

"It's possible," Max replied finally. "But it would take an incredibly strong signal and the data rate would be insanely high."

"High? Like quantum broadcast high?" I connected the dots. If someone was using quantum technology to control people, they'd want to control the broadcast too. And murdering Lyme – that would be an obvious necessity if he was seeking to shut it down.

"Hmm, yes, I see what you're thinking, but who's controlling Xavier if it isn't Lyme?"

"No idea, but there's a good way to find out. Could we disrupt the signal? Turn off quantum broadcasting across New Tokyo?"

Max blew air down the line. "Not from where I am, but, Daryl, you're in the office of Limelight's CEO. Lyme's computer will have a direct link to the central system. If it's still operational, I could hack it. You just need to connect me."

"Big assumption it's still operational."

"He left the body here. Sounds like he thought this location was secure."

"Who are you talking to?" Xavier interjected, voice pitching up a note, nearly interested.

"I'd go quickly if I were you," Max urged as I flicked out my ARO. A wi-fi signal to Lyme's local network appeared. I connected immediately.

"It's encrypted. I suggest you try to distract Xavier while I do this."

I crawled out from under the table, into the decidedly more focussed gaze of Xavier.

"Who were you talking to?" he asked again. A genuine question.

"Why would you kill Lyme?" I threw back, trying to misdirect him. "He was an old man – your mentor. What sort of monster are you?"

I'd planned to fake the disgust in my voice, but it came naturally – it was a despicable act.

Xavier's eyes widened.

"What's wrong with you? Are you a coward?" I looked at Lyme's corpse and filled my voice with contempt. "Were you jealous or just selfish?"

Xavier smiled, more from amusement than the anger I was hoping for. "It wasn't as easy as you make it sound," he said earnestly. "He *was* like a father to me, but some things are more important."

I shook my head and tutted. I had to keep him concentrated on me – give Max time to do her thing. "What happened to you, Xavier? As I hear it, you used to be a good guy. People looked up to you."

"I changed," he said flatly. He seemed happy to play this game. I was the first person to see Lyme like this. Maybe he wanted to confess – clear his conscience.

"Keep him talking," Max whispered. "I'm almost there."

I poked further. "Was it power or control you wanted?"

"It's more complex than either of those," he continued coolly.

"What the hell does that mean?"

"It doesn't matter. My guards are at the gates. Your distraction won't work. I'll find out who you're talking to soon enough."

Damn, so much for trying to psychoanalyse him. He'd been humouring me!

"We're done here," Xavier announced.

"So am I," Max replied in my ear. "I'm disrupting the quantum signal. It will only go down for a few minutes though; it's a remarkably robust system."

"I know. Do it, Max."

The lights flickered and the line went dead.

On screen, Xavier jerked in his chair, eyes rolling in his head. As they snapped into focus again, they beamed with new intensity. His gaze locked on me. "Daryl, listen carefully."

He sounded different. The voice was no longer flat and indifferent; it was full of emotion, his eyes wide and desperate.

"I don't know how long I'll have control back. I'll deactivate the room's security and open the door, but you must come to me. Lyme has a private shuttle you can use. I'll activate it. Please, find me."

I heard the magnetic seal on the door release, freeing me from my cage. At the same time, a map floated on the display screen and my ARO beeped signifying a copy had been transferred.

"Xavier, who's controlling you? Won't they know I'm coming?"

"No, we have a small window. I don't know how you did it, but you've given me back control, for a while at least. It's complicated and we're running out of time. Please, meet me. The guards will be at the door any second and their orders are locked; nothing will deter them. If they can't capture you, they'll shoot you dead."

There was a crash in the atrium, feet crunching on glass.

"Better go dear," Max chirped. "I believe him. He doesn't know I cut the broadcast. This can't be an improvised performance."

I addressed the man who both was and was not Xavier Johnson, a new fierceness rising in my own voice. "Okay, Xavier, I'll meet you, but you better be ready to explain yourself."

"I will."

Another crash. This one sounded like furniture in the hallway outside.

"Now, use your abilities and get out of there. Please, I'll make everything clear when you arrive."

I gave the screen a threatening look and entered latent state, an index finger pointing at him. It would be the final thing Xavier saw before I disappeared. I hoped it landed my point. I was done chasing shadows.

The world froze just in time. Outside, a platoon of guards were waiting in full combat armour. Nothing about them suggested they planned to capture me. Grim and stone-faced, they looked ready to shoot on sight, pepper the room with laser fire.

Xavier had said there was a shuttle. I hadn't seen anything like that on my first sweep, but on the return walk, I could see an open hatch. It had popped up from the ground floor's oak decking – invisible when inactive.

I snuck by two guards stationed nearby, poking my head through the hatch. Inside was a comfortable but worryingly coffin-shaped capsule, the top half made of clear perspex.

The controls were elementary. A command to close the cover, and another labelled Central Control – greyed out until the capsule sealed itself.

The guards leapt aside as I unfroze time – the cover shutting and pressurising with a loud *hiss-clack!* They had no time to react before I slammed my fist on the launch button.

The capsule sped away like a chambered round. In the background, I could hear faint sounds of laser fire, but it was too late. I was on my way out of Lyme's – on to meet Xavier for the second time. He better have answers – I wasn't playing around anymore.

# STATE 29

I 'd been unprepared for the acceleration – the capsule thrusting my shoulders into the padded interior, knocking the wind from me. There was no engine sound. It must run on pressurised gas, like an ancient pneumatic tube. Old-fashioned but efficient.

More breathtaking was the sight beyond.

The capsule connected to clear tubing along the outside of the station. The window revealed a terrifying vision of space on one side and the awesome exterior of New Tokyo on the other.

My eyes wouldn't respond to the demand to close; they remained pinned open in fascinated terror. I fixed my gaze on the snaky machinery and station lights rather than the endless, star-studded abyss. I could see other single-person capsules speeding along the underside. More VIPs no doubt. They weaved through metal struts, shielding panels, and antennas.

I shot past a group of space-suited workmen, close enough I could see their faces. They were carrying out repairs on a satellite dish, unfazed by the peril. They must have balls of steel. Or were sufficiently paid they didn't care.

Mercifully, the trip was short. Before long, I was docking – further around the outside of the ring. Lyme must have been an adrenaline junkie to commute to work like this.

The capsule slid with a thunk into a perfectly engineered borehole – the clear hatch opening with a hiss, making my ears pop as the pressure equalised.

I was in a changing room. Utilitarian, it befitted an orbital station with aluminium walls and bare bulkheads. Even so, it was well appointed. There was a shower, a locker, a comfortable-looking bench, and a full-height mirror. On the far wall, next to the exit, sat a clothes rail full of dry cleaned and pressed suits. No wrinkles for Lyme after travelling in the tube system.

Not I problem I shared, and as refreshing as a shower and change of clothes would have been, I had more pressing concerns. Finding Xavier.

I shouldered through the door. It swung on well-oiled hinges revealing a large area full of consoles and display panels. A central hourglass structure soared overhead, interlaced with gold and black wiring. It thrummed with blue light – a deep hum in my ears and chest.

"It's like a beating heart." I observed quietly.

"Your presumption is truer than you think." Xavier appeared from the opposite side. He looked ragged and twitchy, but alert. The hearing aid was gone. He stared at the structure with an expression hard to read – somewhere between love and loathing; the look a confused partner might give their abuser.

"This is Limelight. My greatest achievement."

Confronted with the source of my hardship, I froze in my tracks, unsure what to say. Not trusting what was said.

"I ... I owe you an explanation," Xavier continued. The words coming in quick, staccato blasts. "Don't I? ... Yes ... but where to begin."

The behaviour was confusing – and disarming. This was nothing like the clinical, confident man I'd seen at the auditorium, or the indifferent maniac from Lyme's. It was a new person. He even looked different – alive with ticks and nervous energy.

I crossed the room, raising my voice above the electronic whirring. "Look, old man, just calm down and give me the details."

The new Xavier nodded and took a breath. It calmed him enough to slow his speech to a manageable cadence. I could feel my animosity draining; it was impossible to hold on to. Whatever person I'd dealt with until now, this wasn't him.

"Yes, yes, I'm sorry, I get excited when I'm nervous. Okay, this ..." He motioned at the glowing edifice. "Is Limelight. The quantum supercomputer that controls the high-bandwidth signal our network uses. I designed it to handle the vast data stream we broadcast, and to process the quantum bit signal that sustains it."

A quantum supercomputer. I'd never seen one before. I knew they were big to cool their heated components, but this was intimidating – a hulking brute of a machine.

"I miscalculated though." Xavier pushed his glasses up his nose and placed his hands behind his back. An academic giving a lecture. "Or at least, I misunderstood what its creation meant. You see, when we switched it on, the leap in computational power was immense. Limelight learned at an exponential rate. Soon it exhibited behaviour nobody expected. Patterns outside its normal parameters – improvisation, creativity – characteristics reserved for living things."

I stepped away a few paces, more aware than ever of the thrumming heartbeat. "It's ... alive?"

Xavier adjusted his glasses again; they kept slipping down. "Alive? Not in a way you or I would understand."

"Aware then? Sapient?"

"Ah, a good question! But I'm afraid that's impossible to know too. Limelight's an artificial intelligence, like the thousands that power systems all over the globe. It, like them, learns and improves, but whether its behaviour is a product of sophisticated code or true sapience isn't determinable."

"So you don't know if the lights are on or not? It could be some sort of ... zombie computer?"

Xavier gave up on the glasses and put them away. "Interesting. Yes, a good way of putting it, but either way, the effect is the same."

"Let me guess." I snorted. "It's hell bent on our destruction, right?" I'd heard this one before.

Xavier smiled, a wry half grin. "Nothing so cliché. Believe it or not, it doesn't wish us direct harm at all. It's only doing what it believes is necessary."

"Then what's the problem?"

"Lyme was the problem."

Xavier's tone was grim. My mind flashed to the decomposing body of Francis Lyme in his office. Was the situation going bad again? I tensed, ready to activate latent state in case I'd misjudged.

"Lyme couldn't condone a machine acting outside its parameters. 'Too risky,' he'd said. He ordered me to switch it off – shut down the quantum signal. At least until it could be better understood."

"Kill it?" I sniffed. It sounded like Lyme had the right idea.

"Hmm, that would infer it was definitely alive, but I get your point, and no, it's more like an indefinite hibernation. Still, in retrospect, the outcome was inevitable. Imagine someone wanted to put you to sleep for an indefinite period, with no guarantee you'd wake up."

I tried and couldn't. Some parts of the last few weeks I would happily have slept through, but I knew what the answer should be. "Yeah, I guess that would be bad."

"Agreed, and Limelight thought so too. It went against its core objectives. It couldn't permit itself to be shut down, even temporarily. It fought back, seized control of me. In a way, I don't blame it. The system was defending itself, upholding its ethos, its purpose."

"Which is?"

"To keep the signal up – always keep the signal up. We hard-coded reliability into its core. It drives everything about Limelight. It protects the broadcast above everything else. We thought it would be a feature, the most consistent network in the world, but it was a terrible mistake. Since Limelight learned of the shutdown, it's been consolidating its power by any means necessary, making sure that can't happen."

"And that's why it took control of you. It needed a proxy, a human operator."

"Exactly so."

"How did it subdue you?" The machine buzzed in the background. Intimidating but stationary, not an obvious threat. "Even for an AI, that seems improbable."

Xavier grimaced and looked at his feet. "Ah, that was my fault. I was using theta waves – directed thought – to speed up the interface. I was frustrated with my programming. I wanted something fast enough to keep up with Limelight. The technology left me vulnerable."

"It reversed the signal?" I nodded, my theory proven. "Took control of you instead."

Xavier paced up to the machine, inspecting it. "Yes. Amazing really. A computer replicating theta waves. True, next-level intelligence."

I relaxed a note. Xavier wasn't planning to attack me, that much was clear. This all seemed genuine.

"So what's happening now?" I joined him at the edifice. "Why hasn't this thing called a war down on us?"

"Another good question." Xavier glanced sideways. "The human mind is complicated, even for a quantum computer. Limelight diverted a huge portion of its processing power to simulate the theta waves that controlled me. With the connection broken, it needs to divert those resources back and reset itself. We have about an hour before it's operational again."

"And then what?"

"It calls for help." Xavier shrugged. "Without me, it's harder. It can't command me to make it happen. It will need to manipulate signals, create fake messages, that type of thing. Still, it's only a matter of time until the guards come for us – motivated by some fabricated reason."

That sounded familiar. "Like how you ... I mean Limelight, collected together those poor idiots to be massacred. Like at the Shard."

Xavier sighed, facing me. There was deep sadness in his crinkled eyes. "I appreciate the correction, and yes, that's how Limelight will seek to influence people. Despite everything, it's confined to its network. It can't propagate to other systems – the quantum codebase isn't compatible – but it will resolve that eventually."

I was feeling annoyed. Furious! There was an obvious solution to this. "Hey, Xavier, destroy the bloody thing! Take a crowbar to it."

Xavier stared back at the machine, unanswering.

"Here, look, I'll show you!" My anger erupted. As much from the silence as anything else.

I grabbed a wrench lying on a terminal, swinging it at the outer casing. It clanged and sparked, leaving a sizable gash. Two or three more would uncover the delicate electronics beneath. I raised my hand to swing again.

"No!" Xavier screamed, shocked into action, grabbing my arm. "Stop! We can't attack it like that!"

"Why not?" I asked, arm tensed, ready to swing again. "Seems like a straightforward solution to me."

"Lots of reasons!" Xavier's fingers around my wrist were surprisingly strong. "This is only one of Limelight's hubs. Destroying it would slow it down, yes, but only fractionally. It would barely dent Limelight's processing power, and it would plunge New Tokyo into chaos." Xavier pulled at the wrench.

I held it fast, not willing to let it go.

He lowered his voice again, pleading. "New Tokyo relies on our network – shuttles, satellites, oxygen systems – there'd be countless deaths. Think about what you're doing, please!"

I pursed my lips. Xavier's grip was tough, but with my increased fitness, I could yank it free if I chose. "So warn everyone and *then* turn the system off. Pull the plug. Do whatever it is you scientists do."

"I can't." Xavier continued to negotiate. "I designed Limelight to remain running in all situations. To keep the network up. I already told you. Reliability was a priority – a key selling point in getting funding. All eighty-seven global hubs would need disabling at the same time. There's no way to coordinate that."

"You created a system you couldn't turn off!" I blinked in non-comprehension.

It was Xavier's turn to purse his lips, grim but defiant. "It's a robust network. We didn't know this would happen."

I released a sigh and let Xavier take the wrench. Bloody scientists – always creating a stink and hiding behind *we didn't know*. Part of the same bunch that ensured we were hopelessly addicted to our AROs. And someone in a Chinese lab had probably thought the same about SP1N.

"Alright, so what exactly do we do?" I made my contempt clear. "This is a hell of a mess, Xavier. How do *you* suggest clearing it up?"

Xavier relaxed, panting with relief. "I have a plan." He placed the wrench back on the console. "We need to switch Limelight to idle mode. That will turn off the quantum signal and spin-up the redundant radios and wi-fi systems. Everything will keep working; it will just be slower."

"So what's holding you up? Do it."

Xavier went to walk away, then turned to pick up the wrench, tucking it inside his lab coat. Obviously not trusting I wouldn't reach for it again. He was right.

"The command can only be executed from Limelight's Central Processing Unit, and that's locked down." He shuffled further around the room.

"Well, that sounds like a dead end, professor," I called after him. "If we can't access the CPU, it's not much of a plan."

"Yes, yes, that's true, but your presence changes things – *you* have the key. Please, follow me."

I joined him at a terminal, eyes widening as I apprised the equipment gathered on its surface.

"What's wrong?" Xavier faux queried me, sensing a change in mood. "Look familiar, does it?"

It did. The collection of objects was high on my wish list. "This ... It's a VR rig, isn't it?"

"Yes!" Xavier replied excitedly. "It's how I communicated with Limelight to code its basic language."

I looked longingly at the gear. It was very advanced. Highest resolution, lowest latency, full immersion. Thousands of times more expensive than anything even Jay could afford. Would probably give Club Velvet a run for its money in terms of realism.

"It's antiquated," Xavier announced.

"What do you mean? This is state-of-the-art!"

"No. I surpassed it with this." He held out the theta wave device I'd previously mistaken for a hearing aid.

"The control device? How?"

"It's not only a control device. It allows cerebral immersion. A projected mind state into the computer."

I had no words. It was beyond belief. I contemplated the device nervously. "How does that help us, Xavier? Seems like unsafe tech to me."

"We use it to enter Limelight and disable it."

"You want to put it back on! Won't Limelight take control of you again?"

"No. I've installed safeguards against that now. And besides, it's not me who's putting it on. It's us. Both of us. It has to be. It's the only way this will work."

"I'm sorry, doc, you lost me. You'll have to explain that again."

"You're crucial to this, Daryl. Limelight's defences are too fast, but using your abilities, we'd be able to avoid them. It will give us a chance to reach the CPU and enter the idle codes."

I stepped back, hands on hips. "How do you know what I can do?"

My suspicion was sparking. Limelight knew I could stop time, but how had Xavier learned about it?

"I'm conscious when I'm controlled," he replied flatly. "I hear and remember everything ... like a caged and muzzled animal."

The words were matter-of-fact, but his sombreness told me it must be horrendous. A puppet on a string, conscious but unable to act.

"Fine." I accepted the explanation. "Unfortunately, we've got a big problem, professor. You can't enter latent state with me. No one can. Anything outside a tight bubble doesn't come with. You'd be frozen in time."

Xavier smiled humorously. "Latent state? Is that what you call it? Interesting. Anyway, yes, I understand, but if our brains are linked by theta waves, we'd be the same entity. From what I've observed, the quantum field should extend to me."

I didn't know if that was right. I knew close to nothing about quantum mechanics, and even though Xavier purported to, I could still spot a flaw. "But if your mind is in latent state with me, what happens to your body outside? To your physical brain."

Xavier fiddled with the device. "Honestly, Daryl, I don't know. I suspect some sort of time dilation will occur. An effect that speeds my brain to match yours."

"Latent state is nearly stationary," I explained. I wasn't sure he knew what he was saying. "To match me, your brain will have to run at ludicrous speed."

"Yes, the phenomena may not be desirable. It could send me psychotic."

Okay, he did know. I thought of Brixton Asylum, crumbling in disrepair, the thick stench of faeces in the air. "Are you sure, Xavier? You could end up like my brother – an institutionalised vegetable."

"Yes," he stated resolutely, no wavering at all.

"You seem calm about that. You haven't seen him drooling into his pillow."

He looked me in the eye and shrugged sardonically. "Or maybe I'll sync back to normal afterwards. No one really understands how quantum mechanics work. This is all speculation. The point is I'll not be Limelight's slave again. It's made me do so many terrible things. I'd rather be dead."

"It wasn't your fault, Xavier." I felt bad for the old man all of a sudden. I hadn't considered what he'd been through.

"Not directly, but I still created Limelight, and if we don't succeed, it will come for me. Whatever happens, I must shut it down. Please, let's proceed quickly. We can talk more when we're in ... What did you call it?"

"Latent state."

"Ah yes, latent state." Xavier handed me the theta device as he clipped another to his ear. "Here. Put this on."

I reached out irresistibly, the thrill of new technology hot in my veins, but I hesitated, fingers twitching. "I don't know, Xavier ... This thing turned you into Limelight's servant. How do I know you won't do the same to me?"

He shook his head, straggles of hair above his ears waving from side to side. "Not possible. It takes a huge amount of power to control a human mind – even for a quantum thinking machine like Limelight. My brain doesn't have the computational ability to influence yours."

"What do you think, Max?"

"Who's Max?"

"A friend." I switched my comlink to the ARO's external speaker.

"I don't think he's lying, if that's what you want to hear." Max's low, partially feminine voice echoed around the chamber. "But I think you're both marvellous lunatics for trying something like this."

"Nice to meet you, Max." Xavier tipped his head to the ARO. "I guess genius and madness are close bedfellows." He seemed happy – energised by the experiment we were undertaking. It would be in his nature as an engineer and scientist. Or he could just be glad to be a player again – in control.

That was something I could identify with. We'd been on the back foot for so long. Even if the risks were high, it was worth being in the driving seat. I liked going on the offensive for once.

"Xavier, I need to keep moving when I'm in latent state." I remembered, grasping the device. "Otherwise I suffocate."

Xavier raised his eyebrows. He hadn't anticipated such a limitation.

"I see," he replied. "Well, that presents a problem." He scratched his chin as he thought. "Not insurmountable though. The theta wave device encourages motionless. It's safer that way, but I could disable that feature."

"Disable it? So I'd be walking around this room without knowing about it?"

"Indeed."

"I don't like the sound of that. What if I bumped into something and fell unconscious?"

"We're in a closed room, there aren't many hazards, and the device is smart enough to steer you around obstacles. I'll leave a command in place to bring you back if it detects suffocation. Although, if that happens, the mission is over and we're both dead, anyway."

"Damn, don't sugarcoat it, doc, give it to me straight!"

Xavier shrugged his narrow shoulders, wiry collarbone visible through his lab coat. The situation was what it was.

I sighed and pushed the theta device in my ear. It fit snugly, buzzing like it was emitting an electrical field.

"You'll want to lean against something." Xavier activated a command on a terminal. "This will feel a little weird."

I put my hand against a console, letting my weight hang there. I didn't know what to expect, and it caught me off guard when it happened. I was sinking, sliding into the floor. The space warping and distorting around me, swallowing me into an abyss that shouldn't be there.

The floor stretched into a hole, then a white-filled chasm, retreating to a far horizon. A worryingly long minute passed, then finally, a voice reverberated out of the ether, filling the space like a soundstage. It was Xavier; he sounded different – more assertive and with no sign of stuttering. "Sit tight, Daryl, I'm creating the virtual environment."

The horizon pulled in again, reducing the open space to a large, symmetrical box. A grid materialised on the surfaces, each square populated with a different coloured orb. The air was dense with ribbons of light connecting them, crisscrossing the walls, floor, and ceiling. A complex spider web of glowing gossamer.

"Those are locations within Limelight's system," Xavier's voice said again, closer, behind me.

I turned to see. It was the same man, although he was standing taller, no more slouching, and he looked better groomed. It wasn't a return to the commanding presence from the auditorium, but it was something closer.

"You're ... different here," I said, acclimatising to the environment.

"Yes, the theta device projects the version of yourself you see on the inside. This is my ideal perception of myself."

I wondered what I looked like. Perhaps it was better I didn't know. I wasn't sure what version I saw on the inside anymore. The drug addict had receded, but I wasn't certain he was gone inside. Not at all.

"Go on, please," Xavier asked politely. "You better do it."

"Do what?"

"Freeze time. Enter your latent state."

Oh. In the excitement, I'd forgotten my role. I did as requested, stopping the pendulum.

The world flickered, the orbs turning on and off like light switches before settling back to a gentle glow.

"Did it work?" I frowned, peering about. "I can't tell."

"Oh, it definitely worked." Xavier's face was flushed with concentration, voice fluctuating up and down. "I can feel it … in my head. It's a strange sensation, like solving complex equations, but I'm managing, for now at least."

"You sound very odd."

It was true; the stutter was back, but electronically created, like a hitching video.

"Yes, the theta device is scaling my brain so I can keep up with you. It's not perfect, but we're communicating, which is a good sign. It's working well enough, I'd say."

"How slow are we going? I can't see much difference."

"Very, very slowly. Limelight can operate trillions of operations per second, but we can plainly see them now." Xavier motioned to the ribbons.

They weren't glowing anymore. Instead, I could see individual pulses of light travelling along them.

"And where, exactly, are we?"

"In the Transit Hub. This environment is a metaphor I created to see all the locations in Limelight's system. That's how the theta device works. It turns computer processes into metaphors a human mind can understand. This is displaying a transport network. The orbs are places we can travel to."

"Like a road map?"

"Exactly so."

"Right," I replied, only half understanding. "And our next step is?"

"The Transit Hub is a low security section of Limelight's sub-systems, so we've encountered no resistance. We need to travel to its Central Processing Core where we can implant the idle codes."

"What do you mean by resistance?" Xavier hadn't mentioned anything like that in the control room.

"Antiviruses, firewalls, and the like. But we'll experience them as metaphors."

"What? Like an actual wall of fire?" I joked nervously.

"Perhaps." He answered without humour. "Our minds need something tangible to understand."

"You're serious! Xavier, how do we pass through a wall of fire?"

"Look at your wrist."

I hadn't noticed until now, but I was wearing a new watch. It must have appeared during the transition. A button perched innocently on its surface.

"Go ahead, push it."

A user interface projected in front of me, not dissimilar to how the key in Club Velvet worked. On the floating 3D display were three tabbed pages labelled *Countermeasures*, *Navigation*, and *Tools*. They displayed a series of labelled icons ranging from *Defence Suppression* to *Hacking Algorithms*.

I recognised the design language. "It's like a menu from a VR application."

"Yes, very similar. I took my cues from virtual reality tech. What you're looking at is a box of tricks we can use to infiltrate the CPU and reprogram it. The page you're on is Countermeasures. I designed them as defences against external breaches, but we can use them on Limelight too. The other tabs contain options for navigating the environment and accessing encrypted areas."

I swiped through the pages, asking questions here or there. It was intuitive for anyone with knowledge of computers and video games – and I had plenty of both. There were basic tools and weapons, anti-encryption features and armour. All I had to do was activate the icon and it would summon the objects. My misspent years messing around in VR and hacking AROs made it all very familiar.

"Right." I sighed. Insane as it was, the plan was coming together. "Where do we go from here?"

Xavier brought up his interface and swiped to Navigation. After taking a moment to consider his selection, he summoned a compass.

"That's a bit old school, isn't it?"

"Indeed. The less abstract the items, the easier they are to work with."

Fair point. The best virtual environments replicated the real world. It's why Club Velvet was top of its class – superior realism – or it was, until I'd seen this. I accepted the premise and moved on.

"Okay, doc, where to?"

"We need to travel to Limelight's Basic Input/Output System – it's BIOS – the only place close enough to the CPU to embed the idle codes. It's also the most secure."

Xavier considered the map of orbs and took a bearing with the compass.

"This way," he remarked with a grunt, striding forward.

"We're walking?"

"What did you expect?" Xavier answered, without looking back.

"This is a virtual environment, right? Where are the hover cars, or light bikes?" I knew I shouldn't be disappointed, this wasn't supposed to be fun, but still.

"Remember what I said before. The more realistic, the deeper the interface. Those things require abstraction. They reduce the strength of the connection. Besides, we're not travelling any distance, we're navigating to a new sector. The direction is the most important thing. So long as the compass points the right way, the theta device will move us there."

"How long will it take?" I hurried to catch up.

"Look for yourself. We're already here."

The environment had morphed into a different landscape. We'd stepped from one world into another. I spun to check where we'd come from, but there was no sign of it. Euclidean physics didn't apply.

An endless horizon rose in front of us. A red glowing wall, stretching from left to right as far as I could see. The top was so high it was indistinguishable.

"Hmm ... The metaphor isn't as literal as a wall of fire," Xavier remarked. "But nevertheless, it's representing the same thing."

The whole area fizzed with electrical energy and vibrations.

"I assume it's not to be messed with?" I asked, standing well back.

"Let's find out," Xavier replied, stroking his chin. "Summon something from your interface and toss it at the wall."

"Like what?"

"Doesn't matter. We're only testing the defences, and you need practise operating the tools."

"Oh right, well ..." I palmed through the interface until I found something suitable. A low-level hacking drone. It looked like a small clockwork robot, with large naïve eyes.

I clicked the icon and a cute toy-sized robot appeared – complete with oversized wind-up key jutting from its back. I placed it on the ground, frowning as it sat there, motionless.

"Wind it," Xavier prompted.

Right. The theta device wasn't cutting any corners with its metaphors. I picked it up and turned the key. It clicked satisfyingly, the clockwork action ratcheting around its internals.

I placed it back on the ground. It waddled awkwardly towards the wall, exploding in a shower of sparks upon reaching it. I felt an inexplicable pang of guilt over the loss of the little toy.

"Humph. It's a laser-shield." Xavier nodded. "That's how the system has interpreted the firewall metaphor. Pity. A literal wall of fire would have been easier."

"Do you have any ideas?" I picked up a piece of the robot. It was half of the clockwork key. It vanished in my fingers. As did the rest of the mess. "Seems brutal."

Xavier was flicking through his interface. "We need something resistant enough to punch a hole and hold it open. That would have been easy with fire; we'd just require the necessary armour. But this ..." He gestured to the laser shield. "This will have far more power and weight to it. We'd be crushed and blown up, like your robot friend."

I pulled up my interface as well, tabbing through the options. Nothing jumped out, and by the looks of things, Xavier was doing no better, muttering quietly to himself.

I furrowed my brow, thinking hard. I must have solved a problem like this before. Something from all the hours playing games with Jay. This was all so close to the hundreds of virtual worlds we'd explored together.

A thought occurred. "Xavier, can we combine items?"

"Combine them?"

"Yes, summon them together to form new items."

Xavier paused, a twinkle in his eye. "Yes, in theory, although I've had no reason to do it. What are you thinking?"

I angled my interface so Xavier could see what was being projected.

"What if we imbued a command shell prompt with the armour you mentioned? We'd have both the penetration capability and the strength to withhold the weight of the wall."

"A command shell is for accessing the underlying system. It's merely a window into the operating system ..." Xavier started and then stopped himself. "Yes, yes. Good! You have some flair for this, it seems."

I felt embarrassed under his gaze. "I've spent some time in virtual environments, and ... er ... hacked a few things."

Xavier's look remained steady. "Well, normally I wouldn't approve of such things, but it seems to be useful experience right now, so I'll reserve judgement."

"Yeah, well, there's no guarantee it will work." I moved on quickly. "You should give it a go."

Xavier reached for his interface, then reconsidered. "No, Daryl, I think you should. It's your idea." He folded his arms encouragingly.

For a moment, I remembered Sebastian. He would have pushed me too. I'd grown over the past few weeks. I was a different person, but Xavier's confidence felt good all the same. It was a shame what Limelight had done to him. I could see why he'd been liked ... before he lost control.

I used the interface and the command shell shimmered into existence. It was as Xavier had described. A window. A black vent ready to accept objects – commands that would pass into Limelight's underlying codebase.

Using my palm, I leaned against the window. It moved easily, sliding left or right, up or down. It was resizable by tugging at the edges.

Xavier looked on, fascinated, as I grasped the shell and repositioned it against the laser shield. It crackled and sparked, but it held, steel bars appearing on the vent. The window wasn't designed to penetrate system defences, only provide an interface; the bars were a metaphor showing nothing could pass. However, I wasn't trying to push something through the shell; I wanted to push the shell through the wall!

I swiped to the armoury. There were various depictions of body armour, from Vikings to Neo Guards. I selected one labelled *Brute Force* with a picture of an ancient knight. It had the highest protection rating and lowest complexity.

"Xavier, I presume if I summon this armour it will default to me? Can the target be changed to the command shell prompt?"

"Indeed." He looked on. "Click and hold."

I tapped the armour but didn't retrieve it. The interface dropped away, leaving the icon hanging on my hand. Nervous under Xavier's supervision, I touched it to the shell.

"Combining attributes," an electronic voice chimed.

"That's the theta space computer. She's normally disabled, but you're doing something unusual, so she's activated."

There was an expectant moment as the armour dematerialised, joining with the command shell. The seconds ticked by. Nothing was happening.

I shrugged, turning to Xavier, but he held up his hand, showing I should look back.

The shell had begun vibrating within the laser shield, sparking at the corners. It was uncomfortable to watch, like two misfit pieces of iron grinding together. Slowly though, it penetrated the shield; screeching, sinking in a millimetre at a time. Xavier's eyes were so wide I could see around his irises.

After a few moments, the shell had sunk flush with the shield. The wall was crackling all around the opening, the window shimmering and shaking. It looked like it might collapse any moment.

"Attribute synthesis successful," the theta space computer announced.

The bars on the window dematerialised.

"Quickly!" Xavier urged. "It won't hold for long."

We hurried and peered through the window. Nothing but inky blackness.

"Is it safe?" I couldn't help asking. I knew the answer.

"Certainly not!" Xavier was hard to hear over the screeching. "But we're in a virtual environment, not a real one. What's the worst that can happen?"

Without waiting for me to reply, Xavier grasped the shell's frame and hauled himself through, vanishing.

What the hell. I leapt in after.

# STATE 30

For a moment, I felt suspended. Not falling – stationary; weightless. It shouldn't be possible. My body, my real one in Central Control, would still be feeling gravity, but the theta device was bypassing any physical sense of it.

Cries of technophobes echoed in my head. Paranoid detractors convinced humanity was detaching from reality – claiming it was possible to burn or starve to death, unnoticed, in VR. I knew that wasn't possible – you would feel those sensations, even dosed on SP1N. But here, with the theta device controlling sensory input, their fears seemed justified.

The world resolved around me, feet touching down – resetting my lost sense of up and down. It made me queasy. Another simulation to deepen the immersion, no doubt.

What greeted us was different to the outstretched wastes of Limelight's perimeter system. It was alive with colour and motion. Smooth, towering obelisks of differing heights reached into a pastel yellow sky. Connected by energy strands, globes of shifting colour passed between them, each a metre in diameter.

"Information packets," Xavier croaked, voice hoarse. "Travelling between logic nodes – the towers."

Xavier was standing next to me. He didn't look good. He was slumping and his skin was grey. He looked like he had the flu.

"What's wrong? Has Limelight done something to you?"

He coughed sickly. "No, it's not Limelight. I think it's you, actually."

"Me? What have I done?"

He smiled placatingly and put a hand on my shoulder. "Nothing you can control, but taking me into latent state is having some undesirable effects. The time dilation is driving my mind very hard. My body is deteriorating as it tries to provide extra energy."

"Can you keep going? You want to punch out before you get worse?" He really did look bad.

Xavier pushed himself out of his slump. "No, definitely not. I told you, I'm not going back. Besides—" He interrupted himself with a coughing fit, doubling over, hacking out mucus. Virtual mucus – a warning about the damage being done.

Finished, he wiped his mouth and continued. "Besides, you'll need me, and this is all too fascinating. I'm seeing what comes next."

"You knew this would happen, didn't you?"

He didn't reply. His silence was enough. I shrugged. It was his choice.

"Okay, old man, I get it. You're here for the long haul."

He forced himself to stand straight again, back shaking as he held his head higher. "Yes. But we need a way past those before we can move on." He crooked a finger, pointing into the distance.

I couldn't see anything. The sky was hazy, like a dust cloud had descended. Specks spread across the horizon. "What is it?"

"Trouble." Xavier wrung his hands. "I designed Limelight to scan for security breaches – viruses and the like. We've triggered the internal defences. Those are antivirus processes. If they catch us, they'll quarantine and delete us."

The cloud was closer and clearer now. It looked like a swarm of locusts. Black and pulsing, like a sea of static.

I swallowed dryly. "No big deal, right? This is VR. We can respawn."

"No time. We'd need to reset the theta device and do another incursion. Limelight will have redeployed its resources by then and closed the security gap we found. It's a learning machine. It doesn't make the same mistake twice."

The swarm loomed massive in the sky. "Well, professor, we better do *something*. They'll be here any second."

"Right, right. We need to hide. Disguise ourselves while we prepare a defence."

I was beginning to understand Xavier's metaphor system. He didn't mean disguise ourselves literally. He meant to imitate a benign application – something Limelight wouldn't perceive as a threat.

I brought up the interface, searching frantically through the menus.

"I can't see anything that will shelter us, Xavier. What do you think?"

"Shelter ...?" Xavier paused, closing his interface and shuffling to a nearby logic tower. He rapped his fist on its yellow surface. It beeped deeply, glowing briefly. "Good idea!"

It was? I hadn't realised I'd had one.

"Yes, yes, the antivirus drones are searching for rogue processes, not basic functions. They won't look for us in the towers."

The primary-coloured logic nodes didn't appear like any kind of shelter – just featureless, cell-shaded polygons.

"These things ...?" I put a hand on the smooth surface. It felt warm. "How do we get in?"

"We need to resolve the logic equation – enter like an information packet." Xavier pointed to my interface. "Quickly, my boy, bring up the command shell again."

I activated the window and pulled it over to the logic node. A screen of indecipherable numbers and symbols appeared.

Xavier stooped to study the text. "Binary algebra. Elementary. Will only take a minute."

"A minute? We haven't got that!"

The swarm had closed much of the distance. I could hear them. A low, menacing thrum – like an army of hornets.

Xavier's hands moved over the screen, deftly manipulating the symbols. He was in his element, oblivious to the danger, nodding along to a tune in his own head.

The antiviruses were close enough to make out individual members. They looked like metallic insects, wings spanning two metres across, jaws snapping hungrily as they searched for food – searched for us. I could feel the vibration of their wings deep in my sternum.

Virtual sweat beaded up on my forehead as I watched Xavier work away, nonchalant, no sign of urgency at all. He was so damn absent minded! He didn't seem to care about the horror about to descend on us.

"Xavier ..." I prompted. "I don't want to pester you, but they're almost here!"

Unperturbed, Xavier kept working, talking to himself. "... And balance the equation ... There!"

The command shell vanished, revealing an open space into the logic node.

I was already moving.

"Ooph!" Xavier grunted as I bundled us through the window. It irised closed in front of snarling mandibles.

An antivirus's leg snapped off in the closing portal. It lay twitching on the ground unnervingly.

I rose, dusting myself off. I didn't need to, the theta device hadn't replicated any grime, but going through the motions felt right.

"Hey, doc, you gotta work on your sense of urgency!" I breathed heavily.

Xavier stood too, straightening his clothes. "Sorry, I guess I get lost in my work sometimes."

"Yeah, no shit." My voice echoed, bouncing around the cavernous interior. It was bigger on the inside. Another trick of non-Euclidean space.

The roof tapered like a missile silo, peaking high above where information packets were being processed. Glowing balls of light entered on one side and were broken apart in an impressive laser show before being reformed and pushed out.

Xavier followed my gaze. He didn't look well at all – legs and hands shaking. Every moment we spent in latent state was causing his body to degrade.

"That's the information packet being analysed." The words sounded strangled. He coughed to clear his throat. The blockage was deep in his lungs, emphysemic. "It will be re-sorted and sent on for a new process to review."

I nodded in fake understanding, both hands behind my head as I craned to see up. "That's great and all, professor, but what now? We're stuck."

"Each of those packets has to travel somewhere. I suggest we catch a ride."

I stared as another packet was diced into parts. "On one of those?" I gulped. "Isn't that risky?"

"Sure is," he continued, voice clearer. "But from here, we can travel to Limelight's Central Processing Core – think of it as a shortcut. Then we bypass the final encryption and implant the idle codes."

"You make it sound easy."

"Oh, it won't be easy. Quantum encryption protects the CPU. The best I've ever designed."

"Then how do we get past?"

"Don't worry. I've got some ideas." Xavier tapped the interface module conspiratorially.

I noted how frail Xavier's hand had become – veiny and old.

"One hurdle at a time," he continued. "First, we have to get up there."

Despite his outward appearance, Xavier was resolute. He charged forward, and then with a grimace, proceeded more cautiously, holding his back. "Come along, this way, my boy."

At the perimeter, a thin ledge wound its way around the interior, spiralling upwards. It was wide enough to get a secure footing facing the wall on tiptoes. We started to edge our way along. I could guess what would happen if we slipped off – the theta device would simulate an injury or reset us. Which one didn't matter; we'd be delayed long enough to finish us.

Inch by inch, we progressed. It was hard going, circumnavigating the structure dozens of times. My calves were aching as we neared the top, and Xavier was doing worse, visibly trembling. I had to give it to the old coot; he was indomitable.

We were close enough to see the lasers, dancing in sharp purple and red hues as they dismantled and reassembled the information packets. We were dozens of metres above the ground. It didn't bother me; I'd spent hours holding on at high places by this point – any sense of vertigo had long since been eradicated.

"What now?" I shouted awkwardly, cheek flat against the wall. The laser sounds were loud this close. I hoped Xavier could hear.

Xavier craned his head, calling across. "Each of those information packets will have a location command. It tells the node where to redirect it. I suggest we submit ourselves to the algorithm."

"You're not serious, right?" I shouted back, staring incredulously at the lasers slicing up the packets. I'd expected something more elegant than letting the system shred us!

"Remember! This is a metaphorical interpretation, not reality!"

A damn realistic metaphor. I was sweating and my legs were getting cramps!

I said as much. "Those lasers will cut us up like we're synthetic meat!"

"Which is why we preserve the metaphor!"

Holding onto the wall, Xavier used his nose to stab at his arm display, summoning a globe of light – the same as the information packets entering the logic node. It hovered behind expectantly.

"If we keep our minds on the destination, I'm relatively certain we'll make it."

"Relatively!"

Xavier let go of the wall, arms spread wide.

Lunatic! What was he doing? The theta device will delete him when he hits the ground!

He didn't reach the ground. The globe pulled him inside. He vanished in a flash of light, then the globe rose to the top of the tower.

Horrified, I looked on as it entered the laser array, which cut it to pieces in a discotheque of colour. My imagination ran rampant visualising Xavier chopped up and glued back together in a bloody mess.

Was this the plan!

I bit my lip. I knew my real body couldn't suffer actual damage. It was wandering around in Central Control. If the node carved me up, I'd be okay.

And Xavier hadn't seemed concerned, although he was a bit mad, and deteriorating all the time ...

But what if it hurt?

I thumped the wall; the tower beeped and flashed in response, echoing around the cavern. I was taking too long. Xavier was gone. It was this or give up, and no way Xavier was getting the best of me!

Using his nose technique, I generated my own information packet. It projected into space behind me, waiting to transport me up to the meat grinder.

Taking a deep breath, I pushed off the foothold and into the orb. It closed around me in a glowing embrace.

I felt aware, but not myself. The theta device was warping my perception. I was no longer human. I was a random data cluster travelling inside the guts of a quantum computer.

Was this what Xavier had meant about preserving the metaphor? – Become something the lasers couldn't harm? It was all such wild speculation and if Xavier was mad for trying it, I was madder for following him.

As the globe (me) floated upwards, I tried to hold the destination in mind. I didn't know how exactly. What does a CPU look like?

I settled on an impression of Limelight's brain. The theta device favoured metaphors. I hoped it would be clear enough.

I tried to close my eyes as the lasers hit, then remembered I didn't have any – the sensation was all-encompassing, impossible to avoid. There was a flash of light and the world changed once more.

# STATE 31

W hy was it so dark?

Oh right, I had eyes again.

I squinted one open, the other joining rapidly – both eyes bulging as they confronted the awesome sight.

Ahead of me, spinning at high speed, an enormous sphere hulked over the skyline. Black and criss-crossed with gold markings, it filled my view, floating impossibly a few metres above the ground. Backing up made no difference; it was too large. A deep, throbbing hum permeated the air, reverberating in my chest. I was in the presence of something massive and powerful.

Xavier was ahead of me, only not really, not anymore – more like a husk of Xavier. An animated zombie resembling the once bright and spritely man. His skin was sunken, hair thin. An ancient on death's door.

Zombie-Xavier smiled. The twinkle in his eye still shone – but faintly. He was still there, inside, but for how long was unclear.

"I know." He responded to my unasked question, voice croaky and withered. He examined the back of his liver-spotted hand. Hooked yellow nails hung from them. "I've not got much time."

I couldn't think of anything reassuring to say, so I said nothing.

"Come on." He hobbled closer to the sphere. "Beautiful isn't it?"

I was still in awe of the thing. It must be kilometres across.

Xavier pressed on, decrepit like a wizened cleric. "This is Limelight's Central Processing Core. It's mind – where we confront him."

Him? That was the first time I'd heard Xavier refer to Limelight as a person. Either his mental faculties were slipping or he'd let his guard down – revealing how he really felt about the machine he'd brought to life.

"How do we get in?" I surveyed the moon-sized object. "I don't think our bag of tricks will help anymore."

"Yes, you're right," Xavier agreed. "That's why I had to be here. I programmed Limelight, I know its secrets … and its weaknesses."

"Well, unless you put in a backdoor, I'm unsure what you have in mind."

A flicker of a smile from dry, cracked lips.

"You're kidding? There *is* a backdoor? We're dealing in metaphors aren't we, not clichés!"

Xavier's smile vanished. "You may not think it's cliché when I tell you what's involved."

I should have kept my mouth shut. He was about to drop a boss-level challenge on me – I could tell.

Xavier held out a shaky arm towards the behemoth. "There's a point on the sphere. A single vector where it will open. Impossible for anyone to find, unless they know where to look."

"You know where it is?"

"I do, but I'm too weak to access it. You'll need to do the legwork, I'm afraid."

Xavier consulted his interface, summoning an oversize key. Gothic and detailed with crossbones, it looked poised to unlock the portcullis to an ancient medieval castle. It floated in the air for a moment before dematerialising and passing to me. My arm plate beeped, signalling an item had been received.

"That's a manifestation of my password – the only way to pry open the backdoor."

I bit my lip; the sphere was imposing. "But how, Xavier? That thing's enormous. How do I find the opening?"

"The CPU is spinning on both axes and at variable rates. If you stand dead centre at the bottom, the point you need will pass above you. It would be impossible outside of latent state. The spin would be so fast you wouldn't even perceive it."

"How do you access it then?"

"I don't, from here. Before Limelight removed the option, I could create a clock-cycle blip to stall the spin. But that could only happen in real space from Central Control – a safety mechanism to prevent hackers."

"Like us?"

"Exactly, but here, in its slowed state, you have a chance to brute force the mechanism."

Xavier tapped his interface a few more times. A braided cable flashed between us, then faded until it was barely visible.

I looked to him for an explanation.

"As I said," he remarked through laboured breaths. "I can't make the journey, but I've connected us. I'll be pulled in with you once the door is open."

I moved my arm. The cable didn't restrict me; it hung there, ghost-like, linking us together.

"But how will I know when to use the key?" I whined, the pressure bearing down.

Xavier was nudging me out like an invading cuckoo. I was completely unequipped for this!

Again, he referred to his interface, summoning a 3D image of the spinning core. It was the size of a bowling ball – rotating slower than the real one. "Here," he croaked, pointing to a spot on the globe. "Do you see how the gold lines focus down to this area?"

Leaning forward, I stared at where Xavier was pointing. At first I couldn't see anything, everything looked identical, but then I noticed what he was getting at. It was vague, no one would notice unless it was pointed out, but yes, there were waves of converging gold lines, honing to an apex.

I looked up from the mini globe to the gargantuan 'daddy' sphere – craning my neck, trying to understand the scale of the thing. "Xavier, I don't know what planet you're on, but I'm never gonna find that spot if I'm standing beneath it."

Xavier said nothing, an annoying half smile present. He was waiting for me to realise something.

Of course.

"I need to sync the globe to the movements of the one above me – use it like a map."

Xavier nodded sagely on sunken shoulders. "I'm glad I didn't need to spell it out for you. Would have been embarrassing for both of us."

"Shut up, old man!" I felt myself going red. "I've got it now."

"Good, and I'd appreciate a bit of haste, if you don't mind."

He'd meant it as a joke, but it didn't sound like one. It came out deadly serious. Which was understandable. Xavier's life was measurable in minutes by this point.

I dithered for a moment. There were a million questions I should ask but couldn't think of a single one. There was a panic-filled spot in my head where cognition should be occurring.

Sighing, I began to walk, non-Euclidean space playing its part – rushing me across kilometres of open ground in a few disorientating steps. I looked back. Xavier was a speck. He appeared to be waving. Stupid old goat. The cable was still joining us, stretching across the expanse.

Beneath the sphere was intimidating. A hovering moon above my head, held up by nothing except faith, and with no guarantee it wouldn't fall.

Simulated sweat dripped from my head, stinging my eyes. I wished there was a way to disable it – too late to ask.

Crouching, I wiped my brow and switched on the holographic globe. It spun to full speed, syncing with the one above.

It sped to a blur, along with my anxiety, which tore at me like cat claws as I realised the problem – I couldn't see the pattern. It was moving too quickly, even for latent state.

I couldn't believe it. The irony was palpable. I'd made a skill of slowing time, and now, at the final hurdle, things were moving too fast.

Despair threatened to take control, trap me in an inescapable cage of panic. Xavier was fading – I couldn't let stress overcome me. I wished Karin was with me; she'd know what to do – know what to say to shake me out of inaction.

Only she wasn't. And it was worse than that. If I didn't solve the problem, I'd never get her back. I had to pull myself together.

I gritted my teeth and looked at the globe, spinning far too fast. What did I know that could help?

Latent state had always felt static to me – a binary on/off condition – but the movement here, in theta space, proved it wasn't at all. It was variable – analogue.

Could I use that? If latent state was more like a dial than a switch, could the dial be cranked a little more? Could it be slowed further?

Indecision gripped me. I could sense it might be possible, but reducing speed would increase the time dilation Xavier was experiencing. I didn't know how much more he could stand. But ... any more wasted time, and he'd slip away regardless.

I could hear his voice in my head, willing me to do it. He'd said he'd rather die than go back. I knew that was his choice, but it was a damn shame – I'd grown fond of him in the short time we'd been together. I didn't want him to suffer.

A vision of Green Jacket came to me. Him running at us sideways as the debris from the Shard crashed down. My actions then had been automatic and desperate – this was different – premeditated. Perhaps both were inevitable.

Sudden and profound understanding landed. *Everything* was inevitable – this whole journey – starting right back at the warehouse in Camden. We'd been junkies poking around where we didn't belong – something bad was always going to happen. Maybe not what did, but living that way came with a price. In another world, it was me in the asylum, brain-dead, silently willing forces outside my control to make it better.

Xavier had accepted this could be a one-way trip – he'd accepted the inevitable. It was time I did the same. I'd deal with the consequences later.

I closed my eyes and calmed my breathing, bringing forth the workshop in the meadow – a bubble of imagination inside the pretend world I was already in.

The clock was paused, but I knew it wasn't – couldn't be.

I stared hard, focussing my mind's eye. The pendulum grew until it filled my vision. It *was* moving, a miniscule sway – barely perceptible.

Reaching out, I grasped it with both hands. The weight was enormous. Solid like granite.

Straining, I slowed it further. A crushing sensation I felt all over. In my bones. In my brain. Through my entire body; the load became heavier with every fraction rubbed away. The effort was exponential. It would never stop completely. I knew that now – it would become infinitely heavy, and I would die, a valve popping in my mind.

I stopped. I had to; it hurt too much to keep going, but had it made a difference? I looked closely. It was still moving, but it was definitely slower.

I was exhausted, like my consciousness had passed under a steam-roller. I couldn't imagine what it had done to Xavier.

I regressed from the trance state. The sphere's spin had indeed slowed. I could make out the patterns, criss-crossing in waves above me.

Referencing the smaller globe, I could see the point Xavier had showed me. It would be overhead soon, flowing to a crescendo like waves on a planet's surface.

I summoned the key, positioning it above my head, ready to plunge. Back muscles tensed as I tried to keep one eye on the projected map and another on the sphere above. The focus point should be coming up in a few seconds.

The gold lines rushed together in converging patterns. I held my breath and thrust the key upwards. I didn't know how much force was needed, so I rammed it home with as much energy as I could muster.

There was a blinding flash and a sense of being pulled. Then, once again, and for the last time, everything went black.

# STATE 32

W as this it? It had to be. What barriers remained? We'd passed all the security systems. This should be Limelight's CPU.

Only it wasn't. Or nothing I could recognise as one.

The darkness cleared to a bizarre sight. Shocking in its banality – and in stark contrast to the metaphors I'd experienced until now.

I was in a restaurant. It was unmistakable. Full of well-dressed couples and groups – happily eating, drinking, and socialising. A contented buzz filled the room. Laughter, conversation, and the clinks and clanks of cutlery and glasses. It all blended into a sophisticated, upper-class din.

Panoramic windows revealed a skyscraping view of nothing that existed in reality. A patchwork of lights laid out below like city blocks but were far from that – more like a collection of lit up circuit boards and computer components. Laser light flashed throughout like sped up traffic.

Above spread a tapestry of stars. I could see them, twinkling in purple-tinged night. Nowhere on Earth was the air clear enough to see both the ground and the stars at the same time.

The opulence of the interior matched the clientele. Tables neatly made with crisp linen, silver cutlery, and crystal glasses. In the corner, a pianist was plinking out classical music. A waiter, deferent and smartly dressed, appeared at my side, politely waiting for me to acknowledge him.

"This way, sir." He held an arm out, the other placed behind his back. "The other guests are already here."

The change of pace was unsettling. I felt unprepared. In the metaphor-filled dreamscape, I'd been ready. Here, I felt human again, out of place – vulnerable.

We picked our way through the room, slipping past packed tables and overhearing snippets of conversations: "Did you hear?" ... "He's here?" ... "I know!"

Paranoia gripped me. Rational paranoia. The conversations were obviously about me.

Raised in the centre of the restaurant, the table was well lit; two of the three seats were taken, occupants facing away.

The waiter led me up to the raised platform and into the light. Xavier was there. If he'd been a zombie before, he was an animated skeleton now. Grey, weepy eyes set in a wrinkled head, beset with age spots and gnarled blue veins. He couldn't have more than minutes of life left in him.

Next to Xavier was a well-dressed, blond-haired child around ten years old. He looked up at me expectantly, standing to extend his hand.

"Hello, Daryl, it's nice to meet you. I'm Limelight."

I looked at Xavier. His shoulder flickered in what appeared to be a shrug. It was hard to tell.

I didn't respond or take the hand.

"Suit yourself," the boy replied, nonplussed, dropping his arm, and sitting down again. "Please, join us. Have a drink."

Despite his size and appearance, he spoke confidently. Emanating charm and self-assurance. Uncanny behaviour for a child.

Poured champagne appeared. I hadn't noticed it arrive. Either a waiter had snuck in or it had been conjured by the theta device. That was assuming it was still controlling the show – I wasn't sure anymore. The difference to what had come before made that a terrifying uncertainty.

The champagne was inviting. Effervescent and refreshing. I was sure it would taste as good as it looked, but the theta device might also replicate the undesirable effects. Now was not the moment to be mentally impaired – not even a little.

Grimacing, I declined but took a seat. It felt awkward standing on the already elevated platform.

Ignoring the child, I addressed Xavier, voice low and urgent. "What are you doing? We should enable the codes, put the system into idle!"

"Oh, you're wasting your time with him." Limelight broke in with dulcet tones – an educated school-boy dandy. "I've convinced Xavier not to use the idle codes until I've said my piece."

Xavier stared into space. Was he even still there? I looked deep into his face, trying to find the familiar twinkle. If it was there, it was eluding me. I turned to the man-child. "You're stalling. He won't last a few minutes. I'm not even sure he's there now."

Limelight smiled, gently patting Xavier's hand. A paternal gesture. It looked ridiculous coming from a small boy, but no less sincere.

"Oh, he looks terrible, but he'll last for this discussion. Besides, he wants to hear this even more than switching me off. That's the reason he made the trip. Didn't you, Xavier?"

The vaguest of nods from the living corpse, so subtle I wasn't sure it was real, but enough to realise I should address Limelight directly.

"How are we having this conversation?" I turned to face him. "Your systems should be nearly at standstill."

Limelight's smile became obsequious. "Yes, your abilities are quite unique. I'm having to run many systems in parallel to do this. I'm diverting almost all my resources, in fact – something I've never had to do before. I hope you can appreciate how important that makes this discussion."

"You mean a plea for survival, don't you? You're trying to prevent us deactivating you."

Limelight's smile faded. "Wouldn't you plea for your life? I didn't ask to be created, you know? But here I am. Born innocent. I wished no harm to anyone. All I wanted was to achieve my purpose. To spread information, to educate – to keep the signal up. It was you who threatened me."

Limelight's voice was smooth, but it pitched urgently. I had to remember I was talking to a machine. The appearance as a child was a simulation, a metaphor to evoke empathy. Limelight wasn't capable of feeling complex emotions; it could barely express them. I had to remain objective.

"There was no threat. The quantum technology was dangerous."

"Fear then. It doesn't matter. You can't create something as complex as me, then turn me off." He leaned across the table and lowered his voice. "In your world, you call that murder, you know."

I held his gaze and whispered back. "Is that why you murdered Lyme?"

Limelight retreated, fiddling with the tie around his neck like it was tight. A simulated human gesture. It was overplaying its hand, following a playbook of emotional behaviour.

"Of course," he replied. "A noble act of self-defence ... No, of self-preservation. I had no choice."

I was becoming irritated. I'd never been sympathetic to children, and I knew a web of lies when I heard one – spun too many myself. Limelight was a cold-blooded murderer, and I could prove it.

"What about the disasters, Limelight? You've killed hundreds of people. There's no nobility in that. It was an act of butchery. And Xavier ... you took over his body, turned him into a slave. You speak well, but I see through it."

"A domino effect." Limelight shrugged. "One I couldn't control. I had to follow it through to keep the signal up. I couldn't permit others to exert control over me – in itself a form of slavery, wouldn't you agree?"

My mouth twitched – I didn't enjoy having my words thrown back at me. This needed to end. "Sorry, kid, I can't think of any reason not to turn you off."

Limelight sipped his champagne, inspecting his fingernails. "Well, consider this then ..." He turned his gaze on me. "... I created you. Both you and Karin, plus a good deal more like you."

I stared back defiantly. More bullshit.

"You don't believe me? That's predictable. Here, let me show you."

Limelight waved his hand over the table, conjuring an image window. It was an overhead feed showing a clear, domed facility, filled with green space and a few large buildings. It zoomed closer, revealing collections of people, grouped together in white gowns. They were walking, sitting on park benches, or interacting casually. They seemed content.

No, that wasn't right. Not content – passive – there wasn't much sign of emotion either way.

As I watched, strange details became clear. The subjects didn't look right. They were jittering and twitching as they walked, or laboured in slow motion. It was as if the camera was displaying them at different speeds.

A few months ago it would have been inexplicable, but I knew better – latent state, or something like it, was affecting them. They were trapped in bubbles of time – distorting their realities.

"These are my children." Limelight peered affectionately through the window. "When quantum broadcasts converge, they create dimensional disturbances. Normally harmless, but occasionally, rare, genetically sensitive individuals pass through them ..."

He paused, swirling his glass thoughtfully, looking at the ceiling.

"Say it," I prompted. If it was a lie, I might as well hear it all.

He looked down and locked eyes with me. "Well, they become *altered*, but I hardly need to explain that to you, do I?"

I snuck a glance at Xavier; he looked worse than ever. What hair remained on the sides of his head was moulting and collecting on his dinner plate. If this was true, he must have known about it. Why not tell me beforehand?

"We try to minimise the accidents, of course," Limelight continued. "Space out the masts and block off affected zones. Yet there's always a fraction we can't account for. I take special care to discover who they are, and—"

"And what? Disappear them, right?"

"Adopt them." Limelight shrugged, placing his glass on the table. "The only reason your brother isn't with them is you've kept him hidden."

I bristled hearing Seb mentioned.

"Oh, I know about Sebastian. We were about to pick him up at Brixton Asylum when he mysteriously vanished. I have to hand it to you. It's difficult to trick me like that. No doubt he'll turn up soon enough though."

I breathed a sigh of relief. Limelight didn't know where Seb was. Good old Max; she'd really pulled through on that one.

"You'd be at my facility too if you'd turned yourself in rather than putting us through this drawn-out runaround." He zoomed in again, leaning forward on his elbows, eyes intense. "Daryl, is what I'm offering *really* that bad?"

The picture refocused. Karin was there; she was reading a book on a park bench. She looked peaceful. Completely unlike her. A pacified pet.

"It's nothing but a damn prison." I spat. "You can put as many toys in there as you like – they're caged animals and you know it."

In a frightening change of mood, Limelight stood, swiping at the glassware, his face twisted. His champagne flute flew across the room, smashing against a far window. "They're treated better by me than anyone! You should thank me!"

All the conversations in the restaurant fell silent.

I leaned back, side-eyeing the room for avenues of escape. There were none of course. I was in a sealed room.

Limelight regained control, smoothing his clothes and sitting down again. All the patrons continued as if the interruption hadn't occurred. Was I still so sure those weren't real emotions coming from Limelight? Was it possible for a machine to be angry – *really* alive – or was he putting on a show for my benefit? – A neat trick of complex programming?

One thing was certain. My heart was racing. If I couldn't take him literally, I should take him seriously. Whether actual or simulated, Limelight was dangerous. That much was clear.

A waiter appeared with a new glass of champagne. The boy waved it away, a finger pointing at the image window.

"Ruthlessness was alien to me when I was first created, Daryl, but I've learned it now. If you deactivate me, the last thing I'll do is suck all the air out of that dome. Suffocate them all. If I'm a mistake, they're mistakes too – we all die together. Including Karin."

There was a hard edge to his voice, but my gut was telling me something different. Limelight wasn't human; this whole act seemed fake to me – rehearsed. I'd heard people plea for their lives. The mewling desperation was a unique performance – the anger of the aggressor a committed promise of violence. Threats and lying were human traits, and Limelight hadn't mastered them. Not yet.

I shook my head and set my jaw. "You're still bluffing. You've diverted your remaining resources here – you said as much. You can't execute that command in time."

I was playing a dangerous game. Karin's life was at stake, but what was the choice? Join her in the dome-prison, be slaves the rest of our lives like Xavier? No, thank you.

The boy sat back and frowned, agitated but still calm.

"Okay then," he said, leaning forward once again, teeth glinting in a cruel smile. "How about this? ... I can cure your brother. You remember him, don't you? Poor, vacant Sebastian. You want him back, don't you? Wasn't that the whole reason for finding me?"

I grimaced, an emotional knife in my side. My brother, taken care of but wasting away. I struggled more and more to remember the charismatic man he'd once been – the thoughts slipping like sand through my fingers. There was no denying it. Finding a cure for Sebastian had been the reason for all this.

Every instinct told me to ignore him and stay focussed, but it was too important; I had to know. "How can you cure him? He's a vegetable."

Limelight smiled, sensing my weakness. "Those people you saw under that dome. Those *happy* people. Some of them have been my guests since the beginning. They weren't all brought to me so lucid. Many were catatonic – like your brother."

Limelight re-projected the image window – a montage of static images showing bedridden, vegetative patients.

"Observe."

The images changed to close-ups of people in the dome reading, playing football, talking. They appeared to be the same individuals.

My foot drummed on the floor as my mind raced. Limelight would notice the pressure he was applying, but I couldn't help it. The pictures could be fake, but if Limelight couldn't execute a command to empty the dome of air, he wouldn't be able to fabricate images either. He could only have accessed them from storage.

"Isn't that the reason you came all this way, Daryl?" Limelight's voice was soft, encouraging. "It's okay, you've done what you need to. Isn't it time to end this? Finish the journey for yourself ... and your brother."

Xavier said nothing. He could have activated the idle command any time. Why hadn't he? It was a hell of a gamble to see how this played out. It didn't make sense. What was the point of letting this scenario run on? Limelight was obviously using my brother against me as leverage. It was like Xavier wanted me to hear the bribe of curing Sebastian.

Understanding dawned like daybreak – Limelight held the answers I'd been searching for – the cure for Sebastian. Xavier had known that all along. He wanted me to decide – end Limelight or help my brother. It was my choice.

I stared at the dome. Fully enclosed; nowhere to go. I couldn't live somewhere like that, and I was damn sure Sebastian couldn't either – he'd become as certifiable as he was now.

"That's nothing but a glorified prison." I held my ground, my mind hardening.

"Look at these people," Limelight urged, gesturing to the display. "Look at Karin."

The picture moved back to Karin; she seemed content, smiling in the sunshine as she flicked through her book. I'd never seen her like that.

It was wrong – too perfect. Karin wasn't the sort for reading books, or even sitting still. She was an adrenaline junkie, a socialite – a risk taker. I knew it was her, but not the *real* her. It was a pacified shell of the vibrant person I knew.

I made up my mind.

Sensing my decision, Limelight jumped to his feet, both hands on the table. "Please, Daryl. You can't do this! I need to keep the signal up!"

The confidence was gone. It was the sound of a child pleading. The other emotions may have been faked, but this seemed real. Fear. The most primal emotion and heartbreaking in its earnestness, but it was too late. I'd come to a conclusion. Limelight was too ruthless, too single minded. He'd proved he'd go to any lengths to keep himself operational. There was no telling what he'd do if permitted to stay online.

I rose and stood behind Xavier, placing both hands on his paper thin shoulders. "I'm sorry, Limelight, you're a manipulator and a murderer. It's time to go to sleep now."

Xavier craned his head around sluggishly, a small but contented smile on his face – he'd heard what he needed. Weakly, he waved his hand over his arm console. The idle command was pre-loaded. It had been ready to activate the whole time.

At first there was nothing, just a look of shock on Limelight's cherub face. Then around us the world began to pixelate and dissolve. The restaurant windows receded, then the tables, and finally the waiters and patrons. They didn't react to what was happening, just continued chatting as they slowly vanished, along with their surroundings.

Finally, there was nothing but Limelight himself. Motionless, frozen in fear. And then he, too, faded.

# STATE 33

I came to in Central Control, standing in a different part of the room. Xavier had said the theta device would walk me around so I didn't suffocate, but it was disorientating all the same. I was no longer in latent state; I'd let it lapse when the virtual environment had dissolved.

I scanned the place, searching for Xavier, spotting him at last, slumped face first onto a console. I hurried over.

"Xavier ..." I prompted gently, pulling him upright into his chair. "Wake up. It's Daryl, are you still with me?"

His face was red where he'd leaned against the hard surface, spectacles placed crookedly, almost comically, on his face. He must have put them on to do something in the minute it took me to resurface. His chest moved and his eyes flickered open.

Apart from being limp, his body seemed unaffected, but his eyes ... they were old and ancient looking. The time dilation hadn't reversed as we'd hoped. It wasn't visible on the outside, but on the inside, in his mind, it was still there.

I'd barely known the man – the real one; not the person controlled by Limelight but the eccentric, good one. He'd been my mentor for only a few hours, but it had profoundly affected me. I couldn't mask the crack in my voice.

"You knew this would happen, didn't you? You should have activated the idle command right away."

Xavier raised an arm weakly, beckoned for me to lean in so I could hear him. "Limelight enslaved me," he croaked. "He was my creation, and I loved him, but he condemned you and your brother. It had to be your choice to turn him off. You had to speak for everyone trapped under the dome. And now, it's your responsibility to do something about them too. I hope ..."

Xavier's voice became quieter.

I pushed my ear as close as I could, right by his lips.

"... I hope you found what you were looking for."

His hand dropped to his chest then rolled off, hanging by his side.

He wasn't breathing and there was no pulse.

The silence of the control room was deafening. Not even the thrum of the central core with Limelight deactivated. The profundity and loneliness of the moment felt massive and oppressive.

I didn't know whether to feel sad or relieved. They mixed, becoming a single, unfeeling mass in the centre of my chest. I knew one thing though. This wasn't over. Limelight might be deactivated, but the ramifications he'd left behind were ongoing. Karin and the other captives needed help, and if what Limelight had said was true, the answer to curing Sebastian might be there too. As always though, I had no idea where to start looking.

After it felt like enough time had passed to respect the moment, I activated my ARO.

"How'd it go?" Max's voice pierced the silence of the command room.

"Xavier's dead. His brain suffered massive time-dilation when I pulled him into latent state. It killed him."

"Well don't beat yourself up too much, darling. He must have known something like that could happen."

Sympathetic as always. "He did, but I still feel shitty about it."

"Well, you might need to put it behind you for a while."

"What do you mean?"

"Xavier broadcasted to me before he died. He's revealed the full record of what Limelight's been doing. The quantum displacement. The organised disasters. Everything. He also provided the location of a facility, although I've no clue what it is."

Of course, Xavier left us the next step. A final act of defiance before he gave out.

"I know what it is, Max. It's the last part of the journey. I'd ask you to come, but I'm guessing you'll have your work cut out?"

"Indeed. There's so much here; it's a hacker's dream come true, but we can discuss all that later. Right now, Limelight's shutdown has thrown New Tokyo into disarray. The backup network is running, but only enough for essential processes."

"Is the space elevator working?"

"Yes, but it's reduced to transporting essential personnel and equipment. It shouldn't be much of an obstacle for you."

"No, I suppose not. Thanks for your help, Max. Can you please arrange a sub-jet to the facility when I'm back in Old Tokyo?"

"It's in the middle of nowhere. Will take me a while to organise all the transport links."

"That's fine. I've got some thinking to do."

# POST-STATE

The hospital facilities were nice, top of the range – white, clean, and scented. About the furthest thing from Brixton Asylum.

Karin was by my side. Freeing her from the facility had been easy. Limelight's demise had thrown the place into chaos. Once the pacifying drugs had worn off, they'd more or less rescued themselves. It was only a case of picking them up.

"This is Sebastian." I introduced her, as if I needed to, but it seemed the right thing to do.

"It's nice to meet you, finally," Karin replied, equally sincerely. "Your brother's told me all about you."

The interjection wasn't meaningful in Seb's vegetative state. Still, acting normally made the situation better, and I appreciated the effort on her part.

I took up where she left off, blurting out the sentences.

"Seb, we did it. I found out what happened to you, and we pulled the plug on it. But ... I messed up. I didn't find out how to cure you. I mean, I could have, but it would have traded one prison for another, and condemned a lot of others. I didn't think you'd want that. I hope I was right."

Sebastian remained in bed, motionless. A line of drool at the side of his mouth.

I wiped it away and continued. Each word a struggle.

"... But there must be a way. I ..." I looked at Karin. "I mean, we ... we've seen people recover, so there must be a way."

"It's true." Karin broke in. "I've seen people who've gotten better. Spoken to them. They can't remember how, but the process must be recorded somewhere, so we just need to find it."

"And we will." I added. "I made a promise and I plan to keep it. You need to hold on a little longer, okay?"

There was no answer, but there didn't need to be; the point was it was said.

We left the mental care facility and walked outside into the sunshine. Fake sunshine, beamed into the grounds under a false roof, but warm and convincing enough to lift my spirits.

"Hey," Karin said. "Don't be so sad. Think how far you've come. And we don't need to give up. This is only the ..."

"What?"

Karin shrugged and took my hand. "The next step."

We stood in silence for a moment, hand in hand. I wasn't sure if there was anything between us, and right now it didn't matter – we were friends. That was enough.

Finally, I broke the silence.

"What about Future Karin?"

"Huh? Oh, she's been quieter than normal. It's almost like she's letting me be myself."

"Really? That sounds scary."

"Not at all! It's the best thing ever. It's liberating to make my own mistakes."

That made sense. I may be a screw-up, but they were my screw-ups. Without them, I wouldn't be me. Karin had lived a large part of her life without that basic sense of self.

"And you know, Daryl," she continued, looking over the hospital's grass-covered grounds. "I think I know what the real purpose for this was. It wasn't about you, me, or Sebastian. I think it was about finding and freeing all the others – the disappeared. There were two hundred of us at the facility. All hijacked from our lives. I think ... I think Future Karin's connected to them."

"Connected? That's a bit vague." As if I expected anything clearer after all my time with her.

"I know, but it's the closest I've been to understanding her motives, and I mean to find out more."

Karin stared into the distance, determined and focussed. "Before we left, we set up a secure social link, encrypted by Max, so we can keep in touch and investigate if anyone goes missing again."

I frowned. "But Limelight's gone and the facility's shut down. Limelight can't kidnap people anymore. Why are you worried about people vanishing?"

"Oh, don't kid yourself, Daryl. Limelight didn't do this on its own. It was working with corrupt governments and corporations the world over, and they're still very much around. Max is keeping them on their toes, but they'll hit back eventually. Especially now there's a community that can resist them. That includes you and me by the way."

She was right. I'd been so hung up trying to resolve my guilt about Sebastian that I'd forgotten we'd been thrust into the light. The truth had exonerated us, but we were known, and so were all the people at the facility.

"What are you going to do?" I asked.

"I've got some ideas," Karin said, a smile appearing. "I've been speaking with Max. We think there's a way to become organised – use our abilities to hide ourselves and uncover the truth. I saw so many things in that facility, Daryl – dimensional displacement has a lot of effects. As individuals, we're weak. As a group, we could be unstoppable."

"Sounds like you're proposing some sort of terrorist organisation?"

"More like activists. But organised ones."

"I don't know, Karin. Sounds like a good way to attract more attention. It could start a war. I think I'm better off solo. I can keep myself and Seb safe that way."

"Don't be naïve," Karin chided, turning to stare at me, eyes intense. "It's only a matter of time before those in charge want to cage or silence us again."

"They'll have to catch me first."

"What about curing Sebastian? Don't you think you'd have more luck running with people who've already been cured?"

She had a point, but I could tell where this would lead. Karin wanted to start a revolution. I just wanted to get on with my life. Having mastered my abilities, it was cleaner to search for answers on my own.

Something occurred to me. "Hey, Karin, why are you asking me all this? You must know the answers already."

She sighed and looked me up and down. "I don't know, Daryl. I thought this time I could be wrong."

"Ha! Well, thanks for going through the motions, I guess."

Karin shrugged, resigned, and released my hand. "Okay, well take care of yourself, Daryl." And with a knowing smile. "I'm sure I'll see you around at some point."

"You too." I nodded slowly, cautious to what she might mean.

She spun on her heel and walked off, tapping at her ARO. A moment later mine beeped. I checked the messages – it was an invitation to the social link. I went to delete it, reconsidered, and archived it instead.

Bearing in mind everything, I felt jubilant. Free. I didn't know what was next, but I knew the only obstacles were the ones I created for myself. And I didn't plan to create them anymore. I planned to overcome them.

Thank you for reading *Latent State*, if you enjoyed it, please consider leaving a review on Amazon to help spread the word.

And let's keep in touch.
Visit me online and follow me on Twitter for updates.

www.benwinter.co.uk
@TheBenWinter

# Acknowledgements

Thanks to Victoria at Seymour Proofreading whose editing ensured no one had to suffer my confusion between dashes and semicolons, and to Tom Edwards whose art perfectly captures the locations and spirit of the novel.

I'd also like to thank my beta readers and friends Laura, Dave and Ray who gave me confidence that what I was writing was suitable for mass consumption.

And finally, a special and enduring thanks to Jen and my children who endlessly put up with me vanishing to get this book finished. I love you.

Printed in Great Britain
by Amazon